PROTECTIVE CUSTODY

Hometown Heroes: book 1

JL CROSSWHITE

SIGNED BY THE AUTHOR

Tandem Services Press
SOUTHERN CALIFORNIA

Tandem Services Press
SOUTHERN CALIFORNIA

Praise for JL Crosswhite

"This is a very suspenseful story and I'm looking forward to the next book in this series."—Ginny, Amazon reviewer

"I was impressed with the suspense in this book as well as the romance. Great storyline. Morality issues were great. An overall great read."—Kindle customer

"Absolutely loved it. Fast paced and kept me guessing concerning the outcome. I highly recommend it to all who like a good mystery or suspense."—Linda Reville

"Very well written, with interwoven stories and well developed characters"—Mary L. Sarrault

Whom have I in heaven but you? And earth has nothing I desire besides you. My flesh and my heart may fail, but God is the strength of my heart and my portion forever.— Psalm 73:25-26

Prologue

Orange County, California, 1992

Kyle's stomach flipped like it did when Captain Hook's ship swooped upward at the beginning of the Peter Pan ride at Disneyland. He scrubbed the back of his hand over his eyes as he straddled his BMX Motocross bicycle and waiting for the signal to change. Yep, he was still watching someone steal a car.

He elbowed Joe on the bike next to him. He heard Scott slide to a stop behind them.

"What?"

"See how he's walking between the cars, looking in the windows?"

The guy glanced around the parking lot, lifted a car door handle, and then moved on to another car.

The light changed. Kyle found his pedal without taking his eyes off the guy and pushed off, standing as he pumped his legs, until they reached 31 Flavors. "I think we should call the police."

"Why?" Joe jumped off his bike and shoved it into the rack. "We don't know for sure he's doing something bad."

"We're witnessing a crime. We have to stop him or we could be accomplices."

"We could not." Scott slotted his bike next to Joe's. "We're not helping him steal the car."

"Yeah, but we're watching him and not doing anything about it." Kyle swung off his bike and jammed it next to Scott's.

"So call the police." Joe crossed his arms. He was a big kid, and standing like that would have scared most of the kids in their class, but Kyle knew Joe had no clue how threatening he looked.

"They won't believe us."

"Yeah, who'd listen to a bunch of kids?" Scott headed toward the ice cream store.

Kyle jingled the change in his pocket, dampening it with his sweaty hands. He studied the parking lot, prickles running down his spine. He hurried over to the pay phone before he lost his nerve. The black receiver, hot from the sun, burned his hand as he picked it up. Hearing the dial tone, he punched the metal buttons. The phone rang on the other end of the line.

The guy lifted the door handle of the last car in the lot, a blue Celica. The door cracked open, and the guy scanned the lot before opening the door wider and slipping inside.

"He's gonna steal it!" Joe whispered.

Kyle bounced the toe of his Vans against the sidewalk. The phone rang again.

"911. What's your emergency?" said an official sounding voice.

"Uh—" Kyle's voice cracked. He had to clear it. "Uh, I'd like to report a crime."

"What's your name?"

"Kyle Taylor. I'm at the shopping center at El Toro and Rockfield, and there's this guy in the parking lot—"

Scott grabbed Kyle's shoulder. "He got it started!"

"—he's stealing a car."

"How old are you, Kyle?"

Kyle bounced his foot faster. What did his age have to do

with anything? But he had been taught to always be respectful to adults. "Eleven, sir. Could you please hurry?"

"Now what makes you think he's stealing a car? How do you know it's not his?"

"Because we saw him check all the doors of the cars in the parking lot. He found one that opened and climbed in. He just got it started."

"All right. We'll send someone to check it out. But, son, you'd better be telling the truth. It's against the law to make a false report of a crime."

"Yes, sir. I'm telling the truth."Kyle swallowed. He should have had Scott call. Scott could get anybody to do anything he wanted, even grownups. 911 wouldn't question Scott about telling the truth.

With a squeal and a lurch, the car pulled out of its spot and crossed the parking lot. Kyle gave the dispatcher his home address, the direction the car was heading, and the kind of car it was before hanging up.

"Aren't they coming?" Scott asked.

"He said they'll have a unit in the area check it out." A siren sounded in the distance. They all turned.

It grew louder. A sheriff 's car barreled down Rockfield. The light was red at El Toro. The unit slowed slightly before turning left and speeding up.

The boys watched until it disappeared.

Kyle wiped his sweaty hands on his shorts. That was that. "Let's go get some ice cream."

They walked inside and ordered their cones. Kyle took his double scoop to a window booth. As he took a bite, a piece of mint chocolate chip fell off. He caught it and flipped it in his mouth.

Joe and Scott sat down across from him.

"Wait! Hear that?" Scott stared out the window.

A siren. Kyle jumped out of the booth and bolted outside, Joe and Scott right behind him. "They're coming back!"

The Celica sped into view, the sheriff's car chasing it.

A farm truck loaded with orange crates crawled across the intersection.

The Celica swerved then slammed on its brakes. Slid- ing across the street, the tires left a black trail. The car barely missed the truck. With a thud and a jerk, the Celica crashed into the curb.

The deputy sheriff's unit slid to a stop. The deputy jumped out, threw open the Celica's door, and hauled the driver out, tossing him against the hood. Two more cop cars screamed up the street and squealed to a stop. A minute later the driver was cuffed and put into the back of the deputy's car.

Kyle looked down. Half his cone had dripped down his hand. He licked it and grinned at his friends. "That was awesome!"

Chapter One

Orange County, California, present day

Not spending money on Bernie's caffeine addiction was almost as good as shooting fifty free throws without missing. Detective Kyle Taylor glanced at his watch as he drove his unmarked Crown Vic back to the station. He was going to make it on time, despite covering a shift for Mark, whose wife just had a baby. And that meant Starbucks would be Bernie's treat.

The radio crackled, the constant background music to his life. "…stolen white Lexus SUV. Suspects are four males, Caucasian, heading northbound on El Toro. Passing Jeronimo."

His attention ratcheted up, along with his pulse. That was three-K twelve, Jeff Griffin. A rookie on his first pursuit. His gut tightened. They were headed his way. Detectives didn't usually get involved in pursuits. But Griffin made this different. Kyle had been his training officer and didn't want to think about what would happen if he hadn't trained Griffin well enough.

He hit the lights and sirens on his unmarked cruiser, making it marginally more visible, then snatched the dashboard mic.

"David fifty-seven to three King twelve, moving to intercept from Trabuco and El Toro."

As he turned the corner on El Toro, he spotted the pursuit in his rearview mirror. They were moving to a section four lanes wide and, on a Sunday morning, not too busy.

The lieutenant's voice snapped over the radio. "All units be advised David fifty-seven has the handle on this pursuit."

Kyle groaned. Not only was he going to be late, he would miss the early service completely. Which meant he'd be getting Bernie a Caffe Mocha. Venti or grande? He could never remember what the sizes meant. None of that would matter if he screwed this up. The lieutenant was like his dad. He expected results, not excuses. And a good outcome of this pursuit was all that mattered.

The Lexus SUV in his rearview mirror grew big in a hurry. Kyle forced himself to scan the street in front of him, to avoid tunnel vision on his mirror. "Pursuit is headed toward Portola Parkway. Any units available to intercept, please respond." He moved across the lanes, trying to keep the suspect behind him. "Three King thirty-two is responding. I'm headed up Lake Forest. ETA two minutes."

"Three King thirty-five responding, currently at Los Alisos and Santa Margarita Parkway."

Mission Viejo, huh? Patino must have been at that hamburger and donut shop—weird combo, but Patino swore by it. At times Kyle wished he could let things roll off his back the way Patino did. But then that's why Kyle had made detective and Patino hadn't. Yet.

A glance at his speedometer. As he pushed the gas pedal down, the needle crept up.

The Lexus jerked into the oncoming lane.

Kyle scanned the road ahead. Around the curve, a delivery truck barreled down on them. He winced. *Lord, don't let anyone get hurt.*

Checking the rearview mirror, he saw the suspect cut in

front of the truck. With a screech of brakes, smoke billowed out behind the truck. Narrowly missing the truck, the Lexus swerved off-road, kicking up dust. Back on the pavement now, he closed in on Portola.

Kyle punched the accelerator. He had to reach the intersection ahead of the suspect. Gauging the distance, he slammed on the brakes. His car slid across the center of the intersection.

The SUV still bore down on Kyle.

He swiped the back of his hand across his forehead. Which way would the suspect go? He scanned the area trying to predict.

Tires skidding and rear end fishtailing—coming within inches of sideswiping Kyle's cruiser—the Lexus swerved, cut the corner, jumped the curb, and headed into the hills.

Kyle floored it, squealing the tires as he willed the big V8 engine to race from a near standstill to now playing catch-up.

His pulse throbbed in his neck. Someone was going to get hurt. So far he had a clean jacket on pursuits, no write ups in his file. But if something went bad, no matter what, Kyle's career was on the line.

There was an elementary school coming up. He tightened his grip on the steering wheel. Kyle closed in as they crested the hill. His breaths came closer together.

They'd soon be out of Laguna Vista city limits. Over the radio, Griffin requested assistance from the sheriff's department.

The Lexus accelerated down the hill, out of the residential area.

He blew a sigh of relief. They had a real shot at ending this now. Glenn Ranch looped around and dead-ended back at El Toro. They had the suspect trapped. Unless he went into the canyons.

The SUV shrieked left onto El Toro and headed back into the hills, destined for either Live Oak or Silverado Canyon.

Kyle followed, all three squad cars now trailing him. They approached Live Oak Canyon at nearly seventy miles an hour. He hoped the suspect wouldn't try to make the cutoff. It was a sharp turn and Cook's Corner, a local biker hangout shack, sat close to the road. He could just see the SUV missing the turn and plowing into the dirt lot full of Harleys.

They passed Live Oak. Another relief.

El Toro Road became Santiago Canyon. Not as twisty as Live Oak, but still plenty of curves. Not many places to turn off, either, other than some private and fire roads. With the sheriff's department coming from the other direction, they should have the suspect trapped soon.

Taillights strobed. Kyle slammed his foot on the brake. The suspect's car slung onto a dirt road. Kyle followed,

the kicked-up dust obscuring his vision. He bounced over the rough terrain, brush scraping the sides of his cruiser. His unit had beefed up suspension, but it wasn't an SUV.

The Lexus attempted a hairpin switchback. Too fast. The back end slid out. It tilted up on two wheels, hovered, then slammed on its side.

Kyle's unit shuddered to a stop. He called for EMS, throwing the mic on the seat as he jumped out. Others pulled in behind.

Drawing his gun, he covered the vehicle, waiting for backup. Dust settled around it, eerily silent. He took a deep breath, trying to slow the adrenaline racing through his veins.

The airbags had deployed, blocking the side windows, but the back liftgate window revealed no movement. A groan came from inside.

It hadn't ended safely for these guys. A twinge ricocheted in Kyle's chest. He didn't like people getting hurt. It was a big part of his job to prevent that. But these guys made their own consequences when they decided to steal a car.

Griffin ran up behind him, his gun also covering the SUV. Lopez and Patino followed.

"Anybody hurt?" Lopez's voice came from behind Kyle.

"Can't tell." Kyle studied the vehicle then squatted, peering through the liftgate window. Looked like two in front, two in back. Tinted windows made it hard to see, especially in the shadows. "Can you hear me in there?"

"Uh, yeah. I think my arm's broken." A young voice, like a teenage boy's.

"Okay, we've got an ambulance on the way. Who else is in there?"

"Hey, Alex. You awake, man? Alex? Cole?" Kyle heard the panic in the voice. "I can't get any of them to answer me." Tears now too. "Trevor's next to me, and he's got blood coming out of his head."

Griffin thumbed his shoulder-mounted radio requesting an ETA for the ambulance. The kids were scared now, but most of the time it didn't stick.

"Three king twelve, that's fifteen plus."

He looked up and holstered his gun. "Let's see what we can do."

Patino nodded and pulled out his baton.

Kyle turned to the window again. "We're going to break out this back window so we can help you. I'll need you to cover your face. What's your name?"

"Justin. Justin Foster." Kyle froze. Justin?

ON A HILL OVERLOOKING THE SCENE OF THE WRECKED SUV, Bull studied the activity through his binoculars. Hiding between two boulders, sand digging into his elbows, Bull yanked the binoculars from his eyes, swearing. Rage pumped up the veins in his arms, fisting his hands. He had to punch something, like Alex's face.

He wanted that SUV, and the quick cash it would bring.

It was so simple, but Pretty Boy managed to screw it up.

One minute farther on the dirt road and the cops would have been too close. Way too close. Bull would have lost more than the SUV. A lot more.

Hearing the *thwap thwap thwap* of the sheriff's helicopter, he double-checked his cover, glad he'd worn desert camos. With the uniforms and what looked like a plainclothes guy down there, that chopper wouldn't hang around long. He and his boys were safe. For now.

But Alex? That was a whole other deal. Bull didn't put up with stupidity.

Too bad.

He'd had high hopes for that boy. Now he'd need a replacement.

Chapter Two

Heather McAlistair crossed the stage and stepped onto the risers under the scorching lights.

Looking out over the church congregation, she was thankful this was the last of three services. The back of her throat tickled. She attempted to cough discreetly. It didn't help. She swallowed. And chewed on the side of her tongue. None of her normal tricks were working. She needed something to drink. Desperately. Why hadn't she grabbed a bottle of water before she left this morning? Because she was running late as usual.

"You okay?" Bernie nudged her shoulder.

His curly hair was sticking up from running his hands through it. She never could decide if his plastic-rimmed glasses were nerdy or trendy. Most likely he didn't care. For all his life-of-the-party personality, he was pretty aware—for a guy.

"I've got something in my throat and no water."

"Here." He handed her a cough drop. "Not as good as water but better than nothing."

"Thanks." She popped it in her mouth, scanning the congregation while the rest of the choir filed in.

A few people stood in the back of the worship center. One man in particular caught her attention. He leaned against the wall holding two coffee cups. Why did he look familiar? She didn't know why. He smiled at her.

She slid her gaze away and fiddled with one of her bracelets. This was the worst part, everyone watching before she could lose herself in the music and forget the audience. She smiled and hoped it looked genuine.

Absently, she scanned the rest of the congregation, looking for familiar faces. She spotted a few and smiled.

She had moved on before her brain registered a face.

A sharp intake of breath and the cough drop slid partway down her throat and stuck. She coughed to dislodge it. Her eyes watered. She blinked rapidly and took a breath.

Afraid of what she might have seen, she couldn't bring herself to look again. Surely her mind was playing tricks on her. He wasn't here. He was in New York.

Wasn't he?

Working to keep her expression neutral, she snuck a glance. Third row, aisle seat.

Yep, he was there. Quinn.

Grinning up at her.

Her stomach lurched, and she was afraid she was going to be sick. Why was he here?

A million questions raced through her mind. But some- one stepped into her field of view. Ryan Bradley, their worship leader, raised his eyebrows at her.

She stepped forward to pick up the mic. She pressed her lips together and forced down the twitches in her stomach. If she got nervous, her voice would tighten and shake, and she'd sound terrible. She couldn't deal with Quinn now. Forcibly, she pushed him out of her mind.

Closing her eyes, she focused on the words of the song. Audience of One, right? She wasn't doing this for Quinn or anyone else out there.

Before she brought the mic up, she tried to hum the note she needed. But nothing happened. Her voice locked up. Panic rose from her diaphragm threatening to drown her. Disaster stared at her, wearing Quinn's face.

She glanced over her shoulder, hoping to catch Ryan's eye, to warn him or something. He was focused on the choir. She took a step back, wanting to rush back and blend into the choir.

It was too late. Ryan turned and pointed at her. The drummer counted out the beat.

She had to sing the first word before the band played the note. She had to be right on.

Everyone was waiting on her.

She swallowed, trying to loosen the knot. Closing her eyes and imagining the music in her mind, she let her breath out and back in.

And sang. The first line. Right on. She opened her eyes.

The room faded away, and Heather was only aware of the music and voices flowing around her. Her voice seemed to be singing on its own, without any direction from her.

On the chorus, the choir and congregation joined in. Heather lowered the mic and stepped back into the safety of the choir, legs barely holding her.

As one of the pastors gave the announcements, Heather looked to the man in the back. He gave her a thumbs-up and a smile that caused a flicker of warmth—it fought against the panic that filled her heart.

Kyle eased out of the worship center and into the courtyard as the choir left the stage. He plopped down on the wide edge of a concrete planter, setting the coffee cups next to him, waiting for Bernie to come out. As people passed him, meandering into church, he let himself relax, still trying to shake the dregs of the adrenaline rush from the car chase. Loud-speakers broadcast the announcements so those coming in late or sitting outside wouldn't miss anything. He'd have to get the sermon online later.

The woman singing had a beautiful voice. There was something to it that made him believe what she was singing. He enjoyed watching her too, with her soft brown eyes and light brown hair, cut just below her chin but with something done to it so it didn't quite look like a basic cut. He guessed her height to be about five seven, slender build. Classic, understated beauty that was a perfect backdrop for her fun sense of fashion. He didn't know much about that, but her long, multicolored print skirt and about twenty bracelets on her arms revealed a unique sense of style.

And her playing with those same bracelets revealed her nervousness. Interesting. He hadn't noticed that before. Something had disturbed her. More than that, at one point she looked downright panicked. His radar for something wrong pinged.

Maybe he should head back to the green room to find Bernie. He'd deliver the coffee and maybe even run into her. Figure out what had spooked her. He wasn't going to sort out if it was personal or professional interest.

It'd been an adventurous morning already. After the car chase, he had to call Justin's mom, Claire, and break the news to her. Kyle had taught Justin's fifth grade Sunday school class. He was about the last kid Kyle expected to pull out of that wrecked SUV. Made him wonder how many of the lessons had stuck with the kids.

Claire came to the station to pick up Justin dressed like she was ready to go to Fashion Island or South Coast Plaza instead of church. How she hadn't noticed Justin was missing was something he didn't understand, but Kyle hadn't been in touch with the Fosters much the last few years.

She'd ranted at the station about how Justin's father, who lived in New York, was already catching a flight to Orange County and was not pleased. He'd felt helpless, as usual, in the face of women's emotions.

"But then, when is he ever pleased about anything involving his son?" She waved her hand as if that wiped the thought away. Her tone softened. "Anyway, if Justin was trying to get his dad's attention, he got it. Thanks for all you've done. I know it could have been much worse for him."

He'd talked to Claire a bit longer, trying to figure out how to get Justin involved with some kids who would be a better influence on him. He refused to go to the church youth group, saying all the kids were losers. But hanging around Alex and his friends wasn't a good move either. Just because this time the car they took happened to belong to Alex's stepmom didn't mean that next one wouldn't really be stolen. Justin was lucky he only suffered a sprained shoulder, but next time could be worse.

And there would be a next time. Kyle had been at this job long enough to know that. Justin's dad, living way across the country, didn't have time for him. His mom was frustrated and didn't have any control over him. She was doing her best, but she needed more help than she was getting. Kyle mentally scrolled through a list of people he could call. How hard was it to point a teenager in the right direction?

He could spend some time with the kid. Would Justin be willing to get up early enough on a Saturday to hit the waves? He'd never gone surfing with someone he'd arrested.

He hopped off the planter and grabbed the coffees. He was going to hunt down Bernie. And maybe that pretty lady too.

SOMETHING GRABBED HEATHER'S SHOULDER. SHE JUMPED, her pulse rocketing into the blue Southern California sky, and spun around.

Bernie.

She let out a breath and hoped he didn't notice. "You okay? You look a little pale."

"I'm fine. It was hot up there. Kind of got to me." She

spotted her purse on a chair in the green room. Grabbing it, she slung it over her shoulder. She had to get out of here before Quinn showed up. It would be like him to duck out of church early to try to catch her. She didn't want to talk to him, see him, or have anything to do with him again. Ever.

"A bunch of us from my small group are going to lunch. Join us?"

"Well—"

"Come on, Heather. It'll be good for you."

Heather let him propel her out the door. Using Bernie as a shield against Quinn was cowardly, especially since she didn't feel in the mood to go to lunch. Her small talk game—never very good to begin with—would be lousy today, and she'd end up sounding stupid. Plus, she liked Bernie, but not in *that* way, and she didn't want him to get any ideas. This was not a good idea, but she couldn't figure out how to tell him no.

"Hey, Kyle." Bernie came to a stop.

Heather licked her suddenly dry lips. A tall man with close-cut sandy blond hair handed a Starbucks cup to Bernie. The same man who'd been standing in the back of the church. The scent of chocolate-laced coffee drifted to her. Good looking, he nicely filled out his polo shirt. She didn't dare look for a ring; she'd get caught for sure and wouldn't that just be humiliating? Instead she searched out his eyes. They were gray, the color of the ocean on a cloudy day.

"Hey, Bernie. You guys sounded great up there."

"Oh, you actually caught some of the service?" Bernie turned to look at Heather, then back at Kyle. "Kyle, do you know Heather?" He took a sip from his cup.

Kyle extended his hand. "No, I haven't had the pleasure, but I know your face from your singing in the choir. I'm Kyle Taylor." His gaze seemed a touch too intense, almost searching, like he'd asked a question she hadn't heard.

"Heather McAlistair." She shook his hand. Warm, large, a little rough with calluses. She couldn't think of a thing to say, as usual. "Nice to meet you." Her tongue stuck like it was glued to the roof of her mouth.

"I covered for Mark last night and had a pursuit this morning. But, as you can see"—he gestured to the Starbucks cup—"I made good on our deal. And I'm planning to go to lunch before I go home and crash. Heather, are you joining us?"

"Yes, she is." Bernie took her arm and started maneuvering her toward the parking lot.

Out of the corner of her eye, she saw Quinn headed straight toward her. She froze. Her breath caught, her heart picked up tempo. It *was* him. Part of her still hadn't been sure, had hoped she'd imagined him.

But there he was grinning at her, sun glinting off his dark, wavy hair, that same spring in his step, like everything in his life was absolutely fantastic.

"Heather!" He wrapped her in a bear hug, trapping her arms at her side, sliding her purse off her shoulder. He stepped back, still grasping her shoulders. "How are you? You look fantastic. And you sounded terrific as always."

And Quinn was still overwhelming. She took a step back, thankful for Bernie's presence and embarrassed by Kyle's. "Fine." She was amazed her voice worked, even sounded somewhat normal.

Kyle stepped forward and introduced himself, forcing Quinn to let go of Heather. She gave him a grateful smile. He smiled back, and her stomach did a funny little jump.

Quinn turned back to her. "Heather, I know it's last minute and you probably already have plans, but I was hoping I could talk you into having lunch with me."

"I have plans." At that moment, she was more than grateful for Bernie's invitation to lunch. No way did she want to go anywhere with Quinn. She couldn't deal with his persistence today.

Quinn's 200-watt smiled dimmed a bit. "Sure. I understand."

What? No argument? He wasn't trying to invite himself along? "I thought you were in New York." She couldn't resist. Her curiosity got the better of her.

"I still am. I'm just out here visiting my folks. Miss this gorgeous California weather."

"I see." She shifted her weight, looking around for a way out.

Kyle's gaze flicked from her to Bernie to Quinn. Was it her imagination or did his eyebrows raise a bit? She wanted to get out of here, even if her escape route involved going to lunch with people she didn't know.

"Okay, well, I'd better get going." Quinn pulled keys out of his pocket. "Heather, I'll call you tomorrow. Still have the same number?"

She nodded reflexively. She did not want Quinn calling her. But she *really* didn't want to make a scene in front of Kyle and Bernie. What kind of impression must she be making on Kyle? Couldn't she ever do anything the normal way?

"Nice to meet you all." Quinn gave a small wave then turned and left.

She couldn't believe he left without putting up more of a fuss, but she wasn't going to complain. Maybe Quinn had changed. Heather stifled a sigh of relief. She was exhausted and it was still morning. She should excuse herself from lunch. She was too flustered, and that increased her foot-to-mouth ratio. And what if Quinn hadn't given up? What if he was waiting to ambush them at a restaurant?

On the other hand, Kyle and Bernie had been helpful in shielding her from Quinn. Though that might get old for them if Quinn was persistent. Neither of them knew what Quinn did last year. She didn't want a repeat.

"We can take my truck." Kyle pulled keys from his pocket and gestured to the parking lot as they started walking.

"Sounds good," Bernie said. "I'd be too nervous to drive with a cop in my car anyway."

Kyle was a cop? Heather glanced at him out of the corner of her eye. It fit.

Kyle clapped Bernie on the shoulder. "I'd go easy on you."

They stepped out of the intermittent shade of the trees and buildings and onto the warm asphalt. The marine layer of low, thick clouds present this morning had burned off, leaving a sapphire blue sky, the hallmark of a typically beautiful Southern California day. She wished she could enjoy it.

At the restaurant, Kyle introduced her around. One of the women, Melissa, flipped her thick chestnut hair over her shoulder, her dark-eyed gaze holding Heather's. Melissa was confident with a slightly exotic beauty. Heather hadn't looked in the mirror, but she was willing to bet her makeup had all but melted off under the stage lights. She resisted the urge to blot her face with her napkin.

Heather glanced around at the other diners before she realized she was looking for Quinn. With his sell-ice-to-an-Eskimo skills, he would get himself invited to sit with these unsuspecting people or at the very least sit across the room where she couldn't miss his presence.

Kyle pulled out the chair next to Melissa, holding it for Heather to slide into. Then he took the seat next to her at the head of the table. That was nice. It'd been a long time since anyone had been so gentlemanly toward her. She took a deep breath to head off a yawn. The adrenaline of the morning was draining off. Quinn hadn't shown up, so maybe she could relax. Now as long as she didn't do anything stupid, maybe she could enjoy Kyle's company.

Melissa was talking to the person on the other side of her and Heather didn't understand the context of the conversation. Something about last summer. But it triggered a thought in Heather's mind, and she studied Melissa while she wasn't watching. Could she be...?

Quinn had dated a Melissa before Heather. Heather had never met her but she'd seen pictures. This Melissa could be the same one. Hard to tell just from pictures. A weird feeling slithered into her stomach. Was this some sort of elaborate set up by Quinn? She surveyed the restaurant more thoroughly.

"Tired?" Kyle's breath brushed her ear, sending shivers down her spine.

"A little," she said, surprised at how perceptive he was. She dropped the thoughts of Melissa with Quinn and turned her attention to Kyle. "My Jitter Bug house special wore off about an hour ago."

"What time did you get to church this morning?"

"Seven."

He winced. "That's early for a Sunday."

"Yes, it is. I'm not sure I've recovered from the Easter marathon last month."

Bernie leaned forward. "Aw, come on, Heather. You'd sing every Sunday if you could."

A smile escaped. "Probably. But ten Easter services were too much even for me."

"The joys of attending a big church."

Bernie brought the discussion around to this morning's sermon, recapping it for Kyle's benefit, he said with a wink.

Heather's gaze strayed to the window and the tropical landscaping brushing against the glass. A car drove by, the sun reflecting off its glass, hiding the driver from her. It was a classic Jaguar, like the one Quinn used to drive. Her pulse notched up as she tried to see where it went. A pause dropped into the conversation, and all eyes seemed to be on her. She tried to remember the subject. Ah, the sermon.

"I'm always amazed at the things people go through that bring them to Christ." That was a safe comment. The speaker today had talked about how the collapse of his business and marriage brought him to Christ and eventually led him to start a ministry in Mexico. She shook her head. "I don't know what I'd have done if I had to go through all that pain and loss."

She snuck a look out the window. The Jaguar was gone.

Besides, he'd have his car with him in New York, wouldn't he? Probably wasn't even Quinn.

Bernie leaned his elbows on the table. "Anybody ever gotten up and given their testimony?"

She'd rather die than get up and talk in front of a group, especially about her spiritual life even though she'd been a Christian her whole life. Yeah, she was a real incorrigible six- year-old. Once she threw a temper tantrum when she had to tie her own shoes before Jesus saved her from a life of anger management classes.

Even talking to others about her work made her cringe. On Friday, she got an email asking her to speak to a group of high school girls about her work at the magazine. She responded, "No thank you." Even if speaking in front of a group didn't terrify her, she didn't have anything worthwhile to say. The kids would find her boring and they'd get restless. It would be just an embarrassing mess like the first—and last—time she spoke in front of a group.

Head shakes and a smattering of "not me" rippled around the table like the Wave at Angel Stadium. Until it got to Melissa. Of course, she had given her testimony in front of a crowd. More than once.

The waitress handed Heather a much-desired glass of iced tea. She sipped the cold liquid, soothing her parched throat. Ah, finally. She closed her eyes, rolling her eyeballs against her lids, trying to moisten them. Something to drink, a guy who knew how to be a gentleman, and no Quinn. Going to lunch might have been a good decision.

Even if it had been made for her.

Voices carried from behind her as the hostess seated another party near them. One voice—male—rose above the rest. Heather jerked around expecting to see Quinn's face.

Her elbow hit something cold. Her glass of iced tea. Sending it sprawling across the table.

"Oh! I'm so sorry!" She jumped up and threw her napkin on

the spreading puddle, trying to stop it.

Kyle grabbed her glass, set it upright, and added his napkin to her efforts.

The hostess hurried over with a wad of napkins. "Here. You might need these."

"Thanks." Kyle responded before Heather could. He grinned at Heather. "No worries. We've got it under control, and no one got doused."

She was such an idiot. She couldn't even look at him. Quinn managed to ruin this lunch without even being here.

HEATHER JUST WANTED TO GET HOME. IT WAS ONLY EARLY afternoon, but she was exhausted from emotions that ran the gamut. Kyle drove her and Bernie back to the church, pulling up next to the only two cars left in the lot.

Bernie hopped out and opened Heather's door, but Kyle got out too.

"This your Miata?" He nodded to the sporty, forest green convertible.

"Yes. It's my baby."

"Nice." Kyle strolled around her car, checking it out.

"I like it." She smiled, but it faded quickly. Under the windshield wiper, a folded piece of paper fluttered. The edge lifted to reveal a masculine scrawl. She reached back to the truck for balance.

Kyle had stopped next to the driver's door and started to grab the paper then stopped. "Someone left you a note." Something odd crept into his voice.

Steadying herself, she walked over to the car. She hesitated, and then reached for the note.

Kyle halted her with a touch to the back of her hand. "Do you know who left it?"

"I think so." She hoped Kyle would leave it at that. She didn't want to talk about Quinn.

He moved his hand.

She lifted the wiper and grabbed the scrap. Flicking it open, she scanned it, rolled her eyes then crumpled it.

"Bad news?" Kyle stood just behind her. Surprisingly, it was comforting, not oppressive.

"No, annoying. Like the person who left it." She clicked on her key fob to disarm the alarm and unlock the door. He took a step and opened her door for her.

"Thanks." She slid in, tossing her purse and the crumpled note on the passenger seat.

He reached for his wallet and pulled out a business card. He handed it to her. "If someone's bothering you, don't be afraid to let me know."

She took it, their fingers briefly brushing. "Thanks. It's nothing, though." She hoped.

He hesitated, looking like he wanted to say more, but didn't. Bernie opened the door to his Honda, leaning on the door, but didn't get in. He leaned down to look in her window.

"Thanks for coming with us, Heather."

"Thanks for inviting me." She glanced up at Kyle. "I had a good time." And she had. Until now. Leave it to Quinn to ruin things.

"My pleasure," he said. "We'll see you Friday."

Friday night Bible study. Something they all had managed to talk her into at lunch. "Looking forward to it. Bye, Bernie." Kyle closed the door for her. She started the car, flipped on the AC, and slowly backed out, waving as she pulled away.

What was she going to do about Quinn?

THE SOUNDS FROM THE TV IN HIS MOM'S ROOM FADED away as Justin tiptoed down the stairs in the dark. In the entryway, he touched in the code on the alarm system and eased opened the front door. Sliding through, he pulled it shut behind him, hoping he was quiet enough. You never knew with moms. It was amazing what they could hear.

He climbed in his car, pulse pounding in his ears loud enough for the neighbors to hear. Man, he didn't want to do this. Did he? The Seventeeners were a gang of tough guys who did pretty much whatever they wanted. Their parents had enough money to get them out of whatever trouble they got into, and they knew it.

Justin knew most of them because they had all grown up together, but he didn't really hang out with them. He couldn't remember the last time he spoke to Alex or Cole until they showed up at Trevor's last Saturday night. Stealing Alex's stepmom's SUV early the next morning when she was sleeping in was supposed to be their initiation. Of course, Justin didn't know that until it was too late, and the cops were chasing them. He was still torqued about that. And hanging with these guys was only going to get him in more trouble. He wasn't a loser, but he didn't want to see the inside of a jail cell, either.

But standing up to a Seventeener wasn't good for anyone's health. The last kid who did that didn't come back to school. Rumor had it he was buried in the desert. If Justin didn't show up tonight, they'd come find him. And a sprained shoulder from a wrecked SUV was nothing compared to what they'd do to him.

Shoving the key in the ignition, he turned it to the on position but didn't start it. He moved the shifter into neutral and released the emergency brake, letting the car roll down the driveway and into the street. Once there, he turned the wheel so the car kept rolling until he was a couple of houses away from his. Then he started the engine and headed out of Coto de Caza.

Maybe it wouldn't be too bad. At school tomorrow the story about the car chase would have spread through the cool kids. Maybe Bree would sit next to him at lunch or ask for his notes from Spanish class. He could get through this. Asking Bree out would be a piece of cake after a Seventeener initiation. Minutes later he was flying through twisty Live Oak Canyon. It would have been an awesome drive if he had something that could really handle those curves, instead of a Honda. Once the road ended at Silverado Canyon, he turned right and headed back into the hills, glancing at his odometer. Even in the daytime the turnoff was hard to see.

Justin found the road and took it, swallowing as he remembered the last time he'd been here. Slowing for the hairpin turn, he didn't want to look, but the gouge in the dirt and the crumpled brush where the SUV had landed had an almost-magnetic power to draw his gaze.

His mind flicked to paramedics pulling Trevor out, blood pouring down his face. He hadn't regained consciousness until they'd gotten him to the hospital. Trevor's parents were threatening to put him in a private school. They sure didn't want him hanging out with Cole or Alex again. They'd all been released to the custody of their parents, who'd pulled some strings so everything ended up being cool.

Tightening his grip on the steering wheel, Justin forced his eyes back on the road. Once past the tree, he blinked his headlights three times slowly, coasting to a stop. As the car slowed, his heart sped up.

A figure materialized out of the darkness, barely more than a shadow, and grabbed Justin's door.

He twitched then ran his hands along his pants, hoping to cover it.

"Didn't bring any company with you tonight, did you?"

"No." His voice cracked and he swallowed. "Uh, no."

"Good. Get out."

Justin's hand shook as he unbuckled the seatbelt. It slapped the side of the door as it returned. He jumped. The *thunk* sounded loud and out of place here. Like him. His breath hurt his lungs as he tried to keep from squealing like a girl.

Outside the Honda, he gripped the door and stood on legs

that felt like spaghetti. He had to put on a game face. Or he'd be called out. The dust his car had kicked up invaded his nose and mouth. He spit, then closed the door and leaned against it, arms crossed over his chest. As his eyes adjusted to the dark, he noticed a bunch of other shadowy forms—some with flashlights pointed down—moving toward him.

Bull stood within arm's reach of Justin. The beam of a flashlight caught his white biceps, making his 17 tattoo that much more threatening. His real name was Bill, but as the biggest kid in school, he'd more than earned the nickname Bull.

Justin swallowed again and shifted his feet.

"You did a better job than your buddy Alex." Bull's gaze bore into Justin before he turned and addressed a figure in the shadows. "What's the matter, Alex? You think we were gonna protect you from the cops?"

A shove from behind sent Alex stumbling out of the darkness a couple of steps toward Bull. Alex glanced up at Bull then down again. "I wasn't thinking," he mumbled. "I didn't know what to do." Sweat poured down his face.

"Not only did the police catch you, they almost caught us, and we didn't even get the ride." Bull's relaxed posture tightened. His arm cocked back.

Justin flinched.

Bull's fist landed squarely on Alex's chest. It knocked him off his feet. The guys behind backed away. Alex sprawled in the dirt. His mouth opened, gasping. He wasn't getting air. His face turned red and darkened.

Justin lunged forward.

A band tightened around his arm, yanked him back. "You want some of that?"

Justin tore his gaze from his friend and met Bull's cold gaze. "But he's not—" He broke off as jolts of pain seared his arm. His bone would snap any minute.

Then the pressure was gone. Justin grabbed his arm and sagged against his car. A coughing sound caught his attention.

Alex rolled to his side and threw up.

"Where's your buddy?" Bull took a couple of steps toward Alex.

"There." One of the Seventeeners pointed.

Cole tripped into a small circle of light, each of his arms gripped by a Seventeener.

Bull bore his gaze into Cole who met it for a second before looking away.

Bull shifted his stare.

When Alex didn't even try to meet it, just stared at the ground he'd collapsed on, Justin's world shifted. Alex was the toughest kid he knew. Up until now, he figured Bull was just like Alex. Now Justin knew he was wrong. And probably dead.

When Bull's gaze pinned Justin, he forced himself to meet it. Saliva pooled in his mouth. He forced himself to not move. His chest felt like it was going to burst.

Bull's eyes narrowed.

Justin fought to control his shaking. Anticipating what Bull would do next, he tensed.

The gaze moved away.

Slowly, Justin released his breath.

"So much for your initiation. You girls are going to have to do it again. This time it's bigger." Bull grinned wickedly. "And I'm going along to make sure you do it right."

Chapter Three

Heather sipped her go-to coffee of choice on rough mornings, the Jitter Bug's Jumpin' Java, then lined up the cup on the conference room table next to her notepad and pen and glanced at her phone to check the time. Her boss, managing editor Susan Tang, was late. Nothing good could come of that.

She stifled a yawn as she glanced around the table at the other members of the editorial team, hoping they didn't notice. Mondays after singing at church were always the hardest. It didn't help that she'd stared at the ceiling above her bed thinking of Kyle's moody-ocean eyes. And reliving her baptizing the table with iced tea.

That was after she'd spent an hour resolving to push Quinn out of her mind. An hour of prayer and reviewing Bible verses on fear. He was just being his persistent self. Once she got used to the idea of his being in town—and leaving soon—she was able to forget about him. Mostly.

Lunch had been informative as well as fun. She'd learned Kyle kept a clean truck, was a detective for the police force here in town, and lived one neighborhood over from her. A neighborhood she often ran in. And he didn't seem to think she was a total idiot even after the iced tea disaster.

It'd been sweet the way he'd been almost protective of her after finding that stupid note Quinn had left on her car yesterday afternoon. Kyle being a cop, the protection thing probably came naturally to him. Still, it was nice to be the recipient of someone watching out for her, even if it was most likely professionally motivated.

Glancing up she caught the gaze of the other assistant editor, Brian. He raised his eyebrows and started to say something but Susan strode in.

"Good morning, everyone. Let's get to work." She slapped her binder on the table as she sat, swiping her practical bob behind her ear. "How's September's issue coming? Are all the stories in?"

This was not going to be a good meeting. Heather looked at her notes. "We flagged one of the stories and sent it back to the writer with some concerns about factual accuracy. It should be back in a day or so."

"Not good enough. Pull it and put it in October. Brian, what do you have?"

"One of the articles came in long—"

"How long?"

"About a thousand words, but—"

"That's not a little long. That's a whole other article. These are moms we're writing for. They don't have time for that. Do we have any articles coming up about blended families or how to deal with a wayward teenager? I think it's about time we put one of those in the rotation."

Heather shot Brian a look, while surreptitiously wiping her palm on her pants. He gave a small shrug. Susan was in rare form this morning. She was firm and demanded a lot, but generally wasn't this harsh.

A cell phone rang. Everyone looked around and checked their phones. Susan had an absolute no-cell-phone policy for meetings. If someone desperately needed you, it could wait until after the meeting. It kept meetings short and on topic. But the way Susan's mood was today, whoever the offender was would probably be looking for a new position.

Susan bent down and came up with her own cell phone. Ringing. A slight chuckle washed through the room. She tapped on her phone and stood, heading for the door. "What did you find out about Alex?" The words drifted back into the room as she pushed open the conference room door and left.

Everyone stared at each other around the table. Susan had never answered her phone before, let alone left a meeting. "Well, that was interesting," Brian tipped his chair back. "Who's Alex?"

"I think that's her stepson." Heather flipped through her notes, trying to be prepared for whatever Susan might bring up next when she got back, but not having much hope that it would even matter. There was no telling what Susan would want so there was no use even trying to prepare. "I hope it's nothing serious."

"It would have to be, don't you think?" Brian said. "To pull her out of a meeting?"

The coffeemaker burbled in response.

"Let's continue without her." Brian picked up his pen. "We do this every week. Okay, like I was saying, we can jump the article to the back ..."

Kyle took a deep sugary swallow of the fake fruit punch. Yeah, he had the taste buds of a ten-year-old. Lunch at his desk wasn't his idea of fun, but he needed to work on the Bedroom Burglar case and figure out what to do about Justin. He moved some papers out of the way and set his burrito on the scarred laminate desktop. His cheap chair squeaked every time he moved.

But he couldn't push Heather out of his mind. Funny thing

was, when he got in his truck this morning, a faint hint of something swirled inside. Fresh and…fruit? Flowers? He didn't know.

Heather. He grinned.

Kyle quietly prayed then bit into his burrito.

He could juggle work and romance without hurting either. Right?

A twinge of uncertainty pinged his gut. He hadn't done it before. He'd failed, and the woman he'd thought he'd marry had left him. She hadn't understood the hours he needed to put in to get ahead.

The lieutenant was a hard man to please, much like his father. In fact, Kyle could only remember his father being proud of him two times. Once, when he was eleven and reported a car being stolen. When the police caught the guy, they found he was behind a rash of vehicle thefts in the area. Kyle got an award, and the picture in the *Orange County Register* showed him shaking the police chief's hand. His dad stood behind him with his hand on Kyle's shoulder, grinning. The other time was when Kyle took the basketball team to the championships his junior year. Two times in thirty-three years.

At least he'd made detective under the lieutenant, and he knew the expectations. He could manage it. This time would be different.

He thought of that note on her car. And who might have left it. Her reaction didn't indicate it was a romantic note, but that didn't mean she was unattached. He'd asked Bernie about it after Heather had left, but he hadn't known anything either. Or at least anything he wanted to share with Kyle. Bernie was hiding something.

He poked a chip into his salsa. Since he'd memorized her number when she'd given it to Melissa for Bible study, he could call and ask her to dinner.

Kyle took another bite then shook his head. But he hadn't asked her for it. Would she find that creepy? Or think it sweet that he had tracked down her number?

Women. Who knew what they were thinking? Was he even sure he was ready to get back into this dating thing?

He could take it slow. But what if she thought that meant he wasn't interested? Why was there so much room for miscommunication in relationships? Why couldn't it just be straightforward?

He wished Heather had let him read the note on her car, but he didn't know her well enough to ask. Something about her reaction. Fear had flickered first; she'd gone a little pale. Like what had happened when she was standing on the stage at church. She recovered quickly with a deep breath and annoyance. But it *was* a cover. He was sure of that. Something in that note scared her. And she didn't want him or Bernie to know that.

He thought about that while he finished off his chips and salsa. An ex-boyfriend? A current boyfriend? Kyle wasn't sure he wanted to get involved in that kind of drama.

He hadn't dated anyone since Christa. She'd hurt him. But that was in the past. He didn't want her to ruin his future too. He thought of how hard it was not to just stare at Heather during lunch. He was pretty sure the chemistry wasn't one sided. He read people for a living.

And he wasn't a chicken.

He crushed his wrapper and threw it at the trash can. Two points.

HEATHER ROLLED BACK FROM HER DESK, EYES TIRED FROM tweaking the text of a two-page spread. She was more than ready for another hit of caffeine. It had been a weird morning. Susan never returned to the meeting, and she and Brian finished it.

Susan still hadn't come out of her office. The whole staff was tiptoeing around.

On her desk, her cell phone vibrated. A quick look

revealed another call from Quinn. The third or fourth of the morning. One touch sent it to voicemail with the rest of them.

Standing, she stretched her arms overhead, tilting her neck to work out the kinks. Her job as a magazine editor came with too many hours hunched over a computer. A sore neck and daily headaches had been her companions, along with visits to the physical therapist and the threat of losing her job, until she'd started lifting weights in addition to running. She wasn't a disciplined person, but wanting to keep her job put enough fear in her to develop a few new habits. Now she just had to remember to take frequent breaks.

She picked up her purse and rounded the office divider. "I'm headed to lunch, Kelsy."

Heather's administrative assistant swiveled her chair, smacking her gum. "Yes, ma'am."

Kelsy dyed her hair again this weekend. Today it appeared to be her natural dark brown on top with the bottom two inches platinum blonde, but Heather wouldn't be willing to bet that even the brown was Kelsy's natural color. She waved goodbye with silver and blue tipped nails. Kelsy's wild hair never bothered Heather. If it did, she wouldn't have long to wait until it changed to something else.

Heather pushed out the door, the cool air of the building giving way to the scent of eucalyptus trees warmed by the sun. She clicked the remote for her car and heard the locks pop open. A minute later, she headed down Lake Forest, the sounds of Hillsong United coming from her phone plugged into the car stereo.

At a stoplight, she glanced in the rearview mirror, threading her fingers through her razor-cut bangs. She wasn't a very creative person if you judged by her hair. Her cut was fun, but it only saw highlights if she stayed in the sun too long. And her nails didn't even have polish on them. She hadn't had time to get them done. She sighed. She didn't want to do anything wild, but her life was boring and conventional for a supposedly creative person.

Except for her ex-fiancé who was trying to become her stalker. Give it up already, Quinn. Not a high point in making her life more interesting.

At Sonshine Christian bookstore, she found the Bible study Melissa had e-mailed her the information on. Flipping through it, she was intrigued.

After buying the book, she headed to Baja Fresh. A spicy burrito with lots of cheese would be a great way to break up a Monday. Inside, she ordered lunch, and when she pulled her wallet out, Kyle's card fell into her hand. She fingered it, thinking about last Sunday, before tucking it into her purse.

She carried her tray to a table and took a bite of her burrito. The soft tortilla wrapped around the spicy meat and creamy cheese hit the spot. Yep, this was a good choice.

"Hi, Heather." Quinn.

She dropped her burrito to the tray with a plop. Tremors shot through her as she jerked around. This time she wasn't imagining his voice.

"You didn't call me back, so I thought I'd see if I could join you." He pulled out the chair across from her and slid into it.

"How'd you know I'd be here?" Had someone in her office said something? She hadn't told Kelsy where she was going.

"It was a good guess. You always came here a couple of times a week."

Great. She was such a creature of habit that even after more than a year her ex-fiancé still knew her routine. This was ridiculous.

And creepy.

But really, what did she think Quinn would do? Just because she never felt she could hold her own in their verbal sparring matches didn't mean he was any kind of danger to her. Right? She tried to grab that peace she had last night, scrambling to remember Bible verses. Nothing would come.

He stared at her with a silly grin. "It's so good to see you."

She nodded and took a sip of her soda. She couldn't say the same. "I need to get back to work. What did you want?" Putting her hands in her lap, she turned her bracelet on her wrist.

"I was hoping I could talk you into dinner tonight." He leaned forward across the table.

The chair back pressed into her. "No. I don't think that's a good idea. Let's just leave it how it is, okay? You're going back to New York. Let's not stir anything up. When are you leaving, by the way?"

"I'm not."

Her stomach turned, the burrito sitting in it like a lump. How close was the bathroom? Or maybe she could throw up on Quinn. That'd be justice. Why couldn't she knock her iced tea over on him? "What do you mean?"

"My company's opening another branch out here they want me to manage."

"I thought you were on vacation." She choked the words out. The only consolation in the midst of all his craziness last year was that he was on the other side of the country. How was she going to live with him being here?

Quinn reached across the table, but Heather kept both hands in her lap. After waiting a moment, he pulled his hands back and gave her a small smile. "I was. I'll be closing things out in New York, and then I'll be back. I was hoping we could have another chance."

Stomach plummeting, Heather gathered enough energy to shoot to her feet. The chair scraped, tipped, and clanged back into place. She had to get out of here. Shrugging her purse over her shoulder, she crumpled the paper around her burrito and grabbed her drink. "I'm going. We're done. Here and everywhere. Get it? We are not getting back together."

She beat him out the door, clicking furiously on her key fob. All she wanted to do was get in her car before he stopped her. She opened the door and slid in. He called after her. Slamming the door shut, out of the corner of her eye she saw him jerk his fingers back. She almost wished she'd caught them in the door. Serve him right.

Not meeting his eyes, she backed out and headed to the office.

She hoped he didn't follow her.

Chapter Four

Kyle tossed his truck keys on the kitchen counter, happy to beat his sister home from work for once. He unbuttoned his shirt as he headed toward his bedroom, thinking of what to do with this unexpected bonus of time.

He'd better call Justin before he forgot.

In his room, he changed into his running clothes. Sitting on the bed, he picked up the phone. He dialed and tucked it under his chin while he pulled on his running shoes.

"Yeah?"

"Justin? It's Kyle. How's that shoulder?" He finished tying his shoes and grabbed the phone with his hand.

"It's okay. Not too sore if I don't try to do too much with it."

"Think you'd be up to catching some waves tomorrow?"

"Yeah, I guess. I'll paddle with one arm or something."

Don't be so enthusiastic. "All right. I'll pick you up at five thirty."

"In the morning?"

Kyle laughed. "Yeah in the morning. Don't forget to tell your mom."

"Okay."

"See you in the morning. Five thirty."

Kyle punched the phone off and tossed it on the nightstand. He did some light stretches to warm up. Satisfied he wouldn't pull anything, he scooped up his phone and clipped it to his waistband, and then headed out the door. He started with a slow jog down his street then hesitated when he got to Pittsford. Did he turn right and head up the hills for a better workout, or jog down to El Toro to the Aliso Creek Trail that ran near Heather's house? She had told him at lunch where she lived and that she was a runner.

He didn't even make the pretense of debating it. He turned left and stretched his legs out into a full run.

Every day he tried to get one in. In the winter, it was more difficult because it got dark earlier, but it was spring. He had daylight and no excuses.

Maybe he could figure out where she lived. He'd also learned she grew up a valley girl, which he got to tease her about. Maybe they could go to the Jitter Bug. She'd mentioned liking the chocolate truffle cheesecake at their neighborhood coffeehouse.

Otherwise—unless he called her—he wouldn't see her until Friday's Bible study.

And then there was the small matter of the softball game Bernie was trying to get together for Saturday. Bernie had teased him at lunch about never showing up. Kyle hadn't made a game yet and dreaded it every time Bernie brought it up.

He was good at basketball—could shoot free throws all day long—but softball was another matter. His dad was rarely around growing up so Kyle hadn't had anyone to throw the ball with and consequently threw like a third grader. While he didn't think the group would care, he couldn't bring himself to parade his lack of talent around.

So. Was he going to call her?

After being with Christa a year and a half, planning a wedding, and buying a house to fix up only to have her decide she couldn't handle being married to a cop, he wasn't too eager to swim in that pool again. In fact, he flat out hadn't. When did women decide those things anyhow? Did they have a list of acceptable occupations?

When Christa had first left him, being alone didn't seem so bad. Rehabbing the house consumed whatever time was left over from his job. Then his sister moved in after graduating college, so the place didn't seem empty.

Why was that not enough anymore?

Because he'd been hearing the voice of an angel in his head. At odd times during the day he'd hear her singing that worship song and found himself humming along.

Lord, I don't think You've called me to a life of singleness. I'm not asking if Heather's The One. I just don't… Show me what to do. And now he was apparently seeing one too. He had reached El Toro Road, traffic whizzing by as he waited for the signal to change.

There she stood. Heather. Across the street from him, wearing a tank top and shorts, her hair pulled back into a pony-tail, stretching her calves by leaning against the light pole.

Pleasure curled through his chest. Did she have the same idea he did? He didn't know, but he was glad to see her. *Thanks, God. That was fast.* And some people didn't think God had a sense of humor.

She looked up, and he watched her face, seeing the moment she realized who he was.

She smiled.

He cupped his hands to his mouth. "Stay there. I'll come over." She nodded.

The light changed and he jogged over. "So, come here often?" He grinned.

"I didn't see anyone on the trail"—she tilted her head toward her right—"and I don't like to run it alone, so I figured I'd chal-lenge myself with the hills in your neighborhood."

A little hope flared at that comment. She'd planned to run in his neighborhood. Had she hoped to cross paths with him?

"You're a wise woman not to run the trail alone." She didn't have earbuds in, he was glad to see, so she could remain aware of her surroundings. He ran a hand through his hair. "I don't mean to sound too cop like, but don't ever go back there alone. I've seen some nasty things happen. However, since I'd decided not to challenge myself and you're not alone now, you want to take the trail?"

She gave him a saucy smile and took off. He had to scramble to catch up, but his legs were longer than hers so he made up the ground.

They jogged in silence for a moment. "How far do you usually go?" Kyle asked, looking over at her. She had good form, a nice, easy stride.

Great legs.

"Two or three miles. About ten minutes out, ten minutes back. Depends how many hills I have to conquer." She flashed him a smile. "What about you?"

"About four."

Heather shook her head. "Then you can hit your friendly neighborhood hills after you drop me back home."

"Aw come on. You could do it." "Yeah, but I'd hate you tomorrow."

He laughed. "Well, I wouldn't want that."

Kyle normally didn't like running with a partner. He didn't want to have to match anyone's stride or make conversation, and it was the only chance he had to let his mind decompress, especially if his phone didn't go off. But running with Heather felt comfortable.

"Do you usually run at this time?" she asked. "I'm surprised I haven't seen you before."

"Usually it's later, but I got off work early." Was she hinting that he'd come over here hoping to see her? He slid a glance her direction. Her eyes focused straight ahead, but her face was relaxed, shoulders down. Well, she didn't seem to mind. Just to be safe, he changed the subject. "You mentioned you work for a magazine. What do you do there?"

"I'm an editor. It's a lifestyle magazine. Mostly it's an e-zine, you know, online. But we do a pretty big print run still. We try to be relevant to what's going on today, help people— mostly moms—realize you can be on trend and be interested in raising a family." Looking over at him, she smiled. "Not as action-packed as your job. What was that you said about a pursuit Sunday?"

Kyle shook his head. "I could do with less of that kind of action. It was actually a kid I know. Justin. He's seventeen and has had a few brushes with the law. His buddy was driving an SUV that had been reported stolen, refused to yield, and began a chase that ended with me pulling them out of a wreck and, luck-ily, not dead."

Heather briefly closed her eyes and shook her head. "Turns out, the car was owned by one of the kids' stepmom. But bottom line, Justin's hanging out with the wrong kind of friends."

"How do you know him?"

"I was his fifth-grade Sunday School teacher. He and his mom go to our church."

"That's a tough situation because they think they know it all already."

"Ah, so you do know teenagers." Kyle chuckled. "I want to tell him, 'Hey, I'm older than you, I know better. Don't do that. It's stupid and it'll mess up your life.' But he doesn't want to hear it. But I have another plan. I'm taking him surfing tomorrow. Maybe he'll see me more as a friend than an authority figure."

"Sounds good. Are you going to be able to get him out of bed?" She gave him a wry grin.

Kyle laughed. "I don't know. He didn't sound too thrilled to be picked up at five thirty."

"I wouldn't be either. I could never be a surfer, having to get up that early to catch the good waves." Heather looked over her shoulder. "Head back?"

"Sure." Kyle glanced at his watch. He half wondered if they could slow to a walk to extend their time together. What did they have in common? Church. He'd fall back on that. "Speaking of church, what'd you think of that guy's testimony?"

"I think it's one of the best things our church does. I love hearing about how other people found Jesus during their darkest times. I've been a believer since forever, so it's not something I've experienced." Heather swiped her arm across her forehead. "It always makes me wonder what I would do if I were in their situation."

"I've bought several sermon CDs to give to people just for the testimonies. It gets rid of the idea that you have to have it all together before you come to Jesus. You can preach it to someone all you like, but sometimes the only thing that will get through is a personal experience."

"If you can get them to listen."

"Yeah, there's that small issue."

They chatted about a few more subjects, and he was surprised when her townhome complex came into view. They slowed to a walk. Words tumbled through his brain, and he hoped he didn't mess this up. "Hey, if you don't already have plans, you want to grab dinner tomorrow night?"

Her whole face lit up.

He'd made the right decision.

His waist vibrated. His phone. He wanted to groan. He unhooked it and looked at the number. Work. He had to take it. "I'm sorry. Give me a minute." He turned to the side and answered. As he talked, he watched Heather do some stretching. He was making a lousy impression, he was sure. He got off the phone as fast as he could.

"Sorry about that. I have to head back into work. There's some new information on a case I've been working on." He took a breath. Now he was going to have to ask her twice. "So, about tomorrow night…?"

"That sounds really nice. I'd like that."

Tension he didn't even know he was carrying drained from him. "Good. How does Las Brisas sound? If we get a window table, we can watch the sunset."

"Ooh, I love that place. They have the best seafood and a great view."

"I'll pick you up at six thirty."

"I'm looking forward to it."

So was he. More than he would have thought.

Kyle didn't want to let her go, but he couldn't linger. He could walk her to her door. He had to know where to pick her up tomorrow, right?

"Looks like someone's got a delivery." The front porch of one house was covered with vases of flowers. He couldn't even see the brick steps. "Which one's yours?"

She was unpinning her key from the waistband of her shorts. "The middle one."

The one with all the flowers.

Heather raised her head and froze. It was the same look on her face as when she saw the note on her car. But this time it didn't fade as quickly. She strode to the steps and moved a vase so she could get to the door.

Kyle counted five vases. That was some secret admirer. He thought about his dinner invitation. He wondered who the competition was. If Kyle had shelled out the bucks for all those flowers he'd be eating PB and Js for lunch for a month. Though it might be worth it if it put a smile on Heather's face.

But she wasn't smiling. She wasn't a woman happy to get a porch full of flowers; she was freaked out.

She was searching through the vases, probably looking for a card.

"Any idea who they're from?"

She turned toward him, almost as if she'd forgotten he was there.

"There's only one person. But surely he didn't…"

Behind her, the front door wasn't latched completely. "Heather, did you shut your door when you left?"

She spun around. With a crash the vase fell to the porch, shattered glass spinning everywhere.

Kyle was at her side in two steps. "Don't touch anything. You locked it when you left?"

"Y-yes. Yes, I always do. See?" She held up the key. "I pinned it to my waistband."

He examined the door and jamb without touching either. "Doesn't look forced. Does anyone else have a key?"

"Sarah, for emergencies. But she's still at work." She chewed on her bottom lip.

Something left unsaid hung between them. "Who else, Heather?"

BULL PULLED FARTHER BACK INTO THE BUSHES SO HE wouldn't be seen. He was good at this surveillance stuff. He could still see them clearly though, the cop talking to the chick on her front steps. The same cop that had nailed Alex. The same cop that was the lead investigator on the Bedroom Burglar case. Stupid name. But what did you expect from the press?

It hadn't been too hard to figure out. The *Orange County Register* did a lot of his investigating for him by interviewing the cops on the case. As for the rest, well, the city put hardly any money into their computer system, so it hadn't been much of a challenge for someone of his skills.

He grinned. The cop was easy to follow, and Bull had gotten a little more info than he'd expected. Not to mention a nice view of that chick's legs in shorts. Discovering where the cop's girlfriend lived was a little gift that dropped into his lap. He hadn't let it go to waste.

HEATHER'S STOMACH DROPPED. QUINN. HE STILL HAD A key. She had planned to change the locks, but then he moved to New York and she didn't think about it again.

So what was the deal? He delivered the flowers and then decided to let himself in? To what purpose? She edged toward the door, wanting to see inside but a little afraid.

She forgot she had the card in her hand until she crushed it with her fist. *Miss you* it said. Yeah, right.

"Heather?"

She didn't want to tell Kyle that Quinn had a key. *Really* didn't want to. He'd probably yank back his invitation to dinner faster than those rabbits that lived along the running trail.

"That guy at church? Quinn? I think he still has a key."

Kyle's expression was unreadable. "And the flowers are from him?"

She nodded, biting her lip.

He didn't say anything for a long moment. Would he ask to see the card?

"He didn't have your permission to come into your house or use the key?"

She shook her head vigorously. "No. I have no interest in having anything to do with him." She wanted to explain why Quinn still had the key but felt like a babbling idiot. Kyle was in cop mode, and she wasn't sure what she thought about it.

He nudged the door open, motioning her to stay put. As if she could move, trapped by fear and flower vases. He disappeared inside. A sense of loss pulled at her chest, surprising her. Kyle's job wasn't the kind you could leave at the office.

Quinn had been so obsessed with moving ahead in his career that he chose a move to New York over their engagement. She didn't want to go through that again. Not to mention Kyle's job dealt with the darker side of life. Could she handle that? She had no experience. Though she was getting a taste of it now.

Her mind didn't know what thoughts to settle on and examine. She looked at the flowers. A nice assortment, but Quinn didn't know what she really liked. He probably had just grabbed whatever the florist had on display, figuring quantity over quality. Classic Quinn. What had she ever seen in him?

She didn't want the flowers in her house. Her mind scrolled through what she could do with them. A senior center? Retirement home? Surely there was someone who would like their day brightened by flowers and wouldn't be tainted by the knowledge of the original giver.

"Heather?"

She jumped again at Kyle's voice, her foot catching the edge of a vase and nearly tipping it over.

"Come in and see if anything's missing or been disturbed." Kyle reached out a hand to help her step over the vases and the broken glass. "Don't touch the door."

The air conditioning raised goose bumps on her arms, or was it the brief moment of her hand in Kyle's? The air was cool compared to the warm, slightly humid air outside. She scanned the room, almost afraid to enter. Everything looked in place. She took a few steps forward, feeling a bit more secure. Maybe she had forgotten to lock the door.

She turned around. "Seems okay. Except my cat usually is here waiting for me, clawing at the door when she hears me come up the steps. Did you see her?"

Kyle shook his head. "I didn't know you had a cat."

"Snowflake? Where are you, girl?" She made scratching noises on the couch with her fingernails. "Not that she comes when I call, but it makes me feel better. It's weird, though. The door was ajar? I don't think she'd run out, but maybe." Heather leaned over the couch. A bit of fur stuck out from under the back of the couch. "There you are." She reached over and dragged the cat out, who resisted with claws unsheathed. "What's wrong with you?"

Hugging the cat close while she squirmed was a chore, so Heather dropped her on the couch. Snowflake shot up the spiral staircase to the loft bedroom like her tail was on fire.

Dusting off the fur Snowflake had spontaneously shed on her, Heather looked around her living room. Nothing was missing or out of place. But Snowflake was scared of something. Was she losing her mind? Maybe she did leave the door unlocked. She never did that, but there didn't seem to be another explanation. Why would Quinn unlock the door? And if he did, why did he leave the flowers outside? And why would he deliver them himself ? He'd never done that. He thrived on big drama and productions. None of this made sense. Her head hurt. And she looked like an idiot in front of a guy she wanted to impress.

"This your painting?" Kyle stood by her drawing table placed in front of the sliding glass door for the good light.

Her face got hot. "Yeah." She moved toward him, wanting to cover it up. "It's just something I do for fun, to relax."

"I'm guessing you didn't do this part."

Her brush lay on the drawing board, dripping cadmium red on the edge of the paper. She never let her brushes sit with paint. But even worse was the giant blood red 17 stroked across her seascape.

She wasn't losing her mind. Someone had been in here.

PARKED ON SOME STREET HE'D NEVER BEEN ON BEFORE, Justin peered into the darkness. Bull sauntered into the glare of the streetlights toward the car. He kicked the Honda's front tire, then pulled the door open and jumped in. "Think you can handle this piece of junk?"

"Yeah." He wouldn't have kicked it if it was a BMW. Stupid parents. Did they live to humiliate their kids?

"Good. Then you can be the driver."

Justin swallowed. The driver for what? But you didn't ask Bull questions. Not if you liked your face in one piece. Rumor was he had dropped out of school and joined the Marines, only to get booted out when he knocked out his drill instructor.

"Drive."

"Where?" Justin's voice cracked and he cleared it. Bull smirked. "I'll let you know."

Justin headed down the street, glancing at Cole and Alex in the backseat. Alex's elbow was propped on the door, his leg jumping to the beat of the music. Cole looked out the window, shifting in his seat. Were they okay with this? Or was he the only one who hated it? Why was he doing this anyway? He didn't even like these guys.

One word. Or rather, one girl. Bree. She'd sat by him at lunch today and invited him over to her house to study tomorrow. He could just imagine telling her he was officially a Seventeener. Yep, he'd be taking her out tomorrow night.

He just had to survive tonight.

Still, if for some reason they couldn't do the job, and it wasn't his fault, that would be the best of all worlds. His mind raced for a way out but came up blank.

They headed down El Toro, almost to the freeway. "Pull in here." Bull pointed to a shopping center with a music store, bank, and Starbucks. Only the Starbucks was open.

Justin turned into the parking lot and nearly stopped.

Two cop cars sat in the parking lot, cops talking to each other. Both looked up when the Honda pulled in.

Justin's heart pounded. Now what? "Uh, Bull?"

"Just relax, man. It's a public place. Park there." Bull pointed to a slot a couple of places down from the cops.

"Yeah, Justin," Alex chimed in from the back. "You're starting to act like one of those perfect little Christian teens in those books my stepmomster leaves around. I swear she's thinking they'll make me see the error of my ways or something."

Justin ignored him and let out a breath. He wanted to get out of here as fast as possible. But they couldn't. The cops were watching, and how would it look if they just pulled out again? Nope, they were stuck.

Bull pushed open his door. "Let's go get some coffee."

The guys followed Bull inside and ordered coffee. Justin stood around waiting for his drink, feeling like everyone was looking at him. Even late on a weeknight was a busy time for this Starbucks. Bull snagged a table, and Justin joined him as soon as his order came up. He messed around with his cup, not looking at Bull. As far as he could tell—the reflection on the glass made it hard to see—the cops were still out there.

Cole and Alex joined them. They sat there saying nothing.

A few minutes later the cops came in, heading directly for their table.

Panic bubbled up in his chest. What had they done?

"Where are you headed tonight?" one of the cops asked.

"Just having some coffee. There's no harm in that, is there, Officer?" Bull had a stupid grin on his face.

Bull was an idiot.

"Finish it up and head home. Curfew's in half an hour."

"Yes, sir." They all mumbled except Bull.

Now was the time to get out of here. If Justin wanted to leave, Bull wouldn't dare stop him. He stood, pulling the keys out of his pocket. "Come on, guys. We're done. Let's go home." He walked out without looking to see if anyone followed him.

No one but him knew the keys in his hands were slicked with sweat.

Chapter Five

K yle rolled over and slammed off the alarm. He stared at the clock a moment then rubbed his hands over his face. Justin was right. This was a ridiculous hour. Especially since he'd been up late dealing with the situation at Heather's place. He'd called that Quinn guy who swore he hadn't been anywhere near her place—he'd had the flowers delivered—and even had forgotten he had a key. Since Kyle couldn't see the connection between Quinn and the Seventeeners he was inclined to believe Quinn.

He stumbled to the kitchen, not turning on the light, and pushed the button to start the coffeepot. It'd be faster than Starbucks. Back in his room, he put on shorts and a T-shirt. He grabbed a towel from the hall closet, carried it to the kitchen and tossed it on the counter. Pulling down a travel mug, he filled it with coffee.

What he couldn't wrap his mind around was how the Seventeeners got mixed up with Heather.

And into her house.

He'd gone to Home Depot and picked up a new lockset for her and installed it. Then he still had to go into the station and deal with the burglary case. He'd fallen into bed about, oh, four hours ago.

He still had to pick up Justin and drive the twenty-some miles to Trestles. They'd be lucky to get in an hour before it got too crowded. It would be nice if the kid appreciated it. Somehow, he doubted it.

Ten minutes later he pulled up to the gate at Coto de Caza. The guard took his name and looked at his clipboard. "You're not on the list. Are they expecting you?"

Kyle closed his eyes. Justin hadn't told his mom. "Supposed to be."

"I'll call up there."

Which would wake Claire. Did teenagers ever use their brains? He should just go back home and get in bed, forget the whole thing.

The guard stuck a paper pass on the truck's dashboard. The gate arm rose. "Have a nice day."

Two minutes later Kyle pulled into the Fosters' driveway. He climbed out of the truck just as the front door opened. Claire stood there in her bathrobe. Kyle hesitated a moment. Never having seen her without makeup or her hair perfectly in place, he felt bad for having clearly disturbed her. "Claire, I'm so sorry. Justin didn't tell you."

"Not until I rolled him out of bed. But when the gatehouse called, I hoped the only reason you were coming here so early was to take him surfing." She moved back from the door. "Come in. He's still staggering around upstairs."

Kyle followed her into the house.

"Besides," she said over her shoulder, "you're not the worst thing to see first thing in the morning. How come some woman hasn't snatched you up yet?" She moved into the kitchen.

What? Claire was at least ten years older than him. She wasn't hitting on him. Was she?

She pulled two mugs out of the cupboard. "I've been wracking my brain, trying to find someone to set you up with, but all my friends have kids Justin's age or older." She poured coffee into the mugs and pushed one over to him.

Relieved, Kyle slid onto a barstool and wrapped his hands around the mug, something normal in this weird situation. He took a sip.

Claire was studying him. He needed to say something. Luckily, Justin clattered down the stairs at that moment. Kyle stood. "You ready, bro?"

"Yeah, my board and wetsuit are in the garage." Justin opened the door to the garage and disappeared.

"Thanks for taking him." Claire tugged her robe tighter around her. "I appreciate it even if he doesn't."

"No problem. See you later."

He went out the front as the garage door clattered up. Justin emerged holding his gear. He tossed the board in the back of the truck with Kyle's before climbing in.

The waves had better be good to redeem this morning.

AT 5:30 THAT AFTERNOON, KYLE EXAMINED HIMSELF IN the mirror. Nope, there was no way to hide it. He had one heck of a shiner on his right eye. Even though he'd kept ice on it all day, it still didn't look much better. The guys at work had given him a hard time about it.

He slammed his hand on the bathroom counter. No good deed goes unpunished. He should have followed his instincts and gone back home this morning. The water was miserably cold, even with a wetsuit. Then his surfboard had popped up, come down and caught him just under his right eye. Heather wasn't going to want to go out with him looking like this.

He trudged into the bedroom and picked up the phone.

Chapter Six

Kyle wiped his hand down his pants before he pressed Heather's doorbell exactly at 6:30. She opened the door a second later and his mind went blank searching for words to express his delight. Her dress kissed her curves. The top part of her hair was pulled up and back, kind of pouffy and the ends were more curly than usual. She wore more makeup than on Sunday, but it looked good. A Siamese cat twined around her legs.

He cleared his throat. "Hi. You look... amazing." He was glad he hadn't called and canceled.

She gave him a wide smile. "Thanks. Come on in."

He stepped into the entryway, not sure what to do with his hands. He stuffed them in his pockets and rocked back on his heels.

She studied his face a minute then giggled.

"So, what do you think? Too horrible to go out with?"

She touched his forearm, and he felt it burn through his shirtsleeve. "No, not at all." She moved her hand and tilted her head, giving him a wicked grin. "A little rakish. I always wanted to go out with one of those bad boy types."

He raised an eyebrow.

"Just kidding." A look of concern crossed her face. "Does it hurt?"

For a moment, he thought she would reach up to touch the bruise under his eye. He found himself desperately hoping she would, imagining her cool, soft fingers on his face.

His mouth went dry. "No, not really."

She nodded and stepped back, the moment broken. "What happened?"

"A misbehaving surfboard."

She laughed. "Not the answer I was expecting. I left my purse upstairs. I'll be right back."

The cat blinked its blue eyes at him, and then followed Heather up the spiral staircase.

He looked around her living room, the sounds from the Fray's latest album filling the room. He'd been in cop mode last time he was here. Now he tried to see her living space as reflective of her. Crammed bookcases covered the wall, filling the strange angles made by the staircase. A floral couch with lots of pillows and a stuffed chair furnished the living room, and a small round table sat in the dining area. Watercolors covered walls painted a light greenish gray that matched the furniture. He was sure there was a designer name for the color, like Misty Sea or Meadow Smoke or some such name that told you absolutely nothing about the color. This place looked like Heather.

He strolled over to one of the watercolors on the wall. It was an ocean-scape, looked like Laguna Beach as seen from the bluffs of Heisler Park. It captured the coolness of the ocean as well as the heat of the day. He looked at the signature in the corner. Heather N. McAlistair.

The cat came back and rubbed up against his legs. He reached down to scratch its ears and got a loud purr in return. He knew she liked to paint, but he didn't know she was this good. He straightened and stepped over to another painting on the wall. It was hers too.

He walked toward the sliding glass door, examining it, remembering what he had found last time he was here. Glancing down at the drafting table he saw it was empty. The painting had been taken for evidence, but she hadn't replaced it. An odd sadness settled in his stomach.

Footsteps sounded overhead, and he did a quick final look around. Her kitchen was red along the backsplash and above the small window over the sink. He never would have thought to do that, but it did look good.

She rounded the last curve on the stairs and reached over to the docked iPod to turn it off. "Ready?"

"Yep." He gave the room one last glance as they moved to the door. "I like your red kitchen. I might even let you and my sister, Kim, gang up on me and talk me into painting my walls something other than beige. She is a clothing designer and is always trying to get me to do stuff to the house since she lives there too. I only let her paint her room. She used some purple blue color. It actually doesn't look too bad, but letting her do any other part of the house scares me."

She laughed. "It's just paint, Kyle. If you don't like it, you can start over."

His chest tightened. She did something to his heart, and right now he wanted to trigger that soft, throaty laugh again. They drove down to Laguna Beach, pulling into Las Brisas's parking lot as the sun hovered above the horizon, barely touching the edge of the ocean. Kyle took the ignition-only key off his key ring and handed it to the valet. The entrance was on the other side of the building from the parking lot, allowing a picturesque ocean-view walk along the top of a cliff. But Heather's closeness distracted him.

He felt her take a deep breath and slowly release it. "Mmm, I never get tired of the smell of the ocean. There's just something incredibly relaxing about it. I wish I could bottle it and put it on my desk." She looked up at him. "When I can't stand sitting at my desk a moment longer, I print everything out, put it in my bag, put the top down on the Miata, and come to the ocean."

"That sounds like fun."

"One of the perks of the job. My desk can be anywhere." They rounded the corner and walked inside the restaurant where Kyle gave his name to the hostess. She glanced up at his eye; then her gaze flicked to Heather before she led them to their table.

Kyle held Heather's chair for her and then seated himself. Once the hostess left, Heather gave him a conspiratorial grin. "She was just dying to ask you what happened."

He leaned forward. "You're having too much fun with this." She gave him a saucy smirk.

He was incredibly glad she didn't want to cancel tonight. The waiter came up and took their drink orders, and then Heather turned her gaze to the ocean view. "Look, the sun's setting." The sun began its dip into the ocean, turning water into fire.

He watched, but only for a moment. Turning back to Heather, he decided he much preferred watching her. Yeah, he had a great view.

He had that same kind of heightened awareness as when entering the house of a suspect. But in this case, it was all focused on Heather. He had expected to be more nervous. It had been almost two years since he'd been on a date. But she was so easy to be around.

The waiter set a glass in front of him. "Are you ready to order?"

Too busy studying Heather, he hadn't looked at the menu. "Do you know what you want?"

She ordered the catch of the day.

He quickly scanned the menu while the waiter wrote Heather's order down. Anything here would be good. He ordered Snapper Veracruz.

The waiter took their menus and left.

She touched her silverware, moving it slightly, before adjusting her bracelet. Nervous again. Nice to know he wasn't alone in that emotion.

She tucked a strand of hair behind her ear. "It's kind of funny that I've been in the choir with Bernie for a while, and you're in Bible study with him, but you and I never met before now."

"If I'd known that Bernie knew you fairly well, I would have wrangled an introduction out of him long before now."

A smile played around her lips. "I guess it was a good thing you owed him coffee then."

"A very good thing." He held her gaze until she looked away. "Best bet I ever lost."

"How good of friends are you guys?"

Kyle shrugged, not entirely sure what she was getting at. "We ended up rooming together at a men's retreat two years ago then got roped into the singles' group Melissa was starting." He didn't want to talk about Bernie. He turned the conversation back to her and asked her more about her work.

A few minutes later the waiter brought their food, and the conversation slowed as they savored the mouthwatering seafood. Kyle downed two more glasses of iced tea, not sure why he was so thirsty. Their conversation flowed through the meal, comfortable and interesting.

Taking the last bite, Kyle leaned back. "They have great food here, but the Jitter Bug has better desserts. I was thinking we could head there."

Heather gave a contented sigh. "It might take me the whole trip to make room for some of their chocolate mousse cake."

Dinner had gone well. Well enough that he thought she might want to do it again with him. Glancing at his phone, he said a quick prayer of thanks that it hadn't rung. He had told Steve not to call him under any circumstances. Which had resulted in a large dose of harassment. Of course, with his luck, the Bedroom Burglar would strike again tonight. As long as it was after he took Heather home, the guy could break into the mayor's house for all he cared.

Chapter Seven

Justin pulled up in front of Cole's house, coming straight from Bree's. He hadn't wanted to leave. He and Bree had studied for a while... if you could call it studying. Her parents weren't home. But he had to get to Cole. Between the two of them, maybe they could talk Alex into laying low on this Seventeener thing.

As Justin got out of his car, an arm came around from behind him and shoved the door shut. Biceps with a heavily-decorated 17 tattoo blocked him in. His gaze traveled up the arm to Bull's face.

"I've decided what you girls are going to do for your initiation. Since the cops messed up our plans yesterday."

Justin looked around. Cole and Alex were "escorted" over by two other Seventeeners. He'd kind of hoped Bull had forgotten about them. Two failed initiation attempts. At this point, he wasn't sure if it was worth it. Bree had already agreed to go to the movies with him.

Too late now.

"Since you did a decent job yesterday, you get to drive again." Bull jerked his head in Alex and Cole's direction. "You two girls get to do the actual job. You got the gun?"

Cole and Alex exchanged looks. "Yeah." Alex lifted his shirt exposing the black grip of a gun.

Justin had never even seen one before in real life. Alex was a moron. He'd probably get them all killed.

Bull snorted. "You know how to use it?"

Alex stuffed his hands in his pockets. "Sure."

"Good. Here's the plan."

Kyle's hand was warm on Heather's back as he guided her out of the restaurant.

He paused in the entryway. "Do you want to walk along the cliff for a bit, or will you be too cold?"

She pulled on her sweater. She loved walking along the cliffs even if it would be damp and chilly. "Let's walk for a bit."

He reached for the door, but someone opened it from the other side.

Quinn walked in.

Adrenaline pumped through her veins, leaving her weak. What was he doing here? Coincidence? Probably not, given that this was Quinn.

Kyle's hand returned to Heather's back, and she leaned against it, thankful for the support.

"Heather." Quinn stepped forward, but for once didn't crowd her space. "Las Brisas is still a favorite, I see. And, Kyle, was it? Nice shiner." His eyes cut back to Heather, a hard glint to them. "On a date?"

"Yes." Kyle's hand moved up and down her back. "Excuse us. We were just leaving."

She was so glad Kyle was here.

Quinn stepped to the side, but said, "Aren't you the detective working the so-called Bedroom Burglar case?"

Kyle stared at Quinn a beat. "Yes."

Quinn nodded. "Hope you catch him soon. He's hit my parents' neighborhood a couple of times already."

"We're doing our best." Kyle opened the door and guided Heather out. She didn't give Quinn a second look.

The marine layer had rolled in while they were eating, causing a damp chill when they stepped outside of the restaurant.

Kyle held out his hand, and she slipped hers into it. It was warm. He entwined their fingers, and tingles raced up her arm. "You okay?"

She nodded but couldn't resist a glance back toward the restaurant doors. Quinn wasn't going to ruin this date. She forced herself to relax and concentrate on Kyle.

"Sure you're not cold?"

She looked up at him and smiled. "I'm sure." He squeezed her hand. "Good."

They strolled along the sidewalk at the top of the cliff, listening to the waves crash against the beach below, occasionally stopping to lean against the railing and look down.

Heather peered out into the thick blackness. She was with Kyle. Quinn couldn't hurt her. "It's almost a little spooky at night. I can't imagine swimming in the ocean in the dark." She shivered. "But on the weekends, I like to do my quiet times here. For some reason the ocean always reminds me of God. The waves sound like His voice. Both are dangerous and mysterious, but incredibly beautiful." She glanced up at Kyle. "I know my imagination tends to run away with me."

He traced his thumb along the back of her hand. "No, there's something unique about the ocean that I've never been able to quite define. God's like that: indefinable but still incredibly personal. I guess there's a reason so many people come here for solace."

She nodded, then stiffened, trying to hide a shiver. "You're cold, aren't you?"

"Yeah, a little."

"Let's get you warmed up. How about coffee?" She nodded. "Sounds good."

Inside the truck, Kyle turned the heat on and pointed the vents at her. "Warming up?"

"Um hmm." She rubbed her hands together.

He reached over and wrapped one large hand around both of hers. "Heather! The hand I was holding is warm, but your other one is like ice. Why didn't you tell me you were cold?"

"I wasn't really."

He raised his eyebrows at her.

"Okay, a little. But it was worth it. I like walking along the bluffs."

They drove in silence for a few minutes, getting well into Laguna Canyon before Kyle glanced at her. "So how long did you and Quinn date?"

She closed her eyes. Dredging up her whole history with Quinn was not something she wanted to do on her first date with Kyle.

"We don't have to talk about it if you don't want to. It's an occupational hazard, always investigating." He smiled at her.

She sighed. "It's okay. We were together about a year and a half when he got a job transfer to New York. We had talked about getting married, so I was pretty upset when he took the job. He didn't have to; he just wanted to. Anyhow, he assumed I would go with him. But I don't want to leave California. I love it here, and my family's here. I couldn't figure out why he wanted to move to New York. He thought if he just persisted long enough, he'd wear me down. I didn't want a long-distance relationship. He could choose between me and his job, and he chose his job."

Even though she didn't want Quinn now, that thought still stung. At the time, he'd shattered her world. She tugged on the sleeves of her sweater. "When I broke up with him, he didn't give up. He kept sending flowers, calling, texting. Finally, I sent him an e-mail and told him to stop contacting me, that we were through. But he wouldn't stop. I finally blocked his number and his e-mail. After about a month, he stopped calling. I hadn't seen him until Sunday. Then he told me Monday he was being transferred back here."

"And then had all the flowers delivered to your porch."

"Until we broke up, I had no idea he could be so... persistent." The fact she had imagined marrying him made her question her judgment. "Sorry, this isn't great first date conversation."

"I asked." He smiled at her. "People can be unpredictable. I want you to be careful and trust your instincts. I'm not completely buying his story about the flowers. If anything seems strange or creepy, let me know. Anytime. Okay?"

"Okay. I promise." Could she trust her judgment?

JUSTIN TOOK ONE HAND OFF THE WHEEL AND WIPED IT ON his jeans. He hoped Bull didn't notice. Cole and Alex were in the backseat again, the windows back there starting to get steamy. He figured they were as nervous as he was.

Now they were stopped for the light at El Toro. Justin prayed for it to be a long one. He didn't want to do this, but it was too late now. All he had to do was let Cole and Alex do their thing, then drive off. That was it. Then he'd be a Seventeener. He'd get the respect he deserved. Bree would continue to go out with him. He could lay low after that.

The light turned green. Justin made a right.

Chapter Eight

Kyle drove them to the Jitter Bug, a cross between a 1950s diner and Starbucks. In addition to its fabulous desserts, it was just down the street from Heather's place. It was a small shop, with the option of sitting at the counter like a soda fountain. But he guided her to a table in the corner in the back by a window and held out her chair. "I'll be right back."

He brought back their coffees and a slice of chocolate mousse cake. After sitting and talking for over an hour, the dregs of their coffees cold in the bottom of their cups, Heather scooped up the last bite of creamy cake and offered it to Kyle.

"Nope. You have it."

Popping it in her mouth, she closed her eyes. "Mmm. Wonderful."

He was content to just watch her. Other than the little run-in with Quinn, which she seemed to have put out of her mind, it had been a great evening.

Bull scanned the parking lot as they pulled in. This Justin kid was doing okay. Scared, but then again they all were, whether they'd admit it or not. That's what made the rush so great.

"Pull over there." He pointed to a spot in the parking lot away from the lights and headed toward the back exit.

Justin did as he was told. He hadn't been one of Bull's recruits. Alex had because his dad's connections were useful to Bull. Justin had just been along for the ride when Alex stole his stepmom's car. Like it or not, Justin had gotten himself involved. And since he had no valuable connections, the only way he could be useful to Bull was if he did as he was told. Tonight, they'd find out.

Bull turned his attention to the Jitter Bug, its big windows providing a perfect view of the inside. Only two people…

He was seeing things, he was sure of it. Nope. He forced down the laughter, but a grin still spread across his face. He'd come to Detective Kyle Taylor's backyard to stick it to him. And here he was. With that chick. Oh, this was going to be good.

He rubbed his index finger and thumb together, thinking. It would require some reworking of the plan, but this was going to be even better.

Glancing at his watch, Kyle stifled a groan. "Please tell me you don't have to be at work super early."

She ducked her head. "Will you think I'm lazy if I say I planned to sleep in? It's not a production week, and we don't have any meetings so I'm not tied to a time clock."

"Can I take you to lunch tomorrow?"

Heather smiled at him and tapped her cup on the table. "I'd like that." Then she tilted her head. "Besides, I want a report on what everyone has to say about your eye tomorrow. It should start turning a lovely greenish yellow."

"Ah." He pretended indignation. "You wound me."

Someone walked in the front door, and Kyle's gaze slid past Heather's shoulder, watching the newcomer. Male, late teens, early twenties.

Heather turned slightly to see what he was looking at. The kid gave her a grin that bordered on a leer. Kyle gave him a hard look.

The kid sauntered up to the counter and ordered his coffee. That's when Kyle saw it.

The 17 tattooed on his arm in elaborate script. A Seventeener.

He seemed to be alone. No crime in ordering coffee. As much as Kyle didn't like it, there was nothing he could do. But he should get Heather out of here. It was getting late.

They should walk out right now, but he'd had all that iced tea and coffee, and he still had hopes of getting invited in when he dropped her off. He didn't like leaving her alone at all. But he would only be gone a minute.

Kyle squeezed her hand. "Finish your coffee, and I'll take you home. Back in a sec."

He gave the kid another look and headed to the bathroom.

HEATHER WATCHED KYLE DISAPPEAR BEHIND THE DOOR that led to the bathrooms then turned her gaze to the teen who had caught Kyle's attention. Kyle hadn't done anything overtly, but she sensed him shifting into cop mode. She wondered what it was about this kid that caused it.

He stared out the front window while waiting for his drink, rubbing his thumb over his fingers.

Heather found herself drawn to his heavily tattooed arm. When she looked up, he was staring at her, a creepy grin on his face. Great, he probably thought she was checking him out.

She turned away.

Hmm. Something clicked in her head. Maybe *Strive* needed to do an article on body art. Everyone was getting tattoos these days.

She wanted to sit and revel in the pleasure of the night, but if she didn't write down her thoughts now they'd escape her like a leaf in the Santa Ana winds. She tapped her finger against her coffee cup. She'd dream about Kyle tonight, but for now she needed to capture this thought before it escaped. Is tattooing self-expression? Is it prohibited by the Bible?

She pulled out her iPhone and started tapping out ideas in Evernote then shoved it back in her purse. But she wanted to capture that tattoo. She dug around in her purse, looking for a scrap of paper to draw the tat on. Drat. This was her small purse. Ah, she pulled out a receipt. This would work.

Two other boys walked in, younger and clean-cut. Business was beginning to pick up. They glanced at her then at the tattoo guy. They seemed nervous. Well, tattoo guy did seem a little intimidating.

She started doodling the tattoo while she thought about the article. While trying to capture the design, her eyes strayed to its owner.

He was watching her, still smiling. Almost like he knew her.

She gave a tentative smile back. Was it someone she'd met at church or who had heard her sing there? Didn't seem too likely, but you couldn't judge people based on their appearance. Hoping she'd hit the middle road of being friendly without seeming like she was flirting, Heather continued drawing, but she couldn't help but shoot him sideways glances. She shifted in her chair to better see him.

He sat sipping his coffee like anyone else, watching the other two teens order.

The barista, a red-haired college-aged kid, scanned the room, glancing briefly at tattoo guy before spotting Heather. His eyes widened.

The two clean-cut teens had their backs to her, but tension

radiated from their shoulders, their legs in a wide stance. They were angry about something. A raised voice floated back to her.

Her phone rang in her purse.

Heather grabbed her purse, unsnapping it to reach her phone, but keeping her eyes on the college kid.

Were the kids threatening him? Where was Kyle?

Tattoo guy was sitting closer. Maybe he knew what was going on. He watched the exchange with interest, leaning back in his chair, arm popped over the back. Not concerned at all.

Maybe it was nothing.

Where was her phone? This purse wasn't that big. Ah, she'd stuck it in a pocket. It rang again just as her fingers closed around it.

The taller, dark-haired teen turned his head. Met Heather's stare and held it. Then smirked. His eyes were dark, almost dead-looking.

Heather suppressed a shiver, pulling her phone out. Where was Kyle? Her eyes shifted to the restroom door.

The dark-haired teen watched her then lifted the front of his shirt.

KYLE HEARD RAISED VOICES AND CRACKED OPEN THE bathroom door to see what was happening. He didn't like the teens' body language. He wanted Heather out of there *now*. She could meet him outside. He dialed her phone; he could hear it ringing, but she was out of his line of sight.

He hung up and dialed 911.

The barista darted toward the back of the shop.

The teen raised his arm and an explosion reverberated through the shop. The barista disappeared from sight.

Kyle dropped the phone and drew his gun, jumping out from behind the door. "Police! Drop the gun!"

A second shot shattered the glass behind Heather with a light popping sound, like an instant rain shower.

The teens ran.

Heather's body slammed into the floor. Chairs clattered. As he ran for the door he saw Heather lunge through the broken window. Her leg caught on something, scraping across it. Tugging, she pulled it free then stumbled, hands out, and crumpled on the access path at the side of the building and out of his view.

Torn, his body halted. Then forcing himself to move, he reached the front door. Just in time to see a Honda peel out of the parking lot.

And Heather lying on the ground.

SCRAMBLING HER FEET UNDER HER, HEATHER TRIED TO GET up, get safe, hide. The world tipped. She tumbled off the edge of the curb, down a vine-covered slope to the parking lot below. With a dull *thunk*, her head hit a wheel stop.

Stunned, she couldn't move.

A Honda idled in the parking lot, lights off. She couldn't see the driver, but the two teens leaped in, yelling and screaming.

The license plate. Get the license plate! There was enough light from the parking lot lights. She focused on the letters and numbers, muttered it to herself.

The Honda left with a squeal of rubber, out the side entrance of the parking lot, disappeared behind the building, then sped onto El Toro and into the night.

"Heather!"

She moved her head and pain shot through it. What did she do?

"Don't move." Kyle knelt next to her, his hand on her shoulder.

A faint sound grew stronger. Sirens.

"Where are you hurt?" His eyes scanned her body but revealed nothing.

She had a million things to tell him, she just couldn't remember what they were. "I'm okay. My head just hurts." She tried to sit up, but Kyle held her down.

"Paramedics are on their way. Don't move until they look at you." He trailed the back of his hand across her forehead.

The pieces started falling together. Heather realized what she had seen. "Those two kids… where's the barista? Is he okay?"

"Don't worry about him. Just lie still."

Her eyes searched Kyle, looking for any sign of injury. "Are you okay? Where were you? I was worried." Then she noticed the blood on his hand. "You're bleeding. Did you cut yourself?"

Kyle didn't even look at his hand. "I'm fine."

The sirens grew piercingly loud and bright lights swept across her as a cop car pulled into the parking lot. Kyle waved someone over. He squeezed Heather's hand. "Don't move, all right? I'm not going anywhere. I'm just going to talk to Griffin."

She remembered what she needed to tell him. "I got the license plate number." She gave it to him. "It was a Honda, dark blue, I think, new body style. Someone else was driving but I couldn't see who in the dark."

"Good job."

Her eyes followed his hand where it joined hers. Blood covered her arm. She pushed down the fear. It was just blood. It probably looked like more than it was, because nothing really hurt besides her head and the shoulder she was half-lying on. Some of the shattering glass must have cut her. She glanced down her legs. At least her dress wasn't hiked up.

Kyle stood and said something in a low tone to the officer. She saw the gun in Kyle's hand for the first time. The officer moved away, and Kyle holstered his gun and then knelt down. The officer returned and handed Kyle something. A first-aid kit. He opened it and pulled out gauze pads, placing the first one gently on her arm. "Can you hold this here without moving your head?"

She bent her elbow and held the pad in place. "Careful, there's still glass in there."

More people swarmed around, and Heather could hear activity around the Jitter Bug, some sort of commotion. A couple of people shouted orders. She just wanted to close her eyes and go to sleep. Lying in a parking lot was embarrassing.

Kyle moved down to her leg. "Heather, keep your eyes open. Tell me what you saw from the time I left to go to the bathroom."

The officer Kyle had called Griffin pulled out a pad and glanced between Heather and Kyle. Heather told him about her tattoo article idea and then how the dark-haired teen had looked at her.

"Think you could pick him out of a lineup?"

"Yeah. I'd like to take a stab at drawing him." Griffin raised his eyebrows.

"She's an artist," Kyle told him.

"What about the guy with the tattoo?" Griffin asked Kyle.

"He's a Seventeener. I checked him out as I headed to the bathroom, but he didn't seem to be involved."

Heather replayed the tattoo guy's reaction in her head. "He seemed kind of amused by the whole thing. He was watching what was going on. Like he didn't think knocking over the Jitter Bug was any big deal." She paused. "At first I thought those kids were afraid of the tattoo guy. But once they started arguing with the barista, they ignored him. And they only threatened me, not him." She paused. "Where'd he go, anyway?"

Kyle's hand stilled. He and Griffin exchanged a look.

She'd said something of interest to them; she just didn't know what it was.

The clatter of something being pulled across the parking lot caught Heather's attention.

Kyle smoothed her bangs. "The paramedics are here. I'm

going to let them work on you, but don't worry, you're not going anywhere without me." He smiled at her, then leaned over and kissed her forehead.

Okay, she wished that kiss had been under different circumstances, when she could actually enjoy it.

He stood and disappeared from view as a paramedic knelt in front of her and asked her questions. Someone put something hard around her neck. They started to roll her to her side. Pain shot through her shoulder and she groaned.

"Sorry, we'll make it quick."

Something hard slid under her, then she was on her back, and they strapped her down.

"Shoulder hurt?"

"Yeah."

They lifted her onto a gurney, and she started moving. Where was Kyle? Did he know they were taking her? She didn't want to leave without him.

He shouldered a paramedic to the side. "Hey, I'm right here. I'm going to follow the ambulance." He turned to the paramedic. "Saddleback Memorial, right?"

"Yep."

"I'll see you in the emergency room." He found her hand again and squeezed it.

She squeezed back, not wanting to let go. "It'll be okay."

Tears pooled in her eyes. Don't cry now. She couldn't even wipe her own eyes.

With a bump, the gurney under her slid into the ambulance. A minute later the paramedic came into view. He dabbed at her eyes with a tissue. The doors clanked shut, and they were moving.

Chapter Nine

Kyle watched the ambulance drive off then jogged back inside the Jitter Bug.

"Taylor." Griffin walked next to him.

"What?" Kyle didn't stop. He grabbed a handful of napkins, wiping Heather's blood off his hands.

"So, what's with you and her?" Griffin nodded toward the disappearing ambulance.

Kyle picked up Heather's purse and cell phone from the floor, trying to decide how much he wanted on the office grapevine. Ah, what the heck. "We were on a date."

The words sounded odd coming out of his mouth, almost rusty. He let them roll around in his head a few times, loosening them up, as he walked to the back to retrieve his dropped phone. It seemed to have survived the fall. Straightening, he clipped it to his belt. "I've got my cell phone. Call if you need me." He strode toward the door, ignoring the stunned expression on Griffin's face.

Kyle headed toward his truck. The image of Heather lying in the parking lot, blood oozing from her head, arm, and leg—he couldn't get it out of his mind. It was worse than seeing the dead barista behind the counter. He shook his head. Now he was really messed up. Since when was an injury worse than death?

He tried to detach, to find his footing in his professional routine. It was his fault she was hurt. He wouldn't let that happen again.

He heard his name called, but he pulled open his truck door, climbed in, and sped off.

Why? Why that moment? Why didn't those guys walk in two minutes earlier or two minutes later? *God, I thought You were in control here. How could You let this happen to her? Why didn't You let me protect her?*

His heart squeezed in his chest. He fought for breath. All that blood. She'd been shot.

No. He had kneeled beside her and checked her over. No gunshot wounds, just cuts from glass and a nasty gash on her leg he thought corresponded to a jagged piece of metal in the window frame.

She'd be okay. He wouldn't let anything happen to her.

He couldn't say the same for the barista. Gunshot wound to the head.

Kyle swung into the hospital parking lot and jogged to the emergency bay doors where the paramedics were unloading Heather. He pulled his badge out and clipped it to his waistband. In a few steps, he was next to the gurney. Careful to stay out of the paramedics' way, he moved into Heather's line of sight.

Her eyes lit up when she saw him.

He smiled, glad. "Miss me?" He walked alongside the gurney.

That one got a smile. "Yeah, it's been so long."

She still had her sense of humor. He much preferred that to the tears he saw as they put her into the ambulance.

They wheeled her into a treatment room. A nurse came in with them, getting the information she needed from the paramedics, while they transferred Heather to the hospital's gurney.

Kyle moved to the edge of the bed and took her hand, rubbing his thumb along the back of it.

The paramedics left and the nurse came over, barely looking up from the chart she was writing. "You'll have to wait outside, Officer. You can question her later."

Heather's panic-filled eyes met Kyle's. "Please don't make him leave. I want him to stay." Her words were distorted by the C-collar that kept her neck immobile.

The first good feeling since the shooting wrapped itself through his chest. If she wanted him to stay, no one was going to make him leave.

The nurse looked at him, then at their joined hands. A frown creased her forehead. "Sorry, didn't know he was your boyfriend."

Faint pink tinged Heather's cheeks. It added color to her face, which was so pale a sprinkling of freckles he'd never noticed before stood out on her nose and cheeks.

She didn't look at him.

He leaned his arm above her head and bent down close to her ear. "Let her think that."

The blush deepened, but she smiled.

The doctor walked in. Kyle stepped back out of the way, but still where Heather could see him.

"Let's see if we can't get you out of that C-collar and off the backboard." He gave Kyle a quick look. "Want me to look at that eye?"

"Huh? Oh, no. Just got whacked with a surfboard earlier today."

The doctor started examining Heather but still addressed Kyle. "Any vision problems? Headaches?"

"Nope. Just the black eye."

He nodded then ran Heather through a series of tests, then, apparently satisfied she didn't have a neck injury, he removed the collar. The nurse helped him roll Heather off the board.

Some of the tension left Kyle's shoulders.

She groaned when they rolled her on her side. "Ow."

"What hurts?"

"My head, my shoulder, my leg."

The doctor examined the side of her head. "Ooh, nasty gash. Does it hurt?"

"Yeah, especially if I try to move."

"I'll bet. Looks like it needs stitches. Staples, actually, so we won't have to shave your pretty head." He lifted the gauze on her arm then moved down to her leg. He came back to her shoulder, moving her arm in different directions, asking about pain. "Looks like a strain." He turned to the nurse. "Get me a suture tray and clean up her head and hands. I'll be back."

Kyle let out a breath, glad Heather's injuries didn't require anything more than stitches. It could have been so much worse. The vision of her lying in the parking lot covered in blood flooded his mind. He pushed it away, concentrating on the nurse's ministrations to Heather.

The nurse raised the bed so Heather sat at a forty-five-degree angle. She carefully parted Heather's hair, then cleaned the cut.

Heather closed her eyes and clenched her jaw but didn't make a sound. Kyle wished he could do something to ease her pain.

Then the nurse examined the scrapes on Heather's hands. Efficiently, she cleaned them, put on an antibiotic ointment and covered them with gauze pads she taped down. Then she moved to Heather's arm and leg. Her dress was shredded, ruined.

Heather bit her lip. "This was my favorite. I guess it's a good excuse to go shopping."

Kyle winked at her. She was trying hard, despite the pain she must be feeling. He was impressed with how well she was handling this.

The nurse set up the suture tray and then strode out.

Heather closed her eyes. Tight lines formed around her mouth.

"How bad does it hurt?" Kyle moved over to take her hand, wishing he could do something to help her pain.

"On the one-to-ten scale or the smiley-face to the crying-face chart? I land close to the almost-crying face which is I think a nine. I just want to go home and go to bed."

He gave her a soft smile. "Not exactly how I'd planned this evening to end." He put his fingers between hers, being careful of the bandages. She wasn't going to like what he had to say. He'd give anything not to make her feel worse. "Heather, there's a good chance you won't be going home tonight."

She looked up but didn't say anything.

"Once our guys finish up at the scene, they're going to come down here and have a lot of questions for you. The guy with the tattoo is part of the Seventeenth Street gang. Also known as the Seventeeners. A bunch of kids whose parents have a lot of money and not much time to spend with them. Because their parents have money and are well connected, we have difficulty prosecuting cases against them. They hire good lawyers; they apply political pressure."

He took in a deep breath. He didn't want to scare her, but she needed to know the risks. He hoped she'd cooperate. "Witnesses usually don't show up to testify. They get bought off or get pressured financially."

She didn't say anything.

Almost afraid of the silence, he kept talking. "I don't know if that's what's happening here. But I'm not taking any chances. Unless that guy with a tattoo was only there coincidentally, you'll be under protection. So for tonight, that means a safe house."

Since this was now a murder investigation, he doubted she'd be going home anytime soon. But she'd been through enough tonight. She didn't need to know she had witnessed a murder.

The doctor walked back in. "Ready for some stitches?"

Kyle wasn't sure if he resented or was grateful for the interruption.

"And if I say no?" Heather gave a weak smile.

"Oh, you'll pass out from blood loss, and I'll just stitch you up anyway."

Ah, a comedian. Well, it did help with the tension. Heather gave a short laugh. "Since you put it like that."

She squeezed Kyle's hand when the lidocaine injections went in her arm, but after that, watched rather passively.

Pain prickled in Kyle's chest as the doctor picked out glass then squirted saline full force into the wound. Then he began stitching. The needle pierced her skin and came out the other side, the doctor tugging the suture. Kyle had to keep reminding himself she was numb.

The doctor moved to her head. Kyle couldn't quite see what was happening, but it looked like the nurse was hold- ing Heather's hair back. The *cha-ching* of the surgical stapler sounded just like the one he used to put up Christmas lights. It gave him the creeps.

Just as the doctor moved to stitch her leg, Mark and Bruce, the department's gang detail, came in.

Kyle looked away from Heather's leg and took a deep breath. He was starting to feel lightheaded.

While Bruce questioned Heather, Kyle nodded to Mark to step over to the side of the room. "What about the license plate?"

"Came off a stolen truck. Your eye still looks like you went ten rounds."

"Thanks. What'd you find out?"

"It was a holdup. Looks like the barista had just made a drop and all he had was two twenties, some fives, and ones. That probably made them mad. Interesting thing about our tattoo guy. Someone coming out of the ice cream shop saw him run out the back of the Jitter Bug. And then hop in the Honda when it pulled around back."

Kyle closed his eyes and swore under his breath.

"Yep. Stacey will staff the safe house. She's headed over here to get Heather's keys to her place and pack her a bag. I assume you'll go to the safe house too."

Kyle nodded. He trusted the guys he worked with, but Heather didn't know them. This was going to be disruptive to her, on top of her injuries. He wanted to make sure it went as easy as possible for her, something no one else would be as concerned about.

"So Griffin's right. You have a personal relationship with her."

Kyle rubbed his eyes, wincing at the sore one. It was going to be a long night. "Yep. We were on a date."

"Gee, Kyle, didn't know you went on those. Thought you'd sworn off women." Mark grinned.

Kyle wasn't amused. "Not tonight, Mark." His phone rang.

He unclipped it and glanced at the display.

"That's probably the lieutenant. He said he wanted to make sure you understood your role in all of this."

Kyle glanced at the screen. Mark was right. "This is Taylor."

"Kyle, it's Johnson. Mark and Bruce are in charge of the investigation, since you have a conflict of interest and the attorneys would have a field day with that. But I've put you in charge of Ms. McAlistair's security. I figured I wouldn't be able to keep you away anyhow."

"You figured right, sir."

Johnson chuckled. "So it's true, the rumors? You actually have a girlfriend?"

He pinched the bridge of his nose. That would be an exaggeration, but he didn't think the lieutenant wanted a detailed explanation of his social life. "Yes, sir." He was already weary of being the topic of gossip.

"Glad to hear it. It's about time."

"Yes, sir." Kyle wanted to end this conversation. The doctor had finished suturing Heather's leg.

"Keep me updated. And we'll be talking tomorrow about how someone ends up dead when one of my cops is there."

Kyle started to speak.

"No, don't tell me now. Tomorrow. And keep the press out of it. They're still on our case about the Bedroom Burglar. Don't give them something else to hang us out to dry for."

Kyle worked on unclenching his jaw as he tapped his phone off and clipped it to his belt. He'd been hoping for a little more time between professional disasters.

"What do you guys think?" The doctor stood and stepped back from Heather. "Is that a great stitch job or what?"

"Great, Doc." Heather scowled. "Now it looks like I have two black caterpillars crawling on me. Goes nicely with the post-apocalyptic-chic dress."

Though she was bantering with the doctor, her face was pale. The sooner they got her somewhere to rest the better.

"I aim to please." He finished taping gauze over her leg. "And I hope I don't see you in here again. The nurse will bring your discharge orders. Have a good night. What's left of it." He sauntered out of the room.

Heather looked up at Kyle.

Reaching for her hand, he turned to Bruce and Mark. "You guys need anything else?"

"You bringing her in tomorrow?" Mark asked.

"Yeah."

"Okay, we'll talk to you then."

A broad-shouldered woman appeared at the doorway, her dirty blond hair cut in practical style. She spoke briefly to Bruce and Mark as they left.

"This is Officer Stacey Wells. Stacey, this is Heather McAlistair. Stacey's going to be at the safe house tonight. She'll go by your place and pack a bag for you. Just tell her what you need."

The two women talked for a minute, and Heather seemed to relax a bit. Kyle stepped outside the room to see if those discharge orders were coming. He didn't see anyone. He paced back in the room. Now that she was patched up, he wanted her out of here as soon as possible.

Heather laughed at something Stacey said. "So you do know cats."

"I've had a few." Stacey held a set of keys in her hands. "I'll see you guys at the safe house in a few."

She exited the room just as the nurse bustled in with her hands full and dropped stuff on the bed. "Let's get this sling on your shoulder."

She spent a few minutes adjusting straps, securing Heather's left arm across her abdomen. Satisfied, she held out a yellow sheet for Heather to sign. "You have a concussion." She looked at Kyle. "You'll have to wake her every two hours tonight. Talk to her, make sure she's fully awake. If she doesn't seem coherent or her pupils don't equally dilate, bring her back."

Kyle figured that was one benefit of keeping her at the safe house tonight; he'd be able to keep an eye on her. Although he thought it was interesting, and typical, what the nurse was assuming.

She turned back to Heather. "Change the dressings on your stitches twice a day, and don't get them wet for two days." The nurse handed Heather a plastic zip bag of supplies. "You'll still need to see your own doctor in a week to get the staples out and to check that shoulder. Also, you'll want to wash your hair tonight to get all the glass out—you'll probably need help— but be careful of that cut on the side of your head. If it starts showing any of the signs of infection listed on this sheet, come back in."

Mark peered through the doorway. "The press has already found you. Looks like the reporters from the *Register* and the *LA Times*."

This was the last thing they needed. The fact that there was a witness would probably leak, but he wanted to keep her name and face out of it as long as possible. "Where are they?"

"In the emergency room waiting area, badgering the staff."

"Let's take her out through the medical offices wing. We can get someone to open those doors for us."

Mark shook his head. "If they see anyone coming out that way at this time of night, they'll know it's her."

The nurse smiled, the first one Kyle had seen. "I have an idea."

Chapter Ten

A few minutes later, the nurse wheeled Heather out the maternity ward doors right to the door of Kyle's truck, which Mark had brought around. A realistic, but toy doll used for baby care classes nestled in Heather's arms hiding her sling. A blanket covered her legs—and torn dress.

Kyle gingerly helped her from the wheelchair and into the truck. He pulled her seatbelt out then leaned over her to buckle it.

The traces of his aftershave erased the antiseptic smell of the hospital. His jaw was slightly stubbled. She would have reveled in his closeness longer, if she hadn't felt so much like she'd been run over by a train. It had been a long day for both of them, but he was still taking care of her. What a sweetie.

Kyle took the doll from her arms and wrapped it in the blanket from her legs. The truck door hid the wheelchair from the parking lot. He tossed the bundle in the wheelchair and smiled at the nurse. "Thanks for your help."

She glanced between Kyle and Heather, a slight grin on her face. "No problem." She wheeled the chair back inside with Mark following.

Heather closed her eyes and started to lean her head back

but jerked it forward as the bruised part of her scalp touched the headrest. Her reaction sent stars flying through her vision. "Oh, bad idea."

"You okay?"

"Um hum. Just can't make any sudden moves." She kept her eyes closed, but felt the truck move through the parking lot. "I need a shower. I smell like a hospital."

"You can take a bath if you want when we get to the safe house."

She pictured herself trying to maneuver into a bathtub with her bad shoulder while trying to keep her right arm and leg out of the water. Probably not something she wanted to attempt tonight.

Tonight still didn't seem real. A great first date wiped out in a moment. Even running into Quinn paled in comparison.

A while later, they pulled up in front of a local extended-stay motel. It took her a minute to realize where they were. Kyle spoke into a radio she didn't know he had, and a moment later, he slipped his arm around her waist, helping her out of the truck. He ushered her inside and up an elevator to the third floor. When they stepped out, he helped her down a hallway that seemed to go on forever before knocking on a door.

Stacey opened it.

He gently led Heather into the room.

Stacey closed the door behind them. "Heather, your things are on your bed. I fed Snowflake." She smiled. "I have the night shift so feel free to let me know if you need anything."

"Thanks. Sleep sounds good right now." Heather noticed the small living area and kitchen and started to head for what she assumed was the bedroom.

Kyle touched her shoulder. "We still need to wash the glass out of your hair."

She'd forgotten.

"Did Stacey bring you shampoo, or do you want to use the motel's?"

She wrinkled her nose. Motel shampoo would probably leave her hair like straw. "There should be some in my travel bag." She followed Kyle into a room with two queen-sized beds. Her bag sat on the closest one. She opened it and attempted to rummage around. Finally, she just pointed at her toiletry travel bag and a comb. "It's in there."

Kyle picked them up. "Let's try this at the kitchen sink."

Heather bit the inside of her cheek, not sure what she thought of letting Kyle wash her hair. It seemed rather intimate. Yeah, with all the dried blood and broken glass. Real romantic. There wasn't a choice, really. It needed to be done, and she couldn't do it herself, not with one arm strapped down and the other not able to get wet. It was Kyle or Stacey. She took a deep breath and walked out of the room.

The TV was on low, and Stacey sat on the couch, flipping through a magazine.

Kyle moved a chair in front of the sink. A couple of towels sat on the tiny counter. "What do you think? Kneel here and lean forward?"

"That'll work." She situated herself, resting her weight on her good knee and stretching the leg with stitches off to the side. A moment later warm water ran over her head. It felt good. The water stopped, and his hands massaged the suds through her hair, his fingers gentle. The scent of her shampoo wafted around her, erasing the hospital smell. "Let me know if it hurts."

It didn't hurt, not at all. Tingles ran down the back of her neck to her spine. Hopefully, he couldn't tell.

"So that's what smells so good. It's your shampoo. Pear. I've never heard of that."

She wanted to laugh at the relief in his voice, like he'd solved some great mystery. "It's my favorite. There's matching lotion too. And bath gel." With her head inside the sink, her voice echoed around her.

"I never would have guessed it was pear. I didn't even know

pear had a smell." He was silent a moment. "Ooh, found a piece of glass." His hands left her head.

"Did you cut yourself?" "Nope."

A comb gently tugged through her hair.

"Here's a bunch. Let me know if it hurts." A minute later: "I think I got it all."

Warm water ran over her head again, making her sleepy. "Okay, that's it." A towel covered her head, his hands gingerly pressing the water out.

Heather sat up.

He arranged the towel around her shoulders. "You okay?"

"Yeah." She reached for the comb. "I just need to comb it out so it doesn't dry in knots."

Kyle took the comb from her hand. "Let me. I can make sure I got all the glass out."

She turned around in the chair, too tired to argue. She only had one functioning arm. Getting the far side of her head would be difficult.

He pulled the comb through her hair. It felt good.

"Oops, missed a piece."

He tugged on a piece of her hair.

The comb clattered on the counter. "All done."

"Thanks." Heather used the towel to squeeze the ends of her hair. She'd just go to bed with wet hair.

"One more thing." He took the damp towel from her and knelt in front of her chair. Lifting her right foot on to his thigh, he used the towel to wipe the dried blood off her foot.

The image of Jesus washing His disciples' feet flashed through her mind, and she understood it in a way she never had before. Having someone care for your feet was incredibly humbling. Tears pricked her eyes.

"All done." He gently set her foot on the floor and tossed the towel on the counter. Putting his arm around her back, he lifted her from the chair and guided her to her room. "Do you want Stacey to come help you get ready for bed?"

The clock next to the bed read nearly midnight. She couldn't remember the last time she was so exhausted. "I think I can manage. I'll holler if I need help."

He closed the door behind him as Heather yanked out yoga pants and a T-shirt. Easy enough—or as easy as anything would be—to gingerly wiggle into. She brushed her teeth and washed her face, not looking in the mirror.

She opened the door to the main living area. "I'm headed for bed." She glanced at the other bed. Was that where Kyle was sleeping? She didn't see his bag.

Kyle hopped up from his place at the dining room table. "Anything else you need?" He brushed past her and folded back the covers on the bed.

"No. Thank you for everything tonight, Kyle. I don't know what I would have done without you."

"Come here." He carefully pulled her into his arms and rested his chin on her head, holding her a moment before speaking. "I should have gotten you out of there sooner. I should have known." His hand stroked her back.

Being in his arms was wonderful, but she didn't want him blaming himself. "It's not your fault. You're not a mind reader. You can't always predict what people will do."

"I made a decision not to escalate the situation by showing myself. Turned out to be the wrong decision. You paid the price."

She looked up at him. "I will heal. You weren't the one who pulled the trigger."

He didn't answer, just kept stroking her back. She leaned her head against his chest again, knowing she hadn't convinced him.

He kissed her forehead. "Get to bed. We'll talk in the morning."

She raised her eyes to him and smiled, wondering if he'd kiss her again. His eyes searched her face. Did she see indecision there?

Then he pulled back, his hands sliding to her waist.

Disappointment twinged as she stepped back. Well, it wasn't like she looked terrific, and the situation wasn't exactly romantic. Plus, it was technically only their first date. Though did getting shot at change the rules? "Okay."

"I'm waking you in two hours."

She frowned. Why? She needed a lot more than two hours' sleep.

"Doctor's orders. Remember?" Oh. Her concussion.

He stepped out of her room and pulled the door shut.

BULL MOVED THE JOYSTICK AND FIRED, LAYING DOWN A heavy stream of automatic weapons fire. Bodies fell like dominos on the screen in front of him. He glanced at the compass in the upper right corner and moved his man around the building. He ducked inside and grabbed the plans. MISSION COMPLETED flashed on the screen.

"Yeah, dude! That's the fastest time for that level ever!" Bull's buddy, Chad, traded him a beer for the joystick.

Bull took a swig of beer and leaned back on the couch. The rush from the night had drained away leaving him edgy. Not to mention the fact that things hadn't exactly gone as planned.

Alex was becoming more of a liability than an asset. He was going to have to do something about that. The boy was too cocky to realize he was out of his league. All he had to do was follow instructions. They would have hit the place and gotten out of there before the cop realized he had been caught with his pants down. Literally.

Instead, Alex somehow thought this was the wild West and started shooting up the place. What was he thinking? This wasn't South Central LA.

But the lucky break had been finding the cop's girlfriend's door open. He'd just planned to do a little reconnaissance, but finding the door not completely shut had been a gift. The rush of being in her place, knowing they'd be back soon, was sweet. All the things he could have done while he was there flashed through his mind. But how he left his mark? Genius. He chuckled.

He focused on the screen just as Chad's man died. He reached for the joystick. "My turn."

Chapter Eleven

Exhausted as he was, Kyle came fully awake when the alarm went off. Six thirty. The shift change would be soon, so no use going back to sleep. He swung out of the rollaway bed he'd put in the kitchen area last night. Stacey was still up, drinking coffee. He gave her a wave, grabbed his bag out of the closet, and headed for the shower. Heather had been fine and fully coherent each time he'd awoken her last night—or this morning, actually. She could wait a few more minutes.

He turned the shower on hot, letting the steam fill the room. The smell of generic hotel soap swirled around him, a stark contrast to Heather's pear shampoo. He was glad he'd solved the small mystery of why she smelled so good. After getting hammered on the Bedroom Burglar case, it was nice to know he still had a few detective skills left.

He winced as he washed his face. His eye still ached. Soaping up his hair, he thought about washing Heather's. He'd never washed a woman's hair before, but she didn't seem to mind. Hair washing seemed more of a production with women. Her hair was much longer for one thing. It kept getting tangled around his fingers. And she used scented shampoo. Definitely feminine.

Even her toes had little flowers painted on them. It was different taking care of someone else. But good.

Minutes later—shaved, showered, and dressed—Kyle made a check of the safe house. Nothing outside. All the windows were secure. The one window looked out over the fenced pool area and the sloped hill beyond. Nothing could hide up there. Time to wake Sleeping Beauty. Carefully he turned the knob to Heather's room. When the latch clicked free, he pushed the door open.

She lay on the bed, asleep, her arm in a sling propped on a pillow. It seemed as if she'd shrunk since he first took her to the Jitter Bug. The woman he'd picked up for dinner last night had disappeared when the window behind her had shattered. He hoped he could find her again underneath the sling and bandages. But he'd seen too many trauma victims. No way to accurately predict how Heather would handle this.

He sat on the edge of the bed and brushed the hair back from her forehead. "Heather. Time to wake up."

Her eyes opened, and she stared at him a minute. "Has it been two hours already? Feels like I just went to sleep."

"More than two hours. I know it's early, but I need to take you to the station. Mark and Bruce, the detectives you met last night, want your statement. And while there's a buffet breakfast downstairs, I thought I'd take you to one of my favorite places. Ever been to the Original Pancake House?"

Heather started to shake her head, but stopped abruptly, grimacing. "No, but I like pancakes. How's the coffee?"

"Great." She still hadn't moved. "Do you want me to open the blackout drapes and get some light in here?"

"Yeah, but I think you're going to need to help me sit up. Now I know how a turtle on its back feels. I can't get myself up." He reached behind her and lifted her up. He couldn't help tucking a strand of hair behind her ear. "Do you want some more ibuprofen now on an empty stomach or wait until we eat?"

"I'll risk it. Just means I can't take too long getting ready."

"You already look beautiful."

She rolled her eyes. "Please. But I appreciate the effort to bolster my spirits."

He disagreed, but she obviously didn't see herself the way he did, all soft and sleepy-eyed, and utterly kissable. "I'll take your bag into the bathroom and bring you that ibuprofen."

She nodded and pushed back the covers.

He stood and grabbed her bag, taking it into the bathroom. When he returned with a glass of water and the medicine, she was struggling with her sling. He set the glass and pills down. "Here, let me help you." He unfastened the straps until the sling was loose enough to slip over her head. She lowered her arm with a grimace as he pulled the sling off. "Okay?"

She nodded but grabbed for the pills and water.

"Holler if you need anything, and I'll send Stacey in. She's going to be leaving in a little bit when her replacement gets here." He pulled the door shut behind him then went to work folding up the rollaway and putting it back in the closet. Out of the corner of his eye, he saw Stacey watching him. He was glad they were getting out of here for breakfast. He felt too much like a fish in a fishbowl. Not only was everyone amazed he had a date, he was sure the fact they didn't share a bed would also make the rounds. What kind of world was it where *that* was considered more out of the ordinary?

A few minutes later, Heather stepped out of the bathroom. She had the same pants on but a different top and wore a little makeup. "Stacey, could you help me?"

"Sure thing." Stacey tossed her magazine aside and disappeared into the bathroom with Heather.

Kyle collapsed on the couch and picked up the remote, flipping through the channels. He heard giggling from the bathroom. That was a good sign.

Both women emerged a few minutes later, Heather with a little more makeup.

"Ready?"

"Yep. Thanks, Stacey." She walked toward her bedroom.

"You're welcome."

The radio on the coffee table crackled, and Kyle picked it up. The new shift was here. He went to let her in.

Heather reappeared wearing flip-flops, and Kyle introduced her to Officer Hilary Peterson.

"We're going to breakfast and then to the station, so we'll be gone awhile." Kyle took the sling from Heather's hand.

"Great. A cushy assignment. I like that," Hilary said.

Careful of Heather's arm, he slipped it over her head and refastened it. "Is that okay?" Over her shoulder, he saw Stacey and Hilary exchange a glance. He hoped the novelty of his love life would wear off soon and someone else could be the topic of discussion.

Heather gingerly moved her shoulder. "I think so."

Stacey walked with them downstairs, moving ahead to scout, then returning to stand on Heather's other side.

Once he and Heather were safely in the truck, Stacey waved and went to the unmarked unit she had driven here.

They got on the freeway, taking the I-5 south and exiting at Oso Parkway. He turned into a small shopping center. "I can't believe you've never been here."

"You forget I'm a fairly recent transplant. I don't usually get down this far."

He scanned the parking lot. "It's a good thing we're here early. On a weekend, if you're not here by eight thirty, you're waiting."

Kyle parked then helped Heather out. "Let's grab a newspaper over here first." He wanted to see what the reporters had found out about the shooting.

Digging in his pocket, he came up with a quarter and plunked it in the machine then pulled out a paper. He scanned it. At least they hadn't made the front page. He'd look through the rest of it later.

Inside, no one was waiting and there were a couple of empty tables. It was still early.

"Hi, Kyle." The hostess, Jaime, greeted him. "Ooh, icky bruise."

"Surfboard. Does JoAnn have any empty seats in her section?"

Jaime scanned the seating area. "Yep, there's one right over there." She began walking toward the table, and Kyle motioned Heather to follow, his hand lightly at her back.

They slid into a booth at the back of the restaurant in front of a window.

Jaime left two menus. "JoAnn will be right over."

"Thanks."

Heather opened the menu and studied it. He didn't open his; he just watched her. She looked up with a half-smile. "What?"

"Just watching you."

"Oh." Her eyes dropped back to the menu. She flicked the edge with her thumb. "So, what's good here? They have, what, thirty different kinds of pancakes?"

His staring was making her nervous. He needed to take it down a notch; she wasn't going to break. "Something like that. But I'm a creature of habit. I either get the forty-niner, the Dutch baby, or the apple pancake."

She raised her eyebrows.

Out of the corner of his eye, he saw JoAnn heading their way with a coffee carafe. He waved.

"Hey there, Kyle. How are you? What happened to your eye? And who's this you brought with you?"

"This is Heather. Heather, meet JoAnn, my favorite waitress. And the eye is from a disagreement I had with my surfboard."

"Hi, sweetie." She turned over their cups and began pouring. "I ain't never seen him bring in a girl before. Except his sister. Maybe that surfboard knocked some sense into him."

Heather grinned at him. "Well, then, I feel really special."

JoAnn propped a fist on her hip, her Aretha Franklin voice tinged with attitude. "What happened to your arm? Surfboard do that too?"

Heather's eyes darted to Kyle then back to JoAnn. "Oh, I fell and hurt it. Just a strain." She looked at him, longer this time, checking if her story met his approval. He was pleased she hadn't mentioned last night even though they hadn't discussed it.

"Well, I'll leave you two alone if you know what you want."

Heather looked up at JoAnn. "How about the Dutch baby?"

"Then I'll get the forty-niner." He picked up the menus and handed them to JoAnn. "Thanks. Oh, and add a side of bacon."

"Sure thing."

Heather reached for two tiny cups of half and half then looked puzzled. He took them from her, opened them, and dumped them into her coffee. She stirred it and took a sip. "Mmm. Caffeine."

"I could have made you a cup in the room. Stacey was up drinking it all night."

Heather made a face. "Unless hotels have started carrying Starbucks in the room, I doubt it's any good."

"It's drinkable if you're not picky."

She laughed. "Which I am. On some things." She set her cup down and looked at the tabletop. "I miss my cat."

"We can go by there after the station."

Running her finger around the rim of her coffee cup, she looked up. "How long do I have to stay at the safe house?"

Kyle reached over for her hand. He knew he'd have to tell her eventually, but he kept putting it off. She was going to hate this. "Probably for a while. Depends on how long it takes us to catch him, how much of a threat he seems to be to you." He debated telling her about the barista. No, she was already upset. It could wait.

Biting her lip, she looked down at the table and nodded slowly. Sliding her hand out of his, she picked up her cup. "What do I do about work?"

Kyle exhaled, wondering how much of a fuss she would put up. He'd been thinking about it constantly since last night. "As long as your arm's in a sling and people can see your stitches, they're going to ask what happened. What you told JoAnn was good, but people who know you are going to want more details." He glanced around the room. The place was filling up, the volume rising around the hard surfaces. No one could overhear them. "I think you should stay away from church and choir practice this week and call in sick to work. Depending on what the doctor says Wednesday, we'll go from there."

Taking a sip of his coffee, he let her digest what he just told her. "I don't know what those guys saw, if they even knew you were hurt, but we can't take the chance of someone putting together your injuries with what happened at the Jitter Bug." Especially since they were willing to kill. That was an escalation.

She stared out the window. Across the street, a hill divided into horse property. Several horses wandered around. "I understand. It's just the thought of not being home." She turned back to her coffee, swirling it in her cup before taking a drink. "Can I bring Snowflake to the safe house?"

He'd never been a cat person, but if it'd make her happy, he'd do it. "Sure. We'll pick her up when we get your stuff. That way we won't have to visit your place as often."

Using the back of her hand, she pushed her bangs back from her forehead. "What about my job? I can't just be gone indefinitely. I don't have to go into the office. I can work from the safe house. I'll still need to make the editorial meetings." Her eyes got a far-off look before she met his gaze. "Please, Kyle. Don't make me lose my job over this." She blinked quickly several times.

He squeezed her hand. "You won't. I promise. We'll work it out." Once he got a return smile out of her, he let go of her hand and reached for the paper. "Let's see what they found out." He flipped through the pages until he got to the local section.

A short article mentioned the robbery with shots fired, one

person killed and one injured but no details. He tucked the paper away on the seat next to him.

Thankfully, before Heather could ask about the article, JoAnn appeared at the table, arms loaded down with plates. She set the forty-niner in front of him, the thin pancakes hanging over the edge. Heather got a bowl-shaped pancake that took up the whole plate. Powdered sugar and lemons completed it. A plate of bacon and the check landed on the far side of the table.

Heather's eyes widened and Kyle smiled. "I'll warm up your coffees. Anything else?" "Looks wonderful as always, JoAnn."

As soon as JoAnn had refilled their cups, Kyle asked the blessing on the food, with a special request for Heather's healing and peace. When he opened his eyes, her lashes were damp.

Chapter Twelve

Justin rolled over and shoved the pillow over his head, trying to drown out his mom's voice. She wouldn't let him sleep in. It was a school day. He'd gotten in late last night and had a hard time chilling. Even after falling asleep, he hadn't slept well. He never wanted to go through anything like that again. He'd never been so scared.

But they'd gotten away with it. He was a Seventeener, and that's all that mattered.

"Justin!"

Her voice was right outside his door now.

He tossed the pillow aside and rolled onto his back. "I'm coming."

Pulling himself out of bed, he grabbed clothes off his floor and dressed. He yanked open his door. "Where's the fire?"

"Lose the attitude, Justin. Your father called an hour ago wondering why you weren't up. Somehow that was my fault. Besides, you need to get to school."

He pushed past her and headed down the stairs. What had she made for breakfast?

"I left the newspaper open on the breakfast bar. Read the

article. Seems there was a shooting last night at that coffee shop right around the corner from Kyle's."

Justin lost his balance and grabbed for the banister, his feet like lead blocks.

"You okay?" His mom was right behind him.

He hoped she couldn't hear his pounding heart. Taking a deep breath, he let go of the railing. "Yeah, just tripped."

"You didn't loan your car out to any guys with guns and masks, did you? A Honda was the getaway car, apparently."

Justin's head shot up. He felt the blood drain from his face.

What did she know?

His mom was smiling at him. "It's not like it's not the most common car in Orange County. Good grief, Justin, lighten up. You act like adults can't have a sense of humor. You're such a grump in the morning." She passed him on the stairs. "Anyway, call Kyle, make sure he's okay. Maybe the two of you could go surfing again."

Justin didn't answer, just forced his legs to move to the kitchen. He sank onto a barstool and studied the article.

Someone died? He'd heard the shots, but the guys didn't say anything about shooting anyone. Maybe the paper hadn't gotten that part right. Acid ate at his stomach.

He didn't think his mom would be proud he made the paper.

"WE'LL CALL THE DOCTOR AS SOON AS WE TALK TO YOUR boss. Is she in yet?" Kyle held the truck door open for Heather.

"Should be." She eased herself in, feeling a little less stiff now that the ibuprofen was kicking in.

"I'll explain the situation to her and then let you talk to her and work out the details. If you absolutely need to make a meeting, we can arrange it. But I'd prefer you stay in the safe house as much as possible."

"Okay." Using one hand, she flipped open her purse and pulled out her cell phone. She tried to calm her nerves. What would Susan say? She could be a taskmaster, but her no-nonsense approach resulted in a history of successful magazines. She did manage to keep all the creative types at *Strive* focused, and the magazine had taken off. Generally, Heather had a good relationship with her, but then Heather had never asked for anything like this. And given how out of sorts Susan had been this week, all bets were off.

She selected Susan's number then handed the phone to Kyle. Playing with the edge of her sling, she listened to Kyle's part of the conversation as he explained to Susan that she was involved in an investigation and wouldn't be able to come into work for the time being. He sounded so calm and in control of everything.

She wasn't worried about getting fired; she didn't think Susan would do that. But her ability to get the coveted stories could be hurt. There was a good chance she would be relegated to fillers and regular features. Plus, she liked having input on the layout and the look and feel of the magazine. She couldn't do that if she wasn't in the office.

"Heather?"

Kyle's voice brought her head around. He was holding the phone out to her, palm over the mouthpiece. "It's okay. She'll tell everyone else you had a family emergency and are working from home."

"Thanks." She took the phone from him.

He winked at her and turned his attention back to the road.

Five minutes later Heather pushed the end button on the phone and laid it on the seat. She closed her eyes.

God, where are You? I know You're here, but why do I feel like I'm looking into the grave of my career? I didn't do anything wrong. I'm trying to do the right thing, though it's costing me dearly. I trust You to make good come from this, but right now, I just don't see it.

Susan had been polite, but distant. That wasn't unusual for

her, and Susan had been particularly distracted lately dealing with whatever trouble her stepson had gotten into. Though it hadn't seemed to affect her productivity. And that's what she expected out of everyone. Susan had no use for those who couldn't carry their weight. And right now, Heather was deadweight.

Kyle glanced over at her. "What'd she say?"

Heather swallowed the tears that threatened. "She took me off some interviews and is going to send me already written articles to edit. So, hey, I don't have to attend any editorial meetings." She forced a smile.

"So tell me why this is so bad."

"I feel like I've been demoted. I've worked hard to get where I am. Now I'm essentially back to being a copy editor instead of being a force influencing the direction of the magazine." She twirled a piece of hair around her finger. "I don't want to lose my job."

"I know." He squeezed her knee. "I don't think that will happen. But even if it does, it wouldn't be a surprise to God. He'd have something else planned for you."

"I just wish He'd let me in on the plan. I hate not knowing."

"That's why it's called faith."

She made a face at him. "Profound, Kyle."

"Thanks. I thought about it for a long time." He grinned at her.

She rolled her eyes, but she was grateful for the humor. Picking up the phone again, she looked up her doctor's number.

———

HEATHER WAS SURPRISED AT HOW BUSY THE LAGUNA VISTA Police station was. South Orange County wasn't a high crime area. She rarely saw cops doing anything more than writing tickets or responding to traffic accidents.

Kyle kept his hand on her lower back as he guided her down

the halls, introducing her to people whose names she'd never remember. She wished she were wearing something other than yoga pants, a T-shirt, and flip-flops. Probably not making a great impression on Kyle's colleagues.

Kyle showed her into a conference room. The two men inside stood. "You remember Mark and Bruce from last night."

"Yes. Hi."

Bruce pulled out a chair for her. "How are you feeling? A bit sore?"

She sat down. "Yes, I could barely get out of bed. Kyle had to help me." As the last word left her mouth, she felt her cheeks heat and wished the floor would swallow her. She knew what that sounded like, what they must think. "After he, uh, came in to wake me up from, you know, sleeping in the kitchen." She was just making it worse.

Their faces were equally expressionless, probably because they were consciously keeping them that way.

She adjusted her sling, hoping the heat in her cheeks wasn't visible.

Bruce smiled. "Kyle's a nice guy. I'm sure he was happy to help." He flicked a glance over Heather's shoulder to Kyle.

What was Kyle thinking? She didn't dare turn around to see. As usual, she'd blown it, but this time she'd embarrassed Kyle too, and in front of people he worked with. She was terrible with small talk. Why couldn't she think before opening her mouth?

Mark nodded toward the door. "Kyle, let's get some coffee. Heather, do you want anything?"

Yeah, to go back and redo the last few minutes. "No, thanks. I'm fine." Was it wrong to lie like that to a police officer? Or did the fact that she so obviously wasn't fine negate her words?

"I'll let you and Bruce get to work." Kyle touched her good shoulder. "I'll be back."

"Okay." Heather tried to give him a smile, but by the time she'd summoned it, he was out the door. He hadn't stayed with her. She pushed away disappointment. Then again, maybe he was afraid of how else she'd embarrass him. She was a big girl. She should be able to carry on a conversation and answer questions without help.

She hoped.

Gingerly crossing her legs, being careful not to bump her stitches, she leaned toward the conference table, trying to focus on what she was here to do. The more information she could give them, the sooner they could pick the guy up, and her life could go back to normal.

"Let's have you look at some tattoos. Officer Griffin said you described one of the people in the coffee shop as having a fairly elaborate tattoo." He set in front of her a stack of sheets of photographs. Each sheet had six pictures on it.

"Yes. I drew a picture of it, but I guess it got left at the shop." Heather scooted the chair closer to the table, thoughts of her article long vanished from her head. It seemed so long ago. She remembered being excited about it but couldn't remotely call up that enthusiasm.

"No, they picked it up. It's evidence."

Scanning the pictures of tattoos, she picked out the one she had seen almost immediately. "That's it."

Bruce came over and took the sheet from her, replacing it with a sheet of six faces. "Which of these guys, if any, had the tattoo?"

She shook her head at the teenage faces staring at her. What made them do this? What happened to make them so jaded they already were throwing their lives away?

A face jumped out at her. It was the tattoo guy. "Here. This was the guy who was sitting in the coffee shop when the two boys came in."

He took the picture from her, asked her a few questions about tattoo guy, and made notes. "Excuse me a moment." He stepped out the door, and she heard muted voices before he returned. Sitting down, he started asking her questions about the night.

She forced herself to concentrate, pushing aside the fear that lapped at her like waves on the beach. Closing her eyes, she pictured the scene at the Jitter Bug. She reminded herself she was safe here, visualizing Kyle's arms around her while she remembered the robbery as a detached observer.

Chapter Thirteen

Kyle swirled the bitter coffee in his cup as he sat in the cubicle Mark and Bruce shared. He'd just gotten chewed out by the lieutenant. That made twice this month. A personal record. Granted, the press and the city council were putting a lot of pressure on the department to apprehend the Bedroom Burglar. Last night's shooting didn't help.

Mark walked over and handed him a mug shot. "Recognize him?"

"Yep. He was at the Jitter Bug when the two teens walked in."

"Good. You and your girlfriend remember the same thing." Kyle wished everyone would stop calling Heather his girlfriend. She was a key witness in a crime that had the potential to keep her from ever being his girlfriend. "She picked this out?"

"Yeah. Matched the right tattoo to the right guy. Name's Bill McClosky, goes by Bull. He's a Trabuco Hills High School dropout and general troublemaker. He's eighteen now. Aced his GED then did a stint in the Marines before getting a dishonorable discharge. He seems to be the leader or one of the leaders of the Seventeeners. Quite a coincidence he was at the Jitter Bug the night it's robbed."

Kyle dropped the mug shot on Mark's desk. "What else have you found out?"

"We got a ton of fingerprints as you can imagine. And, something interesting. The two boys and tattoo guy all came in, separately, at different times earlier that day. We got them on security video."

"Casing the place."

"That's what we think."

Video was good news. If Heather's eyewitness testimony wasn't key, she wouldn't be in as much danger. "So Heather's description isn't that crucial."

Mark shifted in his chair. "We know it's them because their clothes match your description. You'd probably identify them. But the video isn't good quality, and the kids are careful never to let their faces get caught straight on. Plus, they're wearing base-ball caps."

Kyle frowned. "But they weren't wearing hats during the robbery."

"No, but the security cameras were mysteriously turned off."

Kyle groaned and slumped in the chair. "Why?"

"Haven't been able to figure that out yet. Nobody seems to know."

Taking a deep breath, Kyle pushed out of the chair. He tossed his cold coffee into the trash. "I'm going to go check on her."

"Kyle."

Mark's voice stopped him.

"Don't do anything to compromise this case."

"Like what? Protect the witness?" The sarcasm was probably over the top, but he was frustrated. His job was to protect Heather, and the best way to do that was to put away the bad guys.

"Like getting involved in the investigation."

Kyle stared at him a second, biting back his words before leaving the cubicle. He headed to his own desk to pick up files and his laptop, grudgingly admitting Mark was right. The strength of his desire to protect Heather surprised him. He hoped this case and the forced intimacy it created wouldn't ruin their chance at a relationship.

He loaded the files for the Bedroom Burglar in a box. The lieutenant had made it clear that Kyle needed to continue to work that case with his partner Steve while overseeing Heather's protection detail.

Last week, an article in the *Orange County Register* implied the department was incompetent for not solving the Bedroom Burglar case. The lieutenant had passed along his displeasure at the article and at Kyle and Steve's inability to solve the crime spree already.

Two break-ins over last weekend, making eleven this year. All by the same guy, the Bedroom Burglar. In the case sitting on his desk, a flowerpot with a dead plant was chucked through the fixed window above the sunken tub in the master bath. The family, gone for the weekend, had returned to find only the master bedroom ransacked, every drawer and shelf pawed through. The thief had used the pillowcases off the bed to make off with a handgun, jewelry, and two Rolex watches.

Of course, the homeowners had forgotten to cancel news-paper delivery. Those were stacked up in the driveway. They had set the alarm, but since the fixed window above the tub didn't open, people rarely alarmed them. A fact this burglar took advantage of. Since he never left the master bedroom, he didn't trigger the alarm.

The other three burglaries were similar. Families on vacation, broken window above the tub, only jewelry, cash, or guns taken from the master bedroom. At least the guy got creative with the objects he used to break the windows. One was a river rock from the backyard landscaping, the other was a tree stake, and finally, a wrought-iron patio chair.

And, as usual, no witnesses. For once, Kyle would like to be ahead of this guy, not just taking reports after the fact. The press was hounding them for results. The lieutenant was already on his case about it. If he didn't get a break soon, things were going to be real uncomfortable around here. Heck, they already were.

Kyle walked into the conference room. Heather's face was pale and her bangs stuck up a little, like she'd pressed her hand to her forehead more than once.

"You okay?" He pulled up a chair next to her and took her hand. It was like ice.

Bruce glared at him. "Good thing we're done." Heather nodded without smiling.

She wasn't okay. He glanced at Bruce. He was a good detective, but it wouldn't have been easy on Heather to relive that night.

"What happens next?" Heather asked Bruce.

Bruce shrugged. "We'll keep investigating, see what we can turn up. But we don't have a name to put on the shooter. Until we do—"

"But isn't there something else I can do? I could draw him, and you could see if anyone recognizes him. Don't you do that?" The eyes she turned on Kyle were full of panic.

He moved his hand up her arm to rub it but stopped when he brushed up against the gauze. He'd forgotten about her stitches. "We usually do that when someone's a threat to the public. It's hard to get a sketch that doesn't look like a bunch of other people."

"Can't I try?" Tears welled in her eyes.

Kyle wanted to say yes, to do anything to stop those tears.

He turned to Bruce who was already shaking his head. "What could it hurt?"

Bruce nodded toward the door and stood.

Kyle squeezed Heather's hand and stood. "I'll be right back." She looked at her lap and nodded.

Giving her one last look as he left the room, he saw her reach up and wipe her eyes. *Oh Lord, I have to help her. I hate seeing her like this.*

He'd barely shut the door before Bruce started speaking. "You're too close to this, Kyle. It's affecting your judgment."

That stung. Kyle prided himself on his professionalism. He could argue that with Bruce later. If they got into it now, he'd lose the ability to get Heather what she wanted. "What could it hurt? We take a few minutes to do a computer-generated sketch, she feels better, and we might get something useful out of it."

Bruce stared at him for a minute, and then shook his head. "Do what you want. I'm done." He turned and strode off.

Kyle took a moment then opened the door to the conference room.

Heather looked up, eyes big and questioning, lashes slightly damp.

He smiled at her. "Come on. We're going to go make a picture."

She was out of her chair, good arm flung around his waist.

Wrapping his arms around her, he held her. "Thank you," she whispered into his chest. He'd made the right decision.

———

KYLE INTRODUCED HEATHER TO DAN SOMEBODY. SHE couldn't remember his last name. She was too distracted by the fact he looked more like a CPA than an artist with his too-big-to-be- in-style gold-framed glasses and receding hairline.

Surprisingly, he had a regular office with a desk and a table pushed off to the side. Nothing like what she'd expected.

He shook her hand. "I hear you're an artist. You have the advantage over me. I'm not."

"Really? I thought you were the sketch artist."

"Well, I suppose the title still sticks, but I'm just trained to use the computer program. It does all the work."

That explained the lack of art supplies and the lack of artistic atmosphere of this office. Even at the magazine, where all graphic arts and layouts were done on the computer, the designers' cubicles had a definite artistic flair.

He pulled up a program on the computer. It had two monitors, and one was pointed toward her. An average-looking teenaged boy stared back at her. "Let's start with this and change the features as you tell me how this differs from what you saw."

Concentrating on the dark-haired boy's face, she opened her eyes and compared it to the face on the screen. "The eyes. They need to be darker, more intense. And he's smirking."

They moved over each facial feature, narrowing down choices, making refinements. Heather never would have imagined there were so many variations of each feature. It didn't take long before they all blurred together. How was she supposed to pick out such fine differences when she'd barely gotten a look at him?

They worked for a while longer until a couple of computer-generated sketches lay on her lap, marked up. She rolled her tense neck. "It's the eyes. Something about the eyes." She tossed the pencil on Dan's desk. "I don't know. I can't even see it anymore."

"It's okay, Heather." Dan leaned his elbows on his desk. "If it comes to you later, we can always fix it."

"Can I take this with me?" She held up an unmarked sketch. "Sure."

Kyle squeezed her shoulder. "Thanks, Dan."

She'd almost forgotten he was there. The world disappeared when she focused on a project.

"No problem. Don't let anyone know how good she is at this. I might be out of a job."

Heather gave a half smile as she stood, exhaustion weighing on her. "Can we go now?"

"Sure." Kyle kept his arm securely around her as he guided her out of the station and to his truck.

Chapter Fourteen

They'd been driving for a few minutes, but Kyle noticed her eyes hadn't left the sketch on her lap. At the stoplight, he looked over in time to see her close her eyes for a moment and then open them, boring into the sketch. He reached over and touched her knee.

She jumped, yanking her gaze from the paper.

"Enough, Heather. It's enough. Let it go." She was just making herself feel worse, and he didn't want to see that happen.

After a moment, she put the sketch on the floor.

They pulled up to the fire station. Joe was working today. Heather raised her eyebrows. "New safe house?"

"No. I want you to meet my friend, Joe Romero. We grew up together. And I'm trading trucks with him."

"Ah."

He was still helping Heather out of the truck when Joe came out. Kyle introduced them.

"A pleasure to meet you." Joe shook Heather's hand. "Kyle talks about you incessantly."

Kyle shot Joe a look. Incessantly? A phone call to tell Joe where he'd decided to take Heather on a date didn't seem incessant to him. Joe was usually better about shooting off his mouth than Scott. Scott, now a naval pilot, had always been brash even when they were kids together. But given the fact that Heather was now smiling in a way he hadn't seen all day, he couldn't be too mad.

Joe tossed Kyle his keys. "Have you checked your e-mail?"

"No, I didn't get a chance to at the station."

"Scott thinks he might be coming home this weekend. Wanted to know if we could get together."

Kyle tucked his arm around Heather's waist. "We should be able to swing something."

"Good. You sure you want to trade your silver truck for a red one?"

Kyle laughed. "It's counterintuitive. If it's bright red, it can't be hiding, right?"

He grabbed a few things out of his truck, including the sketch, and handed Joe the keys.

Joe slapped him on the back. "Be careful."

"You too."

They got to Heather's house a few minutes later. She trudged into the living room and sank into the couch. Her cat jumped into her lap, and she absentmindedly scratched its ears.

Other than meeting Joe, she had hardly spoken since they left the police station. She'd been through a lot this morning; he understood that. He wished there was some way he could make it easier on her, something he could do.

He felt helpless. And he didn't do helpless well. She just sat on the couch stroking the cat's ears.

He hesitated for just a second before sitting next to her, close enough to put his arm around her. He trailed his fingers on her upper arm above her sling.

She looked up then snuggled her head to his shoulder. Okay, he must have done something right. He pulled her closer, the cat springing out of her lap with the movement. His other hand settled at her waist, her thigh brushing his. She was so nice to hold. With his cheek on her head, her shoulders moved with each rise and fall of her breath.

After a moment, she spoke. "I'm sorry. I know you want me to hurry."

"We have a few minutes."

"I just wish I could have given a better description."

Kyle kissed the top of her head. "I know." A heaviness fell over him. Her life wouldn't be normal for a long time. And she would always associate him with this terrible time of her life. But would it be a positive memory of him supporting her and being her friend? Or a negative one of him failing to protect her before becoming her jailer and gatekeeper?

Skimming his hand up and down her back, he noticed how small she was. One big hug could crush her. For now, she was in his arms, trusting him. He'd take that for as long as she was willing to give it. *Lord, show me how to help her. Show me what she needs.*

In what seemed like too short of a time, Heather put her hand on his chest and pushed herself to a more upright position. She smiled up at him. "Thanks."

"Anytime." He smiled back, having no idea what he did, but glad she was happy.

"Help me up, and I'll get packing."

Kyle stood and helped her to her feet, bringing her inches away from his chest. Instead of letting go of her hand, he laced his fingers through hers. His eyes searched her face, lingering on her lips. He wanted to kiss her. But was this the right time? Certain milestones were important to women: the first date, the first kiss. He wanted it to be special, a memory she would treasure, not just a kiss he'd given her because she'd been vulnerable.

His eyes met her soft brown ones as she leaned toward him. Lowering his lips to her forehead, he kissed her quickly, not satisfying himself with that. He'd have to come up with a better plan soon. Having her under his protection was putting a serious kink in their dating life.

She looked up at him, a question flickering across her eyes, while she gave a nervous smile and stepped away. Walking over to the dining table, she picked up a thick, oversized envelope. She tapped the package on the table. "These are passes to The Fest, the big band festival a week from Saturday. I was supposed to go and do a couple of interviews, and I had originally thought you might want to come to and bring that teenager you're mentoring. Justin, wasn't it? But Susan pulled me off the interviews."

Kyle figured Justin would like going to see all the bands, even if he didn't let his enthusiasm show. But he wasn't sure about letting Heather go. Still, if he could, he'd make it happen. She needed every bit of normalcy she could get. "Bring the tickets, and we'll talk about it."

In the next half hour, Kyle got a good portion of Heather's belongings in the truck, including the cat in its carrier and the litter box. He let her pack her clothes, but other than that, made her sit on the couch and direct him. She was bringing her laptop, so he hoped being able to work from the safe house would help keep her occupied.

Unfortunately, the cat was seriously annoyed at being in the carrier. It sat in the backseat of the truck howling as if someone were skinning it alive.

At least he let her carry the In N Out bags. Heather suppressed a grin at the perturbed look on Kyle's face while Snowflake loudly protested from her cat carrier, her cries echoing down the motel hall.

"How long is she going to keep this up?"

"Until she's certain we know she's annoyed." "Great."

Their room door swung open, Hilary appearing in the frame. "I heard you coming. I hope some of that In N Out is for me."

Heather held up the bag. "Double-Double okay?" Hilary had the kind of athletic figure that meant she could eat anything. Her straight dark hair and almond-shaped eyes made her look more like a model or a beach volleyball player than a cop.

"Perfect."

Heather walked in and set the food on the desk in the kitchen area.

"Where do you want it?" Kyle lifted the carrier.

"Put it in the bathroom for now. We'll let her get used to one area."

He took the carrier into the bathroom. Heather followed, soothing Snowflake. She stuck her fingers through the wire gate, letting Snowflake sniff them, and then cautiously opened the cage. After petting her for a minute, she eased out of the bathroom, closing the door behind her. An ear-piercing howl followed.

They ate their burgers, but lunch was punctuated by Snowflake's pitiful cries.

"I'd better go get her before someone calls and wants to know what we're doing to her." Heather opened the door to the bathroom.

Snowflake peeked out, ears perked and eyes darting around the room. Stomach nearly on the floor, she crept forward.

Heather bent down and scooped her up in her good arm. "It's okay. You're fine. Such a baby." After a minute of scratching the Siamese's head, Heather finally coaxed a small purr out of her. She carried her to the couch.

"I'm going to bring up the rest of your stuff."

"Okay."

Snowflake startled when the door slammed shut behind Kyle but then jumped down to explore the room in a low crawl. A bath sounded good, if she could manage it. The sponge bath this morning had been okay, but a long soak sounded heavenly.

When Kyle returned with the rest of her bags, she stood up. "Could you help me with my sling? I'm going to take a bath."

He moved next to her and loosened the straps. "Then I think I'll go running and check out the fitness room. Can I change before you start your bath?"

"Sure. It'll take me a bit to get my stuff together anyway." He slipped the sling over her head then handed it to her. Gingerly, she moved her arm around and lowered it, the muscles protesting. She walked to her room and pulled out clean clothes. Her iPod sat on top and she picked it up. That was exactly what she needed.

When she came out carrying her bundle, Kyle was putting on his running shoes. He had changed into his workout clothes, a T-shirt that fit him too well and running shorts that revealed muscular legs.

She sighed. "Have a good run. I wish I were going." And not just to fight off any other women, though that thought made her bite her lip to keep from smiling. She needed to release this tension weighing on her shoulders. Running could do that in a way a bath couldn't. But it wasn't an option.

He stood and reached her in one stride, lifting her chin with his finger. "You will soon enough. Be good while I'm gone. I'm taking my phone, so call if you need anything."

"Okay." She looked into his stormy-ocean eyes and willed him to kiss her.

His eyes darkened. He slid his hand along her jaw to the back of her neck.

Should she?

Leaning forward, she placed her hand on his chest and slid it up to his shoulder. The heat of his skin came through the thin material. She felt his chest move as he took a deep breath.

A yowl shrieked through the room.

"Sorry, cat, sorry," came Hilary's voice from the sitting area. "Didn't mean to scare you."

Heather had forgotten they weren't alone.

Kyle squeezed the back of her neck. "I'll see you when I get back."

A few minutes later Heather sank into the hot water. Or at least half of her did. Luckily the tub was arranged so she could keep her right arm and leg out of the water without having the spout in her back.

Using the washcloth and her own bath gel, she washed until she no longer smelled like a hospital or a motel. Now that the ibuprofen she'd taken before her bath was kicking in, she was ready for the warm water to do its magic. Careful not to drag the cords in the water, she touched the screen on her iPod and tucked the earbuds in. Music swirling around her, she sank as low as she could.

She hummed along until tears clogged her throat and poured down her face. Clutching her iPod, she leaned toward the faucet and turned it on to cover the sound of the sobs heaving her shoulders, her soul unlocked by music.

Chapter Fifteen

Heather walked out of the bathroom and nearly ran into Kyle. Obviously, he'd finished his workout.

She couldn't decide if he looked better sweaty, his shirt sticking to him, or freshly showered and shaved. Either way he looked pretty wonderful.

"I was just going to see if you were okay. How was your bath?"

She took a deep breath. "Good. I just need to change my bandages."

"I'm going to jump in the shower. Then I'll help you."

"Have a good workout?"

"Not bad." He grinned at her.

She was staring, blocking the bathroom door. "Good. Well, I'll get out of your way." She stepped past him into her room, catching a glimpse of Hilary grinning while flipping through a magazine. Having a chaperone was… interesting.

Heather had the bandage-changing supplies on the coffee table when Kyle came out. She had pulled the paper tape and gauze off her leg, but was having trouble doing it one-handed on her arm.

Snowflake had decided the room was safe. She jumped on

the coffee table and kept sniffing and pawing at the bag of bandages. Heather nudged her off.

Kyle sank down next to her on the couch wearing a T-shirt and jeans, barefoot, hair still damp. Motel soap smelled good on him.

"Let me know if this hurts." He picked up her arm and gently peeled off the tape. "So, do you want to get a movie tonight?"

"Can we get a pizza to go with it? And I'll need some Diet Coke."

He got out clean gauze and laid it over her stitches. "Sounds good." He taped it down, then picked up her leg and set it across his lap, gently lifting her pant leg.

She was glad she'd managed to shave her legs, though it'd been tricky around the stitches.

Adding two gauze squares this time, he said, "Any requests?"

"Nope. I haven't seen anything in a while. And you can put whatever you want on the pizza as long as it's got sausage."

"Not picky about pizza. Good. I was wondering."

She crossed her arms. "I'm not picky."

Kyle looked at her and raised his eyebrows. "You just don't like anything that comes with a motel room."

She giggled. "That's different."

"Uh huh." He eased down the final piece of tape, then started rubbing her foot. "Cute feet. How do you get those flowers painted on your toes?"

"You mean Kim has never enlightened you on that secret?"

"I don't notice my sister's feet."

"They're decals."

He kept massaging her foot. It felt good. She stifled a yawn.

"You want to take a nap before our big date?"

She thought for a moment. No, she wanted to be exhausted when she went to sleep. Hopefully, that'd keep the nightmares away.

Shaking her head, she said, "I need to check my e-mail."

He squeezed her foot one last time, then stood up. "I'll set up your computer."

A minute later Kyle had her computer bag unpacked and all the cords hooked up. He stretched them over to her on the chair.

She turned on the computer. Her sister had written her, wanting to plan a girls' day. The cat jumped in her lap. "Drat."

"What?" Kyle looked over from the TV.

"My parents. What do I tell them? And my sister just wrote me." She didn't like the squeaking tone she heard in her voice. But she couldn't believe she'd forgotten to tell them. She rubbed Snowflake's ears. "I'll miss choir practice tonight. I need to let Sarah know."

He rose and came to stand behind her, his hands on her chair. "You can tell Sarah you're not up to choir practice tonight. You can tell her the whole story later as long as you can swear her to secrecy. As for your parents, just briefly tell them you witnessed a robbery, got some cuts and bruises and until we know more about the case, you're under protection. But you can't tell any of them where you are."

She sighed. "My mom's going to freak."

"Want me to call her?"

He really was a sweetie. She shifted around to look at him directly. "Thank you. I'll do it, but it's sweet of you to offer. She'll want to hear my voice to make sure I'm okay. However, my dad will probably want to talk to you."

"No problem. I'd like to talk to your dad. And maybe we can drive up and meet your family somewhere."

"Really?" That was the best news she'd heard all day. The thought of not being able to see her family was more than she could bear.

"As long as it's not at someone's house that could be traced to you."

"Thank you."

He gently put his hand on her good shoulder. "You're

welcome. I'm going to do whatever I can to make this as easy on you as possible."

BULL CRUMPLED UP THE PAPER AND TOSSED IT ASIDE. HE'D read the article twice. He'd even gone online to see if the paper had posted any updates. None. Despite Alex's screw up, it looked like they'd pulled it off. He had no doubts the cops had already figured out who he was, but he'd done nothing, just had a cup of coffee and smiled at the cop's girlfriend.

Alex was the one who'd be in trouble if that girl could ID him as the shooter. The paper hadn't said anything about a witness. It did mention one person injured, though. That had to be the girl. Unless Detective Kyle Taylor hurt himself tripping over his own feet. He snorted at the thought.

It had been his boldest move yet. It hadn't been necessary, and if things went wrong, it could totally screw up his whole plan. But what a rush knowing the cop was right behind that door while the place was being robbed.

It would work out. He was too smart for the cops. He'd still accomplish what he wanted; no cop was going to stop him.

But it never hurt to read the enemy's playbook. He opened a window on his computer and got to work.

Cheap city computer system.

WOULD HEATHER BE THE WOMAN THAT CAME BETWEEN Scott and him? Kyle had typed a reply to Joe and Scott about Saturday's barbecue but hadn't hit send. Scott's line—"don't bother coming unless you bring Heather"—held him back. He was joking. Right?

He glanced over at Heather. She was on the phone, knees pulled up, talking to her mom. She had no idea how beautiful he found her. A strange feeling crept in his chest at the image of her meeting Scott. A naval aviator stationed in China Lake, Scott had a way of charming women. Kyle always wondered if Scott's easy ability to attract women would ever be an issue between them. He and Scott never seemed to be attracted to the same type of women. But what if this time was different?

The thought of Heather drooling over Scott made him sick, though, honestly, Heather wasn't the drooling type. She hadn't drooled over him. Although she'd given him some amazing smiles and gazed at him with those soft brown eyes of hers. Yeah, she liked him. Still, it wouldn't hurt to step up his game a bit. Given their situation, she needed to be reminded they were still dating.

He hit *send* and put his phone back in its holster. Heather was on the phone but kept looking at him, smiling. She was talking about him. Taking the phone from her ear, she covered it with her hand.

"My dad would like to talk to you."

"How'd they take it?" Kyle moved over to the couch and sat down next to her.

"Better than I thought."

He took the phone from her. "Mr. McAlistair, this is Kyle Taylor." Kyle explained Heather's situation and the security precautions they were taking. He left out the part that she had witnessed a murder, since he hadn't told Heather yet, either.

A few minutes later, Kyle hung up, a little relieved and surprised at how well that had gone. He stretched his arm across the back of the couch, being careful of Heather's sore shoulder. "For being under protection, you're going to have a busy social calendar."

She snuggled up next to him, looking up. "What do you mean?"

"We're off to Joe's house Friday for a barbecue so you can meet Scott. And sometime we have to work in a trip to see your folks. You're going to be so worn out you'll be begging for down-time here."

"Did I tell you how grateful I am?"

He grinned. "I never get tired of hearing it."

She leaned up and kissed him on the cheek, her hand brushing across his chest.

He loved the way she touched him.

She held his gaze. "Thank you." Her voice was nearly a whisper.

Leaning forward he started to properly return her kiss before he remembered Hilary sitting across the room. He slumped against the couch, settling for wrapping his hand around Heather's.

Chapter Sixteen

The smell of garlic and sausage preceded Kyle as he came in the door. He juggled the pizza box and a grocery bag. Hilary closed the door tightly behind him while he set everything on the table.

Heather helped him unpack the grocery bag. "Diet Coke. My hero!" She fluttered her eyelashes at him, then grinned. "Popcorn, M&Ms. Kyle, are you trying to impress me?"

"Yes, ma'am." He winked at her.

"Good job."

"Okay you two." Hilary shouldered her way up to the table. "Can I get a piece of that pizza before Stacey gets here to relieve me?"

"Help yourself."

"Heather, pick a movie from whatever the motel has. I'll bring the food over."

She grabbed a Diet Coke and picked up the remote, clicking through the choices. Ooh, the movie version of *Pride and Prejudice*. She selected it.

Her cell phone rang. She looked at the display. Quinn. Drat. She hadn't turned her phone back to silent after waiting for

Sarah to call her back. This was his fifth or sixth call today. She sent it to voicemail.

Kyle brought the food over and sat next to her, putting his arm around her. Then he noticed the phone in her hand. "Who was it?"

She was going to have to tell him. "Quinn."

"He's been calling you?"

"Yes."

"How often?"

"Several times a day."

"Why didn't you tell me? Has he been leaving you messages?"

"A few."

"I'd like to listen to them."

Hesitating only a second, she pulled up her voice mailbox, then gave him the phone. She watched his face, unreadable, as he listened to Quinn's five messages.

He stood up and pressed some buttons on her phone, walking across the room. She thought he was erasing the messages until he started talking. "Quinn. This is Detective Kyle Taylor." Using his no-nonsense cop voice, he walked into her room and closed the door.

She turned to look at Hilary who just grinned. She could only imagine what Kyle was saying. As much as she didn't want to drag Kyle into her past relationship, she was a little relieved not to have to deal with it anymore. She had enough on her plate.

Thirty seconds later he came out. "He won't bother you anymore." He set her phone on the coffee table and settled back down next to her on the couch.

O-kay. She didn't want to know what he'd said. Time to watch the movie anyhow. She nodded at the TV as she started it. "So, are you okay with a chick movie?"

"I'm secure in my masculinity. Plus, I can see what all the fuss is about."

She laughed and took a bite of her pizza. It was good. Or was it just because Kyle sat next to her?

The radio crackled and Kyle picked it up.

Heather suppressed a scowl. Why didn't he let Hilary get it? She was still on duty.

"Stacey's on her way up."

At the knock on the door a few minutes later, Heather paused the movie. Kyle squeezed her knee and stood up. He talked with Stacey and Hilary for a moment.

Heather finished her pizza. Once Hilary left and Stacey was settled, Kyle would come back and they could have their date. She could pop the popcorn while she was waiting.

Kyle watched her get up, and she gave him a smile. He turned back to his conversation.

As soon as the popcorn was done, Heather waved goodbye to Hilary and took the popcorn to the couch. Snowflake jumped up to sniff the bowl then scampered back down when Kyle approached.

He sat next to her a minute later. "Sorry. Just needed to get everyone updated."

"It's fine. Ready now?" "Yeah."

She flipped on the movie. Matthew MacFadyen was cuter than Colin Firth.

Kyle pulled her next to him, and she laid her head on his shoulder. This was nice, even if it took a little bit to get here.

Twenty minutes later his phone rang. He picked it up, looking at the display. "It's Mark. I need to take this."

Heather sat up. Maybe there was a break in the case.

Kyle moved to the table, opening his laptop while talking to Mark. The call ended after a few minutes, but before Kyle could move back to the couch, it rang again.

She closed her eyes. Her head was starting to hurt again. She needed more meds. Levering herself up, she wandered into the bathroom and grabbed the bottle of ibuprofen. She couldn't get it open with one hand. Back out to the living area with the bottle, she shook it slightly.

Stacey looked up and took the bottle from her. "How many do you need?"

"Two should be fine."

Stacey opened the bottle and shook them out into Heather's hand.

"Thanks." She picked up her Diet Coke can. It was too light. She sloshed it around. Only drops were left. Moving to the counter, she grabbed another one off the six pack. Barely cold. That wouldn't do. She hated anything but ice-cold Diet Coke.

Maybe there was ice. She opened the small refrigerator and looked in the freezer compartment. No ice. Grrr. Well, this was a motel. There had to be an ice machine. Yep, there was the bucket sitting on the counter. She looked around.

The bathroom door swung shut.

Kyle was still at his computer on the phone.

She could get the ice herself. It wasn't that big of a deal.

KYLE BARELY TURNED AS HE HEARD THE DOOR SHUT. Stacey must have gone out. He hung up the phone. Nothing new from Mark; Steve's call was routine. Heather would be disappointed. He looked around to tell her. Where was she? The bathroom door was closed. She must be in there.

HEATHER SPOTTED THE ICE MACHINE IN AN ALCOVE NEAR the elevator. The hallway was quiet. Almost too quiet. It was creepy out here alone. She should have waited for Kyle or Stacey to get the ice.

She moved to the ice machine and put the bucket under the

dispenser, looking around. The elevator doors opened. She jumped, her heart racing. A couple walked by, chatting quietly.

Good grief. She was overreacting again. As usual.

She stuck the bucket under the dispenser again, a little more forceful than necessary. The racket of the falling ice made it impossible to hear anything else.

THE BATHROOM DOOR OPENED AND STACEY WALKED OUT. It took Kyle a moment, and then several thoughts collided at once. "Where's Heather?" He started into the bedroom. Maybe she was lying down.

"What do you mean?" Stacey followed him.

"I mean she's not here. I heard the door open and thought you went out." He strode toward the door and flung it open.

Chapter Seventeen

Heather shook the ice bucket. It was almost full. She stuck it back under the dispenser—

Something grabbed her shoulder. She screamed and dropped the bucket. Ice hit her legs and feet as she turned.

Kyle.

"You scared me. Don't do that!"

"Good. We're even. You scared me. Don't ever leave the room again without one of us." His eyes were dark and hard. He was angry with her. Well, fine, she was angry with him too. She brushed past him, shaking the ice off her shoes.

Stacey stood near the door to the room. "There you are."

"Heather." Kyle called after her but she ignored him.

Reaching around Stacey, she opened the door and went in. Her warm Diet Coke and pills sat on the counter. So be it. She walked to her room and shut the door, a touch too forcefully. Snowflake looked up, awakened from her nap on Heather's pillow. But at this point, Heather didn't care if Stacey thought she'd slammed it. Or Kyle either. She hated not having any privacy.

She pulled *Mind of Her Own* out of her bag. She'd been reading Diana Brandmeyer's book about a mom who develops

amnesia and thinks she's a famous writer when a George Fore-
man grill falls on her head. Right now, Heather could use a bit
of amnesia. She'd like to go to sleep, wake up, and find all of this
was just a nightmare.

Pushing the cat off her pillow, she flopped on her bed and
immediately regretted it, pain shooting through her head and
shoulder, reminding her of the reason for the whole ice fiasco to
begin with.

She clenched her teeth and threw the book down, tears
squeezing out of the corners of her eyes. *God, this is so not fair.
What did I do to deserve this?* How did Kyle handle it? Sure, he
wasn't a crime victim, but he had to see it all the time. How did
he deal with the fact that evil seemed to be winning the battle?
Good grief, she couldn't even get ice for her Diet Coke or finish
watching a movie with her date.

She knew it wasn't about fairness or deserving. The rain falls
on the just and the unjust and all that. But still, this was so
rotten. What about the benefits of following God's plan? What
about the abundant life? This definitely wasn't it.

Picking up her Bible, she knew she should look for comfort
in it. But she didn't want to. She was mad at God and planned
to stay that way, at least for the night. She opened the front
cover and took out the picture of her and her sisters.

It was a family vacation photo, over ten years old, from their
family trip up the coast to Big Sur. She hadn't looked at it in a
while, couldn't even remember why she'd stuck it in her Bible.
The three girls stood on a piece of driftwood at the beach, wind
blowing their hair around. Aimee looked like a model even in
her ratty camping sweatshirt. Kellie looked like she was ready for
mischief, which if Heather recalled, involved a bucket of icy
seawater shortly after the picture was taken.

And there Heather was, the middle sister standing between
them, her hair actually streaked a pretty, dark blonde from the
sun. She looked happy. Content. Innocent.

The girl in the picture never would have guessed what she'd

be going through in the future. If she knew, would she have done things differently? Heather could hardly believe they were the same person.

And what was Kyle doing? Did he get more ice? Did he go back to the movie? Did he even care how she felt?

She looked at the photo a moment longer before putting it back in her Bible and laying it on the nightstand. Feeling petulant and immature, she turned out the light.

A minute later she turned it back on. She needed some big sister advice. Aimee should still be up. She grabbed her phone and called her, pushing a pillow up behind her back.

"Are you okay?" Aimee's voice sounded like home. "Mom told me what happened."

"I'm fine. Just stiff and sore." She should have done this earlier. Already she felt better.

"I'm glad you called. Mom's about out of her mind with worry."

Heather laughed and settled into the pillows. "That's nothing new. Mom always needs something to worry about."

"True. And now that I'm married, that just leaves you and Kellie." Aimee laughed.

"Gee, thanks. Do you know she sent me a newspaper clipping, some job ad for an editor up in the Valley? Like I don't have a job I enjoy." She hoped she would still have it at the end of this.

Aimee whispered something—probably to her husband Daryl—then came back on the line. "She's just hoping you'll move home."

"Yeah." Heather got quiet. She kind of wished she were there right now. But it was out of the question. She couldn't go running home every time she wanted comfort. She hadn't done that since Quinn left her.

"What's wrong?" Leave it to Aimee to cut to the chase. "Besides the obvious."

Heather sighed. "I met this guy."

"That's what's wrong?"

"No." Heather hated that dejected sound in her voice. She gave Aimee a rundown of what had happened between her and Kyle this week, keeping her voice low. "We were on a date when the shooting happened, and now he's my bodyguard. I don't even know if I can deal with a cop for a boyfriend, but how can I accurately judge what's happening between us when we're in this situation?" That whiny tone was sneaking back in.

Aimee sighed. "Ah, I don't miss the dating thing at all. That's the great thing about being married. I don't have to worry about dates, or rejections, or if he likes me."

"Thanks, sis. Not sure how that helps me."

"Heather, he sounds like a great guy." Aimee's voice got soft. "You know what I think?"

"Isn't that why I called?" Heather said dryly. "So you could do the big sister thing."

"Look, you're my little sister. We've got a weirdly connected family who always does everything together. You're the only one who's geographically managed to escape the nest. I think most of us thought you'd be back up here long before now— Mom still does. But you've made a life for yourself down there in Laguna Vista. I think there are two things that freak you out about Kyle being a cop. One, you might lose someone you could potentially love. You've never had that happen, unless you count that thing with Quinn. If you miss your family, we're only a two- hour drive away. Two, you've planted your last root in Laguna Vista and firmly shut the door on ever coming back here."

Heather took a deep breath. Aimee had managed to summarize Heather's feelings before she even knew what they were. "When did you get so wise?" Her voice was barely above a whisper.

"I just want you to be happy. And don't let your fears keep you from that." Tenderness colored Aimee's voice.

Now the tears started to flow, washing away the heaviness bit by bit. "Thanks."

"Heather, it's okay to go slow, but guys are kind of dense and he might not get it. You still have to be bold and talk to him about what's on your heart. The risk is worth it."

Heather thought of the way those gray eyes looked at her. "Yeah, I think he is." She sighed. "Guess what else?"

"What?"

"Quinn's back."

"No!"

"Yep." Heather summarized what had transpired.

Now it was Aimee's turn to sigh. "Oh, sis. Just be careful, okay?"

"I will."

They arranged for a girls' day out in a couple of weeks when all of this would be behind her. Heather reached for a tissue then turned out the light.

HE'D SCREWED UP. HE DIDN'T KNOW HOW, BUT HE HAD. Kyle switched off the computer, finished reviewing the files Steve had sent him. He wanted Mark to keep him updated, but it never occurred to Steve that Kyle might have something to do at night other than work. If Steve was working, why shouldn't Kyle? He exhaled. Normally that would have been true.

But now things were different. He had Heather. Or he hoped he did. And she clearly wasn't happy about how things went tonight. He wasn't either, but what could he do? His job didn't always neatly fit into work hours. Especially given how much pressure he was under on both of these cases.

And then she'd left the room, and he'd been scared. He shouldn't have been so hard on her. He hadn't told her not to leave the room, he had just assumed she would know it wasn't safe. But she wasn't a cop and didn't think like one.

Should he check on her? He had heard her voice earlier, too

low to make out words, but he assumed she was talking on the phone. But there'd been no sounds for the last ten minutes.

Maybe she was asleep. Or mad at him.

He rubbed his hands over his face. He hated not knowing what to do. He wasn't staying here tonight, but he hated to leave without saying goodbye. Would she expect him to come in and talk to her, or would she rather be left alone?

He looked around the room and caught Stacey watching him. Great. Nothing like having an audience. He wondered how long it'd take before what happened tonight got around the station.

If only to get out of Stacey's view, he knocked softly on Heather's door. No answer. He turned the knob and pushed the door open. "Heather?"

The light from the living area spilled into the room across her bed. He stepped closer, waiting for his eyes to adjust to the darkness.

She was asleep on her side, curled around a pillow. A tear glinted on her check. The cat slept next to her head.

He was a total jerk. And the worst part was, he didn't know how to fix it.

Chapter Eighteen

Heather had managed to get jeans on this morning. They had a flared leg so they didn't rub her stitches. But at least she felt like she was dressed instead of just slouching around in yoga pants. With a favorite cute top, she felt a little more like herself.

She had just finished brushing her teeth when she heard the front door open and the sound of Kyle's low voice mix with Hilary's higher one. She rinsed her toothbrush and set it on her toiletry bag then opened the bathroom door.

She noticed the bag of Starbucks ground coffee on the counter. She smiled. He was good to her. A few bags with the same logo on it sat on the small table. It was probably more than she deserved after last night.

Kyle's eyes skimmed over her before meeting her gaze. The swelling had gone down under his eye, but there was still a nasty looking bruise there, turning a sickly shade of green.

"Hi." She hesitated, not sure what he thought about how they left things.

"I made you coffee. The good stuff." He stood and poured her a cup, adding a healthy amount of cream. He handed it to her, kissing her on the cheek. "How'd you sleep?"

She took a sip before answering. Oh, this was good. How did anybody ever wake up before Starbucks? And Kyle didn't seem to be mad at her. "Not bad. It's getting up that hurts."

He glanced at Hilary who was helping herself to a muffin. "I'm sorry about last night."

Hilary picked up her radio. "I'll go do a perimeter check now that you're here."

Kyle flashed a grateful look her way. Once the door closed behind her, he blew out a breath and ran his hand through his hair. "Last night was my fault. I should have told you not to leave the room. You didn't know. Mark knows I want to stay updated on your case. And Steve knows he can call me anytime. Like last night. There was never any reason not to. I'll admit I could pull back there. Nothing anyone told me last night was critical. It all could have waited. Everyone's just used to me being available all the time."

Relief warmed her as much as the coffee. She touched his arm. "I owe you an apology too. I overreacted. It's one of my weaknesses. I guess with everything that's going on, I haven't been able to find my emotional equilibrium yet."

She stared into her cup for a second before meeting his gaze. "I like that you're a cop. I don't know how I would have gone through this situation without you. I know I can trust you completely. Being a cop is who you are, and I wouldn't want to change that." She bit her lip. "I guess I just need to know that sometimes you go off duty. That you know where to draw the line between your personal life and your work."

He stepped forward and gently wrapped her in a hug, careful of her shoulder. She slipped one arm around his waist. "I've never been close to a crime victim before. We don't think about the victims much beyond how they help us solve the case. Many people get their lives completely turned upside down often through no fault of their own."

Too soon for her liking, he released her. He took her hand and led her to the couch.

"There's something I need to tell you about the case." He took a breath. "I haven't told you before now because you've been hit with a lot and I wanted to give you time to adjust."

How could this get any worse? She pushed down the first vestiges of panic. "I know I'm going to be here awhile. I figured that out."

"Yes, but you don't know why. The barista died. You witnessed a murder."

His words took a minute to sink in. Numbness enveloped her.

She'd seen someone die.

The images flashed before her. The barista looking at her, scared. She'd tried to reassure him. The dark-haired teen turning, staring at her. His eyes. His dead, lifeless eyes. He lifted his shirt, raised his arm. The barista ran. The image disappeared in a flash of white.

"Heather? You okay?" Kyle covered her hand with his. "I don't know." She stood and moved to the bedroom.

Spotting her Bible on her bedside table, Heather picked it up. The last couple of days had been crazy, but if she was in this protection thing for the long haul, she needed to cling to it. Right now, it felt like a life jacket and she was being tossed in a stormy ocean.

She tried to digest Kyle's words. They played over in her mind but still didn't seem any more real.

Until now the scariest, most dangerous moment of her life had been when a homeless man banged on her car window late at night. That had been her insulated life, a far cry from the dangerous people Kyle dealt with every day.

Like those kids who had killed the barista.

BULL PULLED HIS EXPLORER INTO THE VISITOR SLOT AT HIS mom's town- home complex. This place was a dump. At least forty years old with a rotting shake roof, crumbling stucco, and dead weeds everywhere, it represented the last traces of his old life. He'd get her out of here soon.

He grabbed the laptop off the passenger seat and checked the mirror one last time. Long sleeve striped shirt over jeans. Cool looking but presentable to Mom, and it covered his ink. He'd pass as a smart computer geek making bank, right? He was one of her main interests, and she paid a lot of attention to everything he did.

Didn't mean he couldn't fool her. He'd been fooling her since he was twelve, swiping her cigarettes, selling them to the neighborhood kids. At thirteen, he'd snuck out of the house whenever he wanted, going to parties. Mostly beer, though he'd gotten high a time or two. Wasn't for him, though. He was smart, and he didn't want weed messing with his head. Even high he could pull off most of what he wanted to do and not get caught.

But he had bigger plans.

Rapping on the door, he noticed flyers and ads tucked into the rusty screen. He wadded them up. Two locks snapped open and the chain rattled before he saw his mom's face.

"Hey, Ma. I brought you something."

"Billy! Are you on your lunch break?" She pushed open the screen door, and he stepped inside.

Reflexively, he glanced at the Patek Phillipe watch he'd kept for himself. Eleven. Close enough. "Yeah, Ma. Plus, I can make my own hours."

"Let me make you a sandwich."

He followed her back through the cramped, dark hole she called a home to the kitchen. The gold-brown carpet was ratty. It smelled like a combo of wet dog and old ashtrays in here half the time. And no AC.

He set the laptop on the kitchen table while she pulled things out of the refrigerator.

"How's your knee, Billy? Did the doctor clear you yet to go back to the Marines?"

"It's okay. Uh, Ma, you know with all this money I'm making with computers I'm not going to go back to the Marines. See, I—"

She turned, looking like she was going to cry. He hated it when she did that. "Aw, Ma—"

"I thought you were going back to the Marines. That's why you dropped out of high school and got your GED. You said they'd pay for your college." She began stirring something on the stove.

"But Ma, I'm making plenty of money without a college degree. I don't need that."

"A college degree is never a bad investment." She pointed a red-coated spoon at him. "Of either time or money. Now I know I never could afford to send you to school, but if the military is going to pay for it, that's like looking a gift horse in the mouth. Plus, I always thought the discipline would do you good. Without your father being around, I know I wasn't able to have as firm a hand with you as a boy needs."

He hustled to think of a way to get her off this subject. She'd never know that he couldn't go back to the Marines even if he wanted to. Which he didn't. He'd had enough of their idea of discipline to last him a lifetime. Two lifetimes. "Hey, you didn't even look at what I brought you." He opened the laptop and booted it up.

She glanced at it when she moved over to the counter. "I don't know how to use one of those things."

"It's real easy. I'll teach you. You can get on the Internet—I'll hook you up with a wireless router—and send e-mail. You can even do your scrapbooking stuff on here if you want."

She put a plate in front of him. Grilled cheese with tomato and pickles. A generic can of soda followed. Then a bowl of tomato soup. He'd had this same lunch at least once a week for as long as he could remember.

Pulling out the other chair, she sat down next to him.

"Aren't you going to eat?"

"I'm not hungry." She picked up her pack of cigarettes and lit one. "The police came here yesterday looking for you."

He expected that. "What did they say?"

"They wanted to ask you some questions about a robbery Tuesday night. They wanted to know if I knew where you were."

"I saw that in the paper. I was playing video games over at Chad's."

"You're not involved with those boys again, are you?"

"Nope." Involved wouldn't really describe it.

They were both quiet for a while, him eating, her smoking. "I've got this big project coming up at work. They say if it goes well, we'll all make a ton of money off of it." He grinned at her, raising his soda can in a mock toast. "I'll buy you a new house. What do you think? Want to live in Newport? Or maybe Laguna? Get one of those houses up in the hills with a view of the ocean off your balcony?"

She shook her head, blowing out a stream of smoke, then smiled. "Use that money and go to college."

Bull stood up, his chair legs squealing across the fake brick vinyl floor. "Thanks for lunch, Mom. I'll be back later to show you how to use that thing." He pointed to the computer before reaching into his pocket. He pulled out his money clip and tossed five C notes on the table. "Pick out where you want to live. It's only a matter of time."

She walked him out.

He was down the steps and halfway to his SUV before he heard her say through the screen door, "It doesn't get as hot at the beach, does it? With the sea breeze and all."

"No, it's real nice down there." She waved.

He hopped in his car and drove off, planning.

Chapter Nineteen

K yle hit send on his e-mail. Heather's protection schedule was on its way to the lieutenant. Female officers made up less than ten percent of their force, not giving him much in the way of choice as to who to assign to the detail. He was grateful he'd worked with three of them before and had heard good things about the fourth. It should be okay. That's what he'd keep telling himself.

With that out of the way, it was back to the Bedroom Burglar case. His partner, Steve, had been on the phone all yesterday and today. Nothing stolen last weekend had shown up at any pawn shops in the area. No surprise there. Kyle had pretty much figured out the Bedroom Burglar was fencing the stolen goods out of state, since nothing had ever turned up. Leaning back in his chair, he looked at his watch and stifled a groan. Usually, he didn't mind putting in long hours. But when he was covering the same ground over and over, not making any progress, it wasn't fulfilling.

Clasping his hands behind his head, he wished he could go shoot some hoops to relieve his frustration. Instead, he scanned his e-mail and saw several phone messages from the station. Two were from reporters. He deleted those. He got a couple a day and couldn't be bothered to get himself distorted, misquoted, and generally raked over the coals for being incompetent.

The mouse hovered over the delete button for the third phone message. Then he sat up. He didn't want to make this call within Heather's earshot.

Grabbing the phone and radio he stood up. "Hilary, I'll be outside for a few. I'm taking the radio."

"Okay." She didn't even look away from the TV.

Heather looked up from where she was reading on the couch and smiled.

Once outside the room, he dialed Quinn's number as he walked toward the gym.

HALF AN HOUR LATER, HEATHER WAS SITTING AT A SMALL table in the corner at Dairy Queen, Kyle across from her. They pretty much had the place to themselves. Though it would probably ruin her appetite for dinner, she was glad to get out of the motel.

She bit into her chocolate-dipped cone and a piece of chocolate dropped into her lap. "Drat." She switched her cone to the hand with the sling so she could pick up the broken piece with her free hand and pop it in her mouth.

"Hang on." Kyle jumped up and grabbed a couple of napkins.

Too late. A brown spot marked the chocolate's landing zone. She scrubbed at the spot ineffectually. "Stain remover when I get home." No, she wasn't going home. "Or I guess the sink."

Kyle studied her a minute, shoving the straw up and down in his root beer float.

"What?" She was getting used to catching him looking at her.

"Quinn left me a message at the station."

Panic, confusion, and who knows what else swirled through

her brain. She didn't even know what to think, let alone what to say. "Why?"

"That's what I wanted to know. I called him back, and we talked for a while—"

"When?"

"When did I talk to him? At the motel, when I went outside."

She swallowed, wondering what hammer was going to fall next.

"Anyway, he apologized for coming on too strong. He said he was hoping the two of you would get back together, but he's resigned himself to that not happening. However, he still needs to talk to you."

This was interesting. Having a message from her ex-boyfriend being delivered to her by her... well, Kyle wasn't exactly her boyfriend. They were in that nebulous stage between expressing interest in each other and making some kind of commitment. And now with this whole protective custody thing, who knew where their relationship would end up?

She licked her cone. Weird. Quinn was persistent, but she had to give him credit for going to Kyle. He really must want to talk to her. "Why?" She was saying that a lot lately.

"Apparently, you guys still own some property together."

"What?" She sat up. "No, we sold that." The cone was going to mush in her hand, and she'd lost her taste for it. She started to stand to throw it away, but Kyle did it for her.

She wiped the sticky off her hands. "When we were engaged, we bought a townhome together. Renters were in it, and we just let them stay since we weren't getting married for a while. Then when he got transferred, we sold it."

He finished his root beer float with a loud sucking noise. It followed her cone into the trash. "Apparently not."

She couldn't read his expression. Was he upset? Annoyed?

"If he wanted to talk to you, this was a good way to do it."

She nodded. "So now what? Am I supposed to call him back?"

"In case you haven't guessed yet, I brought you here for more than ice cream. I figured you were uncomfortable enough with everyone knowing about our relationship. I didn't think you wanted an audience while I told you about Quinn. So, how about this? Joe's available to shoot some hoops with me. While we're doing that, you can call Quinn and straighten this whole thing out."

KYLE DRIBBLED THE BASKETBALL, GLANCING OVER AT Heather. She was on her phone, pacing back and forth, her gesturing restricted by her sling. She was upset at Quinn; Kyle took some small pleasure in that. He moved in for a layup. The ball arced over the top of the rim and down the other side into Joe's waiting hands. Joe grinned and took the ball back up to the top of the key.

Kyle checked on Heather again. Yeah, she was messing up his game, but that's not why he was here anyway. He needed to burn off some stress running up and down the court, and she needed privacy for her call. Now she sat on the bench, legs crossed, phone dangling from her hand.

"So. How's it going?" Joe nodded toward Heather while he dribbled the ball.

His relaxed demeanor didn't fool Kyle. He watched Joe's eyes, trying to figure which way he was going to move. "Hard to say. The case—and her safety—takes priority." He moved so his back was to Heather and lowered his voice. "The close quarters is making it difficult for the relationship to advance at its own pace. Even if we decided it wasn't working, it's not like either of us could just walk away. On the other hand, I don't want her to have a knight-in-shining-armor complex about me either."

Joe laughed, dodged around Kyle, and made his shot while

hardly looking. "I don't think you have to worry about that."

Kyle grabbed the ball. The park had thinned out. It was getting close to dinnertime; most of the moms with kids had left. Which was why the woman standing alone watching them caught his eye. He studied her a moment longer before turning his attention back to the game. "Spending more time shooting baskets than fighting fires?"

"Don't change the subject." Joe shot a look at Heather, and Kyle followed his gaze.

She had finished her call with Quinn and was sitting on a bench watching them. She smiled. After a long look, he dribbled back down the court. "I'm not. I'm just saying it's a difficult situation." The thought had occurred to him that maybe they needed to put their personal relationship on hold during the case. No way was he telling Joe that. The guy already thought Kyle was seriously lacking in the romance department.

Pivoting quickly in the other direction he took a shot. Joe got a finger on it and deflected the ball, making it bounce uselessly against the rim. "I may be rusty, but I'm not stupid." After praying about it, he realized there was no question in his mind that he wanted to date Heather. He might as well let her know it. How he would do that was the problem.

"Never thought you were." Joe wiped his forehead with his arm. "But she's not helping your game." He lifted his chin. "Someone's checking you out."

Kyle glanced at Heather, but she wasn't looking at them. Instead, that woman he had noticed earlier was smiling at them. "I think that's for you, Joe."

She moved over to where Heather sat, said something to her, and sat down. Maybe she was a friend of Heather's. Unease settled over Kyle. He didn't know this woman, and she was sitting too close to Heather for his comfort. But he doubted she had gang connections.

Joe passed him the ball, and Kyle began dribbling. If he didn't concentrate, Joe was going to wipe the court with him.

Chapter Twenty

I hope you don't mind my joining you," the woman said as she sat next to Heather. "My brothers played constantly, so whenever I see guys playing I tend to stop and watch."

"Oh, no problem." Heather scooted a bit to make room for her. She was watching the guys but not focusing on them. Her thoughts were still on her conversation with Quinn. She was so ticked at him. He'd lied to her. He hadn't sold the town- home like he'd told her. All those papers she'd signed? He'd shredded them. The money she got back from the supposed sale? From him. Oh, she was so glad she hadn't married him. If he'd thought the property would appreciate (which it had), why didn't he just tell her he wanted to keep it instead of lying to her about it? He'd said it was because she had turned so hostile toward him after he took the job in New York. Her conscience twinged a bit at that but not enough to check her anger toward him.

"I don't see a ring. Are you attached to either of those cute guys out there?"

It took Heather a minute to register the woman's words.

"Huh? Oh... " She didn't want this woman, who was clearly ga-ga over Joe and Kyle, to think Kyle was available. On the other hand, she didn't have a claim to Kyle. "Um, I'm dating the blond one."

"He's a babe." The woman paused a minute. "He looks really familiar too. I wonder if I know him." She crossed her legs and propped her elbow on her knee, chin in hand. "I know I've seen him somewhere." She looked at Heather, but Heather didn't say anything. She wasn't helping this woman at all. Something seemed off.

"I'm Monica, by the way." She smiled.

Maybe it was because she felt this woman was interested in Kyle. Maybe it was because she was a little freaked out by being under protection. Whatever the reason, Heather hesitated giving this woman her name. But she had to say something, or Monica would think she was rude. "I'm Nicole." Her middle name. It didn't sound right coming out of her mouth, but she'd never see this woman again. And as long as Kyle or Joe didn't call her Heather, she'd be fine.

"I've got it. He was in the paper recently. He's with the police department, right?"

A weird feeling washed over Heather. Kyle had been in the paper last week when he was interviewed on the Bedroom Burglar case. Goosebumps broke out on her arms, and she tried to catch Kyle's eye.

Joe saw her staring and winked at her. She gave him a tight smile back. Kyle saw and looked over, smiling at her. She raised her eyebrows, but he'd already turned his attention back to the game. Men were so clueless.

The woman went on as if she didn't notice Heather hadn't answered her. "What's his name? Kyle? Right?"

Maybe she should just make up some excuse to leave, or pick up her phone and pretend to talk on it. Or maybe she was just overreacting. Kyle was on the police force, that was public knowledge. This was a woman, for goodness sake, not a teenage gang member. "Yeah, that's him."

"Wow, so how does it feel to be dating a famous detective?"

The woman stared at Heather with intense interest, as if she were about to reveal the cure for cancer.

"Um, it has its challenges." That was an understatement. Kyle looked over at them again. She smiled to reassure him.

"Hang on a second, Joe." He tossed him the ball and jogged over to the bench. He leaned over to grab a water bottle and stared at Heather, eyebrows raised questioningly.

She started to smile again and then decided to be more proactive. "Kyle, this woman is a fan of yours."

Monica started to say something, but Kyle's eyes went hard and dark. "Joe." He didn't even look to see if Joe heard him, but almost instantly Joe was next to Heather.

Monica continued blathering on about how she loved basketball, and she was following the Bedroom Burglar case with intense interest. Heather watched Kyle. Something was wrong. Her earlier fears came back with a vengeance. He had shifted into cop mode. But what was wrong?

Monica shifted slightly and moved her hand.

Kyle lunged for Monica. Joe caught Heather around the waist, lifting her off the bench and through the air several yards until her feet landed on the grass. "Get in the truck!" His arm was still around her, pushing her to move faster. Her feet felt like lead and wouldn't follow the commands she was sending them.

Joe got to the truck first. He opened the passenger door and shoved her in before racing around to the driver's side. He started the car, and they squealed out of the parking lot.

Heather caught her breath. "What happened?" "I think she was going for a gun."

"WHAT ARE YOU DOING?!" THE WOMAN WAS SCREAMING AT him. Probably because he was sitting on her.

He had knocked her off the bench, grabbing her wrist, and had flipped her over on to her stomach, hand behind her back.

Except that the gun he expected to see in her hand wasn't there. Instead, she clutched a digital recorder.

All the adrenaline drained out of him at once, his muscles turning to water. Breathing hard, he rolled off her. "You can sit up. Who are you? And what were you trying to pull?"

She flipped over and gave him a hard stare. "Monica West. I'm a reporter."

A cold chill froze him. If the press knew about Heather, then the Seventeeners did too. If he found out who leaked that information, they were dead.

"I'd planned to do a feature on you for Sunday. Everyone's so interested in the Bedroom Burglar that's been terrorizing the city I thought people might like to see the man behind the manhunt."

It had nothing to do with Heather. He barely kept himself from sighing with relief. It still didn't explain everything, though. "How did you find me here?"

She smiled, clearly proud of herself. "Since you wouldn't return my calls, I had to do a little detective work of my own. You make no secret of your religion or where you go to church. I just called people I knew until someone knew who your friends were. Joe's name came up. I found out where he lived, and he led me to you. Pretty good, huh?"

Kyle forced a smile. Flattery might be the way out of this. "Yeah. That's good. If that reporter thing doesn't play out, maybe we could hire you to be one of our detectives."

She scowled. Uh-oh. "I don't believe in guns. Or violence." She gave him a pointed look. "Speaking of which, what was with the police brutality bit? You do that to anyone who reaches in their pocket?"

This would take some maneuvering. If she picked up on his overreaction, she might begin speculating on who Heather was. He gave a shrug, then got to his feet and offered her a hand up. Which she declined, getting to her feet on her own.

"Occupational hazard, I guess. I don't know you, and you were sitting next to my girlfriend."

Monica's eyes went wide. "Girlfriend? Nicole said you were dating."

Nicole? Ah, he got it. Good job, Heather. He gave Monica what he hoped was a sheepish, aw-shucks kind of look. When his boss heard about this, it would be chewing out number three. That wasn't a record he was looking to break.

Chapter Twenty-One

Friday morning, armed with a grande mocha frappuccino, Heather walked into the conference room at the police station. Lisa Park, the police officer who had been her bodyguard this morning, showed her inside. She had hoped to spot Kyle as they walked in, but no luck. Heather sat and took a sip of her coffee, studying Lisa over the rim. She looked more like a model than a cop with her straight, glossy black hair and delicate features. Heather started to ask her what made her choose this career when the conference room door opened. Heather hoped it was Kyle.

Kyle poked his head in, winked when he saw her, and came in the room. "Stopped by Starbucks, I see."

"I needed fortification." She gave him a wry grin, which she felt droop a bit when she remembered why she went to Starbucks: because she couldn't go to the Jitter Bug anymore.

"How are you feeling? Did you sleep well?"

She wasn't going to tell him about the nightmares. He couldn't do anything about that. "I'm sore but less stiff. The swelling's gone down around the stitches."

"Good. And I see you met Lisa. Karen will be on duty tonight."

"How'd *your* meeting go?"

His eyes shot toward Lisa, and his expression went blank. He was purposely concealing his emotions, which meant it didn't go well. Kyle had caught up with them at Joe's house yesterday and explained about Monica being a reporter. "About what I expected. We'll just have to see what happens."

Poor guy. He couldn't seem to catch a break. Heather shot up a quick prayer that something positive would happen in one of his cases soon.

The conference room door opened, and a uniformed officer said to someone beyond her vision, "Here you go."

Heather's heart rate shot up in a way that had nothing to do with the caffeine she was drinking.

Quinn strolled in wearing a suit, every hair in perfect place, his aftershave wafting across the room, big grin on his face. A rather plain woman walked in behind him carrying a sheaf of papers. Must be the notary.

He shook hands with Kyle, turned on his charm to Lisa, and finally took a seat at the head of the table. The notary set out papers and pens.

Kyle motioned to Lisa with his head. "Heather, let me know if you need anything. We'll be outside or in my office."

"Thanks." She tried on a brave smile and then the door closed, leaving her with Quinn.

He immediately shifted toward her. "I'm so sorry about what happened. How are you doing?"

She glanced pointedly at the notary. "I'm fine." She and Kyle had decided the police station was the best place to meet Quinn and the notary so she could sign the paperwork and get out of the house she and Quinn still owned. When she discovered that waiting to sell the property had made them double their original profit, her anger had simmered to annoyance over his deception. Quinn was going to use his to buy a bigger house now that he was back here. Heather hadn't figured out what to do with hers yet. Like everything in her life now, that decision was on hold.

Quinn folded his hands and unfolded them, and then finally relaxed his shoulders when the notary asked for their identifications, thumbprints, and signatures.

They didn't say much beyond the notary explaining what they were signing and where to sign. The stack of papers must have been an inch thick. Each one probably generated by some lawsuit.

Finally, Heather's coffee was gone and the notary was done. She packed up her things and left, but Quinn stayed seated. Heather was wary, but after spending nearly an hour in his presence, she'd become re-accustomed to him. She had been engaged to him once, after all.

"I miss you."

Heather stared at him. He looked back at her across the table, but this time it seemed that he was expressing his feelings, not working an angle. Then much to her horror, tears welled up in her eyes and spilled over. She swiped at them, furiously rummaging one handed in her purse for a tissue. Angrily, she dumped the whole thing on the table.

Quinn grabbed a lipstick before it rolled off. "Let me help." She found a tissue, and he started putting things back in her purse.

Sobs welled up and wouldn't be pushed back down. It hurt her shoulder, but she couldn't stop. Her tissue was soaked and her nose was running. Finally, when she caught her breath, she looked up.

He was perched on the edge of the table. "I'm sorry." That started another round of tears, less intense than the first. "I hated New York."

She wiped her face with the soggy tissue.

"I don't know what I was thinking. Yes, I do. I was thinking that if I was in the corporate office I would get noticed by the big boys. My career was all that mattered. I was incredibly short-sighted. And frustrated that I couldn't get you to see things my way." He leaned back. "Turns out you were the smart one." He gave her a sad smile. "I'm so sorry I didn't see that earlier."

She bit her lip to keep from crying. She didn't know what to make of Quinn's words. She believed him, but with Kyle in the picture now, it was easier to be mad at Quinn than to like him. "I'm sorry I shut you out. You were always so persuasive that I knew I couldn't hold my own against you. I was afraid you'd talk me into moving to New York."

He grinned. "Be glad you didn't. It was a bad experience. Who would ever want to leave OC anyway? You've got the beach and the mountains and the desert all within driving distance. This winter I really am going to ski and surf in one day." She laughed with him, feeling like she was with the old Quinn, the one she fell in love with.

The door opened and Kyle walked in. She knew the instant he saw her red eyes and nose: his face went blank. "Everything okay? I saw the notary leave."

Quinn eased off the table. "I just wanted to apologize to Heather." He turned to her. "Take care of yourself, okay?"

She nodded, unable to speak past the tears clogging her throat again.

He shook Kyle's hand and then left.

Kyle came and sat next to her. "What happened?"

But "he apologized" was all she could get out before the tears started again. Good grief, what was wrong with her?

Kyle put his arms around her. She laid her head on his chest and thoroughly soaked the front of his shirt.

BULL OPENED HIS COMPUTER, NOT TOO DIFFERENT THAN the one he'd tweaked out for his mom. Obviously Detective Taylor ID'd him. But even if they picked him up, so what? He was just having coffee. So the police had been around asking questions. He'd figured they would, so the less his mom knew the better. Besides, she'd be grateful when she was sitting on her deck, sipping a glass of wine and watching the sunset over the ocean. He got into the police department's system with no problem. He wasn't sure what he was looking for. He started searching police reports and logs for that night. The paper had said one was injured and one dead. That corresponded with the call for both an ambulance and the coroner.

So who got hurt? Probably the chick. There was a lot of glass. He didn't think Alex had actually shot her.

He skimmed through files. Nothing here pointed to Alex and Cole. Good. Might be time to go back and start taunting Detective Taylor again. Out of curiosity, he pulled up the shift schedule. Scrolling through, he was bored, but he kept going. Experience had told him things that could help you often turned up in the oddest of places.

Well, what was this? Four officers assigned special duty. Not expecting to find anything, but having nothing better to do, he wrote down their names and did some research on each of them.

Half an hour later he discovered all were female. Now what kind of special duty would require four female officers?

They wouldn't be protecting her if she didn't know something.

He had to find her.

Chapter Twenty-Two

Heather tossed aside the month-old magazine she'd borrowed from Lisa. She was bored. Kyle had called and said he was tied up with a case and wouldn't make it over until probably just before time to pick her up to go to Joe's. She'd finished the book she'd brought and read her Bible. What she wanted to do was to see her friend, Sarah.

"Do you think it would be okay if I met a friend for coffee? You'd be there of course. But she has a key to my place and could bring me my mail and more books to read."

Lisa looked upward. "How much do I value my job? Correction, my life." She looked back at Heather. "I'll call Kyle. But she can't go by your house. That's too risky. And you guys are going to have to meet someplace away from either of your houses."

Heather grinned. "Sounds to me like South Coast Plaza would be the perfect place."

Lisa thought a moment then nodded. "Not bad. I'll call Kyle."

HEATHER THANKED THE WAITRESS FOR HER ICED TEA AND
scanned the room at Vie de France. Good. No one else she knew
was here. Lisa was at the table next to her looking for all the
world like she was listening to music and reading a magazine.

Sarah spotted Heather and hurried over, giving her a hug.
She grabbed a chair, scooting into the table and sloshing the tea.
"You were very mysterious on the phone." Sarah cut her eyes
toward Lisa. "That your bodyguard?" Her voice was low.

Heather nodded. "Thanks for coming. I needed to get out of
that place."

Sarah lifted a bag. "I brought you a bunch of books."

"Ah, you're a lifesaver. I'm so bored. I wish I had my paints. I
grabbed my sketchbook, though."

The waitress came and took their orders. A minute later she
was back with Sarah's iced tea. When she left, Sarah asked,
"What's up with Quinn? Is he still calling you?"

Heather told her about the property and the meeting with
the notary.

"Sounds like you guys had a peaceful resolution."

"I think so. I feel okay about how it finally worked out."

Sarah glanced at Lisa and lowered her voice. "Tell me about
Kyle. How is it working out between you now that you're his,
well, job?"

Heather leaned her elbows on the table and drew a circle on
the surface with her finger. "I don't know. His job obviously
keeps him busy. He's working today. But I also admire him for
his sense of duty, his desire for justice. He's very protective." She
smiled, thinking of his comments about her running the trail
alone and Quinn's note. "One thing's certain, he's not boring."

Sarah nodded slowly. "He runs in a different world than you
do. You don't even like to kill bugs, and his job is to go after the
bad guys. Normally, you have your own life, things to keep you
busy so you're not waiting around for him to get free to see you.
I guess you just have to find out if you're both running down the
same road in life or headed in different directions." Sarah sighed.

"Remember Tracey, my college roommate? She went skiing with us in Big Bear."

"I remember her."

"She married a cop right out of college, couple of weeks after graduation. She got tired of him never being home. He brought his work home with him and saw the worst in everyone. Don't get me wrong; she had her own issues too. But their marriage only lasted two years.

"All that is to say, marriage is hard, or so I've been told. Don't grab someone who's interested in you just because you hear the clock ticking. The problem with waiting until you get older to get married is that you get more set in your ways. Kyle may have developed the habit of letting his job run his life." She looked at Heather directly. "Don't let it run yours."

Heather sat back, chewing her lip. "It's hardly time to start thinking about marriage."

"You're wrong. It's exactly the time. There's no point in dating someone you can't marry. What if you fall in love with him and then find out he's addicted to his work? Or you can't deal with the dark side of his job? Wouldn't it be better to find that out up front before your heart gets involved?"

"You're right." Heather rubbed her forehead. "But I'm now officially too tired to think straight."

"I know it's hard. I'm praying for you." "Thanks."

"Besides, I have just the thing to get your mind off this. Retail therapy."

In his truck, heading to Joe's, Kyle glanced over at Heather. He hadn't seen her all day, but whenever he'd had a spare minute, Heather had popped into his mind. He wasn't used to anything but work occupying so many of his thoughts. And that could create problems for him at work if he wasn't careful.

Even in the short time they'd been together, her ability to handle this situation impressed him. She had a great sense of humor and a quirky view of life. But what did she think of him? And did he really want to introduce her to the one best friend women constantly threw themselves at? Not that he thought Heather would. But he could recall times where women would flat out ignore Joe and him, focused only on Scott. A few times it had been girls he'd been interested in.

Heather wouldn't do that. Right?

She was singing along to the radio and caught him looking at her. She smiled.

He turned his attention back to the traffic. "Almost there. It's going to be very low key and casual. If you get too tired, say the word and we'll head back."

"It's good to get out of the safe house. Twice in one day."

Kyle called Joe and in a minute, they were turning into a driveway and pulling through the garage door that had just opened. He waited until it closed before he helped Heather out of the truck.

They entered through the kitchen where Joe, Scott, and a few other friends were hanging around a counter covered with plates of delicious-looking Mexican food. Tamales—he hoped they were Joe's mom's recipe—and taquitos, salsa, guacamole, enchiladas, and more. His stomach growled. He introduced her around, and they filled plates with food. It was a great break from the fast food they'd been eating.

They were talking to Scott when Kyle caught Heather stifling a yawn. Maybe he shouldn't have brought her, let her turn in early instead. She needed her rest. The officers on duty heard her. Nightmares, every night.

But he didn't get to see Scott that often, and he wanted Heather to meet his friends.

Maybe show her off was more accurate.

He bent to whisper in her ear. "Be right back." She nodded.

He headed to Joe's refrigerator and pulled out two sodas.

Closing it, he noticed Scott had stepped over to talk to Heather. Kyle leaned against the counter and watched.

Scott was talking to Heather but wasn't hitting on her. Not that Kyle thought Scott would. After all, he was his best friend. He wasn't sure what he expected. But Scott treated Heather the way he did Kyle's sister, Kim.

Heather nodded at something Scott said then looked over her shoulder around the room until she caught Kyle's eye. And smiled.

He smiled back, holding her gaze until she turned to respond to something Scott said. And in one moment, all his questions about their relationship were clarified. He knew what he wanted to do.

Grabbing the sodas, he pushed away from the counter and went to join her. He handed her a soda and slid his arm around her waist.

Yep, it'd been a successful day.

And if he had his way, tomorrow would be even better.

His phone buzzed. The number didn't come up as one of his contacts, but it still looked vaguely familiar. He gave Heather a squeeze and then moved outside to the patio while answering.

"Kyle, it's Quinn Morgan. My folks' house was broken into. My mom walked in on the burglar. The guys from your department are already here, but since it involved my mom, and I'm a little worried about her, I thought I'd give you a call." Kyle's mind started to work through the possibilities. The Bedroom Burglar again or a random burglary? Not to mention that it was Quinn calling and asking for help. "Let me make some calls and check into it. There's a good chance this would have landed on my desk anyway. I'll get back to you when I know something."

"Thanks, Kyle. I appreciate it."

He rubbed his hand over his face. Not the way he wanted to end the evening. He headed back inside. "Sorry, guys, but duty calls."

The light in Heather's face dimmed. She was having a good

time, and here he was ruining it for her. That killed him. "Leave her here," Scott lightly patted Heather's good shoulder. "One of us can take her back. She's safe."

Heather bit her lip. Kyle was beginning to learn that meant indecision, but he wasn't sure about what. Did she want to stay? Who would want to go back to a dark motel room? His responsibilities tore him in two different directions, something he wasn't familiar with. He didn't doubt her safety here with Joe and Scott, a firefighter and a naval pilot.

"I'll send Lisa to come get you." He squeezed Heather's hand. "Would that be okay?"

She nodded. "Don't worry. I'll be fine."

He gave Scott a hard look. "She'd better be."

Chapter Twenty-Three

K yle set his Diet Coke in the cup holder of the truck as he pulled up to the Morgans' house. A marked unit sat in the driveway. Steve was supposed to be meeting him here any minute. The house was lit inside and out. He got out and rang the doorbell. A stack of papers, mailers, and fliers piled up to the side, an oddity in an otherwise meticulously maintained yard.

An older woman opened the door, hair perfectly in place, make-up and jewelry just so. She reminded him a bit of Claire, which reminded him he needed to check on Justin. Did all the women in South Orange County always look like they were ready to go out? His mind flashed to Heather in her yoga pants and T-shirt. Not all.

Quinn appeared behind his mom. "Hi, Kyle. Come on in. This is my mom, Brenda Morgan."

She extended her hand with a giant square-cut diamond on it. "How do you do? Please come in. Can I get you some- thing to drink?"

"No, thank you. I appreciate the offer, though."

"That's quite a black eye you have. Line of duty injury?"

"Surfboard, I'm afraid." The bruise was fading but not fast

enough. He pulled out his pad and began making notes, the first being a reminder to call Justin. The uniform that had responded to the call was his former trainee, Jeff Griffin. He gave Kyle a quick update of what had been reported and what they'd found.

Griffin had done a good job. Kyle was pleased.

Mrs. Morgan led the way down a travertine-tiled hall into the living room, tastefully decorated in leather and warm woods. Kyle sank into a buttery-soft leather chair, while she took a seat on the couch—although he supposed it was probably more properly termed a sofa—across from him. Quinn perched on the sofa arm next to his mom.

Kyle asked her some basic questions, things Griffin had covered, but it gave her a chance to relax and become comfortable with him before he had to lead her through the events of the night.

"Tell me about your day."

She described shopping at Fashion Island—the sea breeze moderating the heat of the day—lunch with the girls, home for a quick change, and then out to dinner with Quinn. Quinn's dad was on a business trip. It was oddly like a conversation he might have with his sister, Kim, but with more money involved. "What happened when you got home from dinner? Did you come in through the front door or the garage?"

"Oh, we always use the garage. Just pull in and close the door behind us."

"And that leads to the kitchen?"

"Yes, would you like me to show you?"

"Sure."

They stood and made their way to the kitchen.

"We came in. Quinn was going to watch TV in the family room. I went upstairs to change." Her voice quavered a bit.

"Can you show me?"

She nodded and started up the stairs, Kyle following with Quinn close behind him. He glanced around the house. *So this is what Heather almost married into.* He could never afford anything like this. His cop salary would have been considered good money anyplace but Orange County. And if he hadn't bought a fixer just before the market took off, he never would have been able to afford a house. Most of Laguna Vista's cops couldn't even afford to live in the city. They commuted from central Orange County if they were lucky. Or San Bernardino or Riverside if they weren't.

The master bedroom was bigger than his first apartment, complete with its own fireplace and sitting area. Aside from the slightly messed bed, the area looked like something out of a magazine until he stepped farther into the room. The guys had dusted for prints, leaving black smudges. The closets had been torn apart, along with the dresser drawers.

"I walked into the room, coming in halfway when I stopped. I'm not sure what it was that made me do that. And a split second later this man"—her voice broke, but she swallowed and continued—"came out of the walk-in closet carrying one of my good silk pillowcases."

Kyle nodded but didn't say anything.

"It seemed like forever that we just stared at each other. Finally, he came toward me, and somehow I grabbed my Mace out of my purse and sprayed him. I just got so angry. I mean, how dare he come into my house and rummage through my things?" Tears welled in her eyes, and Quinn came to her side, putting an arm around her.

Kyle waited until she was ready to continue. "Can you tell me what happened next?"

"He ran back into the bathroom, and I know it sounds stupid, but I was so angry I went after him. He went out the window over the tub. He must have had a ladder or something, because by the time I got there he had disappeared. I finally remembered to run over and push the panic button for the alarm next to our bed. Quinn came running up a second later. He said I had been screaming at the top of my lungs. I don't even remember doing that, but my throat is a little sore."

Quinn moved his mother over to the sofa in the sitting area. The doorbell rang.

"That's probably my partner." Quinn stood up. "I'll let him in."

"Thanks." Kyle turned back to Mrs. Morgan. "Can you describe the man?"

"He wasn't as tall as you, maybe just under six feet. Heavier than you too. Had a little bit of a paunch. He was wearing jeans and a T-shirt, I don't know about shoes. Funny, he struck me as being too old to be breaking into houses. He would be early forties, I would guess. His hair was receding, and he had it cut short, maybe even shaved."

"Do you think you could identify him if you saw him again?"

She took a breath. "I think so."

He heard Steve and Quinn on the stairs. "Thank you, Mrs. Morgan. You've been a big help. I take it you gave the officer a list of what was stolen?"

She nodded.

"Good. I'd like to take a look at the backyard."

"Certainly."

They stepped out of the bedroom just as Steve and Quinn reached the top of the stairs.

"Mrs. Morgan, this is my partner, Steve Collins." They shook hands. "One more thing before I show him around. When I came in, I noticed a pile of papers and fliers by the front door. Is there a reason for that? Were you out of town?"

Quinn grimaced. "That's my fault, I'm afraid. I've been staying here. Each morning when I go out for a run, I toss the paper on the front porch for them, completely forgetting they never use that door. But since it's around the corner, none of us noticed them piling up."

"It's possible the burglar saw the papers and thought you were out of town. Thank you, Mrs. Morgan, I'll let you know if I need anything else."

"Oh, Detective, one other thing I almost forgot. I didn't think anything of it at the time, but when we were driving up the street, coming home after dinner, there was a construction-type truck parked up the street. It stood out because it's rare for anyone here to park on the street, and I wondered who was having work done."

Quinn took his mom downstairs, and Kyle showed Steve the bedroom.

"Another Bedroom Burglar case?" Steve scanned the room. "Looks like it. At first I wondered, since they were home.

But the piled-up newspapers seem to make sense."

"Now how did you get here before we were officially assigned the case?"

Kyle glanced toward the door to make sure the Morgans had gone downstairs. "Quinn called me."

"He's a friend of yours?"

Kyle sighed. "Not really. He's my—uh, Heather's ex-fiancé."

Steve raised his eyebrows and looked around the bedroom. "That must be, uh, interesting."

That was an understatement.

Chapter Twenty-Four

Heather was barely up and dressed when the radio crackled.

Lisa grinned at her. "Kyle's coming up."

"Why does he have to be such an early riser, especially on a Sunday?"

Lisa laughed and let Kyle in.

He stepped inside, his hands full. One had a bag with grease spots that looked suspiciously like muffins. The other held flowers.

She couldn't help but smile.

He stepped forward and held them out to her. She almost thought he looked a little nervous. Maybe it was because Lisa was watching them intently.

Heather took them and pulled them to her face. He'd gotten an exotic tropical mix, including her favorite, alstroemerias. While they had no scent, the bouquet itself had a spicy sweet smell that reminded her of the beach. She lowered them. And smiled. "Thank you, Kyle. That was very sweet."

"I'll put them in water for you." Lisa took the bouquet from her and then rummaged through cupboards in the kitchenette.

In two steps, she was in his arms. He held her gently, careful of her sling. "I got coffee and muffins and thought you might like to head to the beach this morning since we can't go to church."

"That'd be great." She felt him relax against her.

Fifteen minutes later, they headed down Laguna Canyon in Joe's truck, Lisa following in an unmarked unit. At least they had privacy in the truck. Heather had sipped at her coffee and finished her muffin but hadn't said much, just enjoying something that felt very much like a date.

They got close to the downtown area and traffic picked up. But because it was a Sunday morning, he found a metered spot open on the street next to Heisler Park.

He took her hand, and they started down the path. She finally spotted Lisa a little ways away from them. She didn't think Kyle would shift completely out of cop mode just because Lisa was here, but hopefully he could relax a little.

It was so good to be at the beach. She took a deep breath and lifted her face to the sky, relaxing, enjoying the salt-crusted breeze on her face. The sound of the beach surrounded them. The waves, the seagulls' shouts, the cars on PCH.

They were approaching a wide, grassy area. Serpentine benches with fossils carved in the sides perched in the grass and overlooked the ocean. He tugged her in that direction.

Sitting down, he braced his arms behind him and leaned back. He had a purpose in this trip today, something specific he wanted to tell her. She hoped it wasn't more bad news about the case. She didn't need her enjoyment of the beach ruined too. For once, she just wanted to pretend that they were the couple they must look like to anyone watching them. She tilted her face towards the sun.

She was dying to know what he was going to say, maybe even a little afraid, but she didn't want to rush him.

"The call I got last night? It was Quinn. His parents' house had been burglarized."

Heather dropped her gaze to Kyle's and covered her mouth. "What happened?"

He told her about Quinn's mom walking in on the Bedroom Burglar and using Mace on him.

"Is Brenda okay?"

"Yeah. A little shaken up, but doing okay. She's a strong woman." He looked over at her. "A lot like you." But instead of smiling, his jaw tightened. Probably remembering that Brenda had been her future mother-in-law at one point.

"I should call her." She gnawed on her lip. What must it have been like for her? To face her attacker and to fight back?

"I'm sure she'd appreciate that. Just don't tell her anything about your situation." His voice was more formal than usual. Heather wouldn't have suspected Brenda—the small, perfectly mannered woman she knew—of being strong enough to fight back.

Kyle looked out over the ocean. "Like you, I was engaged once."

The change in subject jolted Heather.

"She broke it off, saying she couldn't handle the idea of being married to a cop. After that, a couple of guys I knew got divorced. I wondered for a while if this job was compatible with a relationship, although there are guys who make it work. I haven't dated anyone since." He leaned forward and lifted his gaze to meet hers, just a trace of his bruise shadowing his eye.

Warmth flooded her chest, overflowing to every limb in her body. His ex-fiancée was an idiot, and Heather was glad. Her sister Aimee's words came back to her. She could almost hear a door slamming shut.

He was worth it. She reached over and laced her fingers with his.

KYLE FOCUSED ON THEIR HANDS, HIS THUMB MOVING BACK and forth in a rhythm. Heather had relaxed more completely here than he'd ever seen her. He needed to get her out of that motel.

Silent for a moment, he reviewed what he was about to do. It felt like the first time he stood on top of the high dive as a kid. The bottom seemed far away and the risk huge. But wasn't Heather worth it? He'd thought Christa was, but he'd been wrong. Still, if he admitted it to himself, the signs were there. Christa never wanted to talk about his work, mostly pretended like it didn't exist. She hated it when he worked overtime, which was a lot.

He wanted Heather in his life, but he needed to know if she could handle his job. If she couldn't, he wouldn't pretend it didn't matter like he did with Christa. He thought Heather might be the one for him. Maybe today he'd find out if that was going to come to a crashing end. He needed to step out and make a move.

Heather squeezed his hand. "I'm sorry she hurt you. But she didn't deserve you."

The smile he offered her lacked energy. "I know my job isn't typical. And it's been my life for a long time. I guess the short answer is that I haven't been doing a good job of keeping my personal life separate from work. Short of church, Bible study, and seeing my folks, I haven't had a need to keep work in perspective." He studied Heather as she watched the ocean. "Until now."

Some ambiguous emotion crossed her face. Pleasure? Fear? Reluctance? She pulled her eyes to his but didn't say anything. Just crossed one leg over the other, shifting toward him.

"I don't play games, Heather, so I'm just going to put it all on the table. I don't think either of us wants to date just for the sake of dating at this stage in our lives. We need to figure out now if my job is going to be an issue between us. This isn't a typical job. You know that. There will be times I'm working nearly around the clock. But not often."

He reached over to cup her jaw. "I'm willing to draw some lines, to be unavailable for work so I can be available to you. I want to see where this goes. I want to make room in my life for you. But I need to know if you can handle dating a cop."

She gave him one of her amazing smiles and leaned toward him. "I can handle it."

That warm feeling curled around his chest again. "Good. I'm probably going to mess this up a few times. If I hurt you or you feel neglected, I want to know."

She laid her hand on his chest. "Deal."

"Good." He shifted into her space, the smell of her pear soap surrounding him. He'd wanted to kiss her for so long. And if she was okay with him being a cop and wanted to make this work... Gently, he slid his hand behind her head and pulled her to him, brushing his lips across hers, softly at first. Her hand slipped up to his chest and tightened on his shirt. Pleased at her reaction, he deepened the kiss, became more possessive. She was so soft and sweet, receptive.

He pulled back, still wanting more, but overwhelmed a little by what he was feeling.

Her eyes slowly opened. A smile blossomed.

Yeah. His job had no chance competing against that.

THEY WERE WALKING ALONG THE PATH THAT FRONTED THE beach, holding hands, when Kyle's phone rang. It was Steve. He pulled his mind from Heather. "What's up?"

"Griffin just picked up this guy, Watson, for a DUI. He matches the description we have of the Bedroom Burglar. He drives a white Ford F-150 with a construction rack, and when

Griffin searched it, he turned up two Patek Philippe watches that ended up matching a couple stolen last month and the gun that was taken from the Morgans'. He apparently hadn't fenced them yet."

Steve had Kyle's full attention. This was good news. It could be the big break they needed. Hopefully the press and his boss would get off his back. "Has he talked yet?"

"Nope. There's some legal wrangling going on, and he seems willing to cut a deal, but since it's a Sunday... " Steve continued. "I'm making up a list of questions and people we want to ask Watson about tomorrow."

"I'll be in shortly." Kyle hated to leave Heather. Not being able to help himself, he stole another kiss from her.

Chapter Twenty-Five

Kyle poked his fork around the remains of his salad bowl. Nothing good left, just iceberg lettuce. Yuck. He stood and threw the plastic bowl and fork into the trash.

Some lunch. This is why he preferred junk food. At least it tasted good.

Stretching, he looked at Steve over the stack of folders on the cubicle desktop. The Bedroom Burglar case was finally going somewhere. It was with great pleasure that he called Monica West to give her an update on the case and put the possible leads out to the public. Maybe something would turn up.

Of course, she seemed equally pleased to tell him to be sure to look in the Features section tomorrow of the *South County Times* for her article on him. Great, he couldn't wait.

Watson had talked. All they had to do was match up what Watson said with what they already knew about the case. Dates, items stolen, methods of entry. They'd been at it all day. Now they were going in circles.

He sank into his chair and stared at the file he'd been working on. He missed Heather. Yesterday had been the right move, and he was glad he did it. He ran his hands through his hair. If he was going to LA, he wanted to see her before he left.

He stood. "Steve, we're just banging our heads against the wall. We've done enough. Wait until we get some of those interviews in LA tomorrow."

Steve looked up from his folder, examining Kyle's face. "Got a hot date?"

"Not yet. But I'm hoping."

Heather tried to turn her attention to Psalms. She'd been staring at the same page for half an hour. Kyle distracted her even when he wasn't present. Her face heated as she thought about that kiss. And the one he gave her before he left. He had followed her into her room and pulled her around the corner so Lisa couldn't see them. That one had made her knees weak.

Good thing they had a chaperone. His kisses could be addictive.

She glanced at her clock then closed her Bible. She'd try again later.

Walking out to the living area, she saw Hilary doing sit ups. Of all the female officers guarding her, Hilary was the most athletic. She'd played basketball, softball, and volleyball in high school and won a full scholarship to college in volleyball.

She'd been encouraging Heather to do some light stretching and loosening up so she didn't get so stiff. It was painful at first, but it got better the more she did it. Her cuts were healing nicely and starting to itch.

"Get down here and join me." Hilary patted the floor next to her.

For the next fifteen minutes, she and Hilary did sit-ups, crunches, and modified leg lifts. Heather's muscles were shaking, and she was sweating. It felt good, though.

The radio sounded, and Hilary pushed herself off the floor. "Good job." She offered Heather a hand up, which she took.

A few minutes later Kyle walked through the door. He looked at Heather. "What have you two been up to?"

"Hilary took it upon herself to be my personal trainer. There's actually a few things I can do."

"Good." He bent forward and kissed her lightly.

"Hey, Kyle, if you're going to be here for a while, do you mind if I go run on the treadmill in the gym for twenty minutes?"

"No problem. Take the radio."

"Thanks."

Hilary grabbed the radio and headed out.

Kyle opened the small refrigerator. "Did you two eat all the Rocky Road? Is that the real reason you were working out?"

"Funny. Yeah, there's some left."

Kyle got out the ice cream and dished it into two bowls. "Steve and I are headed to LA tomorrow. Griffin getting this guy on a DUI was just the break we needed. There's apparently a whole network. He's given us some names, his fencing connections in LA, so we're headed up there to talk to them. We still think he was working with someone else, maybe someone familiar with the neighborhoods, who alerted him to when people were going to be on vacation. Regardless, my boss is a lot happier with me now than he was a few days ago." He handed her a bowl, and they sat down at the table.

She took a bite. "Hmm. Never realized you had boss pressure too. Just figured it was crime-fighting pressure."

"Cute. It's a bureaucracy like any other, complete with politics and game playing. I hate that part, but I don't suppose you can escape it anywhere. As long as I don't screw up again anytime soon, I should be okay."

"Even the press is singing your praises." She pushed the paper towards him. Kyle's official photo dominated the front page of the Features section. He looked so serious. She started giggling.

"Aw, she said she was going to print the story. I wasn't sure if I should believe her."

It was a basic background piece, a compilation of known information about Kyle, like that he was a local boy, how long he'd been an officer, when he'd made detective, and some notable cases from the past. A few quotes from his coworkers and boss. And then there was this great line. "But one of the city's most eligible bachelors may not be much longer. He was seen in the company of a woman named Nicole. Other than calling her his girlfriend, Detective Taylor declined to further identify her."

Heather's giggles turned into laughter. "I see you didn't correct her."

Kyle laughed too. "No. And I forgot to congratulate you on such quick thinking. Good job, *Nicole*."

She made a small bow. "Thank you. She just rubbed me the wrong way."

He picked up the paper. "At least she left out the fact that I tackled her. I never would have lived that down." He finished the last bit of his ice cream. "What else did you do today?"

She pushed her ice cream around with her spoon before answering. "I checked in with Susan this morning after the editorial meeting. She doesn't have anything for me to do except copy editing, and I'm all caught up on that. And she didn't like my idea for a tattoo article. Or rather, it wasn't that she didn't like it; she just said I was going through a difficult time right now and shouldn't worry about work. Which is why she also pulled me off The Fest interviews."

"Come here." He stood and pulled her into his arms. He stroked her hair silently for a moment. "I think we should go anyway."

"To what? The Fest? Why?" She could hear her voice reverberate through his chest.

"Mostly because it'll be fun and get you out of here. I also think it'd be good for Justin. With you under protection, I'm not sure how much time I'm going to get to spend with him, and it'd be a good opportunity to do that."

"True. I'd like to meet him." But it would be weird to be at an event she was supposed to be covering, knowing she wasn't. Still, Kyle was trying to help. If she didn't go, it would only be because she was pouting.

"What's to keep you from working on a story idea on your own? Just because you're not interviewing the bands, maybe you can come up with something else. Best-case scenario, you get a great article she likes. Worst case, you have a good time with me."

"That's the worst case?" She tilted her face up to look at him. "See, even the worst case is pretty good."

She laughed.

"Back to me being gone. It should just be for two days. Should we try dinner again when I get back?"

"Sounds like fun."

"Any requests?"

"Surprise me."

He considered that. "Okay. Any place you *don't* want to go?"

"Let's see. McDonald's, Taco Bell, Carl's Jr..."

"I can guarantee we won't be going any of those places."

"Good. Then whatever you pick should be fine." Something a little louder than a tapping sound reverberated through the motel room. It stopped then came again, from the living room.

Kyle stepped in front of Heather and pulled his gun out, in cop mode. "Get down behind the couch."

Heather started to nod but then realized he was already focused on the window. Her heart picked up its pace as she stumbled toward the couch and crouched down, like a twisted game of hide and seek.

Kyle moved the curtain aside slightly. He was perfectly still for a moment, and then his shoulders relaxed. He pulled the curtains all the way open. "Look."

A bird threw itself against the window then pecked violently at it.

Heather let out a breath she hadn't realized she was holding and stood up.

She didn't know anything about birds. This was just a small brown one. It must have been fighting its own reflection. "Turn on the light. Maybe that will help."

"Sorry. That will make you too visible. The bird will just have to figure it out." Kyle closed the curtains and returned his gun to its waistband holster.

Heather moved the curtains slightly to see if she could tell where the bird went. The hill behind the motel covered with dry grass could have hidden the bird anywhere. She hadn't looked out this window before; the curtains were always closed. She leaned her forehead against the window, envious of the bird. She couldn't handle her cage much longer.

KYLE DIALED JUSTIN'S NUMBER. "HEY, IT'S KYLE. I'VE GOT some tickets and backstage passes to The Fest Saturday and I thought of you. Want to come?"

Silence filled the line. "Um, is it that music thing?"

"Yeah. Should be fun."

"Nah. Thanks, though."

Kyle tilted his head back. He wanted to spend time with this kid, but Justin was making it difficult.

"Sure you won't change your mind? It could be fun."

"That's okay. I'm just not really into that."

"All right. But let me know if you decide to go. I don't know when we'll be able to go surfing again."

"I can go with my buddies."

Justin was pretty clear about not wanting to hang out with him. He didn't want to disappoint Claire, but there wasn't much he could do about it. "Okay, well, I'll catch you later then."

That went well. Considering his luck this morning, he debated making the next call. He hesitated a moment and then decided to do it before he changed his mind. "Quinn, it's Kyle Taylor. I wanted to let you know we got the guy who robbed your parents' house."

"That's great news. How'd that happen?"

"He got pulled over for a DUI. He had your dad's gun in his car, plus watches from two other burglaries. I'm headed up to LA tomorrow to get some more information on his contacts, but I don't think he had time to fence your parents' stuff so they should get it back."

"That's great. Thanks for letting me know. I appreciate that."

"Sure. Given what your mom went through, I thought she might feel a little better knowing we got the guy."

"I'm sure she will, thanks." There was a beat of silence then, "How's Heather doing?"

"She's fine. I'll let her know you asked."

"Thanks. I know you can't tell me anything about what's going on with her, but just let her know I said hi."

"I will." Kyle hung up then sat a minute longer, thinking.

BULL PULLED INTO THE THIRD MOTEL PARKING LOT OF THE night. Laguna Vista only had four, so if his guess was right, he had to be getting close. Figuring the Laguna Vista PD didn't protect too many witnesses, Bull was willing to bet—with the price of real estate around here—that they didn't own an actual safe house. And given that police departments played politics, odds were any money spent on a safe house stayed in Laguna Vista. It was possible they were staying at a hotel in a neighboring city, but most Orange County hotels were either near the beach or Disneyland. Inland from the beach, there weren't many choices.

He really didn't know what he was looking for, but that

didn't mean he might not find it. Plus, it gave him time to try to figure out how to fix Watson's mess. The man was a total moron. All he was supposed to do was get the goods to the fence. Instead, he decided to freelance and play copycat. And got caught. Served him right.

Except that Watson would talk. And all of Bull's contacts were hiding. Bull had goods he needed to move and other jobs in the works. Not to mention looking for that girl, who the paper conveniently named today. Life would be easier if people just did their jobs and he didn't have to clean up their messes. His car headlights panned across the lot. It was close to midnight. Anyone who was staying here would be in for the night. He did a three-point-turn and drove to the other side of the lot.

Bull parked next to a red Chevy Silverado and got out. Wandering around the motel property, he scanned the rooms, rubbing his finger against his thumb.

She was in there, somewhere. He had a gut feeling.

Chapter Twenty-Six

Heather was lying in bed reading when a high- pitched *whoop whoop whoop* reverberated through the room. Bright strobe lights flashed from the fire alarm. Snowflake jumped off the bed and hid under a chair. By the time Heather put her book down and sat up, Stacey was in her room saying something Heather couldn't make out over the noise.

She put her mouth next to Heather's ear. "I'm calling down to the front desk to see what's happening. I don't want to take you out of here unless it's absolutely necessary. It could be a ruse. Stay close to me."

Heather nodded and followed her out to the living area. Even though she was standing next to Stacey, she could barely hear what she was saying on the phone. Her heart pounded. Was there a fire? Or had someone found her and was trying to drive her out in the open like a dog flushing its quarry toward the hunter? She was sure Stacey was competent—Kyle wouldn't have picked her otherwise—but she still wished Kyle were here and not in LA.

Stacey hung up and turned to Heather. "I can't get through. I'm going to keep you up here as long as possible. And I'm calling for backup. Get ready to move if we need to." She moved around the room, checking out the peephole and then the window while talking on the phone. Heather hoped the person on the other end could hear her. Stacey picked up the radio and fitted a wire into it, fitting the earpiece end into her ear and clipping the radio to her belt.

Heather hurried into her room and flipped open the cover of her Bible. The picture of her and her sisters was there under the flap. She grabbed it and then bent down to where Snowflake cowered. Snowflake howled at her. Heather started to say something reassuring but realized it wouldn't do any good. She scratched behind the cat's ears and then went to the closet to get the carrier. Snowflake went in without the usual struggle. Carrying the cat and her photo, she went back to the living room on unsteady legs.

Was that smoke she smelled or was it her over-active imagination again? She rubbed her nose. It was definitely smoke.

Banging at the door caused Heather to jump. Yelling followed, but Heather couldn't hear what they were saying over the alarm. She looked to Stacey for guidance.

Stacey pulled her gun and moved toward the door, looking out the peephole. Cautiously, she cracked open the door and looked out. A second later she shut it but left the safety bar off.

Heather forced herself to breathe calmly. In and out. In and out. But all she could imagine was her life being narrowed down to two choices: remaining in a burning building to die of smoke inhalation, or running the gauntlet set up by someone who wanted her dead.

Stacey stepped over to her. "Stay with me." She glanced at the carrier.

Heather nodded. She could lose everything else in this place now that she had the cat and her picture.

Stacey grabbed her arm. "We're going. Stay right behind me. If it's too smoky, grab my shirt."

Heather nodded. With one arm in the sling and the other

holding the carrier, it wouldn't be easy. But she could always ditch the sling to protect her cat.

Stacey motioned for her to stand to the side, and then she cracked open the door and looked out. Smoke began wafting in the room. Heather resisted the urge to cough.

Stacey moved out into the hall, dragging Heather with her. They hustled down to the stairs at the end of the hall. Stacey opened the door to the stairwell and looked in. Scanning the hallway, she motioned Heather to stay put while she entered the stairwell. A moment later she came back and nodded. Heather followed her down, glad it was only three flights. Her legs were shaking, and she didn't have a spare hand to hold onto the handrail.

When they reached the door to the lobby, Stacey again checked before she would let Heather out. She replaced her gun in her waistband holster before opening the door to the lobby. The alarms blared, but there was no smoke. People were milling around, hotel staff was on the phones, and firemen were hurrying around. Heather wondered if Joe was among them, and she started looking until Stacey bent to yell in her ear. "We're headed out the front. There should be a uniformed officer in a marked unit. If anything happens, run straight to him or her. Don't stop for me. Drop the cat if you need to. Understand?"

Heather nodded, trying not to picture anything happening to Stacey. Or Snowflake.

"Okay, let's go."

Stacey walked briskly across the lobby, Heather following close behind. They headed out the front doors. The marked unit was right out front next to the fire engines. Heather focused on it, keeping her wobbly legs moving. Snowflake was howling again.

Someone grabbed her arm.

Heather jumped and let out a small scream before she saw who it was. A cop in uniform. She was glad the alarms covered her yelp. He must have been just outside the door. She was so focused on Stacey and the beckoning safety of the police car that she didn't see him. He guided her to the car. Stacey had the door open and nearly shoved her in then scrambled in after her. The door was barely closed before they were flying out of the parking lot, Snowflake's howls replacing the fire alarms.

KYLE RUBBED THE BRIDGE OF HIS NOSE AS HE LISTENED TO Stacey's report. Heather was okay and currently at the station in the conference room with Stacey and Patino. Apparently, the cat was there, too, judging by the howling he heard in the background. The latest news from the fire department was that a fire had started in a microwave on the second floor. Some kids traveling with their dad on business had been left alone while their parents were at a dinner function. They were making popcorn and left it in way too long. The fire damage was only limited to that room, with some smoke damage in neighboring rooms. Patino was going to take Heather and Stacey back as soon as they got the all-clear from the fire department.

"How's Heather holding up?"

"A little shaken, but fine. I'm just glad it turned out to be a real fire alarm and not something else."

"Yeah, me too." He hated being away. What if it had been a real threat? But it hadn't, and he needed to be thankful for that. "Do you think it's still a secure safe house?"

"Yes, I do. We were evacuating like anyone else. No one was out front when we put her in the unit except the firefighters, and they were busy doing their jobs. I think it's the best place to keep her for now."

"Okay. I trust your judgment. Call me when you're safely back at the motel. I don't care how late it is. And let me talk to Heather."

"Will do."

"Hi." Heather's voice came over the line, causing another layer of tension to release. He could tell by her voice she was okay. But he asked anyway.

"I'm fine. It was a little scary, and Snowflake's not happy."

"Yeah, I can hear. You going to be okay going back there tonight?"

"Yep. How's it going up there?"

"We're making good progress, and I should be back tomorrow in time to take you to dinner." He ran his hand through his hair, wishing he were there, even though he trusted Stacey.

"Good. It'll give me something to look forward to." He heard her stifle a yawn.

"Try and get some sleep, and I'll see you tomorrow."

"Good night, Kyle. Stay safe."

"You too." But there was much more that he wanted to say.

Chapter Twenty-Seven

Heather, free of her stitches, stepped out of the shower. She didn't have to wear the sling either if she didn't want to. The doctor said not to overdo it or lift anything heavy. In one small way, she was getting her life back. And then there was dinner with Kyle tonight. If she ended up with an article from The Fest that Susan liked, she might feel like everything was back to normal.

Except for the fact that she was in an extended-stay motel and someone probably wanted her dead.

She combed out her wet hair. Well, at least dinner tonight would be nice. Without the sling, she could pretend everything was normal.

KYLE LEANED BACK IN THE PASSENGER SEAT AND RUBBED his eyes, glad Steve was driving. The case was nearly over; they'd left LA in time to beat the traffic. He turned his attention back to the laptop, getting a head start on their report. They were stopping by the DA's office to update him before heading to the station. Kyle still felt someone was tipping off Watson as to who was on vacation. It'd be nice to figure out who. But Watson denied it, and they had enough info for the DA.

Then he'd get to have dinner with Heather tonight. Talking to her on the phone was one thing, but he wanted to see in person that she was okay. Why did something have to happen when he was gone?

He got the number for the Salt Creek Grille off his phone and made a reservation before turning his attention back to his report. The more he got done now, the less he'd have to do later. Nearly two hours later they were pulling off the freeway to head to the District Attorney's office when Kyle's phone rang.

HEATHER SHUT OFF THE iPOD, SILENCING HILLSONG United. Usually she could count on worship songs to calm her and reduce worrying. But since about six fifteen, she hadn't been paying attention. Kyle was supposed to be here at six. She paced around the bedroom, picking up her scattered clothes, straightening the bedspread.

Six thirty and she hadn't heard from Kyle since this morning. Did she call him? What if he was in the middle of something? That would be the only reason he wouldn't call, right? She didn't want to interrupt. And she didn't want to be one of those needy girlfriends who didn't have a life outside of their boyfriends. Though right now, she didn't have much of one.

The door to the motel room opened and she hurried out. It was Stacey coming in to relieve Hilary. With a bag from KFC.

Heather's stomach growled.

KYLE CLIMBED IN THE CRUISER AND CLOSED THE DOOR. Steve started the car. They were finally headed to the station to end this long day. Who would have guessed Watson would have a heart attack and die? But according to the jail personnel and the doctor Kyle interviewed, that's exactly what happened.

It put a twist in their case, but not a fatal one. It was the DA's baby now.

He checked the time on his phone.

Oh no. It couldn't be. He closed his eyes and groaned. Heather.

"WEREN'T YOU SUPPOSED TO HAVE DINNER WITH KYLE tonight?" Stacey asked, handing Heather a piece of chicken.

"Thanks. Yes, but he probably got held up in LA with the case." She took a bite. Mmm, it tasted good. She hadn't realized how hungry she was. She gave Stacey a wry grin. "The cost of dating a cop."

"Tell me about it. It's even harder being a woman and a cop. Most guys don't want to deal with that."

For a few moments, the only sound was of them eating and licking their fingers. "I'm glad you got extra. Thanks for sharing."

"Sure. You never know with this job."

Heather's cell phone rang. Stacey raised her eyebrows as Heather stood, wiping her hands, and grabbed her phone off the coffee table. It was Kyle.

"Hi. You okay?"

"Heather, I'm so sorry. It was this case and—"

"I know. That's what I figured. It's fine." She picked up her soda can and swirled it around.

He was silent for a minute. He probably wasn't somewhere where he could talk. "Thanks. I can be there in about twenty minutes. Did you eat yet?"

"Stacey shared her dinner with me."

"I'll grab something for myself on the way then. How about dessert?"

"Sounds good." Dessert always sounded good. Dating a cop, not so much. Heather was going to tuck her heart safely away.

KYLE STEPPED INSIDE AND CLOSED THE DOOR BEHIND HIM, setting a box on the table. Heather stood up and took a few steps toward him.

Stacey retreated to the living area.

He reached out and ran his hand up and down Heather's arm, a nice feeling now that he didn't have to worry about her sling or stitches. Her skin was so soft. He just wanted to pull her into his arms and bury his face in her hair. They needed to talk, and they needed to go somewhere else to do it.

She was uncharacteristically quiet. What was she thinking? "I really am sorry about missing tonight and not calling. A bunch of stuff happened all at once, and it completely slipped my mind."

He winced. Why did he say that? Now she'd think she was unimportant. He wasn't sure he wanted to tell her how often she did occupy his thoughts. "Sorry. That sounds terrible. I kept thinking I had about another hour and hoped to make it home in time."

She pulled away from his embrace. "I understand. I've been known to get wrapped up in something and totally lose track of time."

"I brought doughnuts as a peace offering. Fresh from the fryer."

"Ooh, yum." She opened the box on the table. "Oh, they're still warm." She bit into one, a look of pleasure consuming her face.

He smiled, glad to have made her happy. But what would happen next time his job got in the way? At some point, a box of doughnuts wasn't going to cut it.

Justin got out of his car a little ways past the oak tree. But this time the faces that appeared out of the shadows seemed less threatening. He was one of them now. A couple of them said hi, slapped his hand or bumped fists.

"Let's go. We've got work to do." Bull's voice came from somewhere in the dark.

With a snap, a green glow from a chem light illuminated Bull's face. He moved over to the hood of Justin's Honda and spread out a large piece of paper, holding the light above it.

"Okay, who's got something to report?"

Alex stepped forward into the pool of green light. He pointed to a spot on what Justin could now see was a map. "This house here is empty. They're friends of my mom's. They're in Europe for a month. And I drive by this one every day. Flyers are piling up on the front door."

Bull looked around the group. "So we have two jobs. Alpha team will hit this house"—he pointed at the one where the owners were in Europe—"tomorrow night. And Saturday night Bravo team will hit this one. But Alex, I want you to do a little more reconnaissance. Dress halfway decently, get a clipboard, and go to the house and look around. Act like you know what you're doing. I want to make sure they're really gone. You, Cole, and Justin are on Bravo team."

Justin felt his stomach turn to liquid. He didn't want to break into a house. What if they got caught? But he couldn't exactly back out. What if Bull knew about his relationship with Kyle? Maybe Justin could be more of a behind-the-scenes guy. "Hey, Bull?"

Bull fixed him with a stare. "Got a problem?"

"Not exactly. It's just that there's this cop that's friends with my mom. He expects me to go to this concert with him Saturday." He could call Kyle and tell him he'd changed his mind.

That should make Kyle happy. "He'll get real suspicious if I back out."

"What's this cop's name?"

"Kyle Taylor. He's a detective or something. He was just in the paper."

Bull stared at him a long second. Justin resisted the urge to swallow. He'd said the wrong thing. He should have just gone along. How was he going to explain it to his mom when Bull rearranged his face?

Finally, Bull nodded. "Go to the concert with him. But take your cell phone. You'll be reporting to me while you're there."

"Sure." Relieved, Justin hardly heard the rest of Bull's orders to the others. He was off the hook. He didn't know why Bull would want him to report from some geeky concert, but anything had to be better than breaking into houses.

Chapter Twenty-Eight

I thought the Bedroom Burglar had a heart attack in his jail cell and died."

Kyle rubbed his hand over his face. A call from the lieutenant was never a good thing. "Yes, sir. That's what happened."

"Then you want to explain to me why we had another one last night?"

"A copycat?"

"Whoever it is, we need to put a stop to it. I'm sending Steve over with the reports from last night. Get on it."

"Yes, sir."

So much for wrapping up one problem.

KYLE AND STEVE HAD JUST DECIDED TO TAKE A BREAK AND get lunch when his phone rang again. Dreading who it might be, he looked at the screen. And frowned. Quinn?

"Hey, Kyle. Sorry to bother you, but when I was leaving my parents' house this morning I saw several police units in front of one of our neighbors' house. Was there another break in?"

Kyle didn't feel like explaining himself to Quinn, though he had to admit Quinn's tone was more curious than questioning. "Yeah, there was. But I can't really tell you more than that."

"Oh, that's okay. I think I have some information for you. I couldn't sleep last night, and I didn't like what Mom had in the refrigerator, so I made a late-night trip to the store, probably around one thirty. There was a dark Explorer parked a few houses down from where the cops were this morning. It struck me as odd last night because everybody parks in the garage or at least the driveway. With the burglaries and all, I was a little suspicious. When I came back from the store I saw a kid getting in the Explorer. He looked right at me, so maybe it was nothing."

Okay, sounded like maybe Quinn was giving him some good news. "Can you give me a description?"

"Sure. And I got a partial plate off the Explorer."

"Good." It was probably a stolen plate but it would still be helpful. "Can you meet me at the station in half an hour?"

"Sure."

"And Quinn? Thanks."

"No problem, Kyle."

Could this case take any more weird turns?

HEATHER TIED HER WARM-UP JACKET AROUND HER WAIST. It had turned out to be a typically gorgeous Orange County day. The perfect day for The Fest, the annual music festival. They'd been here since the gates opened, her passes giving them extra access. Some of her favorite bands were here, as well as some good up-and-coming ones at the stage by the main entrance. Kyle had been right to talk her into this.

Even Justin had morphed from the sullen teen they'd picked up to a grudging fan. She was glad he'd changed his mind about coming.

"You guys want something to drink?" Kyle asked. They stood in front of a booth that sold sodas.

"Yeah, that'd be nice." Justin grunted.

"Be right back." He stepped away and then turned back. "Don't go anywhere."

She smiled up at him. "Justin, I've got an idea for an article. Can I interview you?"

"Sure. I guess."

Unzipping her purse, she pulled out her phone and a small lotion bottle fell out. She picked it up. Her scars had been itchy. She'd grabbed this one from the motel bathroom so it would fit in her purse. It didn't smell too bad, but she wished she'd dumped it out and put in her pear-scented stuff instead. "Hang on a sec." After tucking the phone partway back in her purse, she squeezed some lotion out and rubbed it in. "Want some?" She offered the bottle teasingly to Justin.

He rolled his eyes. "What is that, anyway?"

"Just lotion."

"From a motel? Maybe the Ritz-Carlton."

Heather laughed. "I wish."

"You stayed there recently?"

"The Ritz? Have you been there? That place is amazing. Right on the beach."

Justin gave her his best teenager-disgusted-with-an adult-trying-to-be-funny look.

She pretended to look at the label, trying to think of something. "Oh, you mean the motel. My folks stay there when they come visit." Anxious to change the subject before she got caught in a question she couldn't answer, she tossed the bottle back in her purse and pulled out the phone. "Give me your number."

She punched it in as Kyle came back with their drinks.

She stuffed her phone in her purse and took the cup Kyle held for her. "I'm glad we came. I got an idea for a story. I'm going to interview Justin."

Kyle winked at her. "Told you."

She nudged him with her shoulder. Scanning the area, she tried to decide where they should go next.

Then she spotted him. A sick feeling filled her stomach.

It was Brian Miller, the other assistant editor. The writer who had replaced her.

She turned abruptly around. She didn't want to face him, didn't want to talk to him, didn't want to pretend she was happy with how everything turned out.

Because she wasn't.

Kyle squeezed her arm. "What is it?"

She glanced around. Justin was engrossed watching a group of teenage girls at one of the booths. Considering what they were wearing, she could see why. "I saw a guy from work, the one Susan replaced me with."

"Where?"

Heather pointed him out. She was being petty. It wasn't Brian's fault. "I should go say hi."

"You sure?" "Uh huh."

"Remember what we discussed. He thinks you've had a family emergency."

She strode forward. "Brian!"

Kyle called to Justin from behind her.

He turned around. "Hi, Heather. I didn't expect to see you here. How are things going?"

"Everything's fine, but I'm not sure when things will settle down enough for me to get back to the office." Kyle touched her shoulder.

She introduced the men and Justin. Brian told them who he'd interviewed, and Justin looked interested for the first time that day.

Brian shot a questioning look at Heather, and she nodded.

He turned back to Justin. "Want to meet them?"

Justin shrugged. "Okay, I guess." He stuffed his hands in his pockets and rocked back on his heels.

"Justin, why don't you meet us just over here"—Kyle pointed—"in half an hour?"

"Okay."

"Thanks, Brian." Heather was glad she'd pushed her feelings aside. It had turned out much better this way.

Brian and Justin moved off.

Kyle took Heather's hand. "Have you spotted Lisa yet?"

She let her gaze wander around the festival area until she saw her. Lisa, with her low-slung jeans and tight T-shirt that hinted of skin looked like just about every other girl here. She appeared to be browsing, but Heather could tell she was constantly in Lisa's line of sight. "Found her."

"Keep track of her in case you need her for anything." She nodded, rubbing her arms at the chill that crept over her. Kyle squeezed her hand. "What do you want to do now?" She shrugged. Some of the shine had come off the day, and she felt conscious of Lisa's eyes on her.

"Hey, aren't those some choir people? There's Ryan."

Heather followed his gaze. Sarah, Cait and Grayson, Ryan, and a couple of other people stood in a group waiting for the next band to come onstage. "Want to go say hi?"

"Sure."

Conscious of holding Kyle's hand and wondering how much explaining she'd have to do, she wandered over, matching Kyle's strides.

Sarah spotted them first, her eyes darting between Heather and Kyle and a smile filling her face. "Hey, you. We've missed you. How is everything?" Her eyes said more, though.

The rest of the group had taken notice of their arrival. Sarah had told everyone Heather was sick. All this lying. She was trying to keep it straight.

Heather introduced Kyle around, noticing as she did that Ryan, their worship leader, was standing close behind Sarah's shoulder. Interesting.

Ryan was telling them about how he knew the guys in the band when Kyle whispered in her ear. "You think you're going to be here awhile?"

She nodded.

He turned and scanned the area, then made a small motion before bending close to her ear again. "Lisa's about fifty feet behind you. I'm going to talk to some of the Irvine PD guys, and then I'll get Justin. Don't leave this spot until I get back."

"Okay."

He squeezed her shoulder and left.

The band started a moment later, too loud to talk over, relieving Heather of trying to think of what was safe to say. Please, let this be over soon. But Ryan seemed to be keeping a lot of Sarah's attention, leaning toward her to speak to her often. Cait and Grayson were in their own world, and Heather was feeling decidedly left out.

After a couple of songs, Kyle and Justin returned. Kyle had to practically shout into Heather's ear to be heard. "Justin wants to walk to the main entrance to see one of the bands there. Any objections?"

She shook her head. Being out in the open was grating on her nerves. Besides, she didn't think Sarah would miss her with Ryan around. Touching Sarah's shoulder, she leaned in and said goodbye. She waved to Cait and Grayson.

They headed down the hill, Justin lagging a bit behind them. Heather figured it was because he didn't want to be seen with them. Teenagers. Good grief, it wasn't like she and Kyle were old enough to be his parents.

A loud pop filled Heather's ears. She started and ducked, expecting falling glass to rain down on her. She threw herself against Kyle. His arms went around her. He wasn't moving. Shouldn't he be dragging her to safety?

He massaged her back. "You okay? A balloon popped."

Shakily, she nodded. The adrenaline faded, replaced by

embarrassment. Pulling back, she looked around. No one seemed to have noticed her reaction.

Justin stopped next to them, scowling. "What's the big deal? It was just a balloon." He sauntered on ahead of them.

Chapter Twenty-Nine

Sitting at a stoplight, Kyle studied Heather as she leaned against the truck door. Her eyes had slid closed before they left the parking lot of The Fest. The day had taken a lot out of her.

He scanned the mirrors. That same Explorer was behind him, had been since they'd left The Fest. Probably a coincidence, but he kept his eyes on it anyway. They got on the I-5 freeway and Kyle soon lost the Explorer in traffic.

Heather was still asleep when they pulled up to Justin's house.

Justin hopped out of the truck. "Hey, thanks." He nodded to Heather. "Tell her thanks too, when she wakes up."

"I will." Kyle watched Justin go inside before he left. He seemed happier than when they'd picked him up. Kyle had only caught him texting twice, so he couldn't have been too bored. He and Heather had hit it off. That was good. The more positive people in that kid's life the better.

He left the gate at Coto de Caza. After driving down Santa Margarita Parkway awhile, he noticed a dark green Explorer behind him. It was a common car, but still, it matched Quinn's description of the car he saw the night of the burglary. Maybe Kyle could get a look at the plate.

Heather was still asleep. He had time.

He tried slowing down so he could get behind it, but the SUV slowed with him, changing lanes when he did, even though it always stayed a couple of cars back. Continuing until Bake Parkway, he headed south. If he hadn't noticed the SUV earlier, it might not have popped back on his radar. He made a left on Trabuco. Because he had to wait for the light, there was only one car between him and the Explorer. He turned left again on Lake Forest, nearly completing a loop. This guy was following him on purpose.

He called dispatch and requested any unit in the area to come to his location.

———

ADRENALINE FILLED BULL'S BLOODSTREAM AS HE REALIZED Kyle had spotted him. He knew it was only a matter of time. It was difficult enough to tail someone with one car, impossible to do once they'd made you. Bull kept his eyes scanning in front and behind. He'd bet his last take that Kyle would radio for help. He was a by-the-book guy.

Yep, there it was. A black-and-white coming the other way. Bull laughed. For once he appreciated the concrete medians that ran down the center of every street, only allowing left turns at signals.

He swung into a neighborhood close to where he grew up. A couple of quick turns, and he came out of the subdivision on the other side. No sign of any cop units or that red truck, which he was sure he'd seen somewhere before, even before Justin had texted him. Just to be sure, he took a circuitous route home. Parked in the garage, he sat for a moment, listening to his heart-beat and his quickened breathing.

What a rush!

Justin stared at the phone in his room, then at the crumpled paper in his hand. He had a number. The question was, would he use it?

He'd done what Bull had asked him. He'd called when they were leaving and told Bull they were in a red Chevy Silverado. He didn't know why Bull wanted to know; Justin was probably better off not knowing.

But he had discovered something else. Knowledge that might keep him out of breaking into any homes. Information that might prove to Bull that he was better used as the brains of an operation instead of the muscle.

Something wasn't right with Heather. People kept asking Heather where she'd been, but she didn't look like she'd been sick. And she didn't seem like the type to play hooky. Too much of a goody-goody.

So what was up? The lotion bottle with the name of a local motel, the way she jumped at the balloon, the woman who he'd seen watching them a couple of times. There could be a logical explanation for it all.

Maybe there was. But if Heather had fingered Bull and could identify Cole and Alex, they were all in trouble. If Bull went down, he'd take them with him and laugh doing it.

This sucked. He didn't want to be in trouble with the law or with Bull. There had to be a way out.

He picked up the phone but stuck the paper back in his pocket.

"Alex, what'd that girl look like in the Jitter Bug?"

One thing was clear. Someone was looking for them. Kyle had ensconced Heather in the conference room with a Diet Coke. He'd left a message for the lieutenant that he wanted

Heather moved to a new safe house. Then he'd requisitioned an unmarked unit and called Joe to say he'd be dropping off the keys to the truck. Now that Joe's truck had been identified, it was worthless to Kyle. But he didn't want Joe driving it either in case someone mistook him for Kyle.

Something was going on here. It was like he had all the pieces but couldn't quite see how they fit. A dark green Explorer followed them today. The partial plate Quinn had given him was from a dark green Explorer. As far as it went, the partial matched the plate Heather saw on the black Honda at the Jitter Bug shooting. They knew the plate was stolen off the truck. So, assuming it was the same plate, was there a connection between the Bedroom Burglar and the Jitter Bug shooting? Or was it a coincidence? Four out of seven letters and numbers still left quite a few possible combinations. Then what was Watson's role in all of this? More questions than answers.

He had just sat down at his desk when his phone rang.

The lieutenant.

He listened, the sick feeling in his stomach growing the longer the lieutenant talked. With a final "yes, sir" Kyle hung up. Though it was couched in complimentary terms—Kyle had done a good job with evasion so whoever was following them didn't know where the safe house was—the bottom line was still the same.

No new safe house for Heather.

Chapter Thirty

On the way back to the motel in the unmarked police car, Heather smoothed her dress. She was glad she had packed this summer one. From the way Kyle had been looking at her all morning at the Pancake House, she thought he probably appreciated it too. And finally, her shoulder didn't bother her too much, so she was able to blow-dry her hair the way she liked it.

She hadn't been sure she wanted to date a cop, but when she was with Kyle, he was so considerate and focused on her. She felt safe and protected. Underneath that handsome exterior was a man with true character. That was a rare commodity. Maybe it was her trust issues getting in the way. Could she trust God to protect Kyle and to take care of her no matter what happened?

She slid a glance at Kyle.

He caught her staring and gave her a slow smile as they turned into the motel parking lot.

She swallowed. Her pulse picked up its pace. She busied herself picking up her purse. They had planned on watching the church service on her computer.

"Heather."

She raised her eyes.

He turned toward her, his eyes dark gray. Oh my. She didn't dare breathe.

He picked up the radio on the seat between them and put it on the dash.

"Come here." She slid closer.

He removed her purse from her hands, setting it behind her, never taking his eyes off her face. His hands brushed hers, and jolts shot up her arm. He tucked a strand of hair behind her ear, leaving his hand alongside her face.

She slipped her hand up his shoulder and around to the back of his neck, running the tips of her fingers along his close-cropped hair.

With a soft groan, he leaned forward and captured her mouth with his.

Closing her eyes, she felt him slide his hand around her waist. He pulled her closer, his kiss possessive, exploring.

A dull *thunk* rocked the car. Breaking glass crackled around the interior. Loud pops echoed outside. Kyle's solid weight pushed her down, off the seat. Something scraped her arm. It burned. The floor of the car pressed into her back. Her breath left in a rush. For a moment, everything went black. Kyle pinned her down. What was happening? She couldn't see anything but the roof of the car over her. "What—"

"Shh."

His weight shifted on her. He twisted, gun in hand.

All the pieces clicked together. Someone was shooting at them. Her heart pounded and she started to shake. Her arm burned, got warm and wet.

Hilary's voice cracked over the radio, echoing through the car. Heather couldn't understand what she was saying.

Kyle levered himself up with a grunt, his hip digging into her thigh. Then he moved back down.

Hilary's voice came again, panic lacing her tone.

"Are you hurt?" Kyle wasn't looking at her. A dark stain spread across his shirtsleeve.

Heather had to take inventory. "I think only my arm. What about you?"

Sirens sounded in the distance.

"It's nothing, just grazed me. Did you reinjure your shoulder?" He glanced down at her. "Show me."

"The other one." Her arm was under the dash; she couldn't move it. But she could feel blood running down it.

The door opened behind her head. Hilary leaned in, staying low. "Either of you hurt? Why didn't you answer the radio?"

"Couldn't reach it. It's on the dash. Heather hurt her arm, but I can't see how bad it is from this angle. See anyone?"

"Just a black sports car taking off."

A car screeched up next to them. Kyle pushed off her, with a wince, broken glass crunching as he moved to the car seat. Hilary grabbed her under the shoulders.

Fiery pain shot through her arm. "Ow!"

Hilary stopped. "Okay, we just need to get you out of here." She adjusted her grip lower around Heather's ribs and pulled her out of the car.

Blood ran down Heather's arm, soaking her dress, and dripping over the car floor. But it barely registered as Hilary hauled her into the backseat of a police car. Kyle piled in after her, and they sped off.

Once she caught her breath, it hit her. She'd been shot.

It was all Kyle could do not to slam the conference room door as he left. Only the fact that Heather was in there, and she didn't need to be shaken up any more than she already was, stopped him. She was lucky. The bullet had passed through muscle, not hitting anything vital. But she'd needed two layers of stitches. Kyle had only needed three stitches to patch him up.

He didn't want to leave her. But he needed to talk to Mark. Hilary was with her. That decided it. Purposely, he unclenched his fists as he strode down the hall. He'd told the lieutenant yesterday that he wanted Heather moved. That motel was a bad place for a safe house. There was no way to protect the entry and exit of witnesses. But the lieutenant hadn't been convinced its safety had been compromised. It was all the city could afford, and they didn't protect witnesses often.

Well, now they were doing it Kyle's way.

Mark was just sitting down in his cubicle when Kyle came around the corner. "What'd you find out?"

"Recovered bullets—one embedded in the passenger side seat of your unit—casings, some footprints. The shooter was in the bushes in the business park next door."

"That's where I saw him."

"Get a description?"

"Didn't get a good look. Dark hair, male. A black sports car—an Acura maybe—sped off just after the shooting from one of the far exits. That's it. Could be the same shooter from the Jitter Bug."

"No one else has any reason to shoot you or Heather. How is she? Did she see anything?"

"Nope. I heard the gunshots and shoved her to the floor."

"What happened before the shots? Were they shooting at you as you pulled in?"

"We had pulled in and parked."

"So you hadn't gotten out of the unit yet."

"No."

Mark looked at him intently. "Why?"

Kyle closed his eyes. He was never going to hear the end of this. "I was kissing her."

Mark struggled to keep a smile off his face. A face Kyle wanted to punch.

"Okay. Well that's all I need for now. By the way, the lieutenant wants to see you in his office."

Great. Kyle headed to his boss's office.

The lieutenant looked up. "Come in and shut the door."

HEATHER COULDN'T STOP SHAKING. HER JAW HURT FROM clenching it to stop her teeth from chattering.

"Here." Hilary handed her a jacket.

She pulled it tight around her but still couldn't get warm. The coffee cup warmed her hands, but she hadn't been able to take more than a sip. She wanted to be sick.

Probing the tender spot on her thigh, she figured it'd be a nice bruise tomorrow. Someday she'd be up to teasing Kyle about it. Nothing about it seemed funny now.

Hilary eased into the conference room chair next to her. "When I heard the shots and Kyle didn't answer the radio—" Her voice broke. "When I got outside, the whole driver's side of the unit was shot up. It looked bad."

"It's real, isn't it?" Heather looked at Hilary. "Someone really is trying to hurt me. It's not just an accident."

Hilary squeezed Heather's good shoulder. "We're not going to let anything happen to you."

She was safe here; she had to keep reminding herself. Kyle would protect her. He would keep her safe. But she wanted to be anywhere but here.

KYLE SAT ON THE BACK PORCH OF HIS HOUSE, THE CITY lights blinking on as the sky bruised to dusk. He had what the real estate agent had called a peek-a-boo view. To him that meant he had to scoot his chair to the edge of the patio to see the valley.

The team was in the house, along with Heather and Kim.

He needed a moment alone.

He'd never been so scared.

Today his body had been the only thing between Heather

and a fatal bullet. And he was lucky that bullet hadn't done more damage to her before he realized what was happening.

Because he'd been distracted. By her.

He stretched his legs out on the patio chair and considered the view, its peaceful appearance deceiving. If something had happened to her... He didn't even want to think about it. The thought that she'd come so close to being seriously injured made his stomach turn.

He'd been on protection detail before. And while he'd been concerned for the safety of the people he protected, none had come close to affecting him the way Heather did. The strength of his feelings for her scared him a little too. Was he falling for her? Yeah.

But love? He didn't know. She'd certainly invaded his heart. And if he cared for her, there was one thing he had to do. Keep her safe.

She'd hardly asked any questions about today, about the changes. Just looked up at him, trust in her eyes, accepting. Before, he would have been confident in that trust. But now? She was her own biggest danger: a distraction to him.

He'd been taking her protection too lightly, putting her comfort above her safety. Well, the safest place for her was inside his house. And that's where she was staying. He wouldn't make the same mistake twice.

BULL SWORE, TOSSING HIS PHONE ON THE COUCH. IF ALEX wasn't so useful, he'd be dead. What was he thinking shooting up that motel parking lot in the middle of the day? All of Bull's work wasted. After Alex's snafu, the chick had most certainly been moved. They'd be driving a different car and security would be tighter.

The only advantage they had now was Justin. He hoped that kid kept his mouth shut. As long as the detective didn't know about Justin's association with the Seventeeners, they might actually get some good intel.

Alex was a loose cannon. He was used to doing whatever he wanted and not facing any consequences. His boldness was helpful, but not his stupidity. His dad's connections with the city council were valuable. Right now, that was outweighing Alex's stupidity.

But he didn't need much longer. The last two hits had netted him almost all that he needed. He still had the problem of rebuilding his fences. Watson had ruined that. Good thing the dude was dead. But as soon as he could move the goods, he'd be almost set. He should tell his mom to start looking at houses. He opened his laptop. One more thing. With the Internet, it was easy to reach out and touch someone. A little gift to Heather might keep Detective Taylor on his toes.

Chapter Thirty-One

Heather awoke to an unfamiliar room. Staring at the walls, it took her a minute to figure out where she was. Kyle's guest bedroom. She half expected to see shattered glass sprinkle her bed. She'd dreamed about it enough last night.

Rolling out of bed, she grabbed a few things from her bag that Hilary had packed at the motel for her. The bathroom was down the tile-lined hall that ended in the kitchen. She didn't see anyone but heard the TV playing faintly.

Turning on the faucet, she stripped off her sweats, noticing that there was indeed a bruise the size of a softball on her thigh. It was already a lovely shade of eggplant. Stepping into the tub, she let the hot water lap at her neck and shoulders, turning sideways to keep her stitches out of the water. She wanted to go running to burn off the dregs of adrenaline that laced her system but knew Kyle wouldn't allow it.

Someone wanted to kill her.

Her mind couldn't wrap around that. Was she looking at her own mortality, possibly the end of her life? Did she like what she saw? Had she accomplished all she'd hoped to? Of course not. What would she have done differently? She didn't know.

It was too early to contemplate such deep things without coffee.

After soaking a while longer, she dressed, and then blow-dried her hair. Opening the door, she found Snowflake perched outside. Heather picked her up and, scratching behind those sable ears, wandered into the kitchen.

Kyle sat at the kitchen table with coffee and the paper spread open. Something about that picture made her heart squeeze. What would it be like to wake up to that image every morning? Or wake up alone when he wasn't home?

He looked up, smiled, and then stood.

"Thanks for letting Snowflake stay here. I know you're not a cat person."

He brushed a kiss on her forehead as he passed her. "Kim was thrilled. She's been wanting an animal for a long time." He poured a cup of coffee and handed it to Heather. "Cream's in the refrigerator. She wanted to know why you got to bring over a cat and she didn't."

Heather raised her eyebrows. This was interesting. "And?"

"She's my bratty little sister. You're my girlfriend."

"I'm sure she appreciated the bratty little sister part."

"Hey, if she doesn't like it, she can get her own place. Her problem is she likes clothes too much. She spends her paycheck on the most ridiculous stuff."

Heather sipped her coffee. "Obviously, you don't follow the must-have clothes of the season."

Kyle gave her a you've-got-to-be-kidding look. "So, how are you this morning?"

"Thanks to you, I have a lovely bruise on my thigh." She smiled as she said it. It felt good to have something to smile about.

He winced. "Sorry about that."

She put her cup on the counter and stepped forward, touching his arm. "Don't be. You were protecting me. And you got hurt too."

He slid his arms around her waist and pulled her closer. "I don't know how good of a job I did. I got distracted, and that shouldn't have happened."

It sounded vaguely like an insult, but she knew he didn't mean it that way. He was just being hard on himself. With her finger, she traced his collarbone through his shirt. "Do you ever make mistakes?"

"Of course I do. Everyone does."

"On the job?"

"Sure. Not often, but yeah, I've made my share of mistakes."

"Before yesterday, did you think someone would try to shoot me?"

He was silent a moment, staring past her shoulder. "No. We had no reason to suspect they even knew who you were. On the off chance they found out, our main goal was to keep you away from your house and work, places they could easily trace to you. Now we have three things to figure out: how they knew who you were, how they knew where you were staying, and who they are."

"Kyle, think about it. Even if we hadn't been, uh, kissing, we would have either still been in the car or just getting out of it. Wouldn't it have been worse if we were out of the car?"

"Yeah, but if I had been paying attention, looking around, I might have seen something."

"Or not."

He lifted his chin but didn't say anything.

She hadn't convinced him, not that she expected to. Sighing, she laid her head against his chest.

"Heather, I can't take that chance again. I can protect you best inside this house. With the security system, the break-proof Mylar-coated windows, and a couple more security cameras I'm installing today, this is the best place for you to be. You're not going to be able to leave unless absolutely necessary.

I'm sorry. I know that'll be hard for you. But I have an idea that might help." He pulled back to look at her.

"That's okay. After yesterday, I kind of like the idea of not going anywhere."

"Don't you want to hear my idea?"

She smiled. "What's your idea?"

"You can paint my house."

At the pleased look on his face, she laughed. "Oh, I can?"

"Yeah, I thought it might take your mind off things if you had a project. Think your arm is up to that?"

Her arm ached, but she'd manage. She could paint left-handed. Her mental health was more important at this point than her physical comfort.

Glancing around the kitchen, she considered it. She hadn't seen much of the house yesterday, hadn't cared. But all these beige walls had possibility. "Hmm. Any color I want?" She couldn't resist teasing him.

He paled a bit but said, "I trust you."

"Uh huh. I can tell." She ran her palm along his jaw. Freshly shaven. Nice. "It's okay. Color's good for you."

He turned his head and kissed her palm. "If it makes you happy." Pulling away from her, he turned to the refrigerator. "Want some scrambled eggs? We need to start brainstorming about how someone might have figured out where you were."

ALL MORNING KYLE AND HEATHER HAD GONE OVER WHOM she'd talked to each day. If it wasn't something in an e-mail, then the leak had to be somewhere else. There was a good chance they'd never find it, but he was determined to rule out everything he could. Heather opened her laptop, accessed her e-mail, and then turned the machine to him. "You can read through it all if you want. I don't think I said anything to anyone, but you might be able to tell that better than I could."

Kyle tapped on the track pad, scrolling through a very long

list of e-mails. "Don't you ever clean out your inbox? You've got over two hundred e-mails in here."

"I delete the boring ones right away."

He scrolled past several e-mails from his address with a little surge of pleasure. She'd saved the little notes he'd sent her during the day. "Mine are still in here."

She flashed him a sassy smile. "That's because they weren't boring." She turned to the paper still open on the table.

He looked from her to the kitchen. Breakfast dishes, glasses, silverware, and the skillet still littered the counter and sink. It was almost as messy as her inbox. She couldn't possibly miss the chaos. He suppressed a sigh. Yeah, she could. Neatness was not her strong suit. In the motel, he noticed her clothes spilled from her suitcase and piled up in the corner. The bathroom counter was cluttered with her stuff. When she noticed it, she'd pick up, but more often than not, she'd get distracted and the mess would remain.

For a few seconds, he tried to think of a good way to ask her to clean the kitchen while he was going through her e-mails. It would be the best use of their time. But he couldn't think of one. He'd end up doing what he usually did, start cleaning. She'd see and offer to help.

Turning back to the computer, he looked at the dates and started with the e-mails from two weeks ago. There weren't near as many. Her sisters, work, Sarah. He forced himself to check the e-mails in order so he didn't miss anything. So far, she hadn't written anything different than if she were sitting at home.

He sat thinking over the list of people who knew Heather was under protection. Her family, her boss, Joe, people at the station. It was a large number of people, and anyone could have let something slip to the wrong person. The families of these Seventeener kids had a lot of money and power. If they wanted to find something out, they could.

He closed the computer. If Heather was going to be living in his house, they were going to have to work out this messiness thing.

On second thought… He opened the computer again and turned on iTunes. Setting it to shuffle, he clicked play.

Heather looked up as the music poured out of the computer's speakers.

He held out his hand. "Come help me clean the kitchen."

———

HEATHER ADJUSTED THE COMPUTER SCREEN AWAY FROM the changing sun. She loved the big wooden slider leading to Kyle's patio. He wouldn't let her sit outside in the sun, but the light streaming through the glass was the next best thing.

She'd spent all morning on home-decorating websites, looking at colors and designs, comparing them to Kyle's house. The kitchen, breakfast area, and family room all opened into each other, so she decided to treat them as one room. A doorway from the kitchen led to the more formal living and dining room. She particularly liked the sites that had sample rooms where she could try different color combinations on the walls. As much as she could tell, his house had a Spanish flare typical of many homes in the area. Three creamy stuccoed arches covered a front porch. A grouping of palms and other tropicals graced the front yard, terraced to accommodate the sloped street. It was nicely kept up. Did Kyle have time to do it himself, or did he hire it out?

He'd kept the Spanish theme when he had remodeled the house, installing Mexican tile throughout the main living areas and hallway. But beyond that, the rooms were open spaces without much design to them. Other than Kim's room, which had periwinkle walls and a French glam vibe.

Kyle and a couple other members of the protection team worked on the house's security, coming and going through the day, but except for stopping for lunch, Heather pretty much ignored them, engrossed in her project. She hadn't had this much fun in a long time.

Part of her—though she refused to dwell on it—wondered what it would be like if this were *their* home. She gazed around, imagining.

The thought stopped her. Was she falling for Kyle? The way he'd protected her during the shooting, she had no doubts about his ability to keep her physically safe. But her heart? It might already be too late.

Yep, she was falling for him. Big-time. And that meant it would hurt that much more if their relationship couldn't survive her being under his protection. Or real life, if they ever got back to that.

Not wanting to follow that thought trail, she went back to designing the room.

She'd narrowed her choices down to two when Kyle walked in the room.

"Come look at something." She angled the screen so he could see.

Kyle stopped next to her, bending over to pick up the glass, plate, and crumpled up napkin next to her chair. "What?"

She pointed to the screen. "What do you think? Which one do you like better?"

He stared for a moment, then kissed the top of her head. "Sweetheart, whatever you want to do is fine."

She felt a little deflated that he didn't share her enthusiasm. Well, he was a guy. What did she expect? He'd like it when it was all done.

She blinked. He'd just called her sweetheart.

Chapter Thirty-Two

Heather stared at the printouts she'd made of the rooms and noticed her hand shaking. She dropped the paper to her side and hoped Lisa didn't notice. Nope.

She was sitting on the couch, paperwork spread over the coffee table. Lisa had made it clear she didn't paint.

Not knowing how to still her nerves, Heather set her papers on the island and pulled a Diet Coke out of the refrigerator. Popping open the can and taking a sip, she looked around the room. When Kyle was here, it always seemed safe, comforting. Now she was aware of just how much of the house she couldn't see. That she and Lisa were alone.

This was ridiculous. Kyle would be back soon. He needed to get more supplies from Home Depot, so she'd asked him to pick up paint chips while he was there. In the meantime, she'd go read her Bible. That should soothe her nerves.

In her room, she flopped on the bed. She'd forgotten to make it this morning. She hated being out of her routine. Getting up, she straightened the sheets and pulled the comforter up before plumping the pillows and plopping on them.

She picked up her Bible and flipped it open to Psalms, where she'd left off. The parallels between David running for his life and her situation had spoken to her. God had protected David. She had to believe He would protect her too.

Or would He? Christians got hurt every day, died in car accidents, got sick and died. What made her think she was different? She skimmed, hoping to find a verse to cling to that would banish the tension in her heart.

A verse caught her eye in chapter seventy-three: "Surely in vain I have kept my heart pure and have washed my hands in innocence. All day long I have been afflicted, and every morning brings new punishments."

She stopped reading. You got that right. *This is exactly my point, God. I've always been the good girl. I've lived my life for You. So why this?*

It's not about rewards; it's about faith.

The thought seeped into her soul. Okay. That was true. Was she looking at this all wrong? Hadn't she always envied a little bit the people who had great testimonies of how real God had been to them at their darkest moments? Was this about strengthening her faith? *God, couldn't You have found an easier way?*

She finished reading the psalm. What had Asaph, the writer, concluded? That he still belonged to God, that God would guide him, leading him to a "glorious destiny." She read verses twenty-five and twenty-six over several times: "Whom have I in heaven but you? And earth has nothing I desire besides you. My flesh and my heart may fail, but God is the strength of my heart and my portion forever."

He is mine forever. Here or in heaven.

The Matt Redman song, "Let My Words Be Few," played through her head. The second time around she sang along, eyes closed, praying the words.

As her voice faded away, she realized God could have asked her to go through this alone. But maybe her faith wasn't as strong as she thought. Maybe she wasn't ready to walk this path alone. He'd given her Kyle to go through this with her.

And, for this moment at least, it felt like God knew what He was doing.

KYLE WATCHED THE GARAGE DOOR *WHIRR* DOWN, THEN stepped over to throw the bolts that secured it to the house frame. Stepping from the garage into the laundry room, he dropped his bags and was struck by the quiet. It reminded him of the muted stillness when he ran in the fog. He stopped a moment, enjoying the break from the constant activity of the past days.

Walking into the kitchen, he tossed his keys on the counter.

Lisa looked up. "You're back."

"Where's Heather? Sleeping?"

"Maybe. She went into her room about an hour ago."

Not sure if he should be worried or not, he took the bag that had the paint chips in them and knocked on her door. No response. He pushed it open, calling her name.

She lay back on her bed, eyes closed. She was asleep. Her lips twitched. Talking in her sleep? Then he saw the little white cords. She was listening to her iPod.

"Heather."

Her eyes opened and she gave him a lazy smile, pulling out the earbuds as she sat up. "You're back."

"So everyone keeps telling me."

She cocked her head at him and raised an eyebrow.

"Never mind. I brought you something." He shook the bag of paint chips.

She scooted off the bed. "Oh goody. Let's go look at them in the right light." Taking the bag from him, she squeezed past him and out into the living room.

He was glad it was this easy to make her happy.

HEATHER STOOD BACK AND LOOKED AT THE PAINT CHIPS she taped to the walls. The shades appeared to be different on each wall depending on how the light hit them. The butter-scotch for the living and dining area looked great with the light that poured in from the south-facing windows. But the kitchen had two different light sources, and the paint had to comple-ment the countertops, floors, and cabinets. Finally, she chose one that looked good everywhere, a light terra-cotta. It compli-mented the oak cabinets, went with the Spanish style of the house, and adding a dark red accent color, it would be striking.

"What do you think?" She tapped the top color on the chip.

Kyle stared at it a moment. "You want to paint my kitchen orange?"

"It's not orange, it's terra-cotta. There's a big difference." He looked skeptical.

"Trust me. It'll be great." She bit her lip. Maybe he was changing his mind. "You did say whatever I picked would be fine." And called her sweetheart. "But if you don't like it, I could go with something else."

He pulled her into his arms and kissed her forehead. "It's fine. I like it."

"Good." She'd leave the paint chips up tonight to see how the changing daylight affected the colors, but she was fairly certain she'd made her choice.

Wrapping her arms loosely around Kyle's waist, she relaxed against him, finding it difficult to conjure up her earlier fear. He'd have to leave again, probably tomorrow, to get the paint and the list of supplies she'd made. She shivered at the thought.

He pulled back. "You okay?"

"Mmm hmm." She mumbled into his shirt, not lifting her head, not wanting to let her fear disturb the peace. She'd be okay while he was gone. She might be safer, considering both times she'd been shot at had been with Kyle. Funny, she hadn't felt scared at the time. Kyle had been there, and she knew he'd handle it. It was just afterward that the shakes started.

It was kind of ironic, and she started to make a joke about it to Kyle. Her brain engaged in time, and she closed her mouth. Kyle wouldn't find it funny. He still blamed himself.

He pulled back again, and this time Heather let him. "So tomorrow, I'll go get that whatever-color-you-call-it paint, and we can get started."

"We? You're helping? Is your arm up to it?"

"It was just a scratch. You pick the colors, and I'll provide the labor. I might even get Joe in on the act."

"Is he still speaking to you even though he can't drive his own truck?"

"Hey, he gets to drive my truck, which is better anyway. Besides, we've done worse to each other."

She could only imagine. "Hilary's on tomorrow, right?"

"Yep."

"Good. Unlike Lisa"—Heather purposely raised her voice —"I bet Hilary likes to paint."

"Hey," Lisa protested from the other end of the room. "Nothing in my job description says I have to paint."

"But what's not to like about painting? With a little effort, you can transform a room."

"It's that effort part."

Heather laughed. This was turning out to be a decent day. Tomorrow should be even better. She couldn't wait to see Kyle's face when they finished painting.

———

KYLE HAD TO ADMIT THIS ORANGE WHATEVER-SHE-CALLED-it looked good. He'd half expected his kitchen to look like the inside of a basketball. He was willing to put up with it if it gave Heather something to do and made her happy. But this was nice, kind of warm, and it made the cabinets stand out.

With Joe and Hilary helping, the painting had gone quickly. The yellowish color in the living room had been easy to paint since there wasn't much furniture in there. The kitchen and family room had required more taping and furniture moving. They still had to paint the hallway, but that wouldn't take long.

Heather was touching up the backsplash under the cabinets. He watched her struggle to get the paintbrush up into the odd angle, before climbing onto the countertop and stretching out on her back. A blob of orange paint decorated one knee. The bruise he'd given her was visible under the hem of her shorts. Living in close proximity to her, he found himself watching her often. The way she moved, her mannerisms had become familiar to him. Like now, she seemed clueless to his attentiveness. He let his eyes skim her body, liking the fact that she often wore shorts and went barefoot. Like today.

Grabbing a rag, he stood in front of the counter, effectively trapping her.

She glanced his way. "I'm almost done."

He nodded and began rubbing the rag over her knee, mostly smearing the paint. He scrubbed harder. The night of the Jitter Bug shooting flashed through his mind, when he'd washed the blood off her feet. Not even two weeks ago and yet so much had changed between them. He knew she wanted her life to go back to normal, but he liked having her around. Paint now gone, he took the trim brush from her and helped her off the counter. Setting the brush on top of the rag and putting them to the side, he bracketed her against the counter with his arms.

She looked up at him with those eyes of hers and wet her lips.

He was such a goner for this woman.

"So, what do you think?" Heather's gaze traveled around the room and back to his.

He briefly glanced around. Joe and Hilary were nowhere to be seen. They'd probably started on the hall. "I think you're beautiful."

She rolled her eyes and gave her head a slight shake. "About the room."

Leaning close, he whispered, "I like it. I like you."

But his plan to follow that up with a kiss was disrupted when Joe walked back in the room. "Oops. Sorry. Don't mean to interrupt."

Kyle moved away, winking at Heather. "Great timing."

Heather craned her head to look around Kyle. "Joe, what do you think about the color? Honestly."

Curious as to what Joe would say, Kyle leaned on the counter next to Heather. He hoped Joe wouldn't say something stupid and hurt Heather's feelings.

Joe studied the room with a slow nod. "Never thought I'd say this when we opened those paint cans, but I like it. Looks good."

Good. Joe could live another day. Kyle pushed away from the counter. "How about lunch? Pizza okay?"

"You know me. I work for food." Joe moved the couch back in front of the TV, found the remote, and settled in with a soda. Kyle ordered the pizza then headed to the laundry room.

Heather had filled the utility sink with water and was rinsing out brushes and rollers. The clean ones rested on rags on the washer.

He plunged his hands into the cream-of-pumpkin-soup colored water, grabbing a roller. Conscious of her nearness, her pear-scented soap over the smell of latex paint, he couldn't think of a thing to say. They washed in silence, bumping arms occasionally, sending fire up Kyle's arm.

Shaking off the last brush, Heather drained the sink and rinsed her hands. He did the same and took the rag she handed him. They weren't alone often. He was going to take advantage of that.

Tossing the rag aside, he studied her face.

She didn't move away.

Sliding his hand behind her neck, he covered her mouth with his. Both hands ran over her shoulders, down her back, urging her closer. Taking her with him, he turned and leaned against the washer.

Her body melted against his.

Passion fogged his brain, and his only thought was for more of her. His mouth slid across her jaw and down her neck. At the hollow of her throat, he felt more than heard her soft moan. His hands slipped under the hem of her shirt. Her skin was so soft. His body craved hers.

A sound made its way through his drugged mind. His name. Someone was calling his name.

Heather pulled back, adjusting her shirt, and Kyle looked up. Joe stood in the doorway. "Pizza's here."

The quiet voice and lack of a joke hit Kyle hard. "Wallet's on the counter."

Joe nodded and left.

Dragging in a breath, he looked at Heather. It was obvious by looking at her what they'd been doing. Her face was flushed, lips swollen. Her hair was out of its ponytail. He didn't even remember doing that.

She put her arms around his waist.

He lightly rubbed her back. This is the part where he should say he was sorry. But the words wouldn't leave his mouth. He couldn't say it. He wasn't.

Chapter Thirty-Three

Kyle pulled off the last of the painter's tape from the hallway baseboard, turning the wet paint side into the plastic drop cloth. That yellow color even looked good in here. Heather was going to paint the bathroom some shade of green, but she hadn't mentioned his room or the guest room.

Joe appeared at the end of the hallway. "I'm taking off." But he didn't move.

Kyle got the message. "I'll walk you out." They headed out the front door. It was odd to see his own truck parked at the curb instead of in the garage.

Joe clicked off the alarm, but instead of opening the door he leaned against it. "You guys are in pretty close proximity under a stressful situation." He looked down the hill, the peek-a-boo view more view than peek out here. "Be careful. I've been down that road, and I wish more than anything I could take it back."

"I know," Kyle said quietly. Joe had dabbled in partying in high school and college, not coming to Christ until his senior year. Since Kyle and Scott had become Christians through youth group in high school, it had been one thing that had separated the Three Musketeers.

Joe slapped Kyle in the chest then opened the truck door. "Voice of experience, man. Learn from someone else's mistake."

Kyle nodded. "Thanks." He kicked the tire. "Take care of my truck."

Joe grinned and drove off.

Shoving his hands in his pockets, Kyle wandered around the yard. It needed to be mowed. He yanked a couple of weeds out of the driveway. He wouldn't have believed it could be so easy to throw it all away. Even if Heather had been willing to cross that line, he would still be responsible. A mistake that would haunt them forever. He wouldn't do that to her or them.

HEATHER OPENED HER E-MAIL, STILL A LITTLE SHAKEN BY what had happened between her and Kyle yesterday. They hadn't talked about it. Kim had come home and oohed and ahhed over the new paint. Then Stacey had come to relieve Hilary, and Heather and Kyle had turned in early, separately, tired from all the painting.

How did it get so hot so fast? There were probably a lot of physical and psychological reasons for it, from her seeing him as a protector to her living in his house. And of course, add to that he was a great guy and just plain good looking.

She sighed. They'd have to be more careful. Still, it was worse than pushing away chocolate. Who would want to give up something so wonderful?

Except it was more dangerous. She'd never realized how easily things could get out of control. And if they did, there was no going back. Her own weakness scared her.

Not wanting to dwell on it, she scrolled through her e-mail. More fillers to edit from work. Great. But Susan had liked her story idea from The Fest and had given her permission to write it. No guarantee it would run, though. That was okay. It'd keep her busy. Opening Evernote, she made a note to call Justin for the interview.

Back to her e-mail, she saw notes from Sarah and Melissa. Hitting reply, she started to write about painting Kyle's house and then stopped. She couldn't do that. Surprisingly, tears welled up. She brushed them away, angry that she couldn't even share something so simple with her friends. And tonight was choir practice. Another thing she missed. She wasn't even sure what to pray anymore. For more faith? More patience? For this whole stupid thing to be over?

She moved the cursor over to close the program when she saw a new e-mail had come in. It was from Quinn. That's odd. Why would he be e-mailing her? More trouble with the sale of the townhome? She opened it. A chill ran across her back.

"Kyle!"

***

KYLE BENT OVER HEATHER'S SHOULDER, FORCING HIMSELF not to be distracted by her. He read the e-mail a second time.

Hi Heather,

Just wondering how you're doing. I should probably say hi to Detective Taylor, too, as I'm sure, as protective as he is, he's reading all your e-mails. Unless he trusts your judgment. You're not staying at the Comfort Suites anymore, are you? Probably not driving that cool red truck anymore either.

By the way, I was just listening to "Run" by Kutless.

Have you heard it? I thought of you, since you sing in the church choir and all.

Secret Admirer

Kyle's blood chilled. "Do you know what song he's talking about?"

Heather nodded and opened iTunes. She clicked on the song and it played.

In any other context, it was a great song about no matter how far we run from God, He's always waiting there to be with us. But coming from whoever this was, the context was warped. Heather rubbed her arms as the song finished and then deleted it from her library. "I used to really like that song. I don't get it. If it were from Quinn, why would he sign it Secret Admirer? He's not stupid. He knows his name will show up as the sender. Do you think—"

Kyle knew what she couldn't bring herself to say. Was he involved in this? He didn't like Quinn, but he found it hard to believe he'd hurt Heather. He picked up his phone. "I don't know, but I'm calling Mark."

———

HEATHER WALKED AROUND THE HOUSE. SHE WAS STUDYING the paint, making sure they hadn't missed anything. She wasn't pacing. Definitely not. Stopping, she looked at the clock again. Only five minutes later than last time.

This was ridiculous. Kyle would call her the minute he had anything to tell her. She just had to keep busy. Work. That was it. Kyle had taken her laptop into the station so the tech guys could figure out where the e-mail had come from. She just couldn't believe it was from Quinn. So she didn't have her laptop. But she could work the old-fashioned way with pen and paper. She could call Justin and set up an interview. What time did he get out of school anyway? Well, she could always leave a message.

Settling in her favorite chair with a pad of paper, she made some preliminary notes. Jotting down Justin's name and number on the page, she picked up her phone and called him.

He answered on the second ring. "Yeah?"

"Hey, Justin. It's Heather."

"Oh. Hi."

"Hi. Hey, my boss gave me the go-ahead on that article we talked about so I was wondering if you were still up for the interview."

"Sure."

"When would be a good time for you?"

"How about now?"

Heather thought quickly. Might as well do it now. It'd take her mind off things. "Okay. It shouldn't take too long."

She spent fifteen minutes asking him questions about his taste in music, the things he and his friends were into, his reaction to The Fest.

She was wrapping up the interview when he asked about Kyle. "Is he there? I haven't talked to him in a while."

Heather hesitated, measuring her words. "No, I'm assuming he's still at work."

"Oh, I thought—never mind. Just tell him I said hi and anytime he wants to go surfing, I'm there."

"Okay, I'll tell him."

KYLE CAME HOME TO FIND HEATHER IN THE BATHROOM washing down the walls.

She didn't look at him. "This room shouldn't take too long. Taping stuff off is going to be the most time consuming. I'm thinking I should paint the ceiling in here too. Make the room look larger."

Was this what she wanted to do? Did it help? Or would she be better off if he made her talk to him? After watching her a moment, he took the rag from her.

She grabbed it back. "Kyle, I need to get this done. I want to get this room painted so I can finish that article. Did I tell you I talked to Justin today?"

Leaning against the doorjamb, he said, "No." He'd let this play out a bit. "What did he say?"

She dunked the rag and wrung it out before answering. "It was a good interview. I think it'll be a good story, if I ever get it written." She looked his way for the first time. "He asked about you. Said he'd like to go surfing again."

"Good. I should call him." Justin had been another casualty of this whole mess. He'd had enough people in his life who didn't have time for him. Kyle didn't need to be on that list too.

She lifted the bucket to the tub and, standing on the edge, began scrubbing the wall above the surround. After a minute, she hurled the rag into the bucket with a splash. "I don't like being disappointed by people."

"It's inevitable."

She stared at him. "I didn't use to think so. Now, I don't know what I'm sure of anymore." Sobs started shaking her shoulders. "How could he do that? I thought we had fixed things. What made him think that was okay to do? I just wish— I don't know." She wiped at her face with the back of her wrist.

Kyle took her elbow, helped her down from the edge of the tub, and held her while she cried.

After a moment, he said, "I don't think Quinn sent that e-mail." It felt a little weird to be defending Quinn to Heather. "The techs said someone made it look like it came from his account, like they do on phishing scams. The bigger question is how someone knows you and Quinn are—or were—connected. I'm guessing the public records of owning the townhome together. But it means that someone is doing research on you. And the only reason they'd be doing that is if they knew you were the witness."

Chapter Thirty-Four

Justin wished he'd never met Cole, Alex, Bull, or any of the other Seventeeners. When Heather had called him today, he'd been glad he was already sitting down or his legs would have gone out from under him. She was okay. He was relieved. He wasn't sure after what Cole had told him at school.

Justin had been heading toward a table when Cole grabbed his arm, grinning. "Hey, guess what?"

"What?"

Cole moved closer to the wall. "We found her."

"Who?"

"The girl from Jitter Bug. She was at the motel you said."

Heat flashed through Justin followed by ice. "What happened?"

Cole glanced around and shifted his weight. "I didn't see it. We waited next door and when they pulled in, Alex jumped out and hid in the bushes. I parked around the corner. I didn't know what he was going to do. I thought we were just going to see if she was really staying there. Next thing I know, I hear gunshots and Alex is jumping back in the car, yelling at me to take off. So I did."

Justin shoved Cole against the wall. "Did he hit anyone? Was anyone hurt?"

Cole swallowed and glanced around. Justin let go of him. The last thing he needed right now was to be pulled into the principal's office for fighting.

"I—I don't know." Cole didn't look too good.

Justin had thought he was going to be sick. He'd gone home and searched the papers, looking for any mention of a shooting. If she'd been hurt, it would have been in the papers. Still, he couldn't shake that fear that something had happened to her or Kyle.

When he talked to her today, she sounded fine on the phone. Still.

That was it, though. He was through with the Seventeeners.

Even Bree wasn't worth this.

HEATHER OPENED THE BROWSER ON HER COMPUTER TO the church's website so she and Kyle could watch a streaming video of the service.

He handed her a cup of coffee and sat next to her, arm around the back of her chair.

Taking a sip, she watched Ryan welcome everybody, and then he and Sarah started the first worship song. The cameras panned over the choir on stage, all faces Heather recognized, singing without her. Longing washed over her. She should be there. Tears blurred her vision of the screen. She set her cup down, not caring it sloshed on the table. Shoving her chair back she nearly ran down the hall to her room. She couldn't watch. It was like she was in prison and life was going on without her. Why was she being punished? She hadn't done anything wrong.

Hugging a pillow to her chest, she hoped the tears would come and bring some relief to the overwhelming pressure in her chest. But she couldn't even cry properly. She threw the pillow. It barely reached the wall before sliding down with a plop. That didn't help. She wanted to throw something that would shatter into a thousand pieces with a sharp noise and shards that would cut her fingers and make her bleed when she picked them up. If she picked them up.

Life sucked.

She sat up. That was it. She was done. She was moving back into her house and living her life again. Who cared if they came after her? It couldn't be any worse than living like this.

Snowflake scratched at the door, and Heather dragged herself to the door to let her in. Picking up the cat, she sat on the bed, scratching the back of Snowflake's head, feeling the rumbling purr.

Why couldn't she be more content? She'd never felt so disconsolate in her life.

She didn't know. Didn't care, either. Nope. As much as she felt like a caged animal, the thought of setting foot outside that door filled her with overwhelming, paralyzing fear. Her brain hurt, and all she wanted to do right now was forget.

Picking up the latest Diana Brandmeyer book next to her bed, she stretched out and forced herself to get lost in the pages until her eyes grew heavy.

But sleep wouldn't come.

She stared at the ceiling, a little surprised Kyle hadn't come to check on her. He was probably watching the service. Good. One of them should.

Sorry, God. I know my attitude stinks. She sighed. *You're trying to tell me something. What?*

She grabbed her Bible and flipped it open, looking briefly at the photo of her and her sisters. She'd have to make another copy; this one was getting a little worn.

In the Bible, James said something about trials, a perfect description of her life right now. Here it was, James chapter one, verses two through four: "Consider it pure joy, my brothers and sisters, whenever you face trials of many kinds, because you know that the testing of your faith produces perseverance. Let perseverance finish its work so that you may be mature and complete, not lacking anything."

Let trouble be an opportunity for joy. Heather chewed on her lip. That was a hard statement to get her mind around. Joy would be the last word she would use to describe her circumstances. Yet she knew from her study of Philippians that joy was not about circumstances; it was looking beyond your circumstances with a heavenly viewpoint.

Okay, so how did she find joy in these circumstances? How did she look beyond them with God's perspective? Well, she already knew she was thankful for Kyle during this situation. And that God was using this to develop and deepen her faith.

But something else felt just out of her reach.

Lord, help me to understand. I don't know how I can find joy here. I've had everything taken away from me: my job, my singing. Everything that defined me is gone. I don't know who I am anymore. Who are you making me to be?

No answer. Just silence.

She sat wrapped in it for a long moment. Finally, she got up and decided to go see Kyle. He had to be wondering.

Kyle was still sitting at the table, his head in his hands. The laptop was closed. Church must be over. She sighed and sank into the chair.

"What?" He raised his head, looking a little concerned.

"How do you deal with all the evil in the world you're exposed to every day?"

He looked like he wasn't expecting that question. Leaning back in his chair, he thought a minute. "I don't have the answers you're looking for, Heather. Ultimately, it all goes back to the fallen world we live in. Yeah, someday there will be justice. God will see to that. But day to day?" He shook his head. "I just can't stand by and let the bad guys win. Yeah, they win a lot. But I have to do my best to keep that number down. Somebody has to stand up to the evil in the world."

Heather nodded. She wasn't sure if that was the answer she wanted. Where did that put her in this battle between good and evil? She wasn't sure.

And the words echoed in her head: Who am I? Who are You making me to be?

HEATHER WASHED OUT THE ROLLERS IN THE UTILITY SINK, feeling a little flushed at the thought of what happened last time she was in here. Using her fingers as a squeegee, she forced the paint out of the roller, watching the water turn green. She'd sent her article off to Susan, hadn't received any more work from her, and had finished painting the bathroom.

She and Kyle had gotten their stitches out this morning. Her arm was sore, but she didn't care. She needed something to do.

Setting the rollers to dry, she headed to the living room. Kyle had been going through files there, away from the distraction of the TV. He probably wasn't much more pleased than she was at being confined to the house. She knew he preferred to work in the field.

He glanced up as she walked in and patted the sofa next to him.

She sank into the soft leather couch. The butterscotch walls were a definite improvement and went nicely with the furniture. Kyle was looking at her. "What?"

"You've run out of things to do." "Yep."

"You haven't painted my room. Or your room."

Hmm. He thought of it as her room, not the guest room. Well, it might as well be. Who knew how long she'd be there?

But for some reason, the thought of painting it didn't thrill her. She didn't want to make that room her own. She wanted her own room back. "What color do you want your room?"

"I don't know. Blue or green, I guess. I kind of like the color in the bathroom."

"You've got a west-facing window, right?" "Yeah. The slider that goes out to the patio."

"Okay, so a cool color would work. Maybe a shade darker than the bathroom."

Kyle's phone rang, and he picked it up. He sat up, his eyes focused on some unseen object, going into cop mode. She watched him until he put down the phone and looked at her. "We're going down to the station. The lab finally ran all the fingerprints from the Jitter Bug, and one came back a match."

Chapter Thirty-Five

Heather sat in the conference room in a much better mood than either of the previous times she'd been there. Just getting out of the house was a nice thing in and of itself. Kyle hadn't said much on the way over, but she hoped this was the beginning of the end of things. He sat next to her, Lisa across the table. They were waiting for Mark and Bruce to come in and tell them what they'd found.

She didn't realize she was fidgeting until Kyle put his hand over hers. "It won't be much longer."

The door opened and Heather startled.

Mark came in, tossing a folder on the table. "Here's what we have. One of the fingerprints in the Jitter Bug shooting came back to Alex Jeffries." He looked at Kyle. "He was the driver of that SUV that was reported stolen and ended up in that pursuit at the beginning of last month."

Kyle rubbed the bridge of his nose.

This didn't seem like good news to him. Heather waited for him to say why, but Mark started talking again.

"Problem is, as you know, he's on the store security camera earlier in the day. So the fingerprint doesn't point to any criminal activity." He turned to Heather. "That's where you come in. We need you to identify him. You're the only one who can prove he was the shooter."

A weight pressed on her shoulders. This whole case rested on her. Her mind flashed through her attempts to come up with an accurate rendering of the shooter. And how she'd failed. What if she failed this time? What if she couldn't remember him? Panic tightened her chest. She didn't want to let them down.

Kyle squeezed her hand. "It's okay, Heather. Just do your best."

"What happens if I can't?"

Mark stopped halfway standing, glanced at Kyle then straightened the rest of the way. "He'd be released until we could find more evidence."

Panic morphed into despair. She heard it in her own voice. "So I'd be under protection indefinitely?" She clenched Kyle's hand.

Mark didn't respond, just looked at Kyle who answered instead, his voice flat. "You'd probably be removed from protection. If you can't identify the shooter, then you're no longer at risk."

"Oh. Then why did someone try to shoot at me at the motel?"

"Probably to intimidate you and keep you from ID'ing someone. They must have figured we were getting close or maybe they just wanted to send a warning. Just like the e-mail. I don't know." He shrugged. "Anyhow, department policy doesn't always jive with reality."

Kyle helped her to her feet, and they followed Mark out of the room. She couldn't help but feel the next few minutes would determine her near future. If she could pick out the shooter, she could conceivably help this case and serve justice. But if she couldn't pick him out, her life would go back to normal.

Wouldn't it?

Only God knew.

In the hallway, Mark explained the process to her.

A man came out of the door. "Hey, Kyle. Figured you'd be here."

"Heather, this is my partner, Steve Collins."

Not as tall as Kyle, with a stockier build and dark, unruly hair, Steve shook her hand. "Nice to finally meet you, although I wish the circumstances were better. Are you ready?"

She looked at Kyle. "Mark and I need to stay out here since we're involved in the case. We don't want a defense attorney implying we coached or influenced you." He rubbed his thumb over the back of her hand. "You going to be okay?"

She nodded with a small smile. "I'll be fine."

Lisa stepped up next to her and put her hand on her shoulder. "I'll go with you."

Heather smiled at her. "Thanks." She took a deep breath and followed Steve into the room, Lisa behind her.

Heather clasped her hands, praying, trying to remember back to that night at the Jitter Bug. The teens came in. Kyle went to the back. The article on tattoos. The loud voices. The look on the barista's face. Her phone ringing. The dark-haired teen turning toward her.

"Heather?"

At the touch on her arm, she jumped. "Are you okay?" Steve asked.

She nodded, taking a deep breath, trying to still her pounding heart.

"We're ready to start."

"Okay." She looked through the window at the young men standing in line. A couple she could eliminate right away. But the rest...

The same frustration of trying to capture his face returned. She studied each face then closed her eyes, picturing him turning toward her.

Pressure closed her throat and tears pricked her eyes. She couldn't do it. She didn't know which one was the shooter. She was letting everyone down. What would Kyle think?

It was over now, wasn't it? She could get her life back. The relief wasn't as sweet, tinged instead with the taste of failure.

"Heather? Have you seen any of these people before?"

Number three shifted his weight.

Heather examined his stance, trying to hold the image in her mind next to the one in front of her.

She took a step toward the glass, that delicate barrier between them. The faint outline of her face reflected dimly in the glass. The two images overlapped, one reflected, one separated. In other circumstances, they wouldn't be that different. On the outside.

The eyes.

He smirked.

In her mind, his arm raised and the glass behind her shattered. "Number three. That's him."

KYLE LEANED AGAINST THE WALL ACROSS THE HALL FROM Mark, wondering how Heather was doing in there. "Has he said anything?"

"Nope. We picked him up at his house for questioning, and his dad had a very expensive lawyer down here before we'd even started." Mark tilted his head. "How do you think she'll do?"

Kyle shrugged. "She'll do her best. I know she was frustrated she couldn't get the composite right, but maybe seeing him in person..."

"We need a positive ID before we can arrest him and get a search warrant for the house. Bruce is out there now just waiting for the word. We really want to get these guys, and right now, other than Bull McClosky 'happening' to be at the Jitter Bug at the same time, we don't have anything tying Alex to the Seventeeners."

"We might. Have you talked to the other boys that were in that SUV?"

Mark raised his eyebrows. "Not yet. None of them are known Seventeeners."

"But Alex is now tied to two criminal activities. If his friends were involved in the first one, there's a good bet at least one of them was involved in the second." Kyle just hoped it wasn't Justin. He would have recognized him from the back running out of the Jitter Bug, wouldn't he? He couldn't be sure. "I know one of them. Justin Foster. He might tell me if there are any Seventeener connections. The other boys, or rather their parents, will probably react like Alex's dad and clam up. But I might be able to get something from Justin."

He massaged the back of his neck. "I guess for personal reasons, I hope he doesn't know anything. Heather and I took him to The Fest, and she interviewed him for an article for her magazine."

"Did he know she was the witness?"

"I don't see how. But I'll go over everything with her again to see if there was anything he possibly could have figured out." He shook his head, a sick feeling filling his stomach. "I don't want to think that. Because it means either he gave the information about Heather to the shooter at the motel, or he was involved."

"Don't jump to conclusions. He'd have to figure out that Heather was the witness and where she was staying. That's a lot of ground to cover."

Kyle nodded, but he didn't like the conclusions he was coming to.

The door opened.

Heather came out, her face pale.

Lisa's hand was at her back, and she was smiling. "She nailed him."

THE DOOR TO THE CONFERENCE ROOM OPENED, AND Heather watched Kyle walk in, looking at his phone. "Ready to go?"

She was. Her legs shook a little as she stood. "Back to prison." Heather gave him a wry grin.

He put his arm around her shoulders. "Hopefully not for too much longer. You did good. Alex was arrested and is being processed, and they're searching his house now."

He held the door for her and Lisa to leave the room. They didn't talk again until they were in the car.

"I'm meeting Justin in two hours at Starbucks."

Heather raised her eyebrows. "Why? I mean, that's great, I was just wondering why now."

"Alex was one of his friends. Remember that pursuit I told you about where Justin was in the car? It was Alex's stepmom's Lexus, and Alex was driving."

Heather felt a little sick. She liked Justin and had just figured him to need a good role model and some attention. But taking part in a shooting? It just didn't seem possible. "Does that mean Justin is involved in this?"

"I don't know. I hope not. But I need you to think back to everything you've said to him. Starting with The Fest." "Well, how did Justin sound on the phone? He seemed fine when I talked to him. If he was guilty, wouldn't he want to avoid you?" Kyle shrugged. "Justin seemed pleased to hear from me. I don't know if I should hope he has information for me or not. Either way, I think there's a chance he might have seen or heard something at school. And I figure he'll tell me more than he would tell Mark or Bruce."

They mentally walked back through the day, starting with when they had picked up Justin.

"When did you talk to him about doing an interview?"

"You had gone to get us sodas. I remember joking with him about staying at the Ritz. I don't know why." Her knee jiggled up and down. Parts of the exchange were missing in her head. "Why can't I remember things better?"

He stilled her knee with his hand. "Stress. It's bad for the memory. Don't try to force it. Just relax. You asked him for the interview. What did he say?"

"It was fine. Then you came back, and he went off with Brian. Then I hung out with the choir people for a while." She turned in her seat. "The balloon. My reaction was so out of proportion. Do you think that's it?"

"A lot of people jump when a balloon pops. I think it'd be hard to draw a conclusion just from that. Besides, that wouldn't tell him where you were staying."

Staying. The word echoed in her head. Justin had said something about it. What was it?

The fragment vanished.

Chapter Thirty-Six

Heather tried to sink deeper under the bubbles, but they were mostly gone, just leaving milky bathwater. The bath had helped relieve the tension of the day, especially since she could get all the way under the water now that her stitches were out. If she could just keep this feeling, maybe she could sleep tonight without nightmares. She should get out; the water was cooling, and Kyle would be leaving soon to meet Justin.

She'd accomplished something today when she'd ID'd Alex. Fighting her fears, she'd stood up for justice. But how brave did she have to be for that? All she did was point her finger. It wasn't like she was physically in danger; glass separated them. How much courage did that take?

What did it say about the level of her faith? Was that all she could handle? What was God trying to do here? What was He telling her?

She'd soak a few more minutes. The questions that had been playing through her mind since yesterday rolled around in her head.

Who am I? Who are You making me to be?

A child of God. At her barest essentials, that's who she was. So, she'd start there.

If she was a child of God, shouldn't her purpose be to grow more and more like a child of God? Develop childlike faith, trusting Him and becoming more like Him? Becoming more childlike felt counterintuitive when she'd strived to become independent and on her own.

And yet, it resonated with something inside.

Wasn't that often the way of God's upside-down kingdom? If you lose your life, you save it. If you're last, you're first. Become childlike to mature.

The water was definitely cold now. She drained the tub and climbed out, toweling off. She grabbed her lotion and squeezed a pale green pool into her hand. Rubbing it on her arms, she tossed the bottle on the counter. It fell over and crashed into a couple of smaller bottles. She reached to straighten them, then stilled.

The bottle of lotion from the motel. The Fest. *"Want some?" She offered the bottle teasingly to Justin.*

He rolled his eyes. "What is that, anyway?"

"Just lotion."

"From a motel? Maybe the Ritz-Carlton."

Heather laughed. "I wish."

"You stayed there recently?"

"The Ritz? Have you been there? That place is amazing. Right on the beach."

Justin gave her his best teenager-disgusted-with-an adult-trying-to-be-funny look.

She pretended to look at the label, trying to think of something. "Oh, you mean the motel. My folks stay there when they come visit." Anxious to change the subject before she got caught in a question she couldn't answer, she tossed the bottle back in her purse and pulled out her phone. "Give me your number."

Heather threw on her robe. She had to catch Kyle before he left to meet with Justin.

JUSTIN SPOTTED KYLE ALREADY AT A TABLE ON THE PATIO. He suddenly wasn't sure if this was a good idea or not. Kyle always made plans in advance. This was short notice.

Kyle stood. "Hey, Justin. Good to see you. What do you want to drink?"

"Caramel macchiato. Thanks, man."

"Sure. I'll be right back."

Justin sat at the table and looked around. Not too busy, but it was still early. He was relieved and worried at the same time. It was good to see Kyle. Justin was glad Kyle was okay and had kind of missed him. For a cop, Kyle was cool to hang with. Better than those stupid Seventeeners. Maybe he should just tell Kyle everything. He'd know what to do.

But that was the problem. Kyle was Mr. Law-and-Order. He'd be disappointed, and Justin couldn't handle one more person being down on him. He got that enough from his dad. Besides, Justin could be in some serious trouble. Kyle couldn't protect him from that.

Kyle came back with their drinks and sat down. "So, how are things?"

"Not too bad."

"How's school?"

"Fine."

"Your mom?"

"Good." He wished they were surfing or shooting hoops or something. This was dumb.

"You hanging out with those guys who stole the SUV?"

Justin snapped his head up. What did Kyle know? Or was he just asking? He'd play it cool. "Nah. Trevor's parents put him in a private school, and I don't talk to Alex or Cole."

"You don't see them at school?"

That would be easy for Kyle to find out. "Well, yeah. I see them around, but we don't hang or anything."

"You know who Bull McClosky is?"

Justin felt heat rush to his face. He took a swig of coffee. Kyle had a reason behind his questions. What did he know? "Sure. Everyone knows him. He has a rep."

"Alex or Cole ever hang out with him?"

Justin shrugged, hoping it was casual. "I don't know. Maybe. They don't run in the same group, though." He drained his coffee.

"You think either of them are Seventeeners?"

Had he talked to Alex or Cole? Did he know they were behind the shootings? No, they would have told him. "Maybe. Like I said, I don't hang out with them anymore."

Kyle tapped his cup on the table. "Good. Those aren't the kind of guys you want to be with. They'll just take you down with them."

Justin nodded. He sure knew that, but he wasn't going to let on to Kyle. Time to change the subject. Put Kyle on the defensive. "So, you and Heather, huh?"

Kyle grinned. "Yeah. What do you think of her?"

"For an older chick, she's hot."

Kyle laughed. "She's younger than me. But I agree with you about the hot part." He drank his coffee. "So, you wouldn't have mentioned to anyone that you thought Heather might be a witness to the Jitter Bug shooting or where she was staying?" His eyes pinned Justin.

The coffee turned to acid in his stomach. He resisted the urge to squirm under Kyle's stare. Kyle did know something. How much and who told him? "I don't know anything about that." Kyle was a cop first, Justin's friend second. He wouldn't understand, and Justin would just be in major trouble.

"You don't seem surprised at the fact Heather was the witness."

Keep cool. Kyle was just fishing. If he knew something, he'd have come out and said it. "I don't know anything about it. My mom showed me the article in the paper because it was close to your house. That's it." He stood up. He had to get out of here before Kyle backed him into a corner and made him say something he didn't want to. "Thanks for the coffee. I gotta run. Call me if you want to go surfing."

Justin climbed into his car and took off without looking back.

KYLE TOSSED HIS KEYS ON THE COUNTER, NOT SURE HOW fruitful his conversation had been. He'd briefly considered meeting Justin at the Jitter Bug—since it had reopened—to hear Justin's reaction to the suggestion and to see how he acted around the scene of the crime. But he'd discarded the idea; he wasn't entirely sure what his own reaction would be.

Justin knew more than he was saying. Kyle was pretty certain Justin had figured out, and probably let slip, that Heather was the witness, especially after what she told him about the lotion. But whether Justin was staying quiet about the Seventeeners out of loyalty or fear, he didn't know.

He went over to the couch, kissed Heather, and then sat next to her. She was dressed in those loose pants and a T-shirt, looking like she was about ready for bed.

"How'd it go?"

He gave her what he hoped was a rakish grin. "Well, Justin thinks you're hot, for an older chick."

She laughed like he'd hoped. "Really? Nice to know I'm still impressing the high school boys."

"How are you doing? It's been a long day."

"Okay. The bath helped, and I've just been watching mindless TV. So, besides saying I was hot, did Justin reveal anything else?"

"Not really. He was uncomfortable, but he said he didn't hang out with those guys anymore."

"Do you think he figured out where I was staying?" Her brow creased.

"He said he didn't know anything about that, and he ended the conversation pretty quick after I mentioned it. But I have a hard time imagining that Justin would put you in danger. Though he might have said something thoughtlessly and is feeling guilty about it now." He scrubbed his face. "On some level, I believe him. But there's something he's not telling me. It could be as simple as he still talks to the guys, or as complex as he's somehow involved in all this. I just wish I knew. If I'd made more time for him, maybe this wouldn't have happened."

Heather leaned over and kissed him on the cheek. "You did the best you could. It'll all come out eventually. It kind of creeps me out a bit to think he might have said something or might know the person who shot me. But I agree with you. I don't think he'd deliberately harm me, or anyone else. Justin's a good kid. If he was involved in something or if he knew anything, I think he'd tell you."

"I hope you're right."

Bull loaded the boxes into the back of his Explorer, closed the hatch, and drove off. Alex had gotten picked up. Bull had expected that—which is why Alex did the job. But his dad had the money and the connections to bail him out. He was sure Alex wouldn't talk; his expensive lawyer wouldn't let him. Still, it wouldn't hurt to get this stuff over to Mom's. They'd be hard pressed to get a search warrant there even if they picked him up. Finding a new fence, one that wanted to play by his rules, was taking longer than he thought.

He couldn't resist sending that e-mail. Sure, it upped the risk, but that upped the rush. Working from behind the computer wasn't the same as doing a job, but it was okay. He hadn't made any mistakes, but they would. He would just have to wait. That was okay. He was patient. Like a sniper waiting for a target. This was going to take a little longer than he thought, but the victory would still be sweet.

His mom wasn't home, so he pulled into his mom's parking spot. He stacked the boxes on each other and headed up to her door. Her key was still on his ring. After opening the door, he set the boxes inside. Where could he put them where she wouldn't get nosy and look inside?

Her bedroom closet. In the back corner of the top shelf should work. He moved some stuff around and shoved the boxes in there. He'd gotten the last one up as he heard her come in the door.

"Billy? Is that you?"

"Yeah, Mom. I'm here."

"I saw your car in my space."

"I'll go move it. Here, give me your keys, and I'll put yours in there."

She handed them over. He moved the cars around and then grabbed his laptop out of his car before heading inside.

"I thought I'd set up that computer for you and show you how to use it."

"All right. I'll make us some dinner while you do it. Just let me change out of my work clothes."

He set up his computer then opened the laptop he'd given her. Looking at the two screens, you couldn't tell them apart. He'd created a separate user account on his computer and hidden all his stuff. He took his mom's laptop and put his on the counter. Now it was hers.

"Billy."

He jumped. She was right over his shoulder. "Sorry. Didn't see you there."

She peered at the computer. "What are you doing?"

"Just getting it set up for you. Are you ready?"

"In a minute. Were you in my closet? Some of my things are pushed around."

He had to decide which way to play this. "Oh, yeah. I brought some boxes over of extra stuff. I thought I had put them out of your way."

"Oh good. I was hoping it was you and not that Bedroom Burglar. Not that I'd have anything to steal." She laughed and then coughed her smoker's cough. "Let me get us something to eat, and then you can show me how to work that thing."

Chapter Thirty-Seven

Kyle had only had one cup of coffee before his phone rang.

It was Mark. "You're going to want to come down here."

"What's up?"

"The lieutenant's removing Heather's protection."

"What!"

"The assistant DA talked to him after Alex's arraignment this morning. He doesn't feel we have much of a case. Especially since we can't connect him to the Seventeeners. Your relationship with Heather complicates her testimony. By the way, Alex's defense attorney has her name now."

Kyle swore.

"Yep. That pretty much sums it up."

"I'll be there in ten minutes."

Punching off his phone, Kyle strode down the hall and knocked on Heather's door.

"Come in."

He opened the door.

She was sitting up in bed. He wondered if she had any idea

how beautiful he found her in the morning. The thought of anything happening to her…

He started to sit on the edge of the bed and then decided it would be better to stay where he was. "I've got to go down to the station."

"Something come up?"

"Alex was arraigned this morning." How much should he tell her? He didn't want her to worry needlessly if there was any chance he could change the lieutenant's mind. "The assistant DA gave Alex's attorney your name." Her eyes widened, and he rushed to explain. "It's not that uncommon, and if he'd refused, the defense attorney would have asked the judge to order him to do so. But they're going to use our relationship to undercut your testimony. Mark and I are going to talk to the lieutenant about what we're going to do next."

She looked a little confused but only said, "Okay. So, I'll see you when you get back?"

"Yep." He stepped over and kissed her on the forehead. "There's still some coffee."

"Thanks."

Ten minutes later, Kyle and Mark sat in Lieutenant Johnson's office.

"Kyle, I understand your position. But the fact is, Mark and Bruce haven't been able to turn up any connection to the Seventeeners. That's the only reason Ms. McAlistair would be under protection. Frankly, witnessing a murder's not enough. Especially when it looks like they're playing it as an accidental shooting. Alex Jeffries comes from a respected and powerful family. There's no reason to think that he poses any threat to Ms. McAlistair. The protection detail is expensive, and I just can't justify it. I have to answer to the city council, and Mr. Jeffries has great influence with them."

Kyle closed his eyes briefly, biting back the words he wanted to say that would probably get him fired.

The lieutenant looked from Kyle to Mark, tapping his

fingers on the desk. "However, I've been at this too long to believe in coincidences. I don't know why Bull McClosky was at the Jitter Bug that night, but I'd bet my pension it wasn't just for coffee. But all our opinions, no matter how well reasoned, won't stand up in court. Here's what I'm going to do. Kyle, you can stay on Ms. McAlistair's protection as long as you work back cases during the day, seeing as you're not making much progress on the Bedroom Burglar case. I don't care what you do at night. But I'm pulling everyone else off.

"Mark, you and Bruce get me that connection to the Seventeeners. You have forty-five days before this thing goes to trial."

This was the best he was going to get, and he should be thankful. He'd been willing to take vacation and personal leave time to keep protecting Heather if need be. "Thank you, sir."

"Dismissed."

Kyle followed Mark back to his cubicle. "Anything turn up from the search?"

He shook his head. "Apparently, Alex is one deprived child. He doesn't have a computer or cell phone. Imagine that."

"Not really a surprise."

"Nope. Hey, at least you're still assigned to Heather."

"Yeah." Kyle rubbed his chin. "I don't know what I'm going to do about that."

"What's there to do? Hey, is it true she's sleeping in your guest room?"

Kyle didn't want to discuss this. "Did it ever occur to you that I'm sick of my personal life feeding the rumor mill?"

"Kyle, you gotta admit it's pretty hard to believe the two of you aren't sleeping together. I mean, if I had a girlfriend who looked like Heather—"

"I'm going home. You know how to reach me." He spun and left the cubicle.

On the drive home, he tried to figure out how to tell Heather. He had no idea how she was going to take it.

And what about their sleeping arrangements? The safest

place for her was in his house. Period. Kim could be their chaperone, but if he was honest with himself, his sister's presence was only a small deterrent. Not that she was even there that much. Mostly she was at work or with her friends. The whole security detail had put her off, and she avoided being at home whenever she could.

Joe would give him advice, whether he wanted it or not.

Right now, he wanted it. He placed the call.

"Good news, bad news. They caught the Jitter Bug shooter, but they can't make a connection to that teen gang, so they're pulling all the protection from Heather except for me."

"Whoa."

"Yeah."

"So what's that mean? Do *you* think she's safe? You've got a shot-up unit that says otherwise."

"No, I don't think she is. Just because we can't prove the connection to the gang doesn't mean it isn't there. But the shooter's dad is influential, so it's become political. At this point, the best thing I can do is keep Heather at my house and drive her to and from work." Just talking to Joe, he felt his frustration at the situation building.

"That's gonna be a problem for the two of you."

"I know."

Silence filled the space between them.

Joe broke it. "How about this? I'll come sleep on your couch the nights I'm not on. That gives you fewer nights to struggle with."

"I was thinking of hiring Hilary to stay. I'm not sure how well I'll sleep anyway without someone else on duty." The money would have to come out of the Kim Fund, as he thought of it. It was the money his sister paid him each month for rent. It was there in case anything major went wrong with the house, but he'd hoped to give it to his sister as a down payment on a house of her own someday. Lord knew she'd never save it on her own.

"You'll go broke. Hire her for the nights I'm not there if you want."

Kyle swallowed. Joe was a good friend. "Thanks, man. I really appreciate it."

"Anything I can do to help, you know that. By the way, stock your fridge. I might cost you as much in food as paying Hilary."

Kyle pulled into the garage. Hilary met him at the laundry room door. "The lieutenant called me, but I didn't say anything to Heather. I figured you'd want to do that yourself."

"Thanks." He started to walk past then stopped. "Hilary, are you interested in earning a little extra money?"

She frowned. "What'd you have in mind?"

How to explain this. "This house is the safest place for Heather to be. I don't want her going back to her townhome."

"Agreed."

"I'd feel better with another body here. I won't sleep well if I'm listening for everything. And if I don't sleep well, I won't be a good cop. I have a firefighter buddy who will stay here, but on the nights he's on duty, I'd like to have another cop here. I'd pay you to stay."

She only hesitated a second before agreeing. "Sure. When do you need me?"

"Thursday and Sunday to begin with. Thanks, Hilary. I really appreciate it."

Hilary hollered goodbye down the hallway to Heather, who raised her eyebrows and looked at Kyle. He sat down next to her and explained the situation.

"So I can go back to work?"

"Heather, this guy knows where you go to church, knows your e-mail address. I'd say it's a safe bet he knows where you work."

"But if I'm not under protection, Susan will expect me to be at work. I can't get fired over this, Kyle." Her voice cracked.

The safest thing was to keep her locked up in his house. He

hated the position this put them in. Either risk her safety or cause her to lose her job. Maybe the lieutenant was right. "Yeah. I'm not thrilled about it, but I'll take you to and from work, and then you can stay here at night." He explained his plan, but he hadn't worked this out completely. For one thing, he didn't have enough rooms for when Hilary came. "I'll sleep on the couch when Hilary's here. You can have my room, and Hilary can have the guest room." The thought of Heather sleeping in his bed flashed through his mind, and he pushed it away.

"Kyle, I hate to put everyone out. You really don't want me to go home?"

"No. Let me put it this way. I'd rather owe friends a few favors than let you be put in unnecessary risk."

"This isn't over, is it?"

"No." He got up and went to the refrigerator and pulled out a soda. "Want one?"

She shook her head, holding up her coffee cup.

Opening the can, he leaned against the island. "There's one other thing we need to talk about." It was weird having no one else in the house with them. "You realize since the shooting we haven't been alone until now."

She nodded slowly, those big brown eyes staring up at him.

Yeah, it was best if he stayed over here in the kitchen.

Looking down, she swirled her coffee around in her cup. "We never did talk about what happened last week."

He could just about feel her in his arms. Dwelling on that right now would not be helpful. "I apologize for that. It was my fault. I let things get out of control."

She looked up. "You weren't alone."

"Still, it's my responsibility."

"I didn't stop you. Probably wouldn't have."

He shifted against the counter. "I didn't need to know that."

She gave him a small smile. "Where do we draw the line?"

"When we start losing our common sense, somewhere before that." *Lord, help me to know where that is.* He straightened and moved to stand next to her. "You want to work on our Bible study together?"

"No way we can go?"

He tucked a strand of hair behind her ear. "Why? Sick of my company?"

"Nope. Feel like I'm in jail, but the jailer's pretty cute." She gave him a sassy smile that curled through his chest.

He'd better go get that Bible study.

Chapter Thirty-Eight

Susan Tang set her briefcase on the granite kitchen counter and rolled her neck in a circle. Jack wasn't home yet. Typical. As long as her hours were at *Strive*, he put in longer ones. She wondered if that's why his first wife left him. Or did he leave her? She couldn't remember.

After kicking off her shoes, she opened the stainless steel Sub-Zero refrigerator. Nothing looked good. She'd call Jack and see what he wanted to do for dinner. The sound of the garage door opening filtered through the kitchen. She wouldn't have to call him after all.

She pulled a bottle of Chardonnay out of the refrigerator door and opened the glass-fronted cupboard.

"Pour me one too." Jack's voice came from behind her.

"How'd the arraignment go?" She grabbed another glass and poured while she talked. "I didn't hear from you, so I assumed it was okay." She handed him a glass.

She was keeping her distance from this whole thing. Alex was her stepson. His parents could handle it. She was still mad at him for taking her SUV. He embarrassed her when, after reporting it stolen, she had to go drag him out of jail because his mother was at the fat farm and Jack was on a business trip.

He took a sip before answering. "He's out on bail with orders to stay away from some gang of kids called the Seventeeners. We haven't figured out what that's all about. We got the name of the witness who identified him in the lineup. The thing is, her boyfriend is the cop who arrested Alex when he took your SUV, so he probably influenced her."

"There was a witness? What else isn't Alex telling us? Why is this the first we're hearing of any of this?" It was a good thing that boy lived with his mother. He frustrated her to no end.

"A woman. Heather McAlistair, I think was her name. And Alex isn't telling us anything. His attorney wants it that way." An odd chill stole over her. Surely she hadn't heard correctly.

"What? Heather McAlistair? Are you sure?"

He nodded. "Pretty sure. Why?"

"One of my editors has been on leave for just over two weeks because she's been under police protection. She's coming back to work tomorrow." She made sure she had Jack's attention before she continued. "Her name's Heather McAlistair."

Jack blinked. He stared at Susan then looked away, draining half his glass of wine. "Okay. This could be the break we need. I need her address, the kind of car she drives, anything you can tell me about her we can use against her."

She should have thought this through before telling Jack. She didn't want to ruin her magazine just to bail out Jack's stupid son. Alex had always been Jack's blind spot. He never thought rationally when it came to that boy. "I don't know that there's anything to use against her."

Jack yanked his tie off. "Look, you still want to spend Christmas in Hawaii? That's not going to happen unless we can make this go away. Good attorneys don't come cheap."

She needed to think this out and come up with a plan, then present it to Jack. Right now he was like a dog with a bone, and she really wished she hadn't brought it up. "I don't think she's staying at her house. She was under police protection."

"Find out where she's staying."

The best thing to do would be to make Jack think she was going along with his plan. She reached into her briefcase on the counter and pulled out her phone. "Here's the name of the police officer that called me to say she was going to be out of work. Detective Kyle Taylor."

He frowned. "I think that's the guy who's her boyfriend. I guess one of Alex's friends, Justin, was in your Lexus. According to Alex's attorney, he's a kid this cop's been mentoring, so he's trying to make Alex out to be a bad influence on Justin when, who knows, it might have all been this Justin's idea from the beginning."

Susan drank her wine, letting Jack talk, nodding her head occasionally. She could develop a plan to deal with this situation. Her brain had always been her best asset.

HEATHER WAS STIRRING THE SPAGHETTI SAUCE WHEN THE doorbell rang. Kyle went to get it, and she heard his and Joe's voices. A minute later they were in the kitchen.

"Hi, Heather." Joe opened the refrigerator and grabbed a soda.

"Hi, Joe." She checked the garlic bread in the oven while the guys moved to the family room. Their voices mixed with the TV and echoed off the tile floor, filling a normally empty room. An overwhelming sense of domesticity and normalcy caught her off guard. She pulled the bread out and set it on the stove then let her gaze wander around the room.

The guys settled into the family room, but Kyle caught her eye and winked at her.

This was nice. She could almost imagine it being normal and forget everything outside the house.

Kyle relaxed against the couch, legs stretched out in front of him. She hadn't seen him like that in a while. Joe was good for him. This whole situation had to be hard on Kyle too. Here she was only thinking of herself and how difficult this was for her. But Kyle was always on duty, always looking out for her safety. It had even followed him into his home.

He was a dedicated cop, but how many officers would go this far above and beyond the call?

The pasta threatened to boil over. She stirred it, and then turned it down, glancing at the timer. Still a few more minutes.

Would he have done this for just anybody? She leaned against the counter and studied him.

Work long hours, yes. Open his home, no. So, did that mean he loved her?

She turned back to the stove and stirred the sauce, not wanting to risk his seeing her thoughts on her face. But she couldn't resist a small smile. Maybe he did love her. How would she know?

And how did she feel about him? Did she love him? Or was this situation making her feel obligated to him?

No, that wasn't it. She didn't feel obligated.

The timer beeped. She pushed it off and turned off the stove. Those thoughts were best contemplated somewhere other than in the same room with Kyle and Joe.

After dinner Heather cleaned the kitchen, shooing Kyle into the family room to watch the Angels' game with Joe. He shot her a few curious looks before getting absorbed in the game. Yeah, she knew he was surprised she was cleaning up. She could clean when she put her mind to it. It was just that she usually got distracted by other things. At home, she had her routine for breakfast and dinner and cleaning house, so everything got done. Here, she had to remember to clean up, and that was hard to do.

After the dishwasher was loaded and the stove and counter-tops wiped down, Heather sat back at the table and opened her computer, which the police department had returned. They never could figure out who had hacked into Quinn's account and sent her that e-mail. Might as well get as prepared as possible for work tomorrow. She scanned through her files. All caught up.

What else could she do? She wanted to be ready. Drumming her fingers on her keyboard, anxiety crept into her chest. She closed her laptop and pushed the feeling away. She was going to enjoy a sense of normalcy tonight.

Slipping next to Kyle on the couch, she kissed him on the cheek.

He glanced over and smiled at her, sliding his arm around her shoulders, before turning back to the game.

Yep, normalcy was nice. It didn't last long.

As soon as the game was over, Kyle took her hand and pulled her into the living room. She thought he wanted to kiss her.

"Since you're going to work tomorrow, I want to make sure you're prepared."

She smiled up at him. "Okay. What'd you have in mind?"

"I'm hoping I can always be there to protect you, but a protection force of one can't always be one hundred percent. So, you need to learn to defend yourself. At least long enough for help to get there."

"Oh." That wasn't very romantic.

They spent the next hour with Kyle teaching her various ways to get out of holds and how to fight back. He made her practice over and over until she was too tired.

She flopped on the couch. "My arm hurts." She rubbed it, hoping she'd never need to use what they were just practicing.

Kyle sat next to her. "The main thing is to get over your socialization to be polite, to be nice, and to not make a scene. That can get you killed. Better to be embarrassed and safe. You want to attract attention. Most fights don't last very long. They're not like boxing matches on TV. They wear you out quickly. If you're too difficult, most attackers will move on. Don't ever give up. Keep fighting and struggling no matter how tired you get." He squeezed her knee. "Don't let the bad guys win."

Chapter Thirty-Nine

Heather had gotten up extra early, hoping it would give her time to get her nerves settled. But what Kyle did before they walked out the door totally negated any chance of that.

"I want to show you something." He handed her a small revolver.

She gingerly took it, holding it like a dead fish. "What do I do with this?"

"I've debated this all morning. I probably should have thought of it sooner so we could have gone to the range. We'll do that tonight. Anyhow, here." He moved her hands so she was holding it properly. Then he showed her how to check to see if it was loaded. "Always assume it is."

By the time she made room for it in her purse, her hands were shaking.

Kyle pulled the car in front of her office. Back at work, and she had mixed feelings about it.

He scanned the parking lot before leaning over to kiss her. "Have a good day. Don't leave the building for any reason, even a fire alarm. Call me if you have any questions or anything feels strange. When you know you're going to be free for lunch, call me and I'll come get you."

"Okay. What are you going to do all day without me?" The gun made her purse feel like lead.

A pained look crossed his face. "Paperwork."

She reached for the door handle. "Well, try and have a good day anyway." She climbed out and shut the door behind her, giving him one last smile through the window. All the way to the door she felt his eyes on her. As she opened it, she turned and waved before going inside.

"Hi, Kelsy."

The receptionist turned around, a huge smile on her face, short purple hair spiking around her head. "Heather! You're back. Everything okay?" She came around the desk and gave Heather a big hug.

"Yeah, it's fine now. It's good to be back. I like the purple. It looks good on you."

Kelsy's hand went to her hair. "You like it? I just did it this weekend."

Susan appeared around the corner before Heather could reply. "Good to see you back. There are some proofs on your desk, and I sent you some work via e-mail. The editorial meeting's at nine thirty."

"Thanks. I'll see you then." Susan nodded and left.

Kelsy moved back behind her desk. "Let me know if you need anything."

"Thanks." Heather went into her cubicle and sat down, turning on her computer. She flipped through the stacks on her desk. She was a little lost on what was happening with this issue. Hopefully, she could get herself up to speed before the meeting.

It was good to be back.

THREE HOURS LATER SHE WAS DRAINED.

She hadn't been able to get fully caught up before the editorial meeting and spent most of the time feeling like she was missing half of what was going on. Susan surprised her at one point by asking if she had anything to add. She'd said no, but by the look on Susan's face, she wondered if that was the right answer. Unfortunately, she had no idea what she could have said instead. It was like swimming in the ocean, waves crashing over her, barely giving her time to catch her breath before the next one caught her.

She went back to her desk perplexed and determined to get up to speed as quickly as possible. Swimming farther out would get her out of the breaking zone just as well as moving toward shore. Engrossed in her work, she startled when her cell phone rang.

It was Kyle. "Ready for lunch?"

Chewing her lip, she thought. "I'd kind of thought about working through lunch."

"You need to eat. How'd your morning go?"

"Okay." She looked around. The cubicle walls were thin.

"Something happened and you can't talk about it. Let me take you to lunch, and you can unload on me."

He knew her too well. It sounded wonderful, but the stacks on her desk and her full inbox tied her to this office. "I don't know if I should."

"Heather, it's your first day back. You need to ease into this. We'll make lunch quick. I'll pull up front in about five minutes. Wait inside until you see me."

It was easier to let him decide. "I'll see you then."

Kyle found them a table in the back corner of Baja Fresh and set their tray down. He waited for Heather to sit down, blessed the food, and then asked, "So what happened?"

She poked a chip into the salsa. There wasn't much to say. "Nothing specific. I just felt a little overwhelmed. Susan seems annoyed with me for some reason, like I'm supposed to know what's going on when I haven't been there in over two weeks. It's not like she gave me anything important to do while I was out." She popped the chip into her mouth, chewed a couple of times, and then talked around it. "I'm sure it'll all work out in a day or two. I'm just feeling tired and sluggish, like my brain's not up to speed yet." The food was helping, though. Or maybe it was the caffeine.

"That's all a normal reaction to what you've been through. Just give yourself time."

"I'm just not sure everyone else around me is willing to be patient."

"Want me to talk to her?"

"No. Thanks for the offer, though. I need to work this out myself." She was already sick of talking about work. "How was your morning?" She started eating, waiting for him to answer.

He told her he updated Mark on his conversation with Justin. Then he met briefly with Steve and now had a stack of files in the trunk of his car. When he looked at his watch, Heather realized how much longer she'd spent at lunch than she'd planned. But it was nice. She was glad Kyle had talked her into it.

He dropped her off again with a warning to wait for him tonight. She nodded, took a deep breath, and went back inside.

———

KYLE LOOKED AT HIS WATCH. ALMOST TIME TO PICK UP Heather from her second day back at work. He hoped she was pleased; he had planned a real date for them. She needed the lift. Besides, he missed being with her during the day. He felt bad about last night. She'd been wiped out from her first day back at work, but he'd made her go through the self-defense moves again and to the shooting range anyway. He was more comfortable with her ability to handle a gun safely, but she had been exhausted.

Flowers with a mushy card sat on the table, and they had

reservations at the Salt Creek Grill for seven. It was ironic that as much time as this situation forced them to spend together, their relationship had taken a backseat to her safety. The forced intimacy the situation demanded pushed them to a level their relationship hadn't naturally progressed to yet. It was necessary, but it was a high price.

This case was forcing him to look at the victim's view of crime in a new way. And the cost they paid for trying to do the right thing.

He picked her up at work. She seemed worn-out. Maybe tonight wasn't a good idea. She'd only been back to work two days and might be too tired. On the other hand, a night out might perk her up. He didn't say anything until they pulled into the garage.

She started to open her door, but he put a hand on her arm. "Go out with me tonight."

A smile lit her face, and she let out a breath. "That sounds nice."

"You're not too tired?"

"Nope. It sounds great."

"Good. We need to leave about six fifteen or so."

"I can do that."

They walked into the house, and he watched her face as she spotted the flowers. She looked at him.

"For you. There's a card."

With a half-smile, she opened the envelope.

A little uncertain if he'd said too much, he watched the faint blush steal over her face and her smile widen.

She turned and threw her arms around his neck. "Thank you," she whispered.

He guessed he'd written the right thing.

The front door opened. "Ooh, mushy stuff. You guys should warn me before I walk in on that."

"Hi to you too, Kim." He clasped his hands loosely behind Heather's back. "Don't worry. We're going out tonight."

"Really? Where?"

"It's a surprise."

She raised her eyebrows, looking exactly like their mother.

She considered Heather. "What are you wearing?"

A look of sheer panic raced across Heather's face. "I don't have anything here. Kyle, I need to go by my house—"

"Don't even worry," Kim interrupted. "I've got a closet full of clothes, and you're only a little taller than me. Kyle, let go of her so we can go do girl stuff."

Chapter Forty

Heather let Kim drag her into her room. The walls were periwinkle, and the room looked like it'd come out of a home design magazine—a miniature studio apartment complete with her own small sitting area.

Kim shut the door behind them then opened a closet packed with more clothes than Heather had ever seen outside the mall. No wonder Kim kept the door closed. Kyle had no idea how many clothes his little sister had. He wouldn't be thrilled.

She sorted through the closet, her back to Heather. "Let's see if I know my brother..." She stopped and turned. "Actually, I have no idea about his dating life. I was still in college when he was dating Christa." She made a face.

Heather laughed. She liked Kim a lot.

"She and I didn't hit it off. I wasn't too bummed when she broke up with him." Kim turned back to the closet and pulled something out, tossing it on the small toile-covered chaise. "I was sad for him, of course. He took it pretty hard. You should have seen this house when he bought it. It was a wreck, a total fixer." Two more hangers hit the chaise. "He added the patio, the landscaping, all the tile." She gave Heather a grin. "Once he got it looking nice, I moved in."

She held up one outfit, then another against Heather, tilting her head. "I'm thinking a skirt, maybe a dress." She moved hangers around. "Here. This is it." She held up a wrap blouse with sheer sleeves and flared skirt to go with it. "And I have just the shoes and necklace for it."

Twenty minutes later Heather was out of the shower and in the borrowed outfit, sitting in front of the mirror in Kim's room while Kim did her hair, chattering a mile a minute. Heather loved the outfit, even though it wasn't something she normally would have picked out. Kim had a great eye. And a great closet. This was fun. Already the tension of the day slid off her shoulders.

Her high heels clicked on the tile when she stepped out of Kim's room, makeup a bit more dramatic than usual. She was a little nervous as to what Kyle would think.

Kyle's head turned; then he stood from the couch, eyes sweeping over her in appreciation. He gave her a lazy grin. "Ready?"

Okay, he liked it. She nodded.

"Be good," Kim called from her doorway.

"Don't wait up," Kyle shot back. "Oh, and let Hilary in when she gets here."

They had a wonderful dinner at the Salt Creek Grill. Heather found herself forgetting about Alex, the Seventeeners, her job... everything except basking in Kyle's attention and appreciation. She loved being with him, especially when it was just the two of them.

He thought she was amazing. She had it in writing. She was falling for him.

Hard.

After dinner, Kyle drove down Pacific Coast Highway a bit to where the Ritz Carlton sat next to Salt Creek State Beach. The path down to the beach was a little steep to attempt in heels, but the hotel had a beautiful walking path along the bluff.

He took her hand, and they strolled along the path. It was a chilly night, but she didn't want it to end.

They hadn't walked far when Kyle tugged her into the shadows. Cupping her head with his hand, he kissed her thoroughly. Everything faded away, and it was just the two of them, the promise of how good it could be. She leaned into him, forgetting she was cold.

He touched his forehead to hers, sliding his hands down to her waist. "I've been wanting to do that all night. And I can't kiss you like that at home. It's too dangerous. It's bad enough that tonight you'll be sleeping in my bed."

She tucked her head against his chest, feeling his heart pound. All she knew was that when he held her like this, she didn't want him to let her go.

KYLE YANKED THE PILLOW OFF HIS BED AND GOT AN EXTRA blanket from the closet. The evening had been electric. Heather was beautiful and alluring. It was probably a good thing Kim and Hilary were still up. He glanced around the room, noticing Heather's clothes in the corner of his room, her things in his bathroom. It felt far too intimate.

He ran a hand over his face. He should have thought this through better. But what was the alternative? If it got too bad, he could go stay at Joe's, he supposed, even if Joe was on duty at the station.

No, he couldn't imagine leaving here. Although he trusted Hilary and respected her skills as a cop, Heather was still his responsibility. If anything happened to her because he couldn't control his libido…

He wasn't going to be doing a lot of sleeping tonight.

KYLE BROUGHT OUT THE STUDY GUIDE AND HIS BIBLE AND set them on the table. Heather was pulling brownies out of the oven, and Kim was supposed to be helping. Mostly she was chattering constantly. Since they couldn't go to Bible study, Kyle was trying to bring it to Heather. He had enjoyed going through it with her. Studying the Bible together was one way to keep temptation at bay.

Heather brought over a plate of brownies, and Kim carried the mugs of coffee. Kyle opened the study with prayer.

When they got to the application part of the study, Heather spoke up quickly. She must have worked ahead because she had an answer ready. "Up 'til now, I pretty much could do what I wanted with my time. Which meant my life was made up of my work and my singing, neither of which I've been able to do lately. I've been frustrated with that, feeling empty and a sense of loss. With nothing but time on my hands, I realized how I had gotten sucked into the society here that values you for what you do and how busy you stay. Your importance rests on how valuable your time is. But now I have nothing but time." She shifted and glanced up at Kyle before looking away.

"So the last couple of days I've been thinking about all this. I know God has a purpose in this, even if I can't see it. But I've been thinking about what it might be and what I have been blessed with during this time. And I realized if the result of all this was just to spend time with you and deepen my faith, isn't that enough? I don't know if that's God's purpose, but I've determined to focus on what I have rather than what I don't have."

Kyle squeezed her hand. She *had* been thinking about this. When they'd worked on the study earlier she had expressed frustration and longing, but clearly she'd come around to a kind of contentment. And it pleased him to no end to be considered part of that.

Kim leaned forward. "Do you think that will change when your life goes back to normal? I know for me, I can go on a great retreat or hear a good speaker and have all these resolutions and good intentions. They might even last for a couple of days. But ultimately I find myself back in the same pattern again. Over and over."

Kyle was a little annoyed. Here Heather had spoken up, shared her heart, and Kim was challenging her.

Heather blew out a breath. "I don't know for sure because I'm not there yet. But I guess the difference is, something shifted in my way of thinking. I saw God in a new light, a different facet of Him, I suppose. It's hard to put into words, but it's like I have a new knowledge that I didn't have before. So I can't go back to where I was. I suppose I could forget, or it could slip back into the recesses of my mind. But I have to trust that God will keep reminding me of what He wants me to be aware of."

Kyle jumped in. "Maybe that's the difference. Maybe we try to change our behavior when we really need to change our thinking."

"But what's the trigger?" Kim asked. "What's the thing that makes your thinking transition into behavior?"

Heather flipped open her Bible. "Romans 12:2 says, 'Do not conform to the pattern of this world, but be transformed by the renewing of your mind. Then you will be able to test and approve what God's will is—his good, pleasing and perfect will.' To me, that says my part is to not copy the behaviors and customs of this world. God's part is to transform me. Now the 'renewing of your mind' part, I'm not clear whether that's God or me."

Kyle was following along. "The note here in my Bible says it means a complete change for the better brought about by the Holy Spirit."

"So maybe that's the difference," Kim said. "Maybe it's relying on God to change our thinking as well. Like what God did with you, giving you a new knowledge and shifting your way of thinking."

Kyle was reaching for another brownie when his phone rang. He looked at the display. It was Mark. "What's up?"

"We picked up Bull."

"When?" Kyle stood and paced in the kitchen.

"About an hour ago."

"Has he said anything?"

He practically heard Mark's scowl over the phone. "Nothing useful. Claims that when the shooting started he ran out the back. He was so afraid the shooter was after him, he just flagged down and jumped in the first car he saw."

Kyle finished Mark's thought. "The Honda the witness saw him get into, which matches the same car Heather saw the shooter and friend drive away in." He kicked at the tile floor.

"Yep. And of course, he can't tell us anything about the guys in the car. Maybe two, maybe three. Maybe teenagers, maybe in their twenties. Probably white but maybe Asian. It was dark and he was scared."

"Where'd they take him?"

"To a buddy's house where they played video games late into the night. His friend confirms his story. The parents apparently were already in bed and didn't know Bull was over. But they said that wasn't unusual."

"Nice parental oversight." Kyle shook his head. What a mess. Everyone covering for everyone else. They just needed one of them to break. "I don't remember Bull's car being one left in the parking lot."

"No, this same buddy apparently dropped him off at Jitter Bug, had something to do, then was supposed to come back and meet Bull there later. After the shooting, Bull decided to get a ride to his house instead. Convenient, huh?" Mark sighed into the phone. "We tried hammering away at their story, but their attorneys came in and that was the end of that. Not enough to get a warrant."

Kyle ran his hand through his hair. "Thanks for letting me know, Mark."

"No problem. I'll call again if anything else turns up."

What was he going to tell Heather?

Chapter Forty-One

Bull popped open a beer and leaned back on his couch. Surprisingly, the cops hadn't followed him back to his place. Time to rethink the battle plan. This wasn't a failure. No plan survived contact with battle. The best commanders read the situation and adjusted.

Getting picked up was inevitable, but he knew they couldn't pin anything on him. His only regret was that it had been at his mom's house. She didn't need to see that. The look on her face when the detectives knocked on the door... A marked unit sat outside like he was a criminal. She'd suspected the worst of him. Even after he'd explained they didn't have a warrant, just wanted to question him as a "person of interest" in a crime.

He had to prove to her he was good enough, make her proud of him. He couldn't let her think he was a loser.

Alex and Justin were going to end this thing now. They screwed up. They could fix it.

KYLE PUSHED THE MOWER ACROSS THE LAWN, MAKING THE last pass. Heather's case frustrated him to no end. For the first time in his law enforcement career, he half wished the whole thing would just fall apart and go away so he and Heather could get back to normal. In this life, justice had its limits.

Shutting the mower off, he scanned the yard. The edging could wait another week. He wanted to get back inside to see what Heather was up for. He'd purposely gotten enough of his paperwork out of the way Friday so he could have today free to spend with her. It was strange with her back at work. He found himself missing her company at different times during the day. He missed finding her Diet Coke cans in the oddest places around the house.

After putting the lawn mower away, he headed into the house, stopping in the kitchen to get a bottle of water before hitting the shower.

Heather sat at the kitchen table, completely engrossed in her computer. She didn't even notice when he came in. He hadn't expected her to be out of bed yet.

When he opened the refrigerator, she looked up. He grabbed a water bottle and shut the door. "What are you doing up so early?"

She raised her eyebrows. "It's nine."

"Early for you." He took a drink.

She gave him a sarcastic grin. "Very funny. I brought home some stuff to work on. I'm hoping to get caught up before next week. And I wanted to turn in that tattoo article. I need something to impress Susan."

"Are you doing all that today?"

"Yeah, why not? It's not like I have anything else to do. I'd rather not work on Sunday."

"All right." Irritation flared. He hadn't planned on her working.

"What? Were we supposed to do something?"

"No. I got stuff I can do around here." He drained the bottle. She stared at him for a minute, indecision written on her face. She'd be a terrible cop. He always knew what she was thinking.

He tossed the bottle in the recycling can. "I'll be in the yard. Send Kim out if you need me." He left the kitchen before she could respond.

In the garage, he got the edger out and headed for the lawn. He wasn't sure why it bugged him so much that she was working today. Maybe he was taking too much for granted. What was their relationship based on anyway? His protecting her? What did she feel for him? Gratitude or genuine affection? How would things have been different if they'd had a chance to have a normal relationship? They'd had a good thing going when they'd decided to take this relationship further that night at the Jitter Bug. Before the shooting. Had the shooting ruined any chance of continuing that?

Yet when they were away from here, when it was just the two of them, there was a connection. Look how he'd missed her this week when she was at work. He couldn't imagine her out of his life.

And she was worried about work. It was the one bit of normalcy that had come back, and she was clinging to it, trying to make it work. He should be supportive of that. He'd just assumed that her plans would always involve him. Maybe he'd better get used to asking about her plans instead of just assuming.

Hmm. He had an idea.

Edging done, he swept up the clippings on the sidewalk and driveway. He checked the planting beds for stray weeds, clipped off dead stems. Putting everything away in the garage, he figured he'd given Heather enough time.

He came in, took a shower, then wandered back to the kitchen. "How's it going?" He leaned over the back of her chair, resting his chin on her head.

"Almost done." She moved out from under him. "Give me ten more minutes."

"Okay. What do you want for lunch?"

She didn't look away from the screen. "I don't know. Whatever. I can't think about it right now."

Ten minutes. He could deal with that. Picking up the remote he turned the TV on, thumbing down the volume so it wouldn't disturb her. He had flipped the channels through a couple of ball games before he heard Heather say, "Okay. I think that's it."

"You done?"

"Yeah. Can you read it and tell me what you think?"

He raised his eyebrows and pushed up from the couch.

She'd never asked that before. "Sure."

She turned the computer toward him, and he scanned the article. He liked the way she wrote. Open, friendly. She obviously knew teens. Maybe she could get more out of Justin than he had. "This is great, Heather. I like it."

"Really? You like it?" She chewed on a fingernail. He hadn't seen that before. Susan must be freaking her out.

"Yeah, I do." He slid his arm around her waist. "So, you feel comfortable setting aside your work?"

"Maybe. I guess. Why?"

"I thought you might want to call Sarah or someone to see if they wanted to watch movies and get a pizza tonight."

"Really? I'd love to see Sarah."

"Yep. I'll have Joe pick her up. He'll make sure he's not followed this time," he said, thinking about Monica West following Joe to the basketball court.

"Okay, I'll call her."

"Good. I'll make us some sandwiches while you do that. If Joe left anything in the fridge."

Heather picked up the phone and flopped on the couch. A minute later she was talking to Sarah.

He watched her as he made lunch. It was good to see her relaxed and happy. Hopefully, having Sarah over would put Heather's job out of her mind. He didn't remember her being that tense about work before. Maybe she had been and he didn't know it.

No, he didn't think so. Even when he was in LA, they talked every night on the phone and work always seemed like a fun, positive thing for her, the one thing that was keeping her sane while she was under protection.

What had changed? He thought back over his conversation with Susan when he told her Heather was under protection. Susan didn't think Heather had anything to do with the crime, did she? She'd seemed supportive and concerned. And Kyle had made it clear Heather was an innocent bystander.

But Heather had said Susan had no use for deadweight. Maybe she was just a very bottom-line oriented person. If that was the case, once Heather got back up to speed she'd be fine. She was an asset to any company.

Heather sauntered over. "She's coming. You know, she lives in the same complex as Joe. Here's the address." She slapped a piece of paper on the counter. "She just moved there."

Kyle glanced at the paper and handed her a plate with a sandwich. They ate lunch and Heather seemed to relax, so he put her job situation out of his mind.

A COUPLE OF HOURS LATER, KYLE HEARD JOE LETTING himself in through the front door, accompanied by feminine laughter.

Heather raised her eyebrows and leaned into Kyle. "I'm impressed. Sarah's normally pretty reserved."

"Joe's got the gift of putting people at ease. Comes in handy when you're pulling someone out of a car wreck."

"I bet."

Joe and Sarah appeared in the arch between the dining room and kitchen.

Heather gave Sarah a big hug. "It's so good to see you. You have to catch me up on all the latest choir stuff."

"Absolutely."

"Let me show you what I've done in my spare time." Heather tugged her friend back into the living room.

Joe tossed the movies on the kitchen island then leaned back, looking toward the living room, before turning to Kyle. "Is she attached?"

"Heather? You bet."

"Funny."

"Heather's never said anything, but I'll ask. You interested?"

The sounds of the women's voices moving through the house floated back to them.

Joe raised his eyebrows. "You owe me. Being here every free night cramps my dating life."

"Yeah, that's real active. When was the last time you dated anyone? Last winter, maybe. Or was it the year before?"

Joe shoved him. "Yeah, well, you can make it up to me. Just have Heather invite Sarah over when I'm here. It's a win-win situation."

"I think I can arrange that."

"Good. Consider it payment for my services."

"And here I thought you were doing it out of the goodness of your heart."

"You know me better than that."

A few minutes later, Kyle tracked down the ladies to see what they wanted on their pizza. Apparently, they hadn't made it farther than Kim's room. Laughter filtered out of the slightly open door. Along with the sharp, chemical smell of nail polish.

He rapped on the door, pushing it open as he did so.

Kim was just closing her closet while Heather and Sarah sat on that couch thing Kim had in her room. Bottles of nail polish scattered across the small table in front of the couch.

Kim moved away from the closet and perched on the arm of

the couch, looking up at him, an innocent expression on her face.

She was so guilty.

Of what, he didn't know. Yet.

"Just came to see what you guys wanted on your pizza. But what's going on in here might be a little more interesting. What's in the closet, Kim?"

"Clothes. What else?" She picked up a bottle and shook it against her palm.

"Can I see?" He stepped toward the closet, but she jumped up and edged in front of him.

"Why? Is this *What Not to Wear*? No, wait. That'd be *your* closet."

"Cute." He reached around her. What was it she didn't want him to see?

"Gotta search warrant?"

"Don't need one. It's my house." Emphasizing slightly the *my* in case she had forgotten.

Heather hurried over in front of him, waving her fingers, pushing him back slightly. "What do you think? Like the color?"

He picked up her hand with her nails painted some purple-red color.

She stiffened. "Careful. Don't smudge them. They're not dry yet." She pushed at his chest with the heels of her hands. "Let's go order the pizza. I know what Sarah likes. They still have to finish their nails."

So, whatever it was, Heather was in on it too. Hmm. He'd get it out of her.

He let her push him out of the room. They were in the hall before he asked, "What's Kim hiding from me?"

She shrugged. "Maybe it's your birthday present."

"My birthday's three months away."

"She's an early shopper?"

He'd never known Kim to think about anything more than five minutes in advance. "Not likely."

She sighed. "Don't be mad. She's a clothing designer. She likes clothes."

He blinked. "What does that have to do with anything?"

"She has a lot of them. Which you should be thankful for. She and I are close enough to the same size that I can raid her wardrobe. Otherwise, I'd be asking you to drag my whole closet over here."

He frowned. "This is about clothes?"

"Don't be mad."

"I'm not. I just don't get it. Why would she hide clothes from me?"

She patted his arm with a smile. "It's a girl thing."

Chapter Forty-Two

Heather had to laugh at the confusion on Kyle's face. Such a guy. He didn't get it. While Kyle ordered the pizza, she ducked back to Kim's room. "You're safe for now."

"Thanks. I owe you."

"I'll collect from your closet." Heather grinned.

"What's mine is yours." Kim swept her arm around the room. "This is a great room, Kim." Sarah blew on her dark red nails. "Did you do it yourself?"

"Yep. I had fun. Too bad Kyle wouldn't let me do the rest of the house." She shot Heather a sly look. "But he let Heather."

Heather gave her a sassy smile in return.

"The house is really terrific, Heather," Sarah said. "You did a great job with the colors."

"Thanks. It was fun, and I think Kyle likes it."

"Kyle would like anything you did," Kim said.

Heather wasn't too sure about that, but she was pleased Kim thought so. "Maybe we'd better join the guys. I wonder what movies Joe brought."

Sarah stood waving her fingers to dry them. "We picked out one classic, one guy movie, and one chick flick."

"So. Joe picked you up before going to Redbox?" Heather tried to keep her voice casual. If Sarah thought she was being pressed, she'd clam up.

"Yeah. I thought that was pretty nice of him. Giving us girls a vote at least."

"Cool. I'd figured you and I'd be talking in the kitchen while they watched some action movie."

"Still might happen."

Heather held Sarah back and let Kim go out ahead of them. "Anything new with Ryan?"

Sarah shrugged. "He's nice. We talk before and after practice and in the green room and at the prayer team meeting. But that's it. I just think he likes singing with me. Our voices blend well."

Heather was a little disappointed for her friend, but Sarah didn't seem too bothered by it. Then again, it could be hard to tell when anything bothered Sarah. Heather reached over and hugged her around the shoulders. "I've missed hanging out with you."

Sarah leaned into her, auburn curls spilling over her shoulder. "Me too."

A RINGING NOISE PULLED KYLE OUT OF HIS SLEEP. AT first, he thought it was his alarm. Already? It was too early. No sunlight filtered into the room. The only light came from his clock. Two thirty.

It was his phone. His hand closed over it and brought it in front of his face. He looked at the display.

A sick feeling hollowed his stomach. This wasn't good news.

HEATHER YAWNED AS SHE WANDERED OUT OF HER ROOM. She was tired from staying up late last night. It had been after midnight when Joe had taken Sarah home. But it had been so good to hang out with friends.

Still, she had woken up earlier than normal and couldn't go back to sleep. She felt compelled to pray, but she didn't know for what. After an hour, she felt a little less pressure on her soul and got up. Maybe Kyle would say they could go to church this morning. She didn't see how it was any different than her going to work.

She'd grabbed the coffeepot before the figure sitting at the kitchen table registered. "Hilary. How come you're here?"

"Grab a cup of coffee and have a seat."

The heaviness returned, and Heather continued to pray as she reached for a cup. "Kyle's okay, right?" She didn't feel that Kyle was whom she was supposed to pray for.

"He's fine."

Hilary didn't elaborate, so Heather sloshed some cream in her cup and hustled to the table. "Where's Joe?"

"He went with Kyle. There was a shooting last night. One of our officers, Jeff Griffin, was shot as he drove up to a convenience store. He's alive, one bullet grazed his head, and somehow, another got under his Kevlar near his waist and lodged near his spine. Kyle was his TO, his training officer."

The pressure increased, and Heather's spirit continued to pray as she asked Hilary questions. "Kyle and Joe went to the hospital then?"

"Yes."

"Why Joe?"

"He knows a lot of the ER staff."

She swirled the coffee in her cup, watching the light brown alternately cover and reveal the sides of the mug. "Does this have anything to do with my case? Is the shooting related?"

"I haven't heard the details, but from what I understand, no. This shooter was in his late thirties. There's surveillance camera footage of him. Patino recognized him. He had arrested him before. So it doesn't look like there's a connection." She pushed up her dark bangs. "Just a stupid, random crime."

"That's got to be hard on all of you. How's Kyle taking it?"

"Professionally. None of us will ever see him shaken. But I suspect he'll need you when he gets home."

"Did he tell you when he expected to be back?"

"Should be soon. I've been here since three. I know Kyle wanted to wait until Griffin got out of surgery."

Heather reached over and squeezed Hilary's hand. "Thanks for coming to stay so Kyle could go. I know that means a lot to him. And to me. I know you'd rather be there with everyone else."

"As much as we'd all like to be at the hospital waiting for word on Griffin, the best thing we can do for him is to do our jobs. The detectives are out there now trying to piece together what happened."

Heather nodded. "I'm going to go get dressed." She had no idea how Kyle would take this and included him in her prayers.

Dressed, with her hair and makeup done, she walked back into the kitchen.

Hilary was gone.

Kyle sat in her place, coffee cup in front of him, staring out the slider.

Heather hugged him from behind, resting her chin on his shoulder. "How are you?"

"Okay." His hand moved up to caress her arm.

"How's Griffin?"

"He came out of surgery okay. The doctors won't know the extent of the damage until some of the swelling goes down, but there's a good chance he'll have some paralysis."

"Oh, Kyle. I'm so sorry." She couldn't imagine, didn't have any words of comfort, just continued to hold Kyle in silence.

After a moment, he turned his head and looked at her. "How come you're dressed?"

She tilted her head. "Originally I thought maybe we could

get out of the house, but you probably don't feel like doing that now."

He started to push back his chair, and she moved out of the way. "I'm sorry. I'd rather just stay here. I don't have the energy to protect you properly."

The flat tone of his words unnerved her. It was like he was too stunned to feel. She didn't know what to do. But there was always food. She moved to the kitchen. "Let me make you some breakfast."

KYLE COULDN'T KEEP HIS MIND ON THE SERMON EVEN though it was on the computer screen right in front of him. The normal routine of worship brought a sense of peace and comfort. He felt that. He just couldn't get his mind to engage. He tried to take notes to focus on what the pastor was saying.

All he could think about was Griffin. Just doing something routine, like stopping for a cup of coffee while on patrol, and nearly getting killed by some wacko who had it in for cops. While Griffin wasn't out of the woods yet, the doctors were optimistic about his chances for survival. But not about whether he could ever walk again, let alone be a cop.

If I couldn't be a cop... Kyle couldn't get past that thought. It was who he was. It was who God made him to be. Yeah, intellectually, he knew if God took that away it was because He had a different purpose, but Kyle couldn't imagine it. Didn't even want to go there. *Lord, please, don't ever...*

You're the man I made you to be. Don't confuse that with what you do.

The truth of the words branded his soul. Painful. Marking him as belonging to The One. The I Am.

For now, it was enough. He only hoped he never had to put that to the test.

Heather picked up the breakfast dishes and cleaned up the kitchen after the service was over on the computer. She was glad to not go to church this morning. Without Kyle's help, she wouldn't have been able to remember who thought she was sick, who thought she had a family emergency. And his mind definitely wasn't here this morning.

Kyle had told her Joe had gone to the station from the hospital, so it was just the two of them—and Kim, if she didn't have plans. She'd gone to church and hadn't come back yet. Maybe Heather could take a nap.

She closed the dishwasher. Kyle caught her hand and pulled her to him. He kissed her, his hand massaging the back of her neck.

"What was that for?"

He gave her a small smile. "Just… because." His eyes were the color of the ocean on a cloudy day. If the eyes truly were the window of the soul, were they reflecting his stormy one?

Sliding his hand away from her neck, he broke eye contact.

Kyle spent the afternoon watching TV, while Heather curled up next to him on the couch with a book.

She must have fallen asleep. The last thing she remembered was her head lying on Kyle's chest, feeling the rhythmic rise and fall, and the tempo of his heart. Now he was gone, and she was on the couch all alone.

Sitting up, she noticed the TV was still on, but she didn't see him anywhere. She stood up and looked around.

The slider was ajar.

She looked out. Kyle stood on the patio, his back to her. He didn't turn when she opened the door and stepped outside.

She came up and slipped her arm around his waist, trying to see what he saw.

He gazed down at her, eyes dark. Not breaking eye contact, he pulled her over to his patio chair and sat down, tumbling her off balance and into his lap. He cupped her face in his hands for a long moment before kissing her, gently at first, then hungrily, tangling his hands in her hair.

The world dissolved around her. Just her and the man who held her heart.

The sound of the sliding door grinding open jerked her back to reality.

"Oops, sorry." Hilary stood in the doorway. "Just wondering where everyone was." She disappeared back inside, sliding the door closed behind her.

Kyle's heart pounded under her hand. She trailed her fingers along his jaw.

She loved him.

She didn't look away, not caring if he could see it in her eyes. Wanting him to see it. Maybe he needed to know.

He kissed her fingers. "Let's go inside."

Chapter Forty-Three

Through the glass-fronted office, Heather could see Kyle waiting out front. She hurried out and climbed in the car.

"Bad morning?"

She shook her head. "Let's just say Susan was less than thrilled about my doctor's appointment this morning. I tried to explain to her that I had no idea when I made it that I would be back at work and that I couldn't reschedule. So, I'd better get lunch after the appointment because I won't be able to take it today. I can't do anything right with her lately."

He reached over and rubbed her knee. "I'm sorry. Maybe it's something completely unrelated to you. Is she like this with everyone?"

She thought for a moment. Was it possible she was over-reacting again? "No, just me. She was very complimentary to Brian's latest project but only mildly interested in my tattoo article." She leaned her head against the headrest and sighed.

Kyle continued to rub her knee. That helped.

An hour later Heather hurried back into the waiting room, glad that the doctor's visit hadn't taken long. Kyle sat waiting, the same pensive look on his face since yesterday. Her heart ached. He was taking Griffin's injury hard, analyzing any possible way he could have failed in his training, Heather was certain. He hadn't gotten to the point where he'd accepted it as one of those horrible, unexplainable tragedies of life. Kyle couldn't control everything. He hadn't figured that out yet.

He stood when he saw her.

She slipped her hand into his and squeezed. "How'd it go?"

They left the doctor's office and headed into the hall, toward the elevators. "Good. I can do a light workout, not to the point of fatigue, as long as I have no pain. So, when you go pick up my mail, can you get my free weights?"

"I think I have some light enough for you to use. Maybe just the bar with no weights on it."

"Kyle—"

"I mean it, Heather. You're going to take it easy." He punched the button on the elevator.

She'd expected that. Still, she wasn't done. "What about running? The doctor said it was okay."

"You know you're safest in the house."

"Oh, so I can run around the living room?" She rolled her eyes. "I'm also going insane. With work and everything, if I don't have a way to blow off some of this tension, I'm going to get ugly real fast."

The elevator opened and they stepped inside. He gave her a patronizing look. "I doubt that."

She nearly stomped her foot in frustration. He wasn't getting it. He'd been through a lot. She shouldn't push him. But she'd been so happy with the doctor's release that she didn't want to come crashing back to reality. She wanted to grab hold of that little piece of her life she could control.

Susan watched Heather enter the reception area and chat with Kelsy. Irritation surged through her again, and she strode back to her office. Sinking into her chair, she knew her feelings were unreasonable. And if she weren't more careful, everyone would wonder why her reactions to Heather were excessive.

Spinning her chair around, she clicked on her e-mail icon, letting the messages download without looking at them. Alex had explained it as a prank that had gone bad. It was stupid—he was stupid—but he hadn't intended to hurt anyone.

And if Susan didn't find a solution soon, Alex would continue to bleed away Jack's time and money.

That, she couldn't allow to happen.

She clicked on the address book icon on her computer. In a minute, she had the number she needed. Picking up the phone, she dialed.

Kyle glanced at his watch. Not much time. There were a couple of things he wanted to do before picking up Heather at work. He hated being helpless, a feeling that was reoccurring with disconcerting frequency. He might not be able to help with her work situation, but he could help with something else.

He dialed. "Joe, I need you and your, uh, my truck."

"Aw man, I still don't have my truck back."

Kyle waited. Joe would come around eventually.

"What do you need?" Joe was using his best put-upon tone.

"Can you meet me at Play It Again Sports in half an hour or so?"

"Sure. I have no life. I live to serve you."

Kyle smiled. "I know."

He swung by Heather's condo to pick up her mail and check her house. He wanted to stop by the hospital to check on Griffin before Heather got off work, if he could squeeze it in. It was going to be tight.

Looking down her street, he noticed a car he hadn't seen before. He passed her street, watching, before turning around and coming back. If he were watching her house, that's exactly where he'd position himself. His senses picked up. That would make this guy a professional.

Or it could be nothing.

He pulled down her street, slowly, eyeing the car. The driver had short, spiky hair, a thick chest, and was talking on a cell phone, looking at home-for-sale flyers. A real estate agent.

Or someone posing as one.

He parked in front of Heather's house and got out, making a note of the license plate. He let himself into Heather's house and hurried upstairs, ignoring the stale and slightly rotten smell. He'd have to track that down later.

Her room still smelled like her, though. He peered through the blinds. The guy was still there, but Kyle couldn't tell what he was doing. He punched in Mark's number, told him what he saw, and gave him the license plate number.

Back downstairs he searched the cupboards until he found the trash bags. He grabbed one and started emptying the trashcans. Then he opened the refrigerator. And tried not to gag. Okay. That was what smelled. He dumped what he could down the garbage disposal and the rest in the trash bag. He was just tying it off when his phone rang.

It was Mark. "That car is registered to a PI, and I'm on my way. Think we should have a little talk with him."

Kyle headed upstairs again. Too bad Heather didn't have a front window downstairs. This was a pain. Didn't look like he'd get to go by the hospital, either. Maybe Mark had some news about Griffin.

The PI's car didn't move. Mark drove in a minute later and parked next to Kyle.

Kyle came downstairs and let him in, looking over Mark's shoulder. "Smile. You're getting your picture taken."

"Always nice when a hunch plays out. Let's hope this guy can give us the connection we need."

Mark started to step over the threshold then spun and strode over to the stranger's car.

Kyle followed, slightly to the side.

Mark whipped out his badge. "Let me see your license. Who hired you?"

The PI looked Mark up and down, then glanced at Kyle. "Just doing some surveillance on a case."

Kyle studied him. The Lexus was the right cover car for a real estate agent, but up close, the guy didn't dress well enough to be an agent in this area.

"Yeah?" Mark took the guy's ID and looked it over. "Why don't you tell me about it?"

"I wouldn't be in business too long if I blabbed about my clients."

"We can do it here or at the station. Easy or hard. Your choice."

The guy shot Kyle a look, working his jaw. "Just typical background stuff on a witness for a legal matter."

"Who are you watching?"

Another hesitation. "Name's Heather McAlistair."

"Who hired you? Obviously the defense. The attorney? Or the defendant?"

"My client list is privileged information."

Mark leaned his forearm against the roof. "We could go down to the station to talk about your loitering."

"I was just leaving. She hasn't been home in three days." He shot a look at Kyle. "Wonder where she's staying." His gaze moved from Kyle to Mark. "That's okay. I know where she works." He grinned and started his car. "Nice talking to you guys."

Mark stepped back and the guy sped off.

Kyle closed his eyes momentarily, trying to stave off the blinding frustration. All right, he shouldn't be surprised. He'd suspected this. Man, he wished he could keep her in the house. He wondered—

"Kyle!" Mark's voice cut through his train of thought. He opened his eyes. "What?"

"I said, what time are you picking her up?" He motioned to the townhome. "Let's go inside."

Mark walked in ahead of Kyle and looked around Heather's place. "Cute."

Kyle nodded, crossing his arms.

"Why don't I follow you when you pick up Heather, to see if you get any company."

"I've been careful, but, yeah, it's a good idea. I've got a stop to make before I pick her up." He gave Mark the *Strive* office address. "By the way, any news on Griffin?"

"He's stable and awake for a few minutes at a time, but the docs are still limiting visits to just family. The lieutenant is talking to Griffin's dad a couple of times a day, staying updated."

"I guess that's about as good as we can expect right now."

"Yeah." Mark headed out the door. "See you in a few."

Kyle took the trash out and picked up her mail from the locked cluster of boxes, scanning the area for anything unusual. Nothing. He locked up and looked at his watch. Joe would probably be waiting for him.

A few minutes later he was at Play It Again Sports. Kyle's truck was parked outside. Kyle looked over a treadmill outside the used sports equipment store then headed inside to see what else they had.

Joe was inside browsing the weight machines. "What are you getting?"

"A treadmill for Heather. The doctor cleared her for light exercise, but I don't want her running outside."

He raised an eyebrow at Kyle but didn't say anything. Kyle was glad. He had a suspicion of what Joe was thinking, and he didn't want to talk about it.

He looked around a little more, finally settling on one,

conscious of the fact he didn't have much time. He paid for it, and he and Joe loaded it into the truck.

Once at the house, Kyle and Joe wrestled it inside. "Where do you want it?" Joe paused in the entryway.

"Good question. I was thinking her room, but now that I'm looking at it, I don't know that it will fit. Let's just put it in the living room for now."

"I'm sure that fits with the decorating scheme she had in mind here."

"Hey, you're here often enough to help move it wherever she wants."

They set the treadmill in the corner. Kyle looked at it. "Think she's going to like it?"

Joe just stared at him. "Man, have you got it bad." He smacked Kyle on the shoulder. "I'm going to grab my stuff out of the truck."

Chapter Forty-Four

Kyle got to the *Strive* office early, taking his time driving around the block of office buildings. He should have asked to borrow the truck again. That PI would recognize this car. Mark's, too, for that matter. But he hated to get Joe involved any more than he already was. Wouldn't matter much anyway, since as soon as the PI saw either Heather or Kyle, he'd know what car they were in.

Third time around the block and he hadn't seen the PI yet. That worried Kyle. He wanted to keep this guy in his sights. Just as he was about to turn the corner, he caught a glimpse of Mark turning in front of him. Different sunglasses, different unit. He picked up his phone. "Pull in behind that building. I'm right behind you."

Once they were in an alley behind an office complex, Kyle drove up next to Mark going the opposite way. "Have you spotted him yet?"

"Nope." Mark handed Kyle a radio through the window.

"Me neither. I'm going to go in and get Heather this time. I don't want this guy to try anything funny."

"He's a former sheriff's deputy."

"Huh. So there's a little professional pride at stake." "That'd be my guess."

Kyle ran his hand through his hair. Great. He didn't need this. "I'll call you when we leave."

Mark nodded and Kyle drove off. His eyes flicked to his rearview mirror. He keyed his radio. "I think I see him."

In an office complex parking lot across the street, nearly hidden behind shrubs and trees, but with a sightline to the *Strive* office door, sat a black Navigator. PIs must do pretty good in Orange County, given this guy's taste in cars.

Kyle only noticed it because it was parked on the side of an office building instead of in the front where there were still a few open spaces. Kyle turned into a parking lot where he could drive parallel to the one the PI was in. Maneuvering until he could get a clear view, he confirmed it was the guy. He gave Mark the info then headed around the back way to Heather's office, using the buildings to shield him from the PI's view.

Parking in a fire lane, he hopped out and strode to the office door, resisting the urge to turn and wave in the direction of the PI.

A young woman with spiky purple hair sat at the receptionist's desk, one of those tall, curved things with some sort of metallic finish on the front. She had to be sitting on a high, adjustable chair. "Can I help you?"

"I'm here to pick up Heather whenever she's done."

The receptionist beamed at him. "I'll let her know you're here."

"Thanks." Kyle found a seat and looked around.

She reached in front of her toward something out of his line of sight, her Bluetooth headset reminding him of that communications officer in the really old Star Treks. He couldn't hear what she said, but he heard a giggle and saw her glance his way. Kyle picked up a magazine and thumbed through it. It looked like last month's issue of *Strive*. With regular glances out the window, he scanned the table of contents. Heather was listed on the masthead and had her name next to a couple of articles. He flipped to them.

He was halfway through the first one when he heard her voice. "Hi." She was smiling at him.

She was a sight for sore eyes. "Ready to go?" he asked, standing.

She nodded, her smile faltering.

He scanned the room. A woman with short, black hair stood in the hallway watching them. His gaze slid past her, and he nodded toward the door. Outside, he used his body to shield Heather as much as possible from the PI, keeping her close to the building until they reached his car. He radioed Mark. "We're leaving."

"I see both of you."

"Let me know what happens."

"Copy that."

He glanced in the rearview mirror. The Navigator followed them, several cars back.

Heather frowned. What was going on? First Kyle met her in the office then herded her to the car like a sheepdog. Now he was talking to someone on the radio. "I thought no one else was on this case."

"Mark's helping me out." He didn't say any more until they were at a stoplight. "There was someone watching your place when I went by there today. He's behind us now. Mark's helping me make sure I lose him before we get home."

A jolt of fear coursed through her body, but she refused to let it get a foothold. Kyle knew what he was doing. It was his job. He'd get them home safely. A glance at him could be deceiving, though. His body was relaxed, arm resting on the car door, hand lightly on the steering wheel. But his eyes were intense, focusing ahead and then in the rear and side mirrors.

Heather didn't want to distract him by unloading her day on him. Once they were safely home she could. But it had been so good to see him in the foyer, tears had welled up and she had forced them back.

She sat quietly, occasionally watching Kyle as he changed lanes, made U-turns, and generally took a circuitous route home. Just as she was wondering how long this would go on, Mark's voice came over the radio. She didn't understand what he said, but Kyle obviously did.

"We lost him." Kyle reached over to squeeze her hand. His eyes lost some of their intensity but still flicked between the mirrors. "I wonder if we'll be playing this game every day. It's going to get old."

Heather swallowed. Her job was becoming more and more of a problem. There was no way Susan was going to give her any more time off. She covered her face with her hands. *God, what am I supposed to do?*

"I have a surprise for you when we get home." Kyle looked pleased with himself.

"Really?" More flowers? That'd be nice. She guessed she'd see when they got home.

They pulled into the garage. Once they were out of the car and entered the house, Kyle took her hand and led her into the living room.

Which now held a treadmill. Was that her surprise?

Kyle tugged her over to it. "I know you miss running, so I thought this might help." He looked at her, waiting for her reaction.

Tears sprang to her eyes. The harder she tried to hold them back, the less she was able to. She tried to speak but couldn't.

"If you don't like it, I can take it back."

She shook her head. Now he thought she didn't want it, and she couldn't speak. She waved her hand in front of her face, barely able to catch her breath.

"Sweetheart, what is it?" Kyle pulled her into his arms and the dam burst. She bawled uncontrollably.

It took a minute before she thought she could say something coherent. She wiped at the wet spot dotted with mascara on his shirt. It would need stain remover. Great, one more thing she'd ruined. Couldn't she do anything right lately?

Kyle rubbed her back and looked at her. "You okay?" She shook her head. "Susan didn't give me any new assignments, just copy editing. And given the look on her face, I didn't dare ask her why. Even Brian noticed it and gave me a sympathetic look. And I hate that. I don't want anyone's pity. I just want to do my job. If I've done something wrong, I wish Susan would just come out and say it. I don't know how much longer I can work under these conditions. I thought maybe it would blow over in time, but now, with this guy following us… Oh, Kyle. I don't know what I'm going to do."

She glanced over at the treadmill. "And that's wonderful. Just what I needed. You're so sweet and good to me. I don't know what I'd do without you."

"Come here." He pulled her over to the couch. He pushed her hair from her eyes, tucking it behind her ear, studying her a moment. "I can't do anything about Susan, but it's not like you to give up. I think you should just keep going to work until she tells you what's wrong. Mark and I will do whatever we need to do to get you there and home safely. Don't worry about that."

She nodded, wiping her eyes with the back of her hands.

"So you like the treadmill?"

"I do. Thank you. That will help a lot."

"I know it's not anything fancy like what Quinn could have gotten you."

She frowned. Where was this coming from?

"Now that you two have made amends, do you ever see yourself going back to him?"

She studied his face. For the first time, she saw vulnerability in his eyes. "No. I'm glad Quinn and I are on good terms now, but I know he wasn't the one for me."

Kyle trailed a finger down her jaw. "Good." The air caught in her lungs.

"Mmm." He leaned in and kissed her softly, tenderly. Did he think *she* was the one for him? Could he *love* her?

He broke the kiss, and she snuggled up against him. This was the perfect way to end a day.

Footsteps sounded on the tile. "So how do you like it?" Joe asked.

Heather tilted her head to see him over the back of the couch. "I love it. I'm going to use it tonight."

"Good. Every once in a while, Kyle has a good idea." Joe winked at her.

Heather patted Kyle's knee. "He's had a few good ones. I'll keep him around."

SUSAN'S CELL PHONE RANG. SHE GRABBED IT OFF HER DESK. It was Jack, probably wondering why she was still at the office. He could work long hours, but when she did... "Are you home?"

"Yes and you must still be at the office." Jack's tense voice came through the phone. "That plate you gave me on the car that picks up Heather is an unmarked cop car. And she hasn't been home since he's been watching her place. You're going to have to get me more info on her soon."

She closed her eyes, resisting the urge to snap back at him. He had no clue what a mess his son was making of her life. "I've given you everything I have. I don't know what else you want."

"I want to end this situation."

"Me too. I'm working on it, okay? I'm making some calls and, hopefully, I'll have an answer tomorrow."

"We need something soon. It's getting expensive." How well

she knew. "I'll be home in half an hour." Jack grumbled then hung up.

She'd have to find a replacement for Heather soon. Susan was tired of figuring out how to shuffle around the work without anyone knowing. That's why she ran the business side of things. But this magazine, and her reputation, wasn't going to suffer because of Heather McAlistair. Soon she'd be out of here, and Susan could breathe easy again. She hoped Alex appreciated it. But being the selfish teenager he was, she was sure he wouldn't.

Chapter Forty-Five

Heather hung up the phone. She'd given Sarah a rundown on the day while Kyle was getting dinner. It helped, but something rolled around in her brain.

She wanted to try out the new treadmill, so that'd be a good time to work out her thoughts.

She changed into a T-shirt, shorts, running shoes, and then grabbed her iPod, and on an impulse, her Bible. She put it on the book rack and flipped through it. Something Sarah had said about our circumstances changing us, about continually being renewed.

There it was. Colossians 3:10: …put on the new self, which is being renewed in knowledge in the image of its Creator.

She started walking on the treadmill, familiarizing herself with the buttons. Confident, she picked up the pace.

The part about continually being renewed struck a chord with her. This experience, as painful as it was, had taken her to a new level.

A renewal.

Heather had been a new creature in Christ most of her life. And yet, this time, this isolation rocked her to the core. It was so unlike anything she'd ever experienced. She'd become complacent. She knew she was saved. She knew God loved her and that she was generally living a life that honored Him. But that passion, that sense of continually being renewed, that sense of clinging to Him every moment had been missing. That sense of awe of who He was making her to be.

Before the shooting, if anyone had asked a deep enough question, Heather would have said she pretty much had her walk with Christ figured out. But now she knew she didn't have a clue, like the ground had shifted under her, and she didn't know how to stand anymore. Everything familiar was gone, and she had been forced to cling to Him.

She tried a light jog. It felt okay, so she kept going. It wasn't like she *enjoyed* what she'd gone through. The stress, the disruption in her life, and now her failure at work. It was horrible, and she hated it. Nothing was routine. There was nothing she could call her own, not even her bed.

And yet, that verse in James that she had memorized long ago in Sunday school, rang oddly true: Consider it pure joy, my brothers and sisters whenever you face trials of many kinds, because you know that the testing of your faith produces perseverance. Let perseverance finish its work so that you may be mature and complete, not lacking anything.

Before, she'd never been able to get past that "consider it pure joy" part. How could trouble be an opportunity for joy?

The fatigue built in her legs, but she pressed on. It was the perfect picture of this verse. She barely tolerated running, but she liked it better than she used to. While she didn't feel it in the moment, over a period of time she felt less tension, more energy, and generally better all around. She'd missed the relief running gave her from tension during one of the most stressful times of her life.

Kyle walked in the room. "How do you like it? Is it working well?"

"I like it." She could barely speak the words she was so out of breath. "I'm out of shape though." She slowed to a walk and took a couple of deep breaths. "Remember that time we went running?"

He grinned. "Yep."

"We talked about running the hills here. I hate running those hills. But maybe if I'd done it more often, I'd be in better shape."

"Maybe. Hard to say. Inactivity's the worst thing, but you were a good runner before. It'll come back to you more quickly than if you were starting from zero."

She nodded. "Probably true. What about you? I know this has messed up your workouts too." She knew Kyle had been running while she was at work or only when he knew someone else was here to protect her. He wouldn't leave her alone.

"Well, I thought maybe if I was nice to you, you'd let me use this too." He tapped the treadmill.

"I think that can be arranged." She stopped and stretched. "Why do you run? Other than to stay in shape. What other benefits do you get?"

"Ultimately, so I'm in better shape than the bad guys. I have to keep challenging myself with hills and longer running times so when the time comes and I need that endurance, I'm glad I have it. Why?"

She switched legs. "I don't know. I was just thinking. Paul often compares an athlete training to the Christian life. I've always known that but lately, it just seems that while my physical training has been completely shot, my spiritual training has been brutal. I've had to use spiritual muscles I didn't know I had. Growing pains, I guess."

"There's definitely a parallel there. Just like you can't expect to run four miles when you don't go more than ten steps out your door, neither can you expect to have instant spiritual maturity when you need it."

Heather plopped down on the couch. "Problem is, I thought I *was* spiritually mature."

"Different levels. You hadn't gone through this before, but

if you didn't have your spiritual grounding, you would have had a more difficult time adjusting, would have spent more time adrift. The comparison to training makes a lot of sense here."

"I suppose. I just want to 'be there' already. Whatever that means."

"I know. Me too." He sat next to her. "Sometimes I think about the things God throws at us or allows to happen to us. Something like what happened to Griffin. It scares me. I don't want that to happen to me. I don't care how mature I'd be on the other side of it. I flat-out don't want to go through it." He picked up her hand and kissed it. "I learned something from you."

She raised an eyebrow. "What's that?"

"You've had your whole life turned upside down, and yet you're still you. *You* define your life. Not your job, not your singing or painting or where you live or what you drive. Just the person God made you to be."

Heather cocked her head. "You see that?"

"Yep. And it's encouraging, because whatever God throws my way, however much I might hate it, I'll still be me. I won't be destroyed." He squeezed her hand. "You taught me that."

She was stunned. Here she'd thought this had all been about what God was teaching her. Just goes to show, it wasn't all about her.

Kyle stood and stepped on the treadmill. "Show me how this thing works."

SOMEONE GRABBED JUSTIN'S SHOULDER AND SPUN HIM around.

Bull.

His stomach twisted. So much for lunch. He'd lost his appetite. Justin had heard Bull was around but had so far been successful at avoiding him. After the last job, and with Bull and Alex getting picked up, everyone was laying low.

"What do you want?" Justin shoved his hands in his pockets and glanced around. Kids moved between classes, talking with their friends, not paying Bull and Justin any attention.

"Alex is in trouble. We need you to get us some info on the girlfriend of that cop friend of yours."

"What do you mean?" He stalled, trying to come up with a way out of this mess while keeping his body intact from the beating that would come if Bull didn't like what he said.

"No one seems to know where she's staying. You helped us out last time. We just need you to do it again."

Justin felt sick. He'd half hoped Alex would have gotten caught last time. He had no clue they had planned on shooting her and Kyle. "I don't know where she's at. No one does."

Bull pounded his shoulder. "I'm sure you'll figure something out. Unless you want them to know you were driving the getaway car. What would your cop friend think about that?" Bull grinned at him. "I'll meet you at your car after school. Think of something by then." He sauntered off, slapping hands with a couple of guys as he walked down the hall.

Justin sagged against the wall. He was in over his head. Glancing over his shoulder, he headed out to the parking lot.

———

KYLE SET THE STACK OF FILES ON HIS DESK THEN wandered over to see if Mark was in.

He was.

Kyle leaned against the cubicle frame. "Making any progress?"

Mark sighed. "Nope. Got any ideas?"

Straightening, Kyle said, "Maybe." He pulled out the other chair and sank into it. "There's something about Heather's boss, Susan Tang. She's been pretty hard on Heather since she's been back. The funny thing is, she seemed accommodating when I talked to her on the phone. I thought I'd look at my notes again and see if I could figure something out. See if it has anything to do with the case. It's a long shot, I know. But I can't just sit by and not try and help her through this."

Mark nodded absently and slid over the box containing the case files. He stopped. "What'd you say her name was?"

"Susan Tang."

Mark frowned. "Hmm." He started digging through the file.

"What?"

"Well, I think… Ah, yeah. Here it is." He flipped through some pages. Then turned one toward Kyle and pointed. "She's Alex's stepmom. It was her Lexus that was reported stolen; then she came and bailed him out."

Kyle looked at the words but didn't see them. Thoughts tumbled through his brain faster than he could make sense of them. "She didn't know Heather was the witness until the arraignment when the defense got Heather's name."

"That makes sense."

"So what's she up to now? Why make Heather miserable and not just come out and be honest?"

"How many people do you know who are honest?"

"You have a point," Kyle conceded. "Keep your friends close and your enemies closer."

"The PI. Susan fed him whatever info she could on Heather."

"That's not much more than he could have gotten anyway." Kyle tossed the paper on the desk in frustration. Knowing why Susan was being hard on Heather didn't help much. Susan hadn't broken any laws.

He didn't like Heather being so close to the suspect's stepmom. He looked at Mark. "Any suggestions?"

"I'll call and talk to the assistant DA. I don't think he'll be pleased about the situation. I'm sure he'll warn Heather not to talk to Susan about the case. And I think it gives us more ammunition with the lieutenant to justify my helping you escort her home. But I think we both know the best thing is for her to be out of there."

He blew out a breath. "Yeah, things aren't going to get better at work if Heather's testimony convicts her boss's stepson. I hate to give her more bad news. It's not like she can really go looking for a new job now anyway." He shook his head. "Never realized the high cost of trying to do the right thing before."

"Not always fair, is it?"

Kyle stood. "I'm going to get some coffee. Want some?"

"No thanks."

Heading to the coffee machine, Kyle tried to figure out what to tell Heather. He'd tell her the truth, of course, but what was she going to do? Was there another opportunity around here for her? Maybe she could freelance. He didn't want her to worry. No matter what happened, he'd take care of her.

He loved her.

The words settled into his heart. He hadn't thought those exact words before, but the realization didn't surprise him. It felt more like the obvious conclusion to a series of questions.

How to tell her? Would it soften the blow about her job, or would she think it was just pity? He needed to do something to show her. Something tangible. Maybe a little more romantic than a treadmill.

She was his.

Chapter Forty-Six

Bull slammed his hand on the hood of his Explorer and swore. Justin had bailed. That little snot was going to pay and big. His friends too. He tossed a glare at Alex in the passenger seat. "The PI hasn't been able to find where she's staying. It's not anywhere on the LVPD computer system. That leaves us one option. We know where she works. We'll have to do it there."

His stomach was churning. He didn't like that feeling.

Made him want to smash something.

Alex crossed his arms. "So? That cop is always there to pick her up and take her home."

"Then we just need to get her out of the building in the middle of the day." Alex had no vision. If Bull didn't take over this plan, Alex was going to screw it up for all of them.

"Or I could get in."

"Yeah, you're so close to your stepmom you always come by." But the idea had possibilities. It was about the only thing they had to go on. But Alex couldn't screw it up again.

"I could say I came to borrow some cash. She'll give it to me just to make me go away."

"Okay, genius, then what? You gonna walk up to her and tell

her not to testify? What are you going to threaten her with? You dumped the gun in the ocean off Trestles when you went surfing, remember? Plus, she'll recognize you and won't go anywhere with you."

Alex smiled. "There's an alley in the back with a back exit. People generally use it for smoking breaks. But I bet we could use it for something else."

This plan had to work. It just had to. He wouldn't be a failure.

———

Kyle drummed his fingers on his desk. What should he get Heather? He looked at his watch. There wasn't much time.

Kim would know. He picked up the phone. "Hey, big brother."

"I need a favor. I want to get Heather something kind of special, but I don't know where to go."

"Ooh, what'd you have in mind? Jewelry?"

"Yeah."

"I knew you were in love with her."

"Kim."

"What?"

Her innocent tone didn't fool him. "Don't say a word to Heather."

"I won't. I promise. I don't want to ruin your surprise."

"Where should I go?"

Kyle wrote down the stores Kim gave him and, after eliciting another promise from her, hung up. He'd have to do this soon. Kim couldn't keep a secret to save her life.

———

Susan smiled as she hung up the phone. It was the call she'd been waiting for, and it was good news. Jack would be pleased. They should go somewhere nice for dinner.

Now to inform Heather she'd just been given the opportunity of a lifetime.

Heather saw the e-mail pop up on her screen. Dread sank into her stomach. Great. Susan wanted to see her. What else could go wrong?

She took a deep breath, said a quick prayer for... Well, she didn't know what, but God knew what she needed. She pushed back from her desk. Might as well get this over with.

She knocked on the door frame of Susan's office. Susan looked up. "Come in. Close the door behind you."

That was not a good sign. She was going to get chewed out or fired; she just knew it.

Heather closed the door then sat, squeezing her hands together in her lap.

Susan watched her for a moment. "I'll get right to the point. I don't think it will come as a surprise to you if I tell you things have been awkward since you've been back. While we value your skills, when you were gone we discovered the team worked well without you."

Here it came. Bad news, just like she thought. Don't cry. Don't cry. Don't cry. *Lord, please, that's the last thing I need.*

Susan took a breath. "Because I value your skills as a writer and the contribution you've made to this magazine, I wanted to find a place for you where you'd work out better. I made a few calls to my contacts and found that there's a managing editor position that's essentially yours for the taking."

Heather couldn't quite process what she was hearing. Susan didn't want Heather here, but instead was offering her a promotion at another company? Maybe this wasn't going to be so bad at all. Just confusing.

Susan slid a business card across the desk. "Here's the publisher's card. He's expecting your call."

As she picked up the card, Heather's hands shook slightly. She hoped Susan didn't see. Not much chance of that. Susan noticed everything.

Heather scanned the card. It took a minute for the pieces to fall together. "This address is in New York. Do they have a local office?"

Susan blinked in what seemed like surprise. "No. They're in New York."

Heather felt like a rock had stuck in her throat. She could barely speak. "But I live here." She almost laughed at the absurdity of it. This was like being in Quinn's shoes a year ago.

"I'm sure they'll arrange to pay your relocation expenses."

Mind whirling, Heather didn't know what to think, but Susan was standing. The discussion was over.

"It's a chance-in-a-lifetime career opportunity, Heather. I went to a lot of trouble to pull strings for you. If you don't want to take it, fine. But you don't have a job here anymore. Take the rest of the day off to think about it."

Somehow, though it didn't seem by her own strength, Heather got out of Susan's office and back to her own. She sank in the chair and stared at the partition. The thought of everyone she'd miss, the projects… Stop it. She was going to make herself cry. Wait until she got home.

Home.

She needed to call Kyle to come get her.

Chapter Forty-Seven

Heather held it together until she got in the car. But the moment Kyle pulled away, she burst into tears. He reached for her hand.

She hadn't told him why she needed him to come get her early. There was no way she could without breaking down. He hadn't asked; he'd just said he'd be there in five minutes.

They were nearly home—with apparently no tail this time—before she could speak coherently, telling him about her meeting with Susan.

"I think I know why." His quiet voice surprised Heather.

He told her what he and Mark had discovered.

Heather's head hurt. There was too much information for her to piece together. "So Susan just wanted me out of the way, hoping that if I went to New York I wouldn't testify?"

"Maybe. Or maybe she just knew she couldn't continue to work with you and really was trying to find a better place for you." He squeezed her hand. "I do know that I feel better not having you in close proximity to her."

"I can't believe this. Just when I think I've got a handle on things, something else gets thrown at me." She laid her head against the headrest and closed her eyes.

"Do you want to go to New York?" She turned her head to look at him.

He stared out the windshield, but his thumb didn't stop

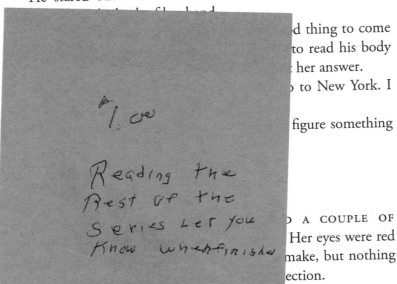

d thing to come
to read his body
her answer.
to New York. I

figure something

A COUPLE OF
Her eyes were red
make, but nothing
ection.

Maybe the price was too high. She didn't want to go to New York, but she had family in the Valley that she would like being close to. Maybe they should both consider leaving the area. He could get a job with another police department. They could start over.

They'd be running away. Wouldn't they?

If they left, all his talk about never giving up, never letting the bad guys win was just a bunch of hot air.

But Heather had already paid a high price. When was it enough?

They needed to get out of the house. He wasn't thinking clearly.

"How does dinner out sound? We could call Sarah, Melissa, bring Joe."

He watched as she tossed down the medicine and swallowed the soda. "Sounds good."

"Okay. I'll make the calls." He thought of the package in his dresser drawer that he'd gotten at lunch. He'd wait for a better time. A time when she wouldn't associate a good memory with a bad one. At this rate, though, he wondered when that would be.

Susan waited for Jack at their favorite restaurant. She felt like celebrating now that the issue with Heather was out of the way, and the problem of Alex should soon be wrapped up.

There he was. Through the window, she saw Jack's black BMW pull up. He got out.

Alex climbed out of the passenger side. Her heart deflated. What was he doing here? He was supposed to be grounded.

Jack came through the door, looking a little harried, and kissed her cheek. "Hi."

She nodded toward Alex. "I thought he was at his mom's." Alex, arms across his chest, smirked at her. Based on those telltale white wires coming out of his ears, he was listening to music. He had no manners. But it wasn't her job to teach him any.

"She had some last-minute thing to go to. I didn't understand it all. Anyhow, we can't leave him alone, so I had to go get him."

So much for a nice dinner.

"Let's just eat, okay?" Jack signaled the hostess.

Once they were seated, drinks ordered, and menus perused, Jack turned to Susan. "How'd it go today?"

"I gave her the news about the job offer in New York. She seemed stunned, but I made it clear she didn't have a job at *Strive* any more. You did call off that private investigator, didn't you? We don't need to be paying his daily rate when the situation's taken care of."

Alex slouched in his chair across the table, playing with his silverware tapping it in time to whatever ridiculous stuff he listened to.

"You know, Alex, you could show a little respect. Your father and I have gone to an awful lot of trouble to get you out of this mess. You could at least be grateful."

He looked up at her without moving anything but his eyes. "I didn't ask for your help."

Susan shoved down the rising irritation. Alex always knew how to push her buttons, and he enjoyed doing it. She wouldn't give him the pleasure. "Well, you got it anyway. Now that we've taken care of everything, I hope you'll learn something from it."

Alex sat up straight, leaning his elbows on the table. "What exactly did you fix? I'm still in the custody of my parents. I still have a hearing coming up. I don't see anything's changed."

Jack stared at his son. "Susan used her professional contacts to find a job for one of her best editors. Not only did she have to pull some strings, but also potentially hurt her own company. Just to help you out. Now I don't think a little gratitude would be out of line."

With a short laugh, Alex leaned back in his chair. "That's it? You got her a job someplace else? How is that supposed to solve anything?"

Susan wanted to strangle this boy. How had Jack raised him to be so ungrateful? She closed her eyes. "It's in New York."

"So? You've never heard of planes? Daily nonstop flights to New York from John Wayne Airport. That's the big solution I'm supposed to be grateful for? You guys are amazing. Are all adults this stupid?" He tossed his silverware on the table, the loud clatter bringing a few stares from neighboring tables.

Jack leaned in close to Alex. "Knock it off. Or so help me I'll make your life miserable."

"Congratulations. You're doing a great job."

A POUNDING AT HIS DOOR MADE ITS WAY THROUGH THE pillow over Justin's head.

"Justin? Are you up?" It was his mom's voice. He heard the door open. "You're going to be late to school."

He yanked the pillow off his head. "I'm not going. I'm sick."

"It's a little late in the year for the flu."

"I think it might have been something I ate. My stomach doesn't feel so good." Which was true. The thought of going to school made him sick. Of course, going to school wouldn't be too good for his health, either.

His mom studied him. He could tell she was considering whether to believe him or not.

It didn't matter. No way was he going to school today.

Maybe not ever.

"Okay, go back to sleep then maybe try and keep some crackers and 7-Up down when you wake up."

Good. She bought it. "Okay." She shut his door.

He needed to call Kyle. Should have done that a long time ago. Kyle was the only one who could help him now.

But first, he was sleeping in.

Chapter Forty-Eight

Heather dressed and wandered out to the kitchen and poured herself a cup of coffee. The moment she told Susan she wasn't going to take the New York job, she'd be fired. She couldn't imagine Susan letting her hang around the office for a couple of weeks. And given what Heather now knew about Susan's connection to Alex, Heather didn't want to hang around there, either.

She reached into the refrigerator and grabbed the cream, dumping a healthy amount into her mug. All that was left for her to do was to tell Susan her decision and go to the office to clean out her desk and say a few good-byes. She choked up at the thought of that. She liked the people she worked with. It was just too bad Susan was their boss. Why couldn't Susan leave? That seemed like the best solution.

Too bad life didn't work out that way.

After taking a sip of coffee, she peered into the living room.

Kyle was already working, laptop open, files spread over the coffee table. He looked up. "Hi. How'd you sleep?"

"Better than I thought I would. I think going to dinner last night with everyone helped. It didn't allow me to brood over this whole thing." She eased down on the couch next to him.

"Are you going to call her this morning?"

"I suppose. Get it over with."

"When do you want to go into the office to get your stuff?"

"When Susan's not there. I'd just as soon not see her again." She sighed. "Although, I guess that's not possible. I don't know, maybe this afternoon? I'd like to say goodbye to everyone before they leave for the day. And if Susan knows that, maybe she'll make herself scarce and knock off early."

"Okay. How about I drop you off, run to check on Griffin for a few minutes, and then come back and get you? Does that work, or do you want me to stay with you?"

"I think I'll be okay. It won't take me too long to pack up my desk, but I imagine I'll be awhile visiting with everyone, especially if Susan isn't there." She didn't want to say goodbye to everyone. "Maybe I can arrange to meet them all for lunch next week when this isn't so raw."

"That's a good idea." He patted her knee. "You'll be okay, you know that, right?"

She gave him a half smile. "Yeah. I know." Leaning over, she kissed his cheek. "I'll go make that call."

SUSAN PINCHED THE BRIDGE OF HER NOSE. HEATHER McAlistair was a fool and an idiot. Susan couldn't believe Heather had basically said thanks but no thanks to the New York job. Had Susan been in Heather's shoes, she'd have jumped at the chance.

Well, it didn't matter much anyway. Without a job, Heather would be susceptible to pressure. And who knew, she might still get desperate enough to take the New York job. Susan wasn't going to worry about it. She'd done her best to help Alex, ungrateful though he was, and she was done with the whole mess.

She was going to Hawaii for Christmas. With or without Jack.

KYLE GLANCED AT HEATHER. SHE'D BEEN A LITTLE ANXIOUS since they left the house. He'd expected that. But once this was behind her, she'd feel better. Especially after what he had planned for tonight. It was Joe's night to work, but Hilary would be happy to help him out. The moon was nearly full, so he was thinking a walk along the beach in the moonlight. Then he could give her his gift and tell her he loved her.

He couldn't wait.

Reaching over, he picked up her hand and kissed it. "You'll do fine."

She nodded.

They pulled in front of the *Strive* office. "Call me when you're ready for me to pick you up. I'll be about ten minutes away. While I'm up in the ICU with Griffin, I won't be able to have my phone on, so if you need me right away, leave me a voice mail. I'll check it often."

Biting her lip, she nodded. She was holding back tears. To cheer her up, he said, "We'll do something fun tonight, okay?" He leaned over to kiss her. "I'll see you in a few."

She climbed out of the car, and he watched her enter the office. She turned inside the door and gave him a small wave.

He waved back.

Through the glass he could see the purple-haired receptionist come around the desk and give Heather a hug.

HEATHER HUGGED KELSY. THIS WAS GOING TO BE HARD.

"Susan said you were leaving us, that you were taking some personal time before possibly taking another job."

Heather squeezed her before pulling back. So that's how Susan was spinning it. Well, if she didn't want the whole office to know her stepson was a juvenile delinquent, it wasn't Heather's place to tell them. As much as she wished everyone knew she was the victim here. No, it wouldn't be right. "I'm not sure what's really happening now. Let's all try and go to lunch next week. Maybe I'll figure it out by then."

Kelsy wiped at her eyes. "Okay. I'll set something up with everyone and let you know. Stop by and see me before you leave."

"I will."

Heather moved into her office without running into anyone else. An empty box sat on her chair, and an envelope was propped up between the keys of her keyboard. She picked up the envelope and slit it open. Her last paycheck, with a bit extra, and a letter of recommendation, somewhat generic but not too bad.

Susan had thought of everything. As usual.

Heather tucked the envelope into her purse, pausing to push the gun to the side. Thinking again, she rearranged things so the gun was the first thing she could grab—and hoped she didn't have to. She put the box on the floor. She pulled out her jump drive and turned on her computer. There were e-mails and a few other documents she wanted to download and then erase.

After she had checked each folder and copied everything to the jump drive, she began packing up her office. There wasn't much; she wasn't the type to fill her office with a ton of stuff from home. But still, there were silly things people in the office had given her, pictures and jokes she'd printed out, photos of people she'd interviewed, copies of every issue she'd worked on. A couple of people stopped by as she packed. That helped break up her propensity for tears. Everyone seemed a bit unsure as to what to say, so Heather simply said Kelsy was setting up a lunch for all of them sometime next week.

She wouldn't be here when the next six issues came out. She wrote a note down for Kelsy to send her a couple of copies of each. She especially wanted the one with Justin's interview, and she was sure he'd want one. She jotted down her phone and address just to make sure Kelsy had them.

The box sat on her desk, nearly full. Her whole career here at *Strive* reduced to the contents of a box. And she thought she'd accomplished so much. Maybe her intangible accomplishments were greater. She hoped so.

She glanced at her watch. The place was unnaturally quiet.

Like a funeral.

She couldn't wait to get out of here.

Chapter Forty-Nine

Justin tossed the remote on the coffee table. It knocked over an empty 7-Up can. His stomach was bothering him, though not for the reasons his mom thought.

Only 7-Up and some pretzels had sounded good. But even with digital cable and five hundred some channels, nothing held his interest. His heart pounded every time the phone rang.

It was only going to get worse, waiting for Bull to come knocking on the front door, being afraid to leave the house.

No sense in putting it off any longer. Kyle might be disappointed in him, but at least he'd be safe. He picked up the phone and dialed Kyle's number.

It went straight to voice mail.

Kyle stepped off the hospital elevator. Griffin's parents were sitting in the waiting area. He'd met them once before. They looked like they'd aged considerably. Having your son get shot could do that to you, he guessed. He couldn't imagine how his parents would react in the same situation.

"Mr. and Mrs. Griffin? I'm Kyle Taylor. I work with Jeff. We met once before." He extended his hand, and Mr. Griffin took it.

"Yes, yes. I remember you. You were Jeff's training officer."

"Yes, sir. I was."

"Please, have a seat," Jeff's mother said.

"Thank you." Kyle sat across from them. "How is he doing?"

Jeff's dad cleared his throat. "Better than we expected. The doctors are optimistic at this point. We keep praying."

"Me too." Kyle glanced around, somewhat surprised there weren't any other officers here. "Has anyone else been here today?"

"Oh sure." Mrs. Griffin looked at her watch. "They come and go throughout the day. There's always someone here."

"Good."

She stood. "It's nearly time for my quick visit with Jeff. Would you like to peek in with me?"

"I'd like that very much." Kyle stood and followed her.

The nurses nodded at them as they passed and entered Griffin's room. Kyle stopped just inside the door.

Half of Griffin's head was shaved and bandaged. He had two black eyes and a couple of cuts and bruises on his face. Kyle recognized the oxygen and IV but none of the other equipment hooked up to Griffin.

His mom walked over to the bed and took his hand. "How's my boy? The doctors are taking good care of you, so you just get yourself well. Kyle's here as well, and all the people you work with keep stopping by. We're all praying for you, so you just get better."

She patted his hand then looked at Kyle. "He wakes up occasionally but isn't really coherent. Still, I hope some of what we say filters in somehow. It can't hurt."

Someone rapped lightly on the door frame and Kyle turned.

Mr. Griffin stood there. "Time to switch."

Mrs. Griffin squeezed her son's hand again then gently

lowered it on the bed before walking toward the door. "Neither of us can bear to wait two hours to see him, so we split the small amount of time we're allotted each hour."

Kyle left the room with Mrs. Griffin. "Thank you for sharing your time with me. Is there anything I can do? Anything you need?"

She stopped and studied him, indecision flickering across her face. "I think Jeff told me you were a believer."

"Yes, ma'am. I am."

"Would you pray with me? There's a small room off the waiting area we can use."

"It'd be my privilege."

ALEX SWUNG OPEN THE DOOR TO *STRIVE*. THE GIRL AT THE front looked confused for a moment before she recognized him. He just waved to her and went on back to Susan's office.

Not bothering to knock, he walked in and sat down in front of her desk.

She looked up, frowning. Not happy to see him. No surprise there. "Alex. What are you doing here?"

"I need some money, and Dad's in a meeting and can't be disturbed."

"But I apparently can be."

He grinned at her. She hated it when he did that.

"I thought you got an allowance."

He shrugged. "I got expenses."

"What could you possibly know about expenses?" But she leaned over and dug around her desk drawer. "Why can't this wait until your father's out of his meeting?"

He hadn't thought of that. Oh man, this whole thing could blow up in his face if Susan didn't buy this. "Because the movie starts in fifteen minutes and the next one gets out too late. You know, Dad's rules."

"I didn't think movies were included in the deal. I thought you were grounded unless you were with one of your parents."

"I called Mom. She said it was okay." Susan and Mom hated each other, so he knew Susan wouldn't call to check. Their hostility was useful at times.

Susan shook her head slightly. He'd won. She handed over fifty bucks.

This worked out better than he expected.

He left Susan's office and sauntered past the receptionist. "Oh, hey. Susan said to tell you to have Heather meet her in the break room."

Chapter Fifty

P hone tucked under her chin, Heather stacked the last item in her box. Drat, Kyle's voice mail again. He must still be with Griffin. She'd try back in a minute.

Okay, she'd talked to everyone. A lot of people had left already. Surprisingly, Susan hadn't been by yet. Well, Heather would have to do the grown-up thing and go seek her out. She'd call Kyle first so he could be on his way. She didn't want to be hanging around here waiting for him any longer than she had to after talking to Susan. If she was lucky, maybe Susan had left too.

Someone was talking to Kelsy. She stood on tiptoe to peer over her cubicle wall. From the back, it looked like—

He turned partially, and she saw his profile. Alex.

The blood rushed to her head and out of her legs. She dropped into her chair, fumbling with her phone. Kyle needed to get here now. What was Alex doing here? Susan was his step-mom, but still. Maybe Susan thought she was already gone. She couldn't think it was a good idea for Alex to be here while Heather was here.

Her fingers kept hitting the wrong buttons. Finally, she brought his number up and hit dial.

It went straight to voice mail.

No, no, no. Kyle, aren't you done yet? "Kyle, it's me. Um, Alex is here. At the *Strive* office. I don't know if he knows that I'm here or not. I don't know what to do, and I'm a little freaked out about it. Call me as soon as you can, okay?" She hung up.

Okay, maybe she was overreacting.

No, this boy had shot at her. Probably twice. But it was possible he didn't know she was here.

Wasn't it?

She had the gun, but would she be able use it? Not wanting to contemplate that scenario, her brain scrambled for an alternative. She needed to get out of here. Who would Kyle trust to pick her up? They could meet Kyle somewhere. Joe was at work. She didn't have Hilary or Lisa or Stacey's numbers. She scrolled through her phone directory.

Quinn.

What would Kyle think? She barely hesitated before selecting the number. She needed whatever help she could get at this point.

"Heather?" Quinn answered the phone.

She let out a breath of relief. She lowered her voice. "Yeah, hi, I need a favor. I'm at the *Strive* office, and I can't get a hold of Kyle. Alex, the kid who shot me, he's here. We found out yesterday his stepmom's my boss. Anyhow, I just need to get out of here. Is there any way you can come get me?"

He hesitated just a second before saying, "Sure. I'll be there in five minutes."

"Thanks, Quinn. I appreciate it."

Hands shaking, she hung up. What to do for five minutes? She didn't want to stay in this cubicle alone. Even Susan's presence would be preferable now, which was such an odd concept Heather didn't bother to try and dissect it.

Five minutes. That's all. She just had to get through the next five minutes.

Picking up her box, she stuck her head around the wall of her cubicle.

No one.

She walked out to the reception area, scanning the area. Kelsy was still there. Good.

But no Alex. Maybe he left.

Heather set her box on the desk, setting her purse on top, and handed Kelsy the note she'd written for her, hoping she couldn't see her hands shake. "When the next few issues come out, could you send me a few copies?" Okay, good. Her voice sounded normal.

"Sure. And here—" Kelsy pressed some business cards into her hand. "These are a few of our advertisers and other people I thought might want to hire someone as awesome as you."

Heather clenched her jaw and forced back tears. She was going to miss this girl. "Thanks, Kelsy. I really appreciate it."

"No problem. I hope something works out for you. I'll call you when I've got lunch set up next week. Everyone really liked the idea."

"Thanks."

"Oh, and Susan wanted to see you. I guess she's in the break room."

She'd nearly forgotten. She had to go talk to Susan. There was no way out of it. She took a deep breath. "Time to face the music I guess."

"Good luck."

She did have one saving grace, though. "My friend, Quinn, is coming to help me. He should be here in a few minutes. When he gets here, can you have him come back to the break room if I'm not out yet?"

Kelsy smiled. "Reinforcements, huh?"

"Something like that."

Heather headed down the hall, her legs feeling a little less shaky with each step. Kelsy was still here. Quinn was coming. All she had to do was say a few polite things to Susan and she could go home: Thanks for the opportunity. I enjoyed working here. I learned a lot. You have a great team here, and I'm going to miss them. Notice I said I'd miss *them*, not you. Okay, she couldn't say that last part. But she wanted to.

She pushed the door open to the break room. She'd walked a few steps in before it hit her.

It was empty.

Huh. She thought—

Arms grabbed her from behind, pulled her backwards, off balance. A hand slapped over her mouth. She scrambled to get her feet under her but couldn't make them move fast enough. Her brain froze. What had Kyle taught her? She couldn't remember a thing. She flailed ineffectively.

The gun.

It was in her purse. On Kelsy's desk.

The outside door to the alley stood open.

Not going there. If something was going to happen, she'd make it happen here.

She shoved her elbow back and felt it connect with a crunch of bone and a grunt. Good. It was coming back to her. Maybe she had a chance.

The hold on her waist loosened, but she was still being dragged closer to the door.

She wiggled and jerked but couldn't get loose. She tried another elbow, but her upper arm was blocked.

"What the—" Another teen boy ran through the doorway and yanked Heather's feet off the ground. His shirt rode up over his biceps as he grabbed her feet. The flash of a black tattoo. "Get her in the car before you screw it up anymore."

Panic at his words surged through her. She kicked hard. The hands clamped tighter on her ankles.

Her resistance wasn't working. They were going to take her anyway. She had to make someone hear her. Kelsy. Susan. Anyone. She grunted then tried to bite the hand over her mouth. The cool air blew across her already sweaty hair as they manhandled her through the door. An Explorer was parked in the alley, engine running, doors open.

Oh, God, please. Help me. What do I do?

The grip on her ankles released. In one move, the guy holding her swung her around and tossed her into the SUV, landing on top of her.

Her face crunched against the floor. Her nose got hot and full. Her teeth cut into her lip. Blood filled her nose, blocking the small airspace above the floor. She couldn't breathe. Couldn't catch her breath. She pushed against the weight on her and got shoved harder in return. Pain shot through her side. Her rib hit some metal part of the seat structure.

Scraping her cheek along the carpet, she moved her head enough to breathe, warm blood pooling over her lip, running down her chin.

Okay, for this moment she was alive. She'd take that as long as she could.

QUINN TAPPED HIS FINGERS ON THE STEERING WHEEL, willing the light to change. Heather wanted him to come help her. He didn't want to let her down. Forget this light. He'd take the back way. Yanking the steering wheel to the right, he pulled into the next lane and turned right. A second later he pulled into the parking lot behind the *Strive* office.

An SUV was parked in the alley behind the building, and a couple people milled around it. He'd driven past it before his mind registered what he saw.

Heather.

Being shoved into that SUV.

He swung a U-turn and sped back. It was probably nothing. He was seeing things.

Wasn't he?

But that Alex kid she'd been worried about…

The Explorer had reached the opposite end of the alley as Quinn turned into it. He tried to keep it in view as it wound through the parking lot and out on to the street.

Two passengers. Both looked male from what he could see. No one who looked like Heather.

Maybe he *was* seeing things. Heather could be back at the office now waiting for him.

Something didn't feel right.

He pulled into the lane next to the Explorer and tried to casually glance over. Two teenagers.

Alex was a teenager.

He reached for his phone. Maybe he could get a hold of Kyle now.

Using voice commands, he called Kyle while keeping an eye on the Explorer. He let it pull ahead of him.

"Quinn. What's up?"

"Glad you answered. Not sure. Heather called me and said she couldn't get a hold of you."

"Yeah, I just left the hospital, I'm in the parking lot now, heading to my car."

"Alex showed up at her office."

"What?"

"Yep, and I don't know, but I thought I saw them shove her into an Explorer. I'm following it now."

"Where are you?"

"On Lake Forest heading south. We just passed Trabuco."

"Okay. I'm going to get some help. License plate?"

Quinn read it off. "You know, it looks like that Explorer I saw parked in my neighborhood the other night. Different plate, though."

"Try not to be too obvious. Hang back but keep them in sight. If we get disconnected I'll call you back."

Chapter Fifty-One

Kyle pushed every feeling away as he strode toward the car, dialing dispatch. By the time he climbed in the car, he had a unit headed to the *Strive* office and one trying to track down the Explorer.

He sped out of the hospital parking lot, turning on the radio Mark had left him. Heather had called three times and left one voicemail. He listened to it. She was scared. He could hear it in her voice.

Alex had been there.

Kyle never should have left her there alone. He slammed his hand on the steering wheel. What had he been thinking?

Time for that later. Now he needed to focus.

The next voicemail played. Justin. He didn't have time for this. He started to hang up but—

"Kyle, I need to talk to you about those guys. Bull and Alex and Cole. I think they're going to do something. Call me."

He called Justin.

Quinn stayed with the Explorer as it got on the freeway. It slipped through a yellow and Quinn ran the red, not missing the honks and gestures that came his way. This time of day traffic was heavy, and Quinn tried to stay close so as not to lose them. He hadn't seen any cop cars yet.

Keeping an eye on the Explorer, he hit redial on his phone. Kyle picked up.

"We're on the I-5 heading north."

"Okay."

It sounded like Kyle repeated that to someone. Kyle came back on the line. "Have you seen anything else?"

Quinn watched the driver. He looked from his rearview mirror to side mirror. The passenger turned in his seat and looked. "I think they just figured out I'm following them."

The Explorer sped up, to well over eighty. Quinn tried to keep up but got hemmed in by traffic. The Explorer cut back over to the off-ramp and exited.

"They got off at Bake Parkway." The taillights flicked on briefly. "They're turning right on Bake." The SUV disappeared from Quinn's sight. He slammed his fist on the steering wheel. "Sorry, Kyle. I can't believe I lost them."

"Don't worry about it, Quinn. You were a big help. We've got people headed for them now. I'll let you know what happens." Kyle hung up.

The next exit was a couple miles down the freeway. Quinn wanted to pull over now.

He'd let Heather down. Again. He wanted to be sick.

Please, God. Keep her safe.

The vibration of the car resonated through her face. It felt like they'd gotten on and off the freeway. She had no idea where they were, but it couldn't be too far from home. They were still stopping at regular intervals, presumably at stoplights.

Her nose had clotted. Dried blood cracked on her face whenever she moved. But as long as she lay still, the pressure on her began to ease up gradually.

There were three of them in the car, from what she could discern of their voices. Probably Alex and the other kid who was with him when they tried to rob the Jitter Bug. And tattoo guy. The tattoo she'd seen on the kid at the Jitter Bug. It finally clicked. He was the one who had grabbed her ankles.

She had no idea what they wanted or where they were taking her. Would they kill her? Or just try to scare her? Panic coursed through her, and she fought against it. She needed her mind to be clear. These were just kids. Surely there was something she could say or do to have the advantage over them.

But they were scared and desperate. That made them unpredictable. And dangerous.

Lord, help me. Give me wisdom. Tell me what to do. It's hard to believe this is my time, that my work here is done. Help me know what to do.

KYLE CLICKED BACK OVER TO THE OTHER CALL AS HE SPED up Bake Parkway. "Justin?" He flipped on the lights on his unmarked unit.

"Yeah."

"They already got her."

"Oh man." Tears clogged Justin's voice. "It's my fault. I should have called you earlier."

"Justin, pull it together. I need your help now. You know these guys. Where are they going? Where would they take her?"

"I don't know. Bull doesn't tell anyone anything. He runs everything himself."

"Where would they take her? To someone's house?"

"I don't know. I don't think so."

Kyle tried to keep the frustration out of his voice. "Where did you guys meet?"

"Out in Silverado Canyon. That's it. I bet that's where they'd take her." Justin's tone turned more confident.

Kyle hoped it was warranted. "Hang on." He picked up the radio. "All units be advised that suspect is possibly headed toward Silverado Canyon. Central dispatch, advise OCSD and request assistance."

"Okay, Justin. Where in the canyon?"

Kyle wove in and out of traffic as Justin gave him directions based on odometer mileage and an old live oak tree. Kyle hoped Justin was right.

For Heather's sake.

Chapter Fifty-Two

The road turned twisty, the movement of the car rolling Heather to her side, pressing her sore rib against whatever had caused the original injury. Then the road got really rough. It felt like Alex half sat up, putting most of his weight on her hip, relieving the pressure on her ribs.

They were off-road now which meant they were probably somewhere back in the canyons. Back where the houses—and help—were few and far between.

Make a run for it.

The thought pressed itself on her heart. How fast could they be going on this dirt road? Should she even try? She tried fighting back before and just got a bloody nose for her trouble. Still, the thought wouldn't leave her. The moment Alex let up... Slowly she moved her head. She could see the door opposite her, pictured herself reaching for the handle. As much as she dared, she moved her toes against the floor.

Was it her imagination, or were they slowing down?

Now!

No time to analyze where it came from. Heather pushed her feet against the floor and arched up.

Alex toppled against the seat.

She stretched for the door handle. A rut knocked her off-balance. She missed.

"Hey!" Alex grabbed at her.

The rocking SUV threw her toward the door. She clutched the handle, yanked.

Arms reached over the front seat. Someone pulled at her legs.

She kicked and scrambled, threw her weight into the door. It opened.

She tumbled out, head first. Her hands collided with the rocky grit, sliding as her legs fell out. The door frame caught her shins, smacking them between the frame and the door. She tumbled.

Run!

Her legs wouldn't work. She tried to get them under her, pushed up with her hand. Finally, like a train leaving the station, everything worked at once. She got up. Stumbled. But stayed upright. And ran.

She heard the car stop behind her, voices yelling. Heather kept running.

After about twenty steps her lungs burned, her rib ached. She couldn't breathe through her nose. Kicked-up dust coated her mouth, choking her.

She wouldn't make it. She could hear footsteps now.

Where'd she think she could run to anyway? As far as she knew, she could be running away from the closest help. These kids were teenagers. She was over thirty and hadn't run in weeks. They'd catch her.

Lord?

Her side pinched. If only she'd been able to run more, get back into shape.

Keep going.

One-two-three-four. Breathe in. One-two-three-four.

Breathe out. Four steps in. Four steps out.

She swallowed, trying to get some moisture into her parched

throat. She needed to catch her breath. A dry creek bed ran across the road, causing a sandy gutter in the dirt road where heavy rains would tumble through in the winter. Dense chaparral and live oaks crowded the banks. Maybe she could hide there.

That hairpin turn might give her the cover she needed.

She ran across the road, the brush and dirt cut away around the turn as if someone hadn't quite made it. Off the road, she hesitated just a second before jumping from the upper level of the road to the lower. The sting that charged up her legs nearly dropped her, but she kept her balance and darted across the lower road and into the creek bed, hoping she hadn't been spotted.

Ducking down, she pushed aside thick, dry brush, scanning for a good hiding place. It was still a couple of hours until sunset, but the shadows were already long in the canyon.

There. Across the creek bed sat a thick bank of brush, deep in the shadows. Leaping from rock to rock so as not to leave footprints in the soft sandy bottom, she crossed and ducked behind the brush. She hoped she didn't have any critters for company, though at this point the four-legged kind was preferable to the two-legged.

Settling into the sand, gasping for air, she realized this spot was better than she thought. She could see the dirt road, hopefully in enough time to jump out and flag down help.

Or watch the boys drive off.

She heard voices and saw a head appear on the top level of the switchback. Then she heard the car engine. The SUV grew larger. Then stopped.

So now what? Sit and wait and hope they didn't find her.

Maybe they'd give up and go home.

The tattoo kid appeared on the top level of the switchback, one foot propped up on a rock like a conquering hero. "We know you're out there. You can't go anywhere, so you might as well give up."

Yeah, right.

THE FIRST UNITS RADIOED THEY WERE AT THE TURNOFF.

Kyle gave them the same directions Justin had given him. He hoped this was it. Otherwise, they were out of options. *God, I need wisdom. Don't let me lose her.*

Kyle turned onto the dirt road. A siren split the air.

"Three King thirty-five. I've spotted the suspect's vehicle." Kyle hoped Patino could catch up to them in time.

THE BOYS DISAPPEARED FROM VIEW, THEIR VOICES growing faint, carried away by the afternoon wind in the canyon. What were they doing? She'd gotten away, so they'd have to give up now, right? She hoped so. In an hour it'd be dark. Maybe then she could slip out—

Something grabbed her shoulder.

Heather bit back a scream, turning to brush off the creature, as she realized it was a hand. Suddenly she felt like she was underwater, everything moving slowly and wavering in her vision. Her eyes traced up the arm from the hand. A black 17 tattoo. It pulled her backward. She lost her balance and was on her back, his face over hers.

She stared at him, eye to eye, for what seemed like an eternity. Then her brain started firing synapses all at once. Her knee came up, caught him in the abdomen.

He groaned and loosened his grip. She twisted out from under him and scrambled to her feet. She turned to run, trying to gain traction in the soft sand, but something caught her foot. She yanked with everything in her, but one quick tug had her back on the ground, the breath expelled from her chest. Everything went black. This was it. It was over. She tried to fight back, but she wasn't good enough or strong enough.

Never give up, Heather. No matter how bad it looks. Don't let the bad guys win.

Kyle. She tried. She couldn't. He was too strong.

Never give up.

Bull's reddened face appeared above hers. He was breathing heavily. She cut her eyes to the side. Rocks, soft sand—

She squeezed her eyes closed and grabbed a handful of grit, flinging it while kicking at his groin.

With a scream, he slapped at his eyes. Heather scrambled from under him. He rolled toward her. She kicked hard, aiming for his knee. Taking off, she ran up the embankment this time, grabbing for foot and handholds. Where were the other two? Looking for her? Had they heard her struggle with Bull?

Crawling over the edge of the road she lay still, listening. Her own breathing was so loud in her ears, she couldn't hear anything else.

The Explorer sat in the road still canted to the side from its quick stop.

Getting to her feet, she dashed to the car. Voices drifted to her on the wind. She couldn't tell from which direction.

She grabbed the door handle and pulled. It came open to her surprise, almost knocking her off her feet. The keys were still in the ignition. A cell phone sat plugged into the charger.

"Hey!"

Not stopping to look, she hopped in the car and turned the key. Pulling the door shut, she threw it in gear as a face appeared at the window. She heard the door locks automatically click down as the car moved and was thankful for that safety feature. They could be opened from the inside but not the outside.

Alex pounded on the window, yelling. She caught a glimpse of Bull behind him, the other kid helping him as she yanked the steering wheel and pushed on the gas pedal, trying to put the big car in a tight circle. She could hear scratching at the door, but she kept going as the car gained momentum. She hoped Alex was out of the way, but she really didn't care.

As she approached the hairpin turn, she forced herself to slow down, despite the fear that they'd catch her. Concentrating on keeping the car on the road, she nearly collided with a police car coming the other way.

Thank You, Lord.

Throwing the car into park, she hopped out and ran toward the cruiser. Her legs gave out, she lost her balance and toppled over.

Chapter Fifty-Three

K yle slammed on the brakes behind Patino's unit, threw it in park, and jumped out of the car.

Patino was helping Heather sit up. Tears coursed, leaving muddy, bloody streaks on her face.

He ran to her, crushing her in his arms. "Sweetheart, you're safe."

She sobbed as he stroked her hair. Patino left them. Kyle heard the SUV being moved, and two more units joined them. He heard his radio crackling in the car. He didn't care. Heather was in his arms. That's all that mattered.

THE HELICOPTER OVERHEAD COMPETED WITH THE SIRENS, making it nearly impossible to think. Bull crawled to the edge of the road, his brain whirling for a way out. The Explorer was almost directly below him, along with a cop car and an unmarked unit. Detective Taylor had his arms around the chick. He could probably get both of them with one shot. He reached into his waistband—

"This is the Sheriff's department." It came from the helicopter loudspeaker. "Put your hands out to the side and slowly get to your feet."

He'd be dead before he could get a shot off. The detective shoved the girl into the unit and closed the door.

Bull did as he was instructed, putting his hands up and slowly getting to his feet. He turned and saw Cole and Alex about fifty feet away with their hands on their heads. Another glance down the road showed multiple police units flying toward him.

Despair threatened to overwhelm him. It wasn't supposed to end this way. His mom was supposed to be proud of him. Not ashamed. He couldn't stand to see that look of disappointment and disgust on her face.

He was running out of time. He had one last card to play.

One last way to remain in control.

He whipped out the gun and pointed it at his head. He ignored the orders to drop the gun. It bought him some time, but not much. "I want to talk to Detective Kyle Taylor! Get him up here now, or I pull the trigger."

HEATHER WAS SAFELY IN THE UNIT, AND HE WAS GETTING ready to take her down to the station when he heard something come over the radio. The noise of the helicopter made it hard to hear, but the two units had stopped at the hairpin turn. Something was going on.

"What's happening?" he asked Patino.

"One of the kids has a gun to his head. Says he wants to talk to you."

Teenagers were panicky and unpredictable. There wasn't time to get a negotiator out there. He could talk to him, maybe talk him out of whatever he wanted to do. He grabbed a tactical vest and shrugged it on.

"Tell them I'm coming up." He opened the door to the unit.

"Heather, I'm going to talk to one of the kids up there. If it takes more than a few minutes, I'm going to have Patino take you back to the station, and I'll meet you there."

She nodded.

He hated to leave her like this. He gently kissed her. "I love you."

"I love you too." She touched his face.

He closed the door and headed up the hairpin turn.

SWEAT TRICKLED DOWN BULL'S HAIRLINE. HE RESISTED THE urge to swipe at it. "C'mon! Where is he?"

Kyle's head and shoulders appeared around the curve. "I'm right here. Let's talk about this."

So he had come. "I didn't think you had the nerve, Detective. Thought you'd be taking your little girlfriend there away from here. Keep her safe. You did a pretty good job. I never did find you. I would have, though, with a little more time."

"What can I do to help you?" The detective's voice was calm and even. He'd been a worthy opponent. Still, Bull was the one in charge here.

"Not much at this point. I know what's going to happen here."

"It doesn't have to be that way. Put down the gun. No one's going to hurt you."

Bull laughed. Yeah, right. "You and I both know I'm not coming off this hill except in a body bag. But you're coming too."

He twitched his hand. He got off at least one, maybe two shots. He hoped one of them found the detective. Lead pounded his body, and everything went black.

Chapter Fifty-Four

Kyle pushed away from the wall as Heather came out of the women's bathroom at the station. She looked a lot better than she had half an hour ago. Lisa had loaned her some clean clothes and with the dirt and blood washed off her face, only the slightly swollen nose and bottom lip clued him in on how rough her evening had been.

He handed her a Diet Coke. "It'll help the swelling on your lip."

She smiled. "Thanks."

He slid his arm around her waist, pulling her tight next to him. He didn't care who was watching. He wasn't letting go of her. He'd come too close to losing her. She'd come pretty close to losing him too, but she didn't need to know that. He could still see some dirt covering his clothes from where he'd hit the ground to avoid Bull's shots. The gouges he'd seen in the dirt and the slugs they'd found were a little too close for comfort.

"Justin and his mom are coming in. He's going to tell Mark everything he knows about the Seventeeners. But I think that means Mark will be too busy to get your statement tonight. Want to go home instead?"

She closed her eyes briefly and nodded.

"Okay, it'll be just a few more minutes. I want to get Justin settled with Mark before I leave."

He guided her over to his desk and handed her his phone. "You'd better call Quinn and tell him you're okay."

"I owe him a big thank you too."

Mark walked up to them. "Justin's mom's coming, too, right?"

Kyle nodded. "Yep. That's what I told him."

"We'll have to tread carefully. We don't want to do anything that the defense can use against us."

"I know. I'll bring them back to the conference room as soon as they get here." Kyle squeezed Heather's shoulder then left her to go up front.

She touched his arm to stop him. "When Justin gets here, can I see him?"

He looked at her a minute. "Sure. I think that'd be good."

When Justin walked into the station a few minutes later, he was pale and shaking. Claire looked worried. "Is he in trouble again?"

"He's trying to do the right thing. He was a big help to us today in finding Heather. I'm not sure we would have found her without his help. But it's better if you're here while he tells us what he knows."

Kyle guided them back to the conference room.

Mark stuck out his hand. "Hi, Justin. I'm Detective Mark Walker. I hear you're the big hero of the day."

Justin shook Mark's hand but glanced at Kyle, then shrugged.

"Justin?" Kyle waited until he had eye contact. "Heather's here. She'd like to say hi."

"You sure? I'd think she'd hate me."

"She doesn't hate you."

Mark opened the door, and Heather walked in. "Hi, Justin." She took two steps and wrapped the teenager in a hug.

Justin's arms hung limply at his side for a second before hugging her back.

She whispered something to Justin that had him nodding and surreptitiously wiping his eyes.

———

HEATHER WOKE UP AND LOOKED AROUND THE GUEST room. What was different?

Her. She was different.

The heaviness was gone. She'd lived with it for so long she wasn't even sure what to call its absence.

Then it came to her. Freedom.

She stretched and smiled. This was very good.

———

"WE'RE ALL DONE?" HEATHER ASKED MARK A COUPLE OF hours later. They were sitting in the conference room at the station, and she had been giving him her report of what had happened yesterday. "That's it. If I need anything else, I know where to find you."

Justin's information, as well as the fact that Alex and Cole were both trying to blame each other, gave the detectives and the assistant DA plenty of work. They had found Bull's computer and stolen goods at his mom's house. It also meant the weight of the whole trial didn't rest on her shoulders.

And the mystery of who had broken into her house? Quinn sheepishly admitted he had remembered he had her key when he dropped off the flowers. He couldn't resist poking around her condo, thinking she might turn to him if she was scared.

Nearly giddy with relief that this whole thing was over, she stood and walked out of the conference room to find Kyle waiting for her.

"Hey, beautiful. Want to have lunch and take a walk on the beach?"

"Sounds great." She smiled up at him. "Today's nice and warm, a break from that string of cool days we had."

"Um hmm."

He had something else on his mind other than the weather. She squeezed his hand. "What?"

"Nothing."

He didn't fool her. She'd get it out of him eventually. And really, she didn't care. It was just nice to feel free again, to not have to look over her shoulder.

They drove down to the coast in Kyle's truck. The way he sank into the seat, made minute adjustments to the mirror, and flopped his arm over the seat made Heather think he was glad to have it back.

"Want to know something funny?" Kyle glanced over at her. "Remember the Bedroom Burglar case, how I thought someone was tipping off Watson about vacant houses? Turns out it was Bull and his buddies who lived in the area. Bull masterminded the thing, the kids did the robbery, and Watson was the fence. He was trying to get a cut of the take the night he broke into the Morgans'."

"So you got two cases wrapped up."

"Yep."

She rolled the window down partway and let the wind blow her hair. She needed a cut.

They got lunch to go and sat on one of the benches at Heisler Park.

Kyle trailed his fingers along her shoulder. "How does it feel to be a free woman again? You get to go back to your house today, sleep in your own bed."

She lifted her face to the sun. "I can't exactly say life is back to normal. Too much has changed." She turned to him. "I guess there's a new normal now. I just have to figure out what it is."

His gaze held hers for a long moment. Expecting to be kissed, Heather smiled slightly.

Instead, he reached into his pocket. "Maybe this will help. There's nearly a full moon tonight, and I had planned on giving it to you then. But I can't wait." He smiled sheepishly and handed her a flat, square box.

This was a surprise. And probably explained his earlier distraction. She untied the ribbon and lifted the lid. Inside was a bracelet of delicate silver links. She picked it up and dangled it from her fingers, letting the sunlight play off it. Engraved on alternate links was either a heart or "I love you" in several languages.

Kyle reached over and turned one of the links. On the back was engraved *Love always, Kyle.*

"It's beautiful." She could barely get the words out.

"So are you. Heather, I love you. I know we've had a crazy time since we've been together. But we've come through it. And I love you more than I ever thought possible."

She touched his cheek. "I love you too."

"Should we see if we can handle normalcy?" He took the bracelet from her and linked it around her wrist.

"Hmm. Sure. Excitement's overrated."

He laughed. "I'm going to miss having you in my house. For now." He leaned forward and kissed her.

She slid her arms around his neck, perfectly content.

Epilogue

The sun had warmed the adobe steps where Heather sat surrounded by little girls whose ages varied as much as their skin tones did. They didn't speak much English, and Heather didn't speak much Spanish, but all those differences seemed to melt under the warm Mexican sun as Heather taught them one of her favorite praise choruses. The girls recognized the word "God" and they broke out in huge smiles when they sang "Jesus."

Heather couldn't imagine why she hadn't gone on a mission trip sooner. But she knew the answer: fear. As simple as that. And after what God had brought her through, she was never going to let fear rule her life again.

She, Kyle, and several others from their small group and the larger singles' ministry had come down to Mexico to do some repair work on the building, bring down donated supplies, and provide help to the overwhelmed workers. Heather didn't think there was much she could do, but she could paint, cook, and help out when needed. What she hadn't expected was how the children responded to her sitting down with them with a simple picture-laden storybook Bible. When she got to the end, she taught them songs. Some silly, like she and her sisters used to sing. And some about Jesus. There was no language barrier with music.

She looked over the dark heads to the cleared dirt area away from the buildings where Kyle and some others were playing baseball, or some form of it, with the boys. She watched as he caught a ball and tossed it to the boy next to him who rocketed it to home plate, or the piece of corrugated metal that served as home plate. Kyle caught Heather's eye and grinned. Mentally she started putting together the talk she and Kyle were going to do next week. She couldn't believe she was going to get up and talk in front of people, but after what she'd been through—after what God had brought her through—how bad could it be? All she had to do was share from her heart about her experiences here at the orphanage and why others should go and be blessed as well.

Because she hadn't expected to receive the blessing coming here. She was supposed to be giving it. The man who organized the trip down here, Hank Valestro, was the very same guy who had given his testimony that first Sunday Heather had met Kyle. The day she couldn't imagine trusting God through so much difficulty and coming out the other side being thankful. When Kyle couldn't imagine putting his flaws out there for everyone to see. They'd both come a long way since that first Sunday.

And Heather wouldn't have it any other way.

Are you curious about what happens next?

Will Joe and Sarah end up together? Or will she end up with Ryan?

And what other adventures await Kyle, Heather, Joe, and Sarah?

Find out by signing up for my latest news and updates at www. JLCrosswhite.com and you'll get the prequel novella, *Promise Me* — Grayson and Cait's story.

You'll be the first to know when the spin-off series, In the Shadows, releases. It will follow the siblings of our Hometown Heroes. And of course all of our original cast will make an appearance as well.

My bimonthly updates include upcoming books written by me and other authors you will enjoy, information on all my latest releases, sneak peeks of yet-to-be-released chapters, and exclusive giveaways. Your email address will never be shared, and you can unsubscribe at any time.

If you enjoyed this book, please leave a review. Reviews can be as simple as "I couldn't put it down. I can't wait for the next one" and help raise the author's visibility and lets other readers find her.

Keep reading for a sneak peak of *Flash Point: Hometown Heroes book 2*

.

Acknowledgments

The expertise on police procedures was provided by my brother, Deputy J. Roy Crosswhite, who came up with some ideas that I wouldn't have thought of. Any liberties taken are my own. This book would not be possible without the patience and willingness to read many, many drafts by Diana Brandmeyer, Malia Spencer, and Jenny Cary. My fellow Pencildancer Liz Tolsma gave me final readings. Special thanks to Sara Benner for her expert proofreading and Danielle Reid and Pamela Martinez for their eagle eyes! Many thanks to my beta readers and reviewers!

Much thanks and love to my children, Caitlyn Elizabeth and Joshua Alexander, for supporting my dream for many years and giving me time to write. And most of all to my Lord Jesus, who makes all things possible and directs my paths.

Author's Note

Laguna Vista isn't a real town, but it's based on the area of Orange County that I lived in for twelve years. As with many stories, a confluence of ideas came together that I wanted to explore. Not to mention it's a beautiful location with the ocean to the west and foothills and mountains to the east and the austere-but-beautiful desert within driving distance.

The area has an interesting juxtaposition of wealth and conservatism. Christianity is both embraced and challenged in this area. It's home to Rick Warren's Saddleback Church, a church I attended and served at. One of the questions I struggled with while living there was how does someone live an authentic Christian life while daily challenged with the trappings of an affluent lifestyle? Cars, houses, jewelry, beauty all add up to one thing in Orange County: image. It's the most valuable commodity.

So how does a Christian reconcile being made in the image of God with society's image? Ultimately, all the characters in the book must deal with this question on their faith journey.

Each of them has their own unique image, yet all are made in the image of God. I hope that is one thing you will take away from reading *Protective Custody* and that you will be encouraged to reflect on how uniquely you are made in the image of God.

About the Author

My favorite thing is discovering how much there is to love about America the Beautiful and the great outdoors. I'm an Amazon bestselling author, a mom to two navigating the young adult years while battling my daughter's juvenile arthritis, exploring the delights of my son's autism, and keeping gluten free.

A California native who's spent significant time in the Midwest, I'm thrilled to be back in the Golden State. Follow me on social media to see all my adventures and how I get inspired for my books!

www.JLCrosswhite.com
Twitter: @jenlcross
Facebook: Author Jennifer Crosswhite

Instagram: jencrosswhite
Pinterest: Author Jennifer Crosswhite

facebook.com/authorjennifercrosswhite

twitter.com/jenlcross

instagram.com/jencrosswhite

pinterest.com/jtiszai

Sneak Peek of Flash Point

Orange County, California, 2000

Dust drifted across the road ahead as Joe Romero sped down nearly deserted Irvine Boulevard, bypassing the infamously jammed El Toro Y, the conflux of Interstates 5 and 405. Were the Santa Ana winds kicking up? But the eucalyptuses lining the road tucked between the foothills and the recently deserted El Toro Marine Corps Air Station weren't swaying. Their leaves remained perfectly still. Eerily so.

So where was the dust—

It wasn't dust. It was smoke.

A car sprawled sideways in the intersection, shards of metal and glass scattered across the pavement. Skid marks across the intersection led to a second car impaled on a light pole, front end crumpled nearly to the windshield.

Orange sparked around the edge of the smashed hood.

A cell phone would be handy about now. As a broke community college student, he couldn't afford one. No pay phones were nearby. He pulled over and hopped out. A man eased out of the car in the intersection.

"You okay?"

The man nodded.

Joe jogged past him. The flames were creeping around the hood of the impaled car.

The driver was a woman with the steering wheel embedded in her chest. Blood ran down her face from a gash in her forehead that corresponded to the spider web of broken glass in the windshield. The woman didn't turn her head. "Please, can you get my baby out?"

He looked in the back seat, the crying just now registering with him. A red-faced toddler screaming his—or her—lungs out. Joe glanced at the approaching flames.

"Please, hurry!"

The mom was in more danger from the flames, but given how she was wedged in there, he didn't think he'd be able to free her. He looked around. A car slowed as it approached Sand Canyon, driving around the debris in the intersection. He tried to make eye contact with the driver but couldn't. He hoped they'd call for help.

Someone came around him to the front of the car. The man from the other car. He carried a fire extinguisher and was reading the instructions. Good, maybe he could get that fire out while Joe worked on the baby. It was the only thing he could do for the mom.

The doors were crunched shut, and the windows had popped out. Lifting the edge of his shirt, he wrapped it around his hand and cleared out the rest of the broken glass. He leaned through the window. "Hey there." He turned to the mom. "What's your baby's name?"

"Brandon."

The other driver must have figured out the fire extinguisher because with a hiss, white powder covered the hood of the car, repelling the flames.

Joe studied the car seat buckles for a minute. "Hey, Brandon. I'll get you right out of here. Okay? How do you work these things anyway, huh? I bet you can figure it out before me." He finally found and pushed the release button, undid the chest strap, and slipped Brandon out of the harness. Making sure the baby didn't graze any of the broken glass, Joe pulled him out of the window.

"See, Mom? We're safe." Though he wasn't too sure about her. The flames were growing again.

The baby nearly threw himself out of Joe's arms, trying to get to his mom. "Whoa, buddy. Hang on there. We'll get your mom in a second." What was he going to do with the baby? He needed to set him down somewhere to get to the woman. His car? It'd have to do. He grabbed a couple of the toys next to the car seat. "I'll be right back." Brandon snatched the red furry one from Joe. With its googly eyes and big orange nose, it had to be some monster from Sesame Street.

The mom didn't say anything. Her face was ashen, and her eyes were closed. They didn't have much time.

He put the baby in his car, giving him the toys. "Stay here, Brandon. I'll be right back."

Brandon stuck a toy in his mouth and grabbed the steering wheel.

This wasn't a great solution, but what choice did he have?

He eased the door shut and ran back to the car.

The other guy was yanking on the door with no success.

Joe went to the other side and leaned in the window. The dashboard was pushed back over the woman's legs, pinning her to the seat. No way were they going to get her out. He eased out of the car. "Where's the fire extinguisher?"

"It's empty."

He scanned the area. No sirens yet. Had anyone even called? The smoke traced across the sky, leaving a clear signal some busybody should notice. "We need to stop this fire. We aren't going to be able to get her out of here ourselves. Got a shovel?"

The man shook his head.

Joe strode around the car. Debris and trash littered the dirt on the side of the road. Maybe there was something here they could use. He grabbed a couple of discarded scraps of wood.

"Here. Use this." He handed one to the guy and then used his to start flinging dirt on the car. The grit pelting the hood of the car sounded like rain. He couldn't tell if it was helping or not. Dust stung his eyes and filtered into his mouth.

He heard something. Was the baby crying? He looked up.

No, Brandon was chewing on the steering wheel.

Sirens.

Relief poured over him. He'd never been so glad to hear that. He tossed another load of dirt on the fire, then ran around to the driver's window. He put his hand on the woman's shoulder. "Did you hear that? The fire department's on its way. You'll be out of here before you know it. And don't worry about Brandon. He's having a good time. I think you've got a future race car driver on your hands, the way he's going after my steering wheel."

That got a faint smile out of her.

The noise was nearly deafening as an Orange County Sheriff's unit drove up followed by the fire engine. Firefighters swarmed the car. Joe stayed next to her, explaining what was happening as they put out the fire and pried the front end of the car off of her.

One of the firefighters leaned over his shoulder. "This part is going to hurt her a bit. Think you can keep her distracted?"

"I can try." Joe could see Brandon, so he gave the mom a running commentary of Brandon's fascination with the lights and activity.

When they were ready to extract her, Joe got out of the way and sprung Brandon from his car. The sheriff's deputy came over to get Joe's statement about the accident. Satisfaction, and something else, mixed in Joe's bloodstream as the cop lifted Brandon from his arms to head to the hospital.

The firefighter from earlier came over. "Good job there. Have any experience with this kind of thing?"

He gave a short laugh. "I'm just a college student." But there had been a time when this was all he'd wanted to do. He had even put out a fire with his friends as a kid. But that dream was gone, smashed in the wreckage of bad choices.

"Well, if you're interested, we're hiring. There's an information meeting Wednesday at seven at the high school. You should check it out."

"I might do that."

The firefighter nodded and walked off.

Joe climbed in his car and sat there a moment before starting it. His steering wheel glistened, and it took him a minute to realize what it was. Baby slobber. He grabbed a napkin and wiped it off.

A firefighter. Huh. He'd thought that dream had died. But maybe ... He'd be graduating in a couple of weeks with a business degree but no firm job prospects. Maybe he'd check it out. After all, it was just an info meeting. Likely nothing would come of it.

He turned the key in the ignition. Something red on the floor caught his eye. He reached down and picked it up.

The furry Sesame Street monster.

Orange County, California, Present day

They were called the devil winds. Fire Captain Joe Romero thought it an apt description of the dry winds that blew down from the desert, funneled through mountains that acted as a chimney, and pushed back the normal Southern California ocean breeze. More often than not, the Santa Anas brought out the arsonists.

A trickle of sweat ran down his neck, adding to the wetness already gluing his shirt to his back under his turnout gear. He rolled his aching shoulders as best he could while holding the hose. The smoke and embers blowing in his face didn't help. He pulled his shroud higher over his nose to block the smell of a campfire gone wrong.

Focus. Fatigue was as big of an enemy as the fire. Scanning the area, he forced himself to be aware of his surroundings and his team. Probationary Firefighter Zach Akino manned the hose with him. "See this expensively landscaped yard we're yanking our hose through?"

The rookie nodded, his eyes widening.

"It won't mean anything if we don't save this house. I know it's our third day on the fire, and we're not going home any time soon. But keep focused and be aware. You can't let your guard down." Joe adjusted the hose on his shoulder. The wind swirled, lifting dust, ash, and smoke in a vortex. The fire made its own weather, the heat sucking the flames skyward into a wall of red-and-black heat.

Joe blinked his eyes to ease the grittiness caused by the smoke, heat, and lack of sleep. Wouldn't be able to put in any study time on his classes that would enable him to move up the fire department ranks. The testing dates moved for no man or woman. Looked like he would miss this round of promotions. A hard ball formed in his stomach at the thought, but he shoved it from his head. No point in dwelling on what he couldn't control.

A crashing noise ended in a metallic clang. A boulder banged into the wrought-iron fence. He swiveled around, looking for more. He closed the nozzle and dropped the hose. Grabbing Akino's shoulder, Joe yanked him back as a chunk of granite shattered where his boot had been. Fragments pelted their turnout gear. A chill raced over his sweat-slicked skin.

Akino gave him a wobbly grin. "Thanks."

Joe snatched up the line again. "With all the noise from the fire, wind, and support aircraft, you won't hear a rock coming until it's usually too late to get out of the way. And there are a lot of big rocks in these foothills that can easily work themselves loose as the fire burns away their support." They needed every man to hold this line. They couldn't do that if any of their thinly-stretched crew got injured.

The Global SuperTanker roared overhead, slightly louder than the fire and the wind. Nineteen thousand gallons of red slurry dropped from the tanker's belly, temporarily pushing back the wall of flames.

Joe nodded at Akino, then braced himself and opened the nozzle. The stream of water knocked down the flames flaring up between the house and the line made by the tanker-dropped fire retardant. Firefighters Jeff McCoy and Andrew Hardin covered the other edge of the house.

More snapping brush. Joe scanned for another rock, but a small deer broke through the chaparral and slammed into the fence. It tried to scramble over. Snakes, rabbits, and mice had been running across the lawn all day. Poor thing. It could see safety, but it just kept pawing at the metal bars, panicked.

"Air Fire 3, coming in for a second pass closer to the line. All personnel be advised." The call came over Joe's radio.

He closed the nozzle. "Akino, this one'll be closer. Move back from the drop zone." Jeff and Andy already loped across the lawn, closer to the house, taking cover under the wide patio.

Joe glanced back at the deer. Wait, it wasn't a deer. It was a dog with dirty, singed fur. If he could get it to follow the fence line around the corner, the dog could escape down the greenbelt.

He ran toward the dog, waving his arms. "Go on. Shoo!" The dog sat and whined, tail thumping.

"Joe! The drop!" Jeff's voice rose above the crackle of the flames and the roar of the approaching plane.

He waved off Jeff and sneaked a quick glance at the sky.

He had time. Hopefully.

The dog pawed harder at the fence, eyes wide, ears flat.

He didn't want to spook the animal into hurting itself. "It's okay, boy. Come on." He patted his leg and moved down the fence, hoping the dog would follow. "You can get out of here."

"Joe!"

He ignored Jeff's voice. The guys were always teasing him for having a soft heart. He liked saving people. And animals. So sue him.

They say smell is the sense most closely related to memory, but Joe always thought it was the adrenaline rush, the split-second decision making, that so often brought back the memory of a steering wheel buried in a young mother's chest and a red-faced toddler screaming in the back seat. Images of his first rescue flashed across his brain at every scene.

He planted his boot on the fence and levered himself halfway over, reaching down. "Come here, boy. Up!"

Someone grabbed his legs. Jeff. "I got you. Get the dumb dog, and let's get out of here."

He grabbed the scruff of the dog's neck and heaved himself back, taking the dog with him over the fence. And toppling over on top of Jeff.

Scrambling to his feet, someone grabbed his collar, yanking him up. Akino.

The roar of the SuperTanker announced its arrival. They ran, ducking under the covering of the house's wide patio as the heavy, red rain fell.

He leaned against the wall, catching his breath. "Thanks, rookie. But obey orders next time." He grinned and looked over at Jeff. Blood ran down his face. "What happened to you?"

"Your boot. You kicked me in the face when you grabbed that stupid dog." Jeff dabbed at his nose with his shroud.

"Aw man, I'm sorry. Do you want—?"

"Nope."

Joe studied Jeff a moment. Deciding there wasn't anything to be done—the bleeding had stopped—he unscrewed the lid on his water bottle, taking a long drink of water nearly as hot as coffee, washing the taste of cinders from his mouth. "Where's the dog?"

Akino gestured to the patio table. "Under there."

"Probably a good move. That drop could have killed him."

Joe squatted down and let the shepherd-collie mix sniff his hand. The dog licked it, and Joe scratched its neck, the fur thick with ash and crispy where it was singed. No collar. Why did people let their dogs out if they didn't have a collar? At a time like this, they'd be lucky to see the mutt again. He was somebody's pet, most likely. He hoped some little kid wasn't going to be heartbroken.

Battalion Commander Dan O'Grady strode around the corner. "Everything under control? Jeff, what happened to your face?"

Jeff tilted his head in Joe's direction. "Oh, you know. Joe was helping. Again."

O'Grady raised his eyebrows and focused on Joe a moment. "Okay. That last drop bought us some time. Gather around." He waited until Andrew Hardin pushed off the wall and joined them. "The heavy winter rains have made these foothills bloom and thickened the growth of the chaparral brush. The winds are sucking the moisture out of every living thing. It's all tinder dry and ready to burn. Wind-driven embers are bursting into spot fires the minute they land. We're making our stand here. If this house goes, the whole neighborhood goes. With tile roofs and a wide greenbelt, these are defensible. Everything north of here is on fire, and the winds aren't forecasted to abate anytime soon. You are the center of our containment line."

He studied each man's face then his gaze drifted beyond.

He frowned. "Hey, you know whose house this is?" Jeff shook his head. Hardin and Akino shrugged.

Joe glanced around. Should he? "The negative edge pool, the outdoor kitchen complete with top-of-the-line stainless steel Weber grill and a fireplace is standard for this neighborhood. So, nope."

"Tony DiMarco, that big land developer." O'Grady tapped the granite countertop he leaned against.

"Really? How do you know?" Joe pulled off his helmet and ran his hand through his sweat-soaked hair.

"My wife dragged me to that charity home tour last Christmas. This was one of them. It'd be ironic if it burned."

What was Joe missing? No one else seemed to get it either. "Oh?"

"Don't you remember? His company was investigated for arson and insurance fraud last year on that empty business park." O'Grady slapped Joe's back then pointed at Hardin and McCoy. "Keep those hot spots down and hold here. Romero, don't give Jeff any more injuries helping. Rookie, listen to your elders. I'll be back with an update." Lifting his radio, he moved off.

"Half the county's burning, and you guys are kicking back. About what I expected." Detective Kyle Taylor appeared around the corner of the house. He wore jeans, boots, and had a bandana around his neck. His Laguna Vista PD badge was clipped to his waistband and his gun visibly holstered.

"Hey, Kyle. Figures you'd bring a gun to a fire. You didn't happen to bring us anything along with your attitude, did you?" Joe stepped forward and fist-bumped his best friend.

"Never go anywhere without it." Kyle handed each of them a cold bottle of water out of the backpack he wore.

Joe drained his without coming up for air. Nothing tasted so good. He capped the empty and tossed it to Kyle. "What brings you up here? Other than your gift of water."

"Checking the neighborhood to make sure everyone's out and nobody's trying to sneak back in. And I don't have to tell you about the pressure from the city council to keep looters out of this neighborhood in particular." Kyle leaned against the wall. His radio squawked, and he turned it down slightly. "So, talked to Sarah?"

"Sarah?" Heat flashed through Joe. No, he hadn't talked to her. Only thought of her nearly every waking moment.

"Sarah?" Kyle echoed. "You know. Sarah, the one you spent

all your spare time with last month, the one you can't stop talking about, the one—"

"Been a little busy. Hate when work interferes with my love life." Joe glared, gesturing to the glowing hills in front of them.

"Wait." Jeff turned. "You have a love life? Since when?"

Hardin snickered. Akino, for once, didn't look terrified.

The tanker overhead, the traffic on the radio, and smelling smoke made for a weird background while discussing his life. They were talking like it was a normal day, like they were shooting hoops or something, instead of protecting people's homes.

Jeff stepped forward. "I've been trying to set you up with my sister. She's a former cheerleader. Perky and happy all the time. She might even appreciate your 'helping.'" He made air quotes.

This wasn't awkward at all. He needed to change the subject quick. "Hey, we need to get after a couple of those hot spots. Akino, grab the hose. Thanks for the water, Kyle."

"No problem. Want me to tell Sarah you said hi?" Kyle grinned, enjoying this too much.

Joe shoved his shoulder. Something exploded off in the distance. The smoke obscured all but a slight brightening to the west.

Hardin peered off in the distance. "Sounds like the fire just hit that grove of eucs off Via de los Arboles."

Joe reached for his radio. "Who's over there?"

"Station 42."

Akino looked from Hardin to Joe. "Eucs?"

"Eucalyptus trees. The volatile oils in their leaves and other desert-adapted plants make them particularly vulnerable to fire. They're basically time bombs, dangerous to anyone or anything around them. Hardin, you and McCoy go check it out. The rookie and I will hold down the fort here."

Joe started to follow Jeff off the patio. Something brushed his leg, and he looked down. The dog stared up at him, whining. Great. Now he had a shadow. Maybe Kyle could take him. No,

Kyle had left. Ah well. Joe gave the dog a final pat then joined Akino at the hose. They searched for hot spots and flare ups. Every time he looked back, the dog was still there, watching him.

"Looks like he knows you saved his life," Akino shouted over the roar of water and fire. "You've got a dog for life."

He didn't want a dog. All he really wanted was a hot meal, a shower, and a long nap. And to call Sarah and see if she would have dinner with him. Yeah, that's what he wanted. But he wasn't going to get it until this fire was contained.

Sarah Brockman dumped her saddle-leather tote purse on her office chair. Coffee. She needed coffee. She slipped her computer out of its sleeve, snapped it into the dock, and booted it up. Twisting open her blinds, she gazed out over her second-story view of tree tops, but she'd take that over a parking lot. Today, billowing smoke filled the skyline as the foothills in the distance burned. Joe must be out there. *Lord, keep him and the other fire-fighters safe.* Maybe Heather would have an update from Kyle, who was also probably working the fire.

The Pandora app opened, and her playlist of soothing music started, which made her office feel more like a spa on a tropical island than an architectural firm. It pulled her mind away from the fires and onto work. While AutoCAD booted, she mentally went down the project list. Final drawings would be due—

Mark Rankin, her boss and mentor, knocked on the door-jamb of her office. "Come see me?"

"Sure. Just let me get some coffee, and I'll be over."

Mark disappeared. He was a great guy, not old enough to be her father, more like a quite-a-bit-older brother. But he was a good boss, and his profit-sharing plan allowed her to make her own hours and do quite well the last couple of years.

She grabbed her mug and headed for the break room and

kitchen area. Popping in her favorite hazelnut pod, she waited for the machine to fill her cup. What did Mark want? It wasn't unusual for him to ask to see her, but never first thing. Which could mean what? Her mind whirled at the possibilities. An unhappy client? Or coworker? A new project? The possibilities were endless.

The machine sputtered out the last of the coffee. She popped the top, pulled out the pod and tossed it, then heavily dosed her coffee with cream. Fortified, she headed to Mark's office.

He gestured to the chair.

She sank into the buttery leather and took a sip. "What's up?"

Mark toyed with a pen. Not a good sign. "Before you say anything, hear me out."

Oookayy.

"You know I've been talking about retiring—"

"But not for a few more years. Your five-year plan, right?"

He tilted his head side to side. "There's been a change. I'm pushing it up." He held up his hand as she opened her mouth. "Just let me finish. Then you can ask questions."

She nodded, gripped her mug tighter.

"Martha's been diagnosed with dementia. It's still early stages, but there are some things we want to do—travel, see the grandkids, things like that—before it gets worse and we can't."

A small gasp escaped Sarah's lips. "Mark, I'm so sorry." She reached for his hand and squeezed it. Tears pooled in her eyes. "What do you need me to do? I'll do anything I can to help." She could pick up more of the workload, handle clients, mentor some of the younger architects—

"Become managing partner."

Her heart stopped. Pressure filled her chest. She sat back in her chair, pulling her hands into her lap. She hadn't expected that. But she hadn't expected Martha to be diagnosed with dementia. If her heart was heavy, Mark must be devastated.

"Sarah, I know how you feel about this. But trust me. I've

watched you over the years. I know what you're capable of. Do you think I'd offer you the job if I didn't think you could handle it?"

He didn't need to be worrying about the firm. That was something she could give him. "Of course, I'll take it. If that's what you really want. Are you sure there's no one else you'd rather have?"

"I know you can do this." He leaned back. "But if you decide not to, I'll ask Eric. But you're still my first choice."

She nodded. "Thanks for thinking that I could do it. That means a lot, your confidence in me." She leaned forward. "Please don't worry about the office. We'll make it work here. I'll be praying for you and Martha, so please let me know if there's anything I can do. Or anything the team can do."

Mark cleared his throat and swallowed. "Thanks."

Recognizing his emotion and not wanting to cause him embarrassment, Sarah stood. "Need anything else?"

He shook his head. "Close the door behind you."

She gave him a soft smile and left, giving him his privacy to grieve. Back in her office, she eased into her chair and opened up her task list for the day. But she couldn't focus on the words.

What had she gotten herself into? Managing partner. Sure, Mark had been hinting for a while, but she thought he'd be around to show her the ropes, answer her questions, ease her into the job, and help her recover from her mistakes. But now, she had to take that load off of him. He didn't need to worry about the firm when he needed to be focused on Martha.

But she could go to Eric and talk to him about it. Maybe there would be a way for the two of them to divvy up the responsibilities. One that kept him away from dealing with the office staff.

Eric Garrity. Why on earth would Mark consider him? Yes, he could handle the financial aspect of the job, but he had no people skills. She could think of two people who would quit the moment they learned Eric was in charge. And they wouldn't be the last once Eric bullied his way through the staff like they were the opposing football team. So maybe that wasn't the best option.

What did *she* want? She didn't really know. She was happy doing just what she was doing. But that wasn't an option. And did it really matter what she wanted? She had to help Mark.

Her peaceful music wasn't helping. Between worrying about Joe and Kyle, and now Mark and Martha, her brain wouldn't settle into work mode. Normally, some fresh air and sunshine would help, but there was none to be found under the smoke-saturated skies. She opened the Bible app on her phone and began to pray through the Psalms.

But her mind wandered. She couldn't wrap her brain around Mark's news. Mark was her mentor. He *knew* her and had guided her career, giving her advice and opportunity. He was more than her boss. Her heart broke at what he and Martha were facing. She didn't want to add to his problems. But she'd never seen herself as managing partner.

However, if she didn't take the job, Eric Garrity would. Creating another set of problems. There was no good solution.

Get it here: www.jlcrosswhite.com/rl/413359

Books by JL Crosswhite

Sign up for my latest updates at www.JLCrosswhite.com and be the first to know when my next series is releasing.

Romantic Suspense

The Hometown Heroes Series

Promise Me

Cait can't catch a break. What she witnessed could cost her job and her beloved farmhouse. Will Greyson help her or only make things worse?

Protective Custody

She's a key witness in a crime shaking the roots of the town's power brokers. He's protecting a woman he'll risk everything for. Doing the right thing may cost her everything. Including her life.

Flash Point

She's a directionally-challenged architect who stumbled on a crime that could destroy her life's work. He's a firefighter protecting his hometown… and the woman he loves.

Special Assignment

A brain-injured Navy pilot must work with the woman in charge of the program he blames for his injury. As they both grasp to save their careers, will their growing attraction hinder them as they attempt solve the mystery of who's really at fault before someone else dies?

In the Shadow Series

Off the Map

For her, it's a road trip adventure. For him, it's his best shot to win her back. But for the stalker after her, it's revenge.

Out of Range (Spring 2021)

It's her chance to prove she's good enough. It's his chance to prove he's more than just a fun guy. Is it their time to find love, or is her secret admirer his deadly competition?

Over Her Head (Summer 2021)

On a church singles' camping trip that no one wants to be on, a weekend away to renew and refresh becomes anything but. A group of friends trying to find their footing do a good deed and get much more than they bargained for.

Writing as Jennifer Crosswhite

Contemporary Romance

The Inn at Cherry Blossom Lane

Can the summer magic of Lake Michigan bring first loves back together? Or will the secret they discover threaten everything they love?

Historical Romance

The Route Home Series

Be Mine

A woman searching for independence. A man searching for education. Can a simple thank you note turn into something more?

Coming Home

He was why she left. Now she's falling for him. Can a woman who turned her back on her hometown come home to find justice for her brother without falling in love with his best friend?

The Road Home

He is a stagecoach driver just trying to do his job. She is returning to her suitor only to find he has died. When a stack of stolen money shows up in her bag, she thinks the past she has desperately tried to hide has come back to haunt her.

Finally Home

The son of a wealthy banker poses as a lumberjack to carve out his own identity. But in a stagecoach robbery gone wrong, he meets the soon-to-be schoolteacher with a vivid imagination, a gift for making things grow, and an obsession with dime novels. As the town is threatened by a past enemy, can he help without revealing who he is? And will she love him when she learns the truth?

Printed in the USA
CPSIA information can be obtained
at www.ICGtesting.com
JSHW020822231223
54065JS00001B/7

9 780997 880236